PRAISE FOR
RIGHT BEHIND YOU

"Gardner knows how to get the reader emotionally hooked into the story, and the police procedure elements of the novel shine. . . . **SHE'S A MASTER OF THE PSYCHOLOGICAL THRILLER, SO DON'T LEAVE THIS ONE BEHIND.**"
—Associated Press

"*Right Behind You* . . . solidifies [Lisa Gardner's] claim as the queen of psychological suspense."
—*Providence Journal*

"DEVILISHLY CLEVER TWISTS PROPEL GARDNER'S TALE."
—*Publishers Weekly* (starred review)

"A long-awaited delight . . . and a thrilling escape."
—*Booklist*

"LISA GARDNER . . . CONTINUES TO RAISE THE BAR."
—*Omnivora*

#1 NEW YORK TIMES BESTSELLER

"Lisa Gardner is the master of the psychological thriller. . . . The world of the FBI, the terror of abduction and victim advocates blend into this tense . . . thriller." —Associated Press

"A psychological thriller both chilling and emotional. Her narrative thrums with heart-pounding scenes and unexpected twists that have you furiously flipping pages." —*USA Today*'s *Happy Ever After*

"Gardner doesn't disappoint. . . . Longtime fans as well as those new to the series . . . will delight in this suspenseful offering." —*Library Journal* (starred review)

"*Find Her* is Lisa Gardner at her all-time best." —*The Huffington Post*

"Superb. . . . Always a great storyteller, Gardner here proves herself a novelist par excellence, fashioning a masterpiece of form as well as function that provides no easy outs for characters struggling to wade through their own moral morass. The first can't-miss thriller of 2016." —*Providence Journal*

"The line between mysteries and thrillers and so-called literary fiction has always been a thin one, but contemporary writers like Lisa Gardner make that sort of arbitrary distinction seem especially foolish. . . . *Find Her* . . . is a taut, brilliantly constructed look at the same sort of horrific situation that powered Emma Donoghue's *Room*." —*Connecticut Post*

"Gardner is known for creating complex, fascinating characters. . . . This is an incredible story." —*RT Book Reviews*

"When it comes to author Lisa Gardner, the tales she writes are always extreme gems in the literary world, and this is no exception." —*Suspense*

Crash & Burn

"With labyrinthine twists and surprises on just about every turn of the page, Gardner has crafted a delight of a suspense novel."
—*New York Journal of Books*

"This page-turner, with its contemporary, hard-edged flavor, is sure to satisfy Gardner's ardent fan base." —*Booklist*

"Expertly crafted." —*Publishers Weekly*

"Lisa Gardner delivers another gut-wrenching emotional thriller with her latest psychological tale, *Crash & Burn* . . . [her] most unpredictable novel to date." —Associated Press

"Lisa Gardner never disappoints." —*Suspense*

Fear Nothing

"Nobody writes about the psychological aspects of working in law enforcement better than Lisa Gardner. . . . She's written another thriller that will keep fans gasping while drawing new readers into the vivid psychological narrative." —Associated Press

"In this strong addition to the series, Gardner retains her place on thrillerdom's top tier." —*Booklist* (starred review)

"Her most intriguing and complex novel to date. . . . Only an author as talented as Gardner could make the book so intensely satisfying."
—*The Huffington Post*

"When it comes to delivering riveting, complex female protagonists, Gardner is in a class by herself." —*RT Book Reviews*

"Gardner repeatedly ratchets up the tension." —*Publishers Weekly*

"If you think Gardner pulled out all the stops in D.D.'s previous cases . . . you ain't seen nothing yet. Better fasten your seat belt for this roller-coaster ride through family hell." —*Kirkus Reviews* (starred review)

"Lisa Gardner delivers an intelligent, sophisticated psychological thriller in her latest installment. . . . Gardner continues to show why she is on the short list of top thriller writers today." —*Suspense*

"Lisa Gardner is her absolute best in *Fear Nothing*."

—Bookreporter.com

Touch & Go

"Lisa Gardner, the master of the psychological thriller, has delivered another tour de force with *Touch & Go*, which exposes the raw nerves of a family imploding, and an investigator trying to escape her past. . . . Gardner does an amazing job of creating realistic situations and characters with emotional resonance. The constant surprises will shock even the most jaded thriller reader." —Associated Press

"Returning home after a date night meant to repair their marriage, Justin and Libby Denbe are abducted along with their teenage daughter from their glamorous Boston town house, leaving cops with no motive or ransom demand. The suspense crackles as the Denbes grapple with their captors' bewildering brutality. But what gives the story heart is Libby's dawning realization that her family may have been broken long before their kidnappers appeared." —*People*

"This no-holds-barred stand-alone from Thriller Award–winner Gardner opens with the brutally efficient kidnapping of the Denbe family. . . . Gardner effectively alternates between the physical and emotional disintegration of the family under the pressure of their captivity and the efforts of [Investigator Tessa] Leoni and company to dig into the secrets of Denbe Construction, its key employees, and its finances, as well as to locate the Denbes. The suspense builds as the action races to a spectacular conclusion and the unmasking of the plot's mastermind." —*Publishers Weekly*

"[A] thrill ride. . . . Even readers who figure out the ringleader long before [Investigators] Tessa and Wyatt will get behind on their sleep turning pages to make sure they're right." —*Kirkus Reviews*

"Gardner's depiction of a woman in the midst of emotional chaos is spot-on, as usual, and she proves herself just as capable when it comes to creating intriguing men. Readers will want to see more of Wyatt."
—*Booklist*

Catch Me

"Gardner always plays in the big leagues, but this scare-your-socks-off thriller is a grand slam, packed with enigmatic characters (some good, some crazily evil), expert procedural detail, and superb storytelling."
—*Library Journal*

"Gardner has become one of the best psychological thriller writers in the business. The compelling characters, the shocking plot, and the realistic atmosphere of how police operate make this a 'must read' for any suspense aficionado." —Associated Press

"The creepy meter is off the charts—though not sensationalized—with children the target of physical, psychological, and sexual abuse at the hands of both strangers and parents. And, somehow, miraculously without any contrivance, Gardner's conclusion delivers a welcome glimmer of hope." —*Booklist* (starred review)

"Gardner's sixth Det. D. D. Warren thriller grabs from the get-go."
—*People*

"A solidly enjoyable thriller that will keep you on the edge of your chair as you turn the pages and listen for any strange noises around you." —*The Huffington Post*

"Irresistible." —*Kirkus Reviews*

LISA GARDNER

RIGHT BEHIND YOU

A NOVEL

DUTTON

DUTTON
An imprint of Penguin Random House LLC
375 Hudson Street
New York, New York 10014

First Dutton trade paperback printing, 2018

DUTTON and the D colophon are registered trademarks of Penguin Random House LLC

The Library of Congress has catalogued this book as follows:
Names: Gardner, Lisa, author.
Title: Right behind you / Lisa Gardner.
Description: | New York : Dutton, [2017]
Identifiers: LCCN 2016041605 | ISBN 9780525954583 (hardcover) | ISBN 9780698411432 (ebook) | ISBN 9781524742812 (trade paperback)
Subjects: LCSH: Government investigators—Fiction. | Murder—Investigation—Fiction. | Brothers and sisters—Fiction. BISAC: FICTION / Suspense. | FICTION / Mystery & Detective / Police Procedural. | GSAFD: Suspense fiction. Mystery fiction.
Classification: LCC PS3557.A7132 R54 2017 | DDC 813/.54—dc23 LC record available at https://lccn.loc.gov/2016041605

Printed in the United States of America
10 9 8 7 6 5 4 3 2 1

To all the once-in-a-lifetime dogs . . .

RIGHT BEHIND YOU

Prologue

*H*AD A FAMILY ONCE.

Father. Mother. Sister. Lived in our very own double-wide. Brown shag carpet. Dirty gold countertops. Peeling linoleum floors. Used to race my Hot Wheels down those food-splattered countertops, double-loop through ramps of curling linoleum, then land in gritty piles of shag. Place was definitely a shit hole. But being a kid, I called it home.

Mornings, wolfing down Cheerios, watching Scooby-Doo without any volume so I wouldn't wake the 'rents. Getting my baby sister up, ready for school. Both of us staggering out the front door, backpacks nearly busting with books.

Important to read. Someone told me that. Mom, Dad, grandparent, teacher? Don't remember now, but somewhere I got the message. Book a day. Like an apple. So after school I headed off to the library, sister still in tow. Read some books, 'cause God knows we didn't have any fruit.

I liked Choose Your Own Adventures. Each scene had a cliffhanger ending, where you had to decide what would happen next. Turn left in the forbidden temple or turn right? Pick up the cursed treasure or walk on by? In the Choose Your Own Adventure books, you were always the one in control.

Then I'd read Clifford the Big Red Dog *to my little sis. Not old enough to read yet, she'd point and laugh at the pictures.*

Sometimes, the librarian would sneak us snacks. She'd say stuff like, Someone left behind their bag of chips. Would you like them? *I'd say*, Nah. *She'd say*, Go on, better you than me. Potato chips aren't good for my girlish figure.

Eventually my sister would grab the chips, eyes greedy. She was always hungry back then. We both were.

After library, home.

Sooner or later, always had to go home.

My mom had this smile. When she was in the right mood, having a "good day," oh, that smile. She'd ruffle my hair. Call me her little man. Say how proud she was of me. And hug me. Big, strong hugs, envelopes of cigarette smoke and cheap perfume. I loved that smell. I loved the days my mother smiled.

Sometimes, if things were going really well, she'd fix dinner. Spaghetti noodles with ketchup—that'll leave a stain, she'd cry gaily, slurping up noodles. Ramen noodles with scrambled eggs—dinner for fifteen cents, now we're living the dream, she'd declare. Or my favorite, Kraft macaroni and cheese—it's the nuclear orange color that makes it special, she'd whisper.

My little sister would giggle. She liked my mother in this mood. Who wouldn't?

Dad was usually at work. Bringing home the bacon. When he had a job. Gas station attendant. Night clerk. Warehouse stocker.

Stay in school, he'd tell me, afternoons when we came home in time to watch him button up yet another grimy uniform. Fucking real world, he'd tell me. Fucking bosses.

Then off he'd go. And my mom would appear from the hazy cloud of their bedroom to start dinner. Or the door would never open, and I'd get out a can opener instead. Chef Boyardee. Campbell's soup. Baked beans.

My sister and I didn't talk those nights. We ate in silence. Then I'd read her more Clifford, or maybe we'd play Go Fish. Quiet games for quiet kids. My sister would fall asleep on the sofa. Then I'd pick her up, carry her off to bed.

"Sorry," she'd say sleepily, though neither of us knew what she was apologizing for.

Had a family once.

Father. Mother. Sister.

But then the father worked less and less and drank more and more. And the mother . . . Dunno. Drugs, booze, her own foggy mind? Parental units appeared less and less to cook, clean, work. More and more to fight, scream, yell. Mom, hurling plastic plates across the kitchen. Dad, punching a hole through the cheap drywall. Then both would guzzle more vodka and do the whole thing all over again.

Sister took to sleeping in my room, while I sat by the door. 'Cause sometimes, the parents had guests over. Other boozers, druggies, losers. Then all bets were off. Three, four, five in the morning. Locked doorknob rattling, strange voices crooning, "Hey, little kids, come out and play with us. . . ."

My sister didn't giggle anymore. She slept with the light on, ragged copy of Clifford *clutched in her hands.*

While I kept watch with a baseball bat balanced across my knees.

Then, morning. House finally quiet. Strangers passed out on the floor. As we crept around them, stealing into the kitchen for the Cheerios box, then grabbing our backpacks and tiptoeing out the door.

Rinse, spin, repeat.

Repeat. Repeat. Repeat.

Had a family once.

But then the father drank or shot up or snorted too much. And the mom started to scream and scream and scream. While my sister and I watched wide-eyed from the sofa.

"Shut up, shut up, shut up," the father yelled.

Scream. Scream. Scream.

"Fucking bitch! What's wrong with you?"

Scream. Scream. Scream.

"I said, SHUT UP!"

Kitchen knife. Big one. Butcher knife, like from a slasher film. Did she grab it? Did he? Don't remember who had it first. Can only tell you who had it last.

My father. Raising the knife up. Bringing the knife down. Then my mother wasn't screaming anymore.

"Shit!"

My father, turning to my sister and me. Bloody knife, drip, drip, drip. And I knew then, what he'd do next.

"Run," I told my little sister as I dragged her off the sofa, shoved her toward the hall.

The shag carpet slowed him down. But the peeling linoleum tripped us up. As we raced through the double-wide, silent in our terror, I passed my sister, scooped her up, little legs still churning through the air.

I could hear him, right behind me. I could feel his breath on my neck, already picture the blade slicing between my bony shoulder blades. I threw my sister into my bedroom.

"Lock the door!"

Then sprinting down the hall, my father and his bloody knife close behind.

I bolted into my parents' bedroom. Leapt onto the bed.

"Fucking kid. Stay still, stay still, stay still."

Knife going up, knife going down. Shredding the bedding. Tearing into the mattress.

I jumped down the other side. Grabbed anything I could find from the top of the bureau. Empty wine bottles, beer cans, perfume. Hurled them into my father's beet-red face.

"Shit shit shit."

Then, as he staggered, I jumped back over the bed, whirling around him. I heard the slash of the knife. Felt the burning pain in my shoulder. But then I was clear, hammering down the hall. If I could make it out the front door, into the yard, cry for the neighbors . . .

And leave my little sister behind?

Then she was there. Standing in my bedroom doorway. Holding out the baseball bat.

I didn't hesitate. I grabbed the wooden bat. I raced into the family room, turning at the last second, assuming the proper stance.

My father. Wild eyes. Flushed face. Lights on, I thought, but no one home.

He raised the bloody knife.

I swung with all my might. Felt the connection, a solid, wet smack, as I knocked it out of the park. My father, falling down, down, down, knife dropping into the carpet.

And still I swung the bat. Bam. Bam. Bam.

Repeat. Repeat. Repeat.

My little sister, suddenly appearing beside me.

"Telly, Telly, Telly."

Myself, looking up. Wild eyes. Flushed face. Lights on but no one home.

"Telly!" my baby sister cried one last time. As I lifted the bat.

Had a family.

Once.

Chapter 1

SHERIFF SHELLY ATKINS wasn't supposed to be in the law enforcement business anymore. Ten years after a fire had left her torso, upper shoulder, and neck a ropey mess of scars, not to mention ruined her hip, she'd hung up her hat, so to speak. Taking up an anonymous benefactor's offer of a once-in-a-lifetime trip to Paris (retired FBI agent Pierce Quincy, she remained certain), she'd initially salved her wounds with French crepes, French wine, and French museums.

Then she came home. Set herself up with a steady schedule of walking the beach, hiking the woods, keeping herself busy. Her replaced hip did best when in motion, the soreness of an active day far better than the knifing ache of idleness. And roaming the great outdoors, she was less likely to remember. A woman with her number of scars was definitely best off not remembering.

Then two years ago, the sitting county sheriff, an outsider whom the locals had never quite taken to, had resigned abruptly. Some whispers of impropriety, but nothing the DA could prove. Either way, the county found itself sheriff-less. And Shelly . . .

She wasn't a beautiful woman. Not even pretty, and that was before the fire had turned half her body into a Picasso painting. She had the solid build of a plow horse and the kind of no-nonsense face that invited men to talk to her at bars while still eyeing the prettier girl three seats down.

She had no family, no children, not even a pet goldfish, because she was never entirely certain she wouldn't take off again.

Basically, eight years after the fire had nearly killed her, Shelly had managed to add nothing and no one to her life. Mostly, she missed her job like hell. Not to mention the people she'd once worked with.

So she'd run for sheriff. And given that she was still remembered as something of a hometown hero for saving a federal agent from that fire, the locals had enthusiastically voted her back into office, bum hip, scarred torso, and all.

Which meant, Shelly reminded herself now as she drove, lights flashing, that she had only herself to blame. A report of shots fired this time of year? Not good for the local sheriff, nor the business leaders who counted on the quaint coastal town's sleepy reputation to remain, well, sleepy.

Hour was still early, just after eight, which argued for either cranky good old boys who were still half-skunked from their excesses the night before, or disillusioned tourists who'd finally figured out that camping in a heat wave wasn't all it was cracked up to be. Normally, August in these parts wasn't so bad, especially with the ocean breeze helping keep temperatures reasonable. But the mercury had been topping a hundred for the past five days and bringing tempers with it.

In a rural community of five thousand, where the number of guns probably did outnumber the total population, maybe a report of shots fired had been only a matter of time. Dispatch had provided the address, a gas station/convenience store at the edge of town, and Shelly had personally taken charge. Both her deputies had already logged overtime working the normal summertime nuisance calls, so she felt it was the least she could do. And while she wasn't happy about gunshots in her town, she wasn't terribly concerned. Overall, Bakersville, Oregon, was most famous for its cheese, trees, and ocean breeze. Sure, it also had a growing meth problem, but policing in these parts was hardly big-city stress.

Headed north, having already made it through the blink-or-you'll-miss-it downtown, Shelly was approaching the county's biggest claim to fame: the cheese factory. Even with lights flashing, she had to blare her horn to weave her way through the thick line of RVs and campers already stacked up, waiting to turn into the parking lot. Given the already hotter-than-hell morning, most of the tourists were probably planning on ice cream for breakfast. When she completed this call, Shelly might join them. Community policing. Eat ice cream, mingle with locals. Sounded like a plan to her.

North of the factory, traffic died down and Shelly picked up speed. Road was narrower here, winding through sharp bends as it twisted its way along the rocky coast. Then, five miles after a turn-in for yet another campground, Shelly arrived at her location: the EZ Gas.

Shelly swung in, killing the lights while appraising the scene. She saw one truck parked in front of the twin gas pumps, a battered Ford that had seen better days. Otherwise the place appeared quiet. Shelly got on her radio, alerted dispatch that she'd arrived. Then, picking up her broad-brimmed hat from the seat beside her, she placed it on her head and climbed out of her white sheriff's SUV.

First thing that struck her: the absence of sound. That, much as anything, set her nerves on edge. In a hot, hazy August, when the local businesses were as busy as they were gonna get, the quiet here . . . It wasn't a good kind of quiet. Shelly's hand went to her holster. She automatically shifted her stance sideways, making herself less of a target, as she approached the front of the worn-looking convenience store.

Smell hit her next. Coppery, thick. An odor even a small-town sheriff knew better than she would've liked.

The faded red pickup, midnineties, was to her left, the open glass door to the small convenience store to her right. Shelly paused, considering. Vehicle appeared unoccupied, which left the store as the main area of concern. She moved closer to the exterior wall, bottom half blocked by giant coolers of ice, upper windows plastered with various posters advertising cheap beer. Hand still on her holster, she tucked herself beside the ice coolers and peered through the open door.

Nothing to see. And again, nothing to hear. Not the ring of the cash register. Not the murmur of voices as the clerk rang up the sale from the truck owner. Just that smell. Thick and pungent in sweltering August heat.

Then, a sound did reach her ears: soft, steady.

The drone of flies. Lots and lots of flies.

Shelly knew then what she'd be finding inside.

A brief pause while she did the smart thing and radioed dispatch for backup. Then, shoulders squared, she unsnapped her holster, removed her Glock 22.

Entered the store.

First victim had gone down ten feet inside the entrance. Body was on its back, spread-eagle, a bag of chips just beyond the twenty-something male's out-flung hand. Local, was Shelly's first guess, as she eyed the worn jeans, unlaced boots, grime-smeared T-shirt. Probably a farm boy, she thought, then caught an extra whiff of something rotten and quickly changed her mind. Fishing. Definitely a boat hand or a particularly pungent job like that. Maybe he'd just gotten in from an early morning haul and had come dashing in for a snack. Now he bore a single shot to the forehead, more bloody holes in the chest. Given the slack features, chances were the kid had never even seen it coming.

Next body was behind the counter. Female this time. Eighteen, nineteen? Second victim. Or certainly shot after the salt-jonesing customer, because the female *had* seen it coming. Body had fallen in a twisted hump, as if she'd turned, tried to run, only to remember she was boxed in, imprisoned by the counter in front and a wall of tobacco products to the back. She'd gotten a hand up. Shelly could see the bullet hole straight through the palm.

She didn't need to see the rest of the damage to know it'd been fatal.

Inside, the sound was louder. The damn flies, drawn by the smell of blood, and now concentrated on twin targets.

It's funny, the things that can get to a woman. Shelly had seen terrible auto accidents, hunting tragedies, even a few combine incidents. She knew gore and dismemberment. Small towns were hardly the idyllic sanctuaries portrayed on TV. And yet the flies.

The damn flies . . .

She focused on breathing through her mouth. Slow, deep breaths. Procedure. Now, more than ever, protocol mattered. She needed to alert her detectives unit, plus the county DA and ME's office. Calls to make, work to do.

A movement to her left.

Shelly whirled, hands together, arms straight, already raising her Glock. End of the candy aisle, right before the wall of cold drinks, she spotted some kind of wire rack, quivering. She tucked closer to the wall making herself less of a target.

She headed down the outer aisle, where she could come at her target from the side. She was sweating profusely, the beads of moisture stinging her eyes. Flies. The drone of flies, interrupted only by the shuffling of her heavy-soled boots against the linoleum floor. Despite her best intentions, her breathing was too loud, ragged in the unnaturally still air.

She wasn't wearing a vest. Too hot, too uncomfortable. And even responding to a call of shots fired . . . Bakersville wasn't that kind of town. Not that kind of community.

She of all people should've known better.

End of aisle, she slowed. Rack wasn't moving anymore. She strained for the sound of movement—say, an unknown shooter creeping down the other side of the aisle or sneaking up behind her.

Nothing.

Deep breath in. Release slowly.

One, two, three.

Sheriff Shelly Atkins pivoted sharply, Glock straight ahead, homing in on the target.

But the aisle was empty, the wire rack of snack bags still. No movement from anywhere in front of the wall of refrigerators housing cold drinks.

Shelly straightened slowly. Aisle by aisle now, step by step.

But whatever had caused the disturbance was long gone. Maybe just an errant breeze or Shelly's own nerves.

Either way, she stood alone in the store. Two bodies. The endless drone of flies. The stench of fresh blood.

Shelly unclipped her radio from her shoulder, preparing to get on with the business of next steps. Just as her gaze came up, she spotted the third victim.

Chapter 2

"STRAWBERRIES OR KIWI?"

"Apple?"

"That's not a strawberry or a kiwi."

"Strawberries and kiwi get too soft. By snack time, nothing but goo."

"Apple it is."

Rainie gives me a wink, then turns to raid the fridge. In response, I push the last of my scrambled eggs around on my plate. This is one of those mornings when I'm supposed to eat a healthy breakfast, get my energy up. I don't feel like it and Rainie knows it.

Beneath the table, Luka thrusts his wet nose against the palm of my hand. In his own way, my dog's trying to cheer me up.

While Rainie's back is to me, I scoop some of the cold, pebbly eggs into my palm, then return my hand to my lap. This time when Luka noses me, I open my fingers and deliver the treat. Now at least one of us is happy.

I'm not supposed to feed Luka human food. He's a former police officer, Quincy likes to remind me. A trained member of law enforcement. He had to retire at five, having torn his ACL twice in one year. Basically, Luka has a bum knee. Not bad enough to hinder him in civilian life, but not strong enough for active duty.

Now Luka is my partner. Quincy got him from a cop friend, a year after I arrived at Rainie and Quincy's house. It's my responsibility to take care of Luka. I feed him, exercise him, and give him his daily joint supplements. I also learned Dutch. I never knew this, but the German shepherds used in police and military training mostly come from Europe, where the bloodlines are purer. Luka came from the Netherlands, so his initial training was in Dutch. His canine officer continued giving his commands in Dutch and now it's my turn.

Do I sound good in Dutch?

I have no idea. But Luka doesn't seem to mind. He listens to me very intently. I like that about Luka. He's a very good listener.

And I sleep better at night when Luka is stretched out beside me. Another no-no, of course. Police canines should be confined to their kennels when off duty. Then, when you let them out, they know it's time to work. Dogs like their kennels, Quincy has explained to me. Many times. Just because Luka is retired is no reason to ignore five years of training. Something, something, something. Blah, blah, blah.

Quincy is very good at lecturing. And I'm a very good foster daughter. I nod obediently at all the right places.

While continuing to take Luka out of his kennel to sleep with me at night.

Rainie cast the deciding vote. I overheard her telling Quincy to let it go. Luka seemed fine and I was sleeping better. Why mess with it?

But I understood what she meant, because some nights, Luka leaves me to search out Rainie instead.

By now, I understand how much Quincy likes his logic and routine. For Rainie and me, however . . . Life is a bit more complicated for us.

I don't call my foster parents—maybe soon-to-be adoptive parents—Mom and Dad. Some fosters, they insist on these things. But I was ten by the time I arrived in this house and had already been placed in too many homes to buy into the instant-family bit. Quincy's full name is Pierce Quincy, but everyone calls him Quincy, even Rainie, so I do, too. He's older than most foster dads. In his sixties. But he carries it well. He and Rainie are out running each morning. Plus

Quincy still works. Once upon a time he was an FBI profiler. That's how he met Rainie—she was a deputy right here in Bakersville when there was a school shooting. Quincy helped with the case and they've been together ever since.

Now Quincy is retired from the FBI and Rainie has retired from policing. Instead, they work together, consulting on cold cases or weird murders outside a police department's normal "purview." Basically, they're experts in monsters.

Which is maybe how they ended up with me?

Rainie doesn't like it when I say such things. I'm just a kid, she likes to remind me. My job isn't to be perfect, but to learn from my mistakes. Some days, that's harder than you'd think.

My parents are dead. I don't have any surviving aunts, uncles, grandparents. Just a brother, four years older than me. I remember him. Kind of. The night my parents died, he went away. No one talks about him, and me being me, I'm not the kind to ask. That would be opening up.

As Quincy would say with his droll smile, *Let's not go nuts.*

In the foster world, being family-less isn't terrible. It means I'm free to be adopted. Which, when I was five and arriving at the first home with nothing but a black trash bag of clothes and threadbare stuffies, made me highly placeable. It wasn't a bad house, either. I mean, the fosters seemed nice enough.

I have trauma. Wait, post-traumatic stress. In the beginning, at least, I was assigned therapy twice a week. My fosters had to take me, all part of the "plan" developed by the family counselor.

But I'm not good at therapy. I don't like to talk. I color. When I was five, the lady counselor encouraged drawing. Especially pictures of my family. Except I never drew a family of four. I always sketched two people. A bigger kid and a little kid. My older brother and me. *Where are your parents?* the lady counselor would ask me.

But I never had an answer.

I don't sleep well. The trauma again. And sometimes, even when I know better, I do bad things. I just do. Impulse control. Apparently, I don't have much. And those first fosters . . . The nicer they were, the less I could stand them.

I don't think that's the trauma. I think that's just me. I'm a little bit broken inside. There are reasons, I'm sure, but having spent the past thirteen years being me, I'm not as convinced as the therapists that the reasons really matter. I mean, if the handle snaps off your coffee mug, do you ask it why it broke? Or do you just glue it back together?

This is Rainie's philosophy, as well, and I like it. We are all a little bit broken, she tells me (the reason she doesn't sleep at night?), but we all work on fixing ourselves.

I like Rainie and Quincy. I've been in this house three years now. Long enough for them to decide to keep me, warts and all. I have Luka and my own room and somewhere in Georgia, a soon-to-be adoptive big sister, Kimberly, with her husband and two kids. In November, if all goes as planned, her daughters will be my nieces. Which is kind of funny, given that they're my age. But I like them. At least as much as I like anyone.

I'm lucky. I know that. And I'm working really hard on gluing and improving and impulse-controlling.

But some days, it's still hard to be me.

I HAVEN'T SEEN QUINCY YET THIS MORNING. Lately, he's been holed up in his office, working on his "project." He won't talk about it, but Rainie and I suspect he's writing a book. His memoirs? Techniques for profiling? At dinner, Rainie and I have been amusing ourselves (and maybe him) by suggesting titles for this unknown great work. Rainie's favorite: *Fibs from a Feebie.* My favorite: *Old Man with Boring Stories to Tell.*

He hasn't confessed yet. Quincy is definitely one of those guys who's mastered the art of silence.

Now, Rainie . . . If Quincy's the quiet one, then Rainie is the emotional one. At least, her face is easier to read. And she's pretty. Long, thick red-brown hair. Blue-gray eyes. She dresses casually, jeans and sweater in the winter, capris and tank top in the summer. But somehow, she always looks put together. At ease.

At summer camp, she would be the girl everyone would want to get to know.

Me, on the other hand, one look and you know I'm a foster kid. I definitely don't have Rainie's reddish hair or Quincy's bright blue eyes. Nope. I've got dirt-brown hair that flips in directions I can't even predict. Jug-handle ears. Dull hazel eyes. Not to mention bony knees and elbows and a too-thin face.

Rainie tells me I will grow into myself. Give it time.

You want to know a secret? I love Rainie and Quincy. I really, really want them to become my real-life forever-and-ever parents. I want to stay in this house. I want to spend every day with Luka by my side.

But I never say these words out loud. Not even the day Rainie and Quincy sat me down and told me they had started adoption procedures.

Not a talker, remember?

I like to think they already know how I feel. Being experts in monsters and all.

Rainie has returned to the kitchen island. She places an apple in the blue insulated lunch bag, then folds over the top, sealing it shut. Done. I can't help myself. I sigh heavily. I don't want to go today. I don't want to do what they've decided I should do. Quincy is a big believer in tough love. Rainie, on the other hand, she's not gonna relent, but at least she feels bad about it.

"It might be fun," she tries now.

I roll my eyes at her. Eggs are gone. I push my fork through little puddles of maple syrup, drawing elaborate designs around random pancake crumbs.

"You like to swim."

I don't dignify this with an eye roll.

Rainie returns to the table, sits down beside me. "If you could do anything you wanted today, what would it be?"

"Stay home. Play with Luka."

"Sharlah, you've done that every day this summer."

"You and Quincy have run most mornings this summer. You still got up and ran today."

"It's swim camp. Four hours at the local Y. You can do this."

I give Rainie a look. I want it to be tough, or sarcastic, or something. But for just one moment . . .

I can't do this. I suck at this. Which is why they're making me go. Not to improve my swimming—who cares about that?—but to work on that whole playing-well-with-others thing. Another one of my broken bits. I don't want to socialize with other kids. I don't trust 'em, I don't like 'em, and best I can tell, the feeling's mutual.

So there. Leave me with Luka. I love Luka. Who's once again licking my hand and whining sympathetically under the table.

"Sharlah . . ."

"If you let me stay home, I'll do chores," I whisper. "I'll clean my room, the entire house. I'll work on learning responsibility. Quincy loves responsibility."

"One week. Four hours each morning. Who knows, you might even make a friend."

Wrong thing to say. Now I am miserable and self-conscious. Rainie seems to get it. She sighs, squeezes my hand.

"Give it two days, honey. If you still hate it by Wednesday . . ." Rainie pushes back her chair. "Come on. Grab your swim bag. Time to get this show on the road."

I rise to standing, dead girl walking.

Luka falls in step beside me.

"Where's Quincy?" I ask as we head for the front door.

"Phone."

"New case?" I ask, already more excited for a potential homicide than swim camp.

"Nah. Local call. Nothing that exciting around here." Rainie opens the front door. "Try smiling," she advises me. "It's as good a start as any."

I plaster a grimace on my face, then trudge out in the scorching heat. Luka takes up position on the front porch, where he will wait till I return.

Except for a second, Luka isn't watching Rainie and me head to the car. His attention has gone left; he's staring off at something in the woods. A squirrel, deer, prized stick?

I follow his gaze.

And feel the fine hairs prickle at the back of my neck.

"Come on," Rainie tells me. "Load up."

But I'm still staring at nothing in the woods, shivering for reasons I can't explain.

"Let's go," Rainie prods again.

Reluctantly, I get into the car. Leaving my dog, still on watch, behind me.

Chapter 3

SHELLY'S LEAD HOMICIDE SERGEANT, Roy Peterson, arrived on the scene first, followed shortly by his team, then Deputy Dan Mitchell. Roy put his detectives to work, then paused long enough to confer with Shelly and Dan outside the EZ Gas. The sweltering August heat had already darkened their uniforms with sweat but was still easier to take than the rapidly increasing stench of blood and gore inside the tiny convenience store.

No sign of media yet, which just went to show there were some advantages to being a backwoods town. Given that Bakersville was nestled equidistant between the bustling metropolis of Portland, Oregon, and political fuss of the state's capital, Salem, Shelly didn't expect that situation to last for long. Ninety minutes was an easy enough drive for a rabid reporter hell-bent on the latest tale of violence. Though sadly, a convenience store shooting was hardly newsworthy in this day and age. Only the location of the murders—the proverbial small town—would make it a story of note.

"Call came into dispatch eight oh four A.M.," Shelly related to her sergeant, tone clipped. "Report of shots fired. I arrived on scene at approximately eight sixteen A.M., discovering two bodies inside. One a young male, approximately midtwenties. Second a young female, eighteen, nineteen years of age. Both appear to have been shot multiple times."

"Owner of the store?" Roy quizzed.

"Don Juarez," Shelly answered, having already asked dispatch the same question. "I spoke to him briefly by phone. He was headed to Salem but is returning now. He tentatively identified the cashier as Erin Hill—at least that's who was scheduled to work this morning, and the body matches her description. She's from a local family. I already contacted Officer Estevan, asked her to pay the parents a visit."

"And the DOA male?" Roy asked.

"No ID, no wallet. Maybe shooter grabbed it on his way out. Truck outside is registered to a fishing charter company. We'll need to fax the vehicle registration over to our counterparts in Nehalem. Maybe one of them can get us a name."

"Got Rebecca and Hal photographing the scene, bagging and tagging evidence," Roy reported. "ME should be here shortly. So far, we've recovered nine shell casings, one slug."

"Nine shots for two victims?" Shelly shook her head. "Seems a bit much."

"Male customer was shot three times to the chest, once to the head. Female clerk the same: single shot to the head, three to the torso, including one slug through the palm of her hand."

"Weapon?" Shelly asked.

"Recovered slug appears to be nine millimeter."

Shelly sighed. Nine-millimeter handguns were common enough, especially around here. Certainly wouldn't narrow their search any.

Dan spoke up. "That's eight bullets."

Roy and Shelly glanced at him.

"Four shots for each victim," Dan supplied. "Eight bullets. But you mentioned nine casings. So where's the last shot?"

"Oh. Haven't gotten to that part yet." Shelly smiled grimly. "Turns out, we got a third victim: store security camera. Which, with any luck at all, might be our lone witness."

HERE WAS THE ISSUE: Security cameras fell under the umbrella of technology. Being a rural county department, Bakersville didn't have a technology expert or forensic computer tech. Meaning their safest bet was to wait for assistance from the state police. Except Shelly didn't feel like waiting.

She had a double homicide in a town that saw only a handful of murders each year. Community leaders would be demanding answers sooner rather than later. Hell, Shelly wanted answers sooner rather than later.

On the other hand, botch recovery of the video, and they'd be ruining one of the only leads they had.

"Business of this size, location," Roy was saying now, "how complicated can the security system be? Odds are, it was picked up at an office superstore. Nothing so sophisticated three well-trained members of law enforcement couldn't figure it out."

Both Roy and Shelly turned to Dan. He was their resident tech expert. Which was to say, he was the youngest member on the force and the one who managed their online community outreach.

"You saw the camera?" he asked Shelly.

"Mounted behind the cash register, up near the ceiling."

"Big, little, old, new?"

"Small. Well, what remained of it. Black plastic," she added helpfully.

"So an electronic eye." Dan nodded. "In that case, actual footage is most likely recorded to a DVR. This place got a back office?"

"Yeah, straight through there."

Shelly pointed to the open door of the EZ Gas, where a flash of light indicated the detectives were still snapping photos. The other downside of attempting to retrieve the security video now; they risked further contamination of the crime scene.

"What do you want to do?" Roy asked her.

"I don't want to wait an hour for state assist," Shelly said.

Roy grimaced. "An hour? I'm guessing more like half a day."

"True. All right. Dan, you're with me. If the security system seems too complicated, we can always call the owner for assistance. But somewhere out there is a double murderer. I want to see his face."

THE FLIES WERE EVERYWHERE. Shelly grimaced as they buzzed thickly over the holes in the male victim's chest, forehead. Her first instinct was to shoo them away, but she knew from experience there wouldn't be any point.

Hal looked up from his camera, greeting her and Dan with a small nod of acknowledgment. They nodded back, none of them speaking. Air was hotter in here, the stench of blood and death forcing them to breathe through their mouths.

Shelly kept as far right as possible, Dan following in her footsteps, so they would disturb the area the least amount possible. They sidled past the body, then tiptoed down the outer aisle to arrive at the wall of cold drinks. In front of the refrigeration units, the air felt marginally cooler, and Shelly exhaled softly. From this vantage point, she could look back toward the front door and take in nearly all of the small, six-aisle store. The front counter, to the right of the door, was partially obscured by bags of chips. But looking up, Shelly could see the camera in question. A small black eye, now dangling haphazardly, the lens shattered by a bullet.

"Good shot," she murmured.

Dan shrugged. "For all we know, he was standing right beneath it at the time."

"All the better to see you with," Shelly agreed, leading the way past the refrigeration units to a plain wooden door marked EMPLOYEES ONLY.

The office door was locked. Dan grimaced, probably already wondering which of them would have to search the dead cashier for the key. Shelly, however, had a better idea. Pulling on gloves, she raised one hand, ran it along the top of the door frame, and sure enough . . .

She smiled. Dan chuckled softly. Then, as if realizing how out of place such a thing sounded, he fell back to silence.

Shelly inserted the plain brass key into the lock, eased the door open.

If the small convenience store was hot, the windowless back office was stifling. In a coastal town known for mild temperatures, plenty of places didn't have air-conditioning, and this store was no exception. When Shelly snapped on the overhead light, she discovered a tiny fan perched on a top shelf, someone's idea of heat relief. Otherwise, the standing-room-only space contained a plank of wood topping two dinged-up metal filing cabinets, a battered-looking laptop, and, sure enough, a DVR, matte black, clearly new, stuck in a back corner with an attached monitor.

"Looks like a recent purchase," Dan said from behind Shelly's shoulder. The small space forced them to stand close, which only made the heat that much more uncomfortable.

"Recent thefts, suspicions?" Shelly murmured. The security system was a lucky break. Even basic models were over a hundred bucks, which, for a business that looked as worn and tired as this one, couldn't have been an easy expense.

She shifted to the side, sucking in her gut as Dan squeezed past, eyeing the DVR.

"Most systems offer immediate playback," Dan said, already punching buttons on the DVR.

He worked his tech magic, then an icon for SuperSecurity appeared on the monitor. A few seconds later, the screen filled with the top-back view of a woman's head.

The cashier, Shelly thought, Erin Hill, who'd started work at four A.M. and dutifully activated the security system.

Dan fiddled again, moving them forward in time: Five A.M. Six. Seven. Seven thirty, then . . .

Not a bad image. Fixed, which was a little disorienting. Black-and-white. Customers appeared and disappeared from the side of the screen, while the back of Erin's head remained dead center. From time to time, she also disappeared, maybe sitting down to read a book, or, more likely, play on her phone, during the lulls.

Seven fifty-three A.M. The male victim appeared. Shelly made out the side of his face as he briefly walked into the store, then disappeared down the aisle in search of chips. Thirty seconds. Forty. Fifty. The man reappeared, full face-shot now as he stood at the counter and dug around in his pocket for a wad of cash.

No audio. They could see but not hear. Given that the guy's mouth was moving, he was saying something to Erin. She must've replied, because he appeared to laugh in response. Then he pocketed his change. Grabbed his bag of chips. Turned toward the entrance.

Suddenly, his arms flew into the air. His body seemed to jerk, then stumble back, then jerk again.

He went down, his head disappearing offscreen till they were left with only the image of his sprawled legs.

Erin turned, her dark hair, their single focal point, suddenly whipping around. She gazed up at the camera, eyes wide, terrified.

Shelly couldn't see her mouth. Only the top half of her face. Was she screaming, was she trying to tell them something? At the side of the screen, a bare forearm came into view. Holding a gun. Pop, pop, pop.

And Erin disappeared from sight.

A life ended. Just like that.

Shelly found herself leaning over Dan's shoulder, staring at the video intently, as the shooter's arm came down, vanished off the screen. No, no, the shooter had to appear. He still had to take out the camera. A lull. Maybe the shooter pausing to check around outside, see if the sound of shots aroused any nearby suspicion. Or maybe he did rifle through the male victim's truck.

But eventually, three, four, five minutes later . . .

A lone figure walked into view. Not a man. A kid. Younger than even his first victim, maybe even younger than Erin Hill. Wearing a bulky black hoodie, sleeves balled up at his elbows but still totally inappropriate for a ninety-degree August morning. The boy approached the counter. He didn't look back at his first victim, nor down at his second. Instead, he peered directly up at the camera. Stared straight at it.

Wearing the flattest expression Shelly had ever seen. No remorse, no glee, not a drop of sweat on his brow.

The dark-eyed boy stared at Shelly through the lens.

Then he raised his arm and fired.

SHELLY HAD TO TAKE A MOMENT to get her breath back. Leaning over the monitor, Dan wasn't doing much better.

"Recognize him at all?" Shelly asked her deputy.

"No."

"Me neither." She doubted it mattered. An image this good, a description this solid, they should have a name within hours.

"He didn't ask for money," Dan murmured.

"No."

"Didn't even talk to them. Just . . . walked in. Murdered two people."

"I know."

"Did you see his eyes?"

Shelly nodded. She understood what her deputy was trying to say.

"What happened here?" Dan asked, his voice more plaintive now.

"I don't know," she told him honestly. "But I know who to ask:

Pierce Quincy. If this video is anything to go by, we're gonna need a profiler's insights. But the shooter's motivation isn't our biggest question yet."

"What's our biggest question?"

"A kid who kills this easily—is he done yet?"

Chapter 4

RETIRED FBI PROFILER PIERCE QUINCY was getting a second shot at life. He wasn't the type to dwell on such things. Maybe, fifteen years ago, not even the type to believe in such things. Raised by a single father after his mother's sudden death, he'd joined the Chicago PD before being recruited by the FBI.

Then, as a young up-and-coming agent, he'd been honored to join the pioneers of profiling, some of the Bureau's most legendary agents. If the work pulled him away from his wife, Bethie, then their two daughters, Mandy and Kimberly, well, hunting serial killers was like that. One could hardly chase down the monsters of the human world and still be home in time for dinner.

The work was a calling. And Quincy . . . he'd lost himself in it.

As his wife left him.

As his two daughters grew up without him.

Until one day, one phone call . . . Mandy had been in an accident. Except it turned out it wasn't an accident. Quincy had brought something home from work after all: a man intent on vengeance. And both Quincy's older daughter and his ex-wife paid the price before Quincy stopped him.

With Rainie, Quincy had found a better balance. And even if he still wasn't a man known for his gift of gab, at least with a former member of law enforcement, he had enough to say. Rainie understood his silence in the same way he understood her demons. She accepted that just because he didn't share his emotions didn't mean he didn't care. And he accepted that she would probably never sleep at night, and every day, all day, she would forever be making the courageous choice not to drink again.

Now here they were. A little older, a little wiser, and heaven help them, with a soon-to-be adopted teenage daughter. They were nervous, they were excited. They were terrified, they were hopeful.

They were parents.

Quincy had spent much of the morning listening to Rainie's low murmur down the hall. Most likely soothing the rabid beast that sometimes posed as their foster daughter, before carting her off to swim camp. Sharlah had come to them with a case history of antisocial tendencies. The paperwork hadn't lied.

With a foster child, bonding was always an issue. Quincy and Rainie had qualified as foster parents, despite his advanced years and her struggles with alcohol, in part because Quincy was considered an expert in bonding. Certainly, interruptions in the bonding process were serial killer 101. Combine the antisocial tendencies with the trauma Sharlah had experienced at a young age, and her caseworker had some concerns.

The first six months, Sharlah had certainly put them through their paces.

But perhaps Quincy was getting soft in his old age, because he looked at his soon-to-be daughter and he didn't see a future predator: He saw a lost little girl. One who'd suffered much and had built the corresponding protective layers. Sharlah didn't trust. Didn't reach out. Didn't have faith.

But she could bond.

Just look at her and Luka.

Quincy had taken the German shepherd on a whim. Some articles on adopting children encouraged adopting pets as well, to give the foster child a companion. Plus, family pets encouraged responsibility, and, yes, Quincy was old-school on that subject. But also . . . as long as he and Rainie were getting a child, why not a dog, too? If you're going to be domestic, might as well do it right.

Sharlah loved that dog. And Luka loved her right back. Two peas in a pod. Maybe not the socialization he and Rainie had been hoping for, but at least it was a start. Certainly he and Rainie liked to hope that one day, if they were really lucky, Sharlah would love them at least as much as she loved her dog.

Again, welcome to parenting.

Now Quincy returned his attention to the phone in his hand. Shelly Atkins, the county sheriff, was on the other end.

"Two dead," she was saying now, "both shot multiple times."

"Robbery?" he asked.

"The cash register's cleaned out. But get this: He took the money after he shot them, not before. According to the security video we watched, he didn't walk in and make demands. He walked in and opened fire. Given that, money feels more like an afterthought. If all he wanted was instant cash, waving around the handgun would've gotten the job done. No need to take out two people who weren't offering any resistance."

"You have a video of the incident?"

"Yeah, which is the real reason I'm calling. Quincy . . . Hell, I don't know how to explain it. But I'd like you to come down, take a look. This kid, the expression on his face as he pulls the trigger. He gunned down those two people because he could. And a boy that cold . . ."

"You're worried he's going to kill again."

"Exactly."

Quincy glanced at his watch. Rainie had already left to drop off Sharlah at the Y.

"Give us forty minutes," he told Sheriff Atkins. "Rainie and I will meet you at your office."

"Park in the back. Media's already caught wind."

"Press conference?"

"Might as well. They're gonna trample all over our crime scene otherwise. Besides, I got work for them."

"You're going to use the media?" Quincy arched a brow. "Tricky proposition."

"I'm a brave soul. Better yet, I'm a brave soul with a still-frame photo of a double murderer. Media broadcasts the image, and with any luck, we'll have our shooter's name by end of day."

Quincy had a thought: "You said the UNSUB shot out the camera."

"That's right."

"*After* he killed the two people?"

"Correct."

"Huh."

"What does *huh* mean?"

"Give me forty minutes, and we'll both find out."

QUINCY CONTACTED RAINIE ON HER CELL and arranged to meet her at the sheriff's office. He could hear Sharlah in the passenger seat, already asking excited questions. In the beginning, he and Rainie had made a conscientious effort to keep their work from their foster daughter. No need to add to Sharlah's trauma. But over time . . . Sharlah was genuinely interested. And bright and passionate. In the end, her own caseworker had green-lighted dinnertime conversations about basic criminology. After all, Sharlah was the kind of kid who already knew bad people existed in the world. For her, policing techniques, the psychology behind how to identify and apprehend criminals, were much more soothing than the traditional parenting placebos of "Don't worry about it" or "We'll take care of you." Sharlah wanted to be able to take care of herself. Which made her a big fan of Rainie's and Quincy's jobs. And maybe also made her exactly the right child for them.

He closed the binder on his desk—the one Rainie and Sharlah had so many questions about—and returned it to its locked drawer.

Then one last item of business, from years of being on the job.

He moved to the wall, to a framed black-and-white photograph of an adorable little girl with a gap-toothed smile peering out from behind a shower curtain. His oldest daughter, Mandy, in the years before life, drinking, and a psychopath had all caught up with her.

He set the photo aside, revealing the gun safe. He'd recently upgraded to a biometrics model. Now he placed his fingertip in the appropriate spot. A whir, a click, and the door swung open.

He selected the twenty-two, a backup piece, because technically speaking, law enforcement consultants weren't required to carry a sidearm. And yet, a man who knew the things he knew . . .

Quincy tucked the gun in his ankle holster.

Then prepared himself to head out into a heat wave.

THE COUNTY SHERIFF'S DEPARTMENT looked the part. Two stories, with squat lines and a beige exterior, it showed off the kind of architecture only budget-conscious local governments could love.

Heeding Shelly's advice, Quincy headed for the rear of the building, his black Lexus slipping past a growing throng of news vans. Ten A.M. Apparently, no one wanted to be late for the press conference at half past the hour.

Quincy shook his head as he made the turn into the parking lot. There were definitely parts of the job he did not miss, and dealing with the press topped the list.

He spotted Rainie's car a moment later. She sat inside, no doubt taking advantage of its air-conditioning for as long as possible. Given the temps outside he didn't blame her.

He pulled in beside her. She opened her door as he unfastened his seat belt, then they both stood in the heat.

"Wow," she said, which pretty much summed up the hot-as-an-oven feel.

Having had drop-off duty for Sharlah, Rainie was dressed casually, black capris and a light green T-shirt with a dark green swirling pattern up one side. She could've been a hot mom on her way to yoga. All these years later, Quincy was still humbled that she was his wife.

In his case, old habits died hard. He wore what Rainie teasingly referred to as FBI casual. Tan slacks and a dark blue polo shirt. Once upon a time, his shirt would've been emblazoned with *FBI*. Today, he'd gone with one advertising the SIG Sauer Academy, where he taught firearms classes from time to time. Law enforcement related, without being false advertising.

"How'd drop-off go?" he asked now, closing his door, then coming around to greet her.

Rainie shrugged. "She's doing her best."

"Which means we have probably an hour before we're called to pick her up?"

"If that." Rainie fell in step beside him as they headed toward the building. "Do you ever think it's ironic that we, of all people, are trying to teach a child social skills?"

"All the time," he assured her. Reaching the door first, he held it open for her, then followed into the relative cool of the building. He already knew from experience the sensation wouldn't last. Temperatures this hot weren't common along the coast, meaning most air-conditioning units couldn't keep up—assuming the building was fortunate enough to have air-conditioning at all.

Having visited before, Quincy and Rainie walked straight to the desk duty officer, flashed their IDs, and were buzzed through the heavy metal door into the heart of the unit. Like most county sheriff's buildings, it housed everything from local lockup to a dispatch center, to several different departments, including the second-floor detectives' unit, which is where Quincy figured they'd find Shelly now. They headed up, and sure enough . . .

Shelly stood in a moderately sized space meant to house four detectives, but not necessarily at the same time. Bone-colored walls, commercial-grade blue carpet, stock fake-wood desks—it looked like any detectives' bull pen Quincy had ever visited, which made it on par with the rest of the building.

Someone had had the foresight to push two of the desks to the side, clearing space in the middle of the room. Shelly, her sergeant Roy Peterson, and a deputy, Dan Mitchell, stood there now, studying an image on the flat-screen mounted on the far wall. Given Rainie and Quincy knew everyone present, hellos were quick, then they were down to business.

"Call came in shortly after eight A.M.," Shelly explained to Rainie and Quincy now. She pointed to the flat-screen. On it appeared a frozen head shot of a white adolescent male, wearing a black hoodie and staring straight back at them. His face was devoid of emotion.

"I personally responded to the call—other deputies having already logged too much overtime," she added upon seeing their questioning looks. The sheriff was rocking lightly on her feet. Tired but wired. Quincy remembered that feeling well.

"But it was all over and done by the time I got there," Shelly said now. "Two dead, perpetrator gone. Given the situation, I made the decision to access the security system on-site, rather than wait for the staties, as it seemed our best option for identifying the shooter."

"Which is this person here?" Quincy gestured to the monitor.

"Yep."

He studied the photo again, feeling a niggling sense of recognition, as if he'd both met this kid once and never seen him before in his life. He glanced over at Rainie, who was also frowning at the image.

"Can we see it from the beginning?" Rainie asked.

"Whatever you think will help."

Shelly picked up the remote. The flat-faced young male disappeared. Then a fresh image appeared, the back of a woman's head. Shelly hit play and the video began.

The resolution was higher quality than Quincy would've expected from a gas station security cam. The video was also short. Gun appeared and within a matter of seconds, much less than a minute, two people were dead. A pause, probably at least a couple minutes in length, then the UNSUB stepped fully into view. Peered directly at them. And raised his gun for one final shot.

"Weapon?" Quincy asked now, the angle of the video making it hard to tell.

"Nine millimeter, at least according to the slug recovered. We'll know more once state's ballistics has had a chance to analyze."

Quincy nodded. Given the shocking nature of this crime—not to mention its soon-to-be-high press profile—the state would no doubt make evidence processing a priority.

Rainie had another question: "How did the shooter arrive on scene? Drive? Walk?" She looked at Shelly.

"Good question. EZ Gas sits off on its own. No neighbors to serve as witnesses. But given its location five miles north on the highway . . . would be a long, hot walk on foot."

"Meaning most likely the shooter drove," Rainie said.

"Only vehicle at the scene is a red pickup, belonging to the male victim."

"So we don't know if the suspect acted on his own or had an accomplice, say, a getaway driver?" Rainie pressed.

"Anything's possible." Shelly clicked back to the still frame of the shooter. "At this moment, this is what we got. Identify this white male—"

"And you have your shooter," Quincy filled in for her.

"That's the plan. Hence the press conference. Which, shit, I should be preparing for." Shelly stared at Quincy and Rainie. "Think he's dangerous?"

"Yes," they both answered without hesitation.

"So I go with the standard lines. Anyone who has any information should contact us directly, do not try to approach this individual on their own."

"Why'd he do this?" Quincy spoke up. "Why did this kid shoot and kill these two people?"

"He ambushed them," Rainie stated. "Which is very heavy-handed if robbery was his sole motivation." She turned to Quincy. "No hesitation," she said.

Shelly caught the implication. "You think he's done this before."

"Highly possible," Quincy murmured. "We need backgrounds on both victims. Particularly the female."

Again, Shelly was no dumb bunny. "She was the real target? She's close enough in age to the shooter. Maybe they had a lover's quarrel, making the chip customer just the poor slob who was in the wrong place at the wrong time."

"I think that scenario would make your life easier," Quincy said. "If this was some kind of breakup gone wrong, the killer's objective has been fulfilled. He did what he set out to do."

"And now?"

Quincy didn't hesitate. "If you're very lucky, he'll go home and shoot himself."

"And if I'm not that lucky?" Shelly asked.

"You're right, his adventures are just beginning. Show the photo to the press," Quincy advised. "Get an ID. But definitely tag him as armed and dangerous. Locals should not approach."

"What do you think the boy will do next?" Shelly asked. "Off the record. Just between us local yokels, who fortunately don't spend a lot of time dealing with these kinds of crimes."

Quincy frowned. He studied the picture. Frowned again.

"I think this boy gunned down two people in less than one minute," he said, "then *made sure* to show us his face. I would say at this point, with this suspect, we don't know nearly enough."

Chapter 5

WE'VE GOT A NAME and an address." Sergeant Peterson stuck his head in Shelly's office, where she was sitting with Quincy and Rainie. They all had cups of coffee, though Quincy knew from experience that Shelly's mug was actually chamomile tea in disguise.

"But I haven't done the press conference yet," Shelly said.

"No need. I e-mailed the photo to a couple of juvenile probation officers." Peterson glanced at Quincy. "You implied the kid had some experience. Turns out you were right. Aly Sanchez hit me right back. Boy's one of hers."

"Is she bringing him in?" Quincy asked with a frown. He'd already risen to his feet, Shelly and Rainie as well.

"Negative. I told her to delay contact for now. I'm worried if he heads to her office, gets any kind of bad vibe off of her at all . . . Kid's already gunned down two; I didn't want to put Aly in that kind of situation."

"Sheet?" Shelly asked.

"Mostly minor offenses, trespassing, criminal mischief. But it's a long record for a seventeen-year-old. Kid's been busy. According to Aly, the suspect currently resides with Sandra and Frank Duvall. Frank is a teacher at Bakersville High, Sandra a homemaker. With their own son off at college, the Duvalls agreed to foster the boy last year. Now get this: Frank Duvall has six firearms registered in his name, including a nine mil."

"Contact the family?" Shelly asked.

"Phoned the house. No answer."

"All right. I'll notify SWAT. When they give the green light, we'll roll."

"It would be best if the suspect didn't feel cornered," Quincy advised.

"I'll be sure to remind them to use their nice voice. Any other advice, Profiler Man?"

"You still have the press waiting outside."

"Ah shit."

"It's okay," Rainie assured her. "If SWAT doesn't have any luck at the Duvalls' place, maybe they can take care of the media for you instead."

THE DUVALLS' ADDRESS TURNED OUT to be a modest, light gray ranch, set far back from the road. One side boasted a grove of towering Douglas firs, the other side a thick hedge of rhododendrons. The front porch was dotted with pots of cheery red flowers, and someone had hung a sign next to the door advertising HOME SWEET HOME.

Apparently, the foster parents cared enough to tend their house. Had their suspected shooter appreciated the effort, Quincy wondered, or was he mostly excited to be placed in a home with six registered firearms?

Quincy and Rainie waited with Shelly while half a dozen SWAT team members spread around the property, made their approach. Shelly picked up her cell, dialed the house number one more time.

All appeared to be quiet. No car in the driveway. No sign of family members through the window.

Still, Quincy felt jittery, on edge. The result of too much coffee. He glanced over at Rainie and saw she felt the same. She glanced at her watch.

"Swim camp," she mouthed back at him.

Right. Picking up Sharlah. Things he should know better than to forget by now. Interesting how three years later domestic life was still something he had to think about. Whereas this, closing in on a suspected murderer, felt as natural as riding a bike.

Static over the radio. Shelly did the honors: "Team leader, come in."

"Team Alpha is in position. Good to go."

"Green light, Team Alpha. Go."

The officers seemed to burst onto the scene. Front of the house, rear of the house. Banging on the doors, then half a second later, when there was still no response, one man dropping low, popping the door with a battering ram. Then heavily armed, heavily armored men poured into the tiny ranch.

Quincy found himself holding his breath. Straining his ears for shouts, screams, shots fired.

Nothing. Nothing, nothing, nothing.

He glanced at Rainie just as Shelly's radio once more crackled to life.

"Team leader to base."

"Go ahead, team leader."

"We have secured the premises."

"Any sign of the suspect?"

"No, ma'am."

"Members of the family?"

"Um, ma'am. You're going to want to see this."

Which told Quincy all he needed to know about the fate of Frank and Sandra Duvall.

FRANK DUVALL NEVER MADE IT out of bed. His body lay flat on its back, thin sheet just pulled to his bare chest, single bullet hole through his forehead. Quincy could see powder burns rimming the edges of the hole, where the barrel of the gun had pressed against the flesh. This shot had been up close and personal.

Which no doubt had woken up Sandra Duvall from her place beside her husband. She'd thrown back the sheet, gotten both feet on the floor, before taking three shots to the back. Tightly clustered, the way all law enforcement officers were taught, Quincy couldn't help but think. The shooter aiming for center mass.

She'd gone down face-first beside the bed, arms flung wide, thin nightgown bunched around her waist.

Two more rooms down the hall. The first was small, with barely enough room for a twin bed and modest desk. The window was open, trying to let in a fresh breeze, except there wasn't any. Similar to the Duvalls' room, a fan droned in the corner, mostly blowing around hot air.

Covers were kicked back, the August heat too sweltering for blankets. No bodies in here. Not much of anything really. The bed, the fan, a lamp. Pile of paperbacks on the bed. Mound of dirty clothes in the opposite corner. Desk held a charger for an electronic device, currently missing.

Quincy knew without being told that this was the foster child's room, their teenage suspect. And it pained him to know Sharlah would recognize this space. Devoid of personalization. Because in a foster's world, possessions were rewards that had to be earned. And given this seventeen-year-old's rap sheet, he'd probably spent more time losing privileges than gaining them.

One more room down the hall. Quincy felt himself falter. A rare and telling moment for a man attempting fatherhood a second time around.

Rainie had opted not to enter the house at all.

"I know my limits," she'd told him, and he'd accepted that.

Door was cracked open, most likely to encourage a cross breeze. Quincy approached alone, the hallway too small, the rooms too tightly bunched to allow for multiple officers. Shelly hadn't even made the rounds yet. Recognizing the limits of the space, and wanting to reduce contamination of the crime scene, she'd asked Quincy to go ahead. Of them all, he was the most qualified.

Roy Peterson had said the Duvalls had a college-age son. Given that it was August, odds were high the boy would be home from school. . . .

With his gloved hand, Quincy pushed open the next wooden door. Another small room. Twin bed, neatly made, brown and blue quilt pulled tight. And devoid of a body. No blood, no drone of flies, no stench of death.

Just . . . a room. Beneath the window was a desk, which appeared completely cleared off. The nightstand held an alarm clock, an old brass lamp, and little more. The only hint of personality came from two posters tacked to the dark paneled walls, both featuring basketball players. The Portland Trail Blazers, Quincy judged by the uniforms, though not being a follower of basketball, he couldn't identify the players.

He stepped back from the empty room and exhaled softly.

He retraced his steps to the modest family room, where Shelly stood next to an afghan-covered oversize gray sofa, hands on her hips, sweat beading on her face in the stifling heat. She stared at him.

"Two down. The Duvalls. Both shot and killed in their bedroom. Single shot for him, three to center mass for her," Quincy reported. "Third bedroom appears unoccupied. Duvalls' son not home from college?"

"Henry Duvall," Shelly relayed. "Just learned he's studying engineering at OSU, and currently in some kind of work-study program at a high-tech firm in Beaverton. So no, he didn't come home for the summer."

"You just spoke to him?" Quincy asked, because it seemed a little early to be contacting family with information of a crime they had no details on.

"Nah, just touched based with Aly Sanchez, the probation officer.

She's the one who personally contacted the Duvalls about taking in her charge. Needless to say, she's a little rattled from the morning's events. Any sign of our suspect?"

"Bed's unmade, as if recently occupied. Also, the fan's still on. Other than that, though . . . The bedroom appears more functional than comforting."

"Eleven months later, kid's not ready to unpack yet?"

"Or he has nothing to unpack." Quincy moved into the kitchen, looked around. Three dinner plates were neatly stacked in the drying rack next to the sink. Same with glasses and silverware. Next he checked the refrigerator, which was solidly stocked with milk, eggs, orange juice, and a hodgepodge collection of Tupperware.

"It appears they ate dinner last night, cleaned up the dishes afterward."

"Shooting was most likely early this morning," Shelly filled in. "If it had been last night, believe it or not, the smell would be even worse."

"Transport options?" Quincy asked.

"Good question." Shelly got on her radio, contacted dispatch. "Vehicles registered to Frank and Sandra Duvall," she requested, rattling off the address. It only took a minute for dispatch to come back with the answer. Two vehicles, a ten-year-old silver Honda and a fifteen-year-old blue Chevy pickup.

"Honda's in the garage," Shelly reported, having walked the outside perimeter.

"But no sign of the truck, which I bet Duvall kept parked in the driveway."

Shelly nodded.

"Gun safe?" Quincy asked next.

"I'm assuming the bedroom," Shelly said.

"Didn't see any sign of one. The garage?"

"Nothing there."

They split up to conduct the search. Shelly was the one who found it first. Down in the basement, which was blessedly cooler than up-stairs. Quincy joined her in the gloom, the overhead light revealing an old Ping-Pong table, a deep freezer, and next to a pile of boxes, a heavy-duty gun safe, tall enough for rifles.

The door to the safe was ajar.

Using a gloved finger, Shelly slowly opened the door.

A couple of loose bullets, and nothing else.

Quincy: "How many guns did you say Frank Duvall had again?"

"Six."

Quincy studied the empty space. "I'm going to guess plenty of ammo to go with them."

"In other words, I've got a seventeen-year-old suspect, heavily armed, with a truck, who's possibly already shot and killed four peo-ple. Quincy, what's going on here? I mean, a troubled kid shooting his foster parents is one thing, but why the two at the convenience store? What the hell does this kid want?"

"He raided the gun safe, then shot the Duvalls," Quincy mur-mured.

"Looks that way."

"Then got in the truck, and . . ."

"Decided to keep on shooting?"

"Spree." Quincy turned, made sure he had the sheriff's full atten-tion. "Our suspect's on a shooting spree. Such incidents generally start with a murder close to home, killing a wife, boss, parent. In-stead of that violence being the end of things, however, the shooter suffers a psychotic break, goes on a rampage. The first target was personal. But from here on out . . . The UNSUB will kill anyone, ev-eryone, unfortunate enough to cross his path. You have a highly dan-gerous offender on the loose, Sheriff Atkins. And he will kill again."

Beneath the sheen of sweat, Shelly's face had grown pale. It made the scars stand out around her neck.

"All right," she said tightly. Then repeated, "All right. We'll need to establish a command center. Issue a BOLO for the missing Chevy. Mobilize SWAT, state reinforcements—hell, anyone and everyone with a badge."

"All public places near the EZ Gas should go into lockdown. Libraries, community centers, day cares, etc." Swim camps, Quincy thought, thankful the Y's pool was on the other end of town.

"Got it."

"We need to learn about this kid, everything there is to know about him. Friends, associates, hobbies, interests. Where would he go under pressure? And how good are his shooting skills?"

"Okay."

"Time matters. The longer this situation drags on . . ."

"More dangerous the boy becomes," Shelly filled in.

"Not to mention the general public, most of whom around these parts—"

"Are heavily armed." Shelly sighed. She nodded, bolstering herself again. She was a good sheriff, Quincy knew, solid under pressure. But like most county sheriffs, more of her time was spent on the war on drugs and domestic cases than crimes of this nature. The next twenty-four hours would be taxing for them all.

Now Shelly unclipped her radio again, contacted dispatch.

"I need a BOLO out on a seventeen-year-old male. Brown hair, brown eyes, last seen wearing a black hoodie and believed to be driving a blue Chevy pickup, license plate . . ." Shelly rattled off the sequence. "He is considered heavily armed and should be approached with extreme caution. I need all neighboring towns notified as well as state police. Also, forest rangers, Fish and Game, local campgrounds. You know the drill. Boy's name is Telly Ray Nash."

Quincy stopped. Felt the blood drain out of his face. "What?"

"Telly Ray Nash," Shelly repeated.

But Quincy wasn't listening anymore. He was charging up the stairs, looking for Rainie.

Chapter 6

"YOU DON'T TRUST ME," *the man said.* Frank. Call me Frank, *he'd told me that first afternoon. Then shook my hand. Actually shook it, while his wife—Sandra—had hovered beside him, clasping and unclasping her fingers. No doubt the hugging type, trying to rein herself in.*

"It's okay," he continued now, looking straight at me. "To be honest, I don't trust you, either. Too early for that. We're still getting to know one another."

I didn't say anything. What was there to say? We were standing in a clearing in the middle of the forest. In front of us, tacked to a beat-up wooden pallet, was a brand-new shooting target, provided by Frank. Around our feet, a litter of spent shells, bottle caps, and cigarette butts. All the locals came out here, Frank had told me as we drove over. A regular redneck shooting range.

I'd been living with the Duvalls for about four weeks. In some fosters, you got, say, a cookie, or even a cake, to mark the one-month anniversary. In the Duvalls' house, apparently you went shooting.

From the back of his truck, Frank removed a folding table. I set it up. Then Frank got out two pairs of safety glasses, a package of earplugs, and boxes of ammo. Finally, from behind the driver's seat, he pulled out a locked black box slightly larger than a lunchbox. The gun. Guns?

I still wasn't sure what I was doing here. I guess it beat taking a kid with my history to a batting cage.

Frank typed a combo into the locked carrying case. He didn't try to hide the screen, so I didn't try not to watch. I don't talk much, my probation officer would tell you. But I'm observant. Again, kid with my history, hard not to be.

Frank raised the lid. Box was lined with black foam, shaped like an egg carton, or maybe the sound buffers they put up in recording studios. Nestled in the middle, black on black, sat the handgun. Smaller than I would've thought. And . . . frightening.

I'd never shot a gun before, assuming video games don't count.

I stuck my hands in my pockets. Cool October morning. My feet and hands were wet with morning dew. Again, what the hell was I doing here?

Frank lifted out the piece. "Ruger SR twenty-two," he declared proudly. "Ten plus one, meaning ten rounds in the magazine, one in the chamber. Now, first things first. A gun's a tool. And a tool must be treated with respect."

He stared at me expectantly. Finally, I nodded, having to look up to meet his eyes. Frank was a big guy. Six four. Solidly built, though more basketballer than footballer. A science teacher at the local high school, he'd grown up in these parts. Local boy, through and through. When he was my age, he'd been working his parents' dairy farm every morning and afternoon, while tearing up the boards as a varsity star, and spending most Saturday nights chugging beer and chasing trouble. He understood being a teenage boy, he'd told me my first night in their home. He understood trouble.

He and his wife, they'd taken me in eyes wide-open. They knew what I'd done. They knew what I was still capable of doing.

They also knew this was it. Seventeen-year-old boy, due to age out of the system in another year. The Duvalls were my last chance to ever be part of something. Not an adopted kid. I'd already entered the system too old for those kinds of pipe dreams. But play my cards right, extend a little trust, hell, clean up my act, and I could at least have a forever foster family. A place to go every Christmas, Thanks-giving. Better yet, as my probation officer explained to me, guidance for all the Big Changes coming my way—getting a job, setting up my own place, paying my own bills. Real world straight ahead. A couple of supportive parental figures in my corner would be a huge help. Or so my probation officer told me.

I didn't have the heart to confide in her, or big, confident, I Know Trouble Frank and cookie-baking, Please Just Let Me Give You a Hug Sandra, that I didn't do family.

Not anymore.

"When it comes to handling firearms," Frank said now, still hold-ing the twenty-two, "safety first. Never point the gun at anything you don't want to shoot. Not even when you think it's unloaded."

He stared at me.

"Never point the gun at anything you don't want to shoot," I re-peated belatedly.

"Some guys, they pretend there's a laser extending out the end of the gun. Anything the laser hits, it slices through. Looking at the Ruger right now, what am I hitting?"

"Um, that tree."

"Can we afford for that tree to be cut in half?"

"Guess so. Sure."

"And now?"

"Just lost your big toe."

"Exactly. And I need my big toe, so I'm not going to dangle the gun like an idiot and risk shooting off my own foot."

"Okay."

"Second cardinal rule: Never assume the gun is unloaded. Even if I hand it to you and say it's clear, you check it for yourself. Always. End of story."

He looked very serious. Even grim. Once again, I nodded.

Frank set the gun on the table, still pointed away from us, at the tree. Tree was a big one. Thick trunk covered in lighter patches of sage-green moss. Or maybe it was lichen. I confused the two. Frank would know the answer. If, of course, I asked him.

"Clearing a gun involves two steps. First, eject the magazine." Frank lifted the Ruger, massive hand wrapped around the grip. "Come here. Take it. Gun won't bite. And if you can't handle it unloaded, then you're certainly not ready for target practice."

I forced my hands out of my pockets. Willed myself to take a step forward. Which was ironic, really, because all Foster Frank had to do was tell me never to touch his firearms, and I would've had my hands on the entire collection in a matter of seconds.

Which, having read my file, most likely he knew. Warn a kid with oppositional defiant disorder not to do something, and you've pretty much guaranteed the crime. Whereas this, granting me permission, offering actual training on how to shoot . . . Now I didn't even want the stupid twenty-two.

Mostly I wished the gun and bullets and moss/lichen-covered trees would go away.

Frank placed the Ruger in my right hand.

It felt heavier than I expected. That was my first thought. But also . . . comfortable. The rubbery grip felt the right size for my palm. The gun was solid but not large.

Certainly it felt easier to wield than a baseball bat.

"'Kay, finger off the trigger. Never touch it till you're ready to shoot. Just a good habit to have. Instead, I recommend placing your finger above the trigger guard. Feel how the grip is rubbery in your palm? That's actually removable—you can slide it on and off. The real gun is matte metal. That's what you're feeling with your trigger finger. It's good to be aware of these things. It will help make the placement of the gun in your hand, the proper position of your trigger finger, more and more automatic. You'll do things based on feel. That's when you'll know you're a good shooter."

I didn't say anything. But he was right. I could feel the different textures, rubber against my palm, matte metal against my index finger. It felt . . . real.

"Now, keeping your finger off the trigger and the gun pointed away, you need to clear your weapon. First step is to eject the magazine. Look on the left side of the grip, right behind the trigger guard; see that small black button? With your thumb, push it."

I did, and immediately the magazine popped out from the bottom of the handle. Not all the way out, but enough that I could slide it out with my left hand. It felt surprisingly light.

"This magazine can hold ten shots. How many bullets do you see?" Frank asked me.

I frowned. "Nothing. It's empty."

"So your gun is cleared?"

I glanced at him. Just because I'd never shot before didn't mean I didn't know when I was being played. "You said first step, meaning there's at least one more."

"Good job. Remember what else I told you about the Ruger? When I first described it?"

"Ten plus one," I recalled slowly. "The chamber. Ten in the magazine, which I just ejected. But that leaves one in the chamber."

"Excellent. Gun is never cleared until you've checked the chamber. So first eject the magazine, then rack back the slide to check the chamber. With the magazine ejected, place your left hand on top of the gun. Smooth metal slide. Again, feel the different texture."

"Yeah."

"Rubber grip. Matte metal body. Smooth metal slide. Yes?"

"Yes."

"Holding the gun out straight-armed, use your left hand to rack back the top slide. Use a little muscle, it's okay."

I tried harder. Abruptly, the slide shot back. I startled, let go, and it slammed forward again.

Frank chuckled. "Easy, buddy. Good way to pinch your hand and lose some skin. You want a smooth motion. Slide it back easily, don't let go."

I fumbled two more times before finally getting it.

"Look in the chamber," he instructed me.

"Clear."

"Now you can ease the slide forward, or, if you want, left side of the gun, above the trigger guard in front of the safety, see that black button? Click it up, and it will hold the slide in the open position."

I found the button, awkwardly got it up.

Frank took the gun from me, placed it on the folding table. "Protocol, you and me. Always present a firearm exactly like this. Magazine out, chamber exposed. That way we both can see, everyone can see, the weapon is clear. Got it?"

"Yeah."

"Okay, now time to get serious. But before we load and start talking shooting, we first must establish your dominant eye."

Turned out my right eye was dominant. And no squeezing one eye shut when pulling the trigger. Instead, concentrate on gazing down the gun sight, homing in on the target, using your dominant eye.

Frank went first. Emptied the magazine. A tight cluster, most in the bull's-eye. Showing off for the foster kid, I thought. But he didn't puff up his chest. More like nodded to himself. Fulfilled his own expectations.

Then it was my turn. Safety glasses. Earplugs. Chasing rolling brass all over the folding table as I struggled to load three bullets into the magazine—just enough to get me started.

Frank positioned me three yards from the target. So close I could've spit on it.

Then, showtime.

The trigger pull was longer than I expected. Then the recoil totally unexpected. The gun jumped up in my hand. I startled. And the tree to the right of the target was now down some moss/lichen.

Frank didn't seem surprised at all. "Concentrate on the trigger pull," he advised. "First pull is long, then the rest of the shots are short. Get used to how it feels. Then we'll work on aim."

Lining up the shot, exhaling all the breath from my lungs, easing back the trigger. By the end of the morning, I at least had control. Standing at five yards, even if I didn't nail the red zone, my shots now showed some semblance of grouping.

"Consistency," Frank acknowledged. "A good start."

He didn't shoot as much as he worked with me. But then, at the end, no doubt to blow off a little steam, he showed off: He turned the paper target sideways, till it faced the trees and we were staring at only its impossibly thin edge. Single shot, he hit the hairsbreadth target, neatly severing the paper in half.

"You been shooting a long time," I said finally, closest I could come to praise.

"Most of my life," he said as he took the gun, cleared the magazine and chamber, and returned it to its padded box. "At home, I'll teach you fieldstripping. Shooting's only half the fun—then you gotta take care of your weapon."

We worked together to pack up the earplugs, safety glasses, boxes of bullets, folding table. I grabbed the remnants of the target. He closed up the back of the truck.

Then he was staring at me again, eyes serious. Face grim.

"You know why we took you in, Telly?"

I didn't say anything.

"We believe in you. We read your file. What happened with your family. Do you remember that night, Telly?"

No need to ask which night he was talking about. My whole life came down to only one evening.

"Not much." I didn't look at him. Went back to studying moss on trees.

"Do you think what you did was right?"

I shook my head.

Frank stilled, studied me for a bit.

"Family counselor thinks you should consider therapy again," he said at last. "We'll take you. We'll do our part, if you think it'll help."

"No thank you."

"Telly, what happened to you, to your whole family, that was a terrible thing. And sometimes, you keep something that terrible inside, it festers, becomes even worse than it was the first time around."

"I don't remember," I heard myself say.

"You don't remember."

"No. My mom screaming, yeah. And my dad . . . But after the baseball bat. Once I got my hands on the bat . . . I don't remember much after that."

"A man does what a man has to do to protect his family," Frank said.

I finally looked at him. I had no idea what he was talking about.

"Your sister defended your actions. Said you saved her, you saved both of you, from your father. That's important, Telly. Means no matter what other people say, you did right that night. You need to hold on to that. It says something about the boy you were, and the man you can become. That's why Sandra and I took you in. Maybe you think what you did was wrong. But Sandra and I . . . We see a boy who did what he had to do. And that boy deserves a better shot at life."

"I hurt my baby sister."

"You broke her arm. She recovered. Surely, if your dad had gotten to her first, it would've been worse."

I didn't have a response to that. I hadn't been lying before: I didn't remember too much from that night. Red haze of battle, maybe even a blackout, the first shrink had tried explaining to me, brought on by terror and trauma and years of abuse. What I did remember was the sound of bone snapping.

And my baby sister's scream. A long, high, thin scream that went on and on and on.

Till eight years later, it was still locked inside my head.

"I don't want to see a shrink," I told Frank.

"All right. But we're gonna talk about it, Telly, because you need to talk about it. Your life is changing. One year from now, you'll be eighteen, ready to head out on your own. Sandra and I, our job is to prepare you for that. Think you're ready to be all alone in the big world?"

I didn't know what to say.

"Telly," he explained patiently, "no one is ready to be all alone in the big world. And no one should have to be. Okay? So here we are. Twelve months to get to know you, twelve months for you to get to know us. Make some sense?"

I still didn't know what to say.

He nodded, seeming to understand. "All right. How about shooting? Would you like to go shooting again?"

I nodded.

He rapped the tailgate of the truck, then headed for the driver's door. "Sounds like a plan. Gotta say, nice work today. You're a real natural, Telly. Calm and controlled. Keep this up, and next time, I'll bring the rifles."

Chapter 7

RAINIE KNEW IT WAS BAD the moment Quincy walked out of the house. It wasn't so much the expression on his face—Quincy prided himself on his New England reserve—as the set of his jaw. Tight. Grim. A man working on the best way to say something he didn't want to say.

She noticed dark splotches on his navy blue polo. Sweat stains from the unbearable heat. To spy such a human element on her notoriously composed husband unnerved her.

"Is the family dead?" she asked softly as he came to a stop before her.

"The foster parents, Frank and Sandra Duvall. Both shot in the bedroom."

"Their son?"

"No. He's in Beaverton, some kind of work-study program. Rainie, the Duvalls' foster son, our suspected shooter, is Telly Ray Nash."

It took her a moment to understand. She found herself thinking in confusion, But that's Sharlah's last name. Then the pieces of the puzzle fell into place and she felt a curious sinking sensation in her stomach.

"Sharlah's older brother," she stated.

"Has she had any contact with him? Mentioned him at all?" When troubled, Sharlah was more likely to confide in Rainie than Quincy, and they both knew it. Having said that, Sharlah wasn't that likely to confide. We are a family of loners, Rainie thought, not for the first time.

"She's never talked about him. Quincy, he killed their parents."

"I know. Baseball bat, not a gun."

"He broke Sharlah's arm."

"I know."

"She's not supposed to have any contact with him. Says so in her file. And severing family ties, that's not something DHS does lightly."

Quincy nodded.

"He killed the Duvalls first, didn't he?" Rainie filled in.

"Yes."

Rainie had been working with Quincy long enough to know the rest. "Telly Ray Nash is on a spree."

"Did you know there's a new term being suggested? Rampage killer." Quincy tucked his hands in his pockets. He wasn't looking at Rainie but staring off in the distance, at the grove of fir trees. Calming himself with logic, Rainie recognized. If he could define and analyze what was going on, then he could control it. And like any parent, Quincy didn't want to feel out of control when it came to his daughter.

"Spree killers and mass murderers are driven by the same psychological need," Quincy continued. "A feeling of isolation, a desire to get revenge on the society that rejected them. Mass murderers confine their violence to one location—a school, a cinema, their former employer. Whereas spree killers by definition kill at more than one location in a short period of time."

"Mass murderers on the go."

"Exactly. But there have been some cases with overlap. Kip Kinkel, who murdered his parents before proceeding on to his high school. Adam Lanza, who shot his mother before attacking Sandy Hook. Are they spree shooters, given that their crimes took place at more than one location? Or are they mass murderers, given that the bulk of their crimes occurred at a single target?"

Rainie waited for Quincy to answer his own question.

"Criminologists like to define," he murmured. "If we can define, then we can understand. Hence the proposal of a third label—rampage killer—to cover both spree and mass murderers."

"The gas station isn't a school or former employer," Rainie said. "As far as we know, it was a random target."

"Spree," Quincy said.

"He isn't done."

"Spree killings only end when the shooter himself is killed."

"I need to pick up Sharlah." Rainie's voice was tight, not quite herself. "What do we tell her?"

"This will be on the news. Such a high-profile manhunt? It will be the talk of the town."

"In other words, we need to be the ones to break it to her first."

"She should stay inside for a bit," Quincy said. "Keep Luka close."

Rainie nodded. He wasn't saying anything she didn't know. And yet she still felt curiously unanchored. Hours ago, she'd been taking her daughter to swim camp, then joining her husband for a local police consult, and now . . .

Her daughter's estranged brother was a suspected spree/rampage killer. Where in the foster training was that class? How exactly did she look into her daughter's eyes and shatter her world yet again?

The antidote to fear and anxiety was strength and self-reliance. Rainie knew that much about basic psychology, and that was before all the parenting classes. A child with Sharlah's history did not want coddling or platitudes. She already knew the worst could happen. What she needed was information, guidance, and reassurance of her own fortitude. Sharlah was strong and Rainie's job was to remind her of her strength.

Which meant, of course, Rainie needed to muster her own. Quickly. "And you?" she asked her husband now.

"I told Sheriff Atkins I'd assist with a profile. But also . . . I want to see if I can find more information on Sharlah's parents' deaths."

"You think what Telly did eight years ago might be relevant to what's happening now." Quincy nodded. A criminal's history always mattered. "But I thought no charges were filed. Given that, are there even records to unseal, check?" Rainie asked.

"Maybe not. But a case that sensational, someone—the DA, investigating detectives, DHS caseworker—is bound to remember something."

"All right. You talk to the experts and I'll talk to Sharlah. She doesn't like to revisit the past, though. And given her age at the time, I don't know how much she even remembers."

"Good luck," Quincy said.

"Where do you think he'll go next?" Rainie asked abruptly, referring to Telly Ray Nash.

"I don't know, but I imagine we'll hear about it soon enough."

RAINIE ARRIVED OUTSIDE THE Y five minutes before pickup. Sharlah was already standing outside, a tall, gangly girl with wet hair dripping down her back and a bright yellow swim bag slung over her shoulder.

Much to Rainie's surprise, her daughter—soon-to-be, close enough, she always thought—was not alone. A little girl of maybe six or seven stood beside Sharlah, talking in an animated manner. In contrast, Sharlah's face was guarded, but she nodded at whatever the girl was saying.

Rainie pulled up, lowered the window.

"Is that your mom?" the little girl asked immediately. "She's very pretty. Are you coming back tomorrow? I think you should come back tomorrow. You did very well today. We should have you swimming by the end of the week!"

"Good-bye," Sharlah said. She opened the car door, slid inside, already leaning toward the blasting air-conditioning. Outside the girl waved madly.

"New swim coach?" Rainie asked, pulling away. She was tapping the steering wheel with her finger. She forced herself to stop, take a deep breath, be more focused.

"Something like that."

"Was it as bad as you thought?"

"I can't swim."

"Sure you can. I've seen you in the ocean often enough."

Sharlah shook her head. "That's not swimming. That's floating. And . . . puttering. I can putter in water. But swim . . . Freestyle, breaststroke, backstroke. I don't know any of that. Which means I was put in with the little kids. And most of them still swim better than I do."

Rainie didn't know what to say. Sharlah was talking swim camp, but all Rainie could picture was crime scenes. Her socially awkward child had had a rough morning. She was about to have an even worse afternoon.

Rainie found herself tapping the steering wheel again. Then noticed Sharlah noticing. Sharlah's face smoothed out. She didn't ask what was wrong, because that wasn't her way. Instead, in a manner Rainie found much more heartbreaking, Sharlah tuned in to the fact that something was awry, then automatically steeled herself for the blow.

The process to become a foster-to-adopt family was as rigorous as most people suspected. The Oregon Department of Human Services, DHS, had subjected Rainie and Quincy to piles of paperwork. There had been home visits, reference checks, security clearance checks. And checklists. The adoption worker seemed to have an endless supply of department-issued checklists.

To receive their certificate of approval as foster parents, Rainie

and Quincy also had to complete thirty hours of foundation training, covering everything from the foster child's rights to the biologi-
cal family's rights to siblings' rights. During this time, they'd learned
Sharlah had an older brother, but he was out of the picture. There
had been an incident. The kids' father had gone on a drug-fueled
rampage and attacked the family. Telly, the oldest sibling, had fought
back with a baseball bat. At the end, both parents were dead and
Sharlah had a shattered arm. The powers that be felt it would be best
if Sharlah didn't see her brother. For that matter, Telly had a note in
his file saying he wasn't to be placed in a household with younger
children.

In the eight years since, Rainie supposed things could've changed.
Counseling for Telly, therapy for Sharlah. The girl had spoken up in
her brother's defense, even with her broken arm, which seemed to
imply she had some feelings for her older sibling.

But Rainie had never heard Sharlah say her brother's name. And
certainly, their phone had never rung with a repentant teenager on
the other end.

For the first time, Rainie wished they'd pushed harder on the subject. As their foundation training instructor had lectured, sibling relationships were often the most important, if not only, stable
relationships in many foster kids' lives. She and Quincy should've
asked more questions, of Sharlah, of DHS, even if both had elected
to ignore them.

The truth was, Rainie and Quincy had liked having the brother
out of the picture. They hadn't wanted to deal with additional family
members. Life had felt cleaner, simpler, with Sharlah all to themselves.

Now Rainie took a deep breath. Given that Sharlah was already
on high alert, it was best to just dive in and keep things straightfor-
ward.

"There was an incident this morning," Rainie said. "A double murder at a local gas station. Police have a video of the shooter. They tracked him to his foster family's house, where, it turns out, he'd already shot and killed his foster parents.

"Sharlah, the shooter has been identified as Telly Ray Nash, your older brother."

Sharlah turned. She sat back, stared out the windshield. "Okay," she said.

Rainie waited. For the initial shock to pass, for Sharlah to ask questions. But the girl remained gazing ahead, face blank.

"Do you remember your brother?" Rainie asked.

"Yes."

"Sharlah . . . do you remember your parents? What happened to them?"

"Yes."

Sharlah moved finally; she started rubbing her left shoulder.

"Have you seen your brother since the incident? Spoken to him?"

"No."

"Would you like to speak to him? Do you miss him?"

Sharlah rubbed her shoulder harder.

"Honey, it's our understanding that you defended your brother's actions that night. According to your statement, he saved both of you from your father."

"He had a knife."

"Your father?"

"He had a knife. And he ran straight at us."

Rainie didn't say anything.

Then, a moment later, so softly Rainie could barely hear the words: "I gave Telly the bat. They were both running down the hall. My father, so close behind. I thought he would catch Telly. I thought he would kill him. So I gave Telly the bat."

"And Telly hit you with the bat?"

"He didn't mean to."

"It was an accident."

"He didn't see me."

"You were hiding? Or somehow got too close? He caught you with the backswing?"

Sharlah shook her head, her face still expressionless, gaze remote. "He couldn't see me. I was there. But he couldn't see me. He looked just like him, you know. Swinging the bat. He looked just like our dad."

Rainie got it then. Her turn to look away. Eight years ago, Telly Ray would've been a scrawny nine-year-old boy. Overpumped on adrenaline and fear, suffering his own sort of out-of-body experience as he beat their father to a pulp. Rainie could only imagine what he must've looked like to a five-year-old girl. Telly's actions that night meant both of them had lived. And yet neither of them had ever been the same.

"Sharlah, do you know what happened to your brother after that night?"

"The police took him away."

"And then?"

"I don't know."

"Did you ask about him? Request to see him?"

"No."

"Why not?"

The girl shrugged, rubbed the top of her arm. She had a scar there. An incision mark where the doctors had had to go in and pin her bone back together. For a five-year-old to have her last memory of her parents, her brother, be colored by such pain . . . It didn't surprise Rainie at all that Sharlah didn't want to revisit the past.

"What do you remember most about Telly?" Rainie asked now.

"What do you mean?" Sharlah finally glanced at her.

"One memory. When I say his name, what's the first image that pops into your head?"

"Cheerios."

"Why Cheerios?"

Sharlah's brow furrowed, the girl thinking hard. "He would get them down for me. Feed me breakfast."

"And your parents?"

"Dunno."

"Were they home?"

"Asleep. Gotta be quiet. Do Not Disturb."

"Did your parents hit you, Sharlah?"

The girl turned away, which Rainie thought was answer enough.

"Did your brother hit you?" Rainie pressed.

A faint no.

"And your mom?"

"No."

"So your father hit—"

"I don't want to talk about it. Whatever happened today. I don't want to talk about it."

"Do you miss your brother?" Rainie asked.

But the girl didn't answer.

"If he reaches out to you now," Rainie said, "tries to contact you in any way—phone calls, e-mails, texts—you need to let us know. Immediately."

Sharlah didn't say anything.

"And for the next few days, at least until we know more, it would be best if you stayed inside."

"He killed his new parents?" Sharlah asked.

"We think so."

"Past parents, future parents," Sharlah murmured. Then: "Any new siblings?"

"The Duvalls had an older son. We think he's all right."

"Then he's not done."

"Why do you say that?"

Sharlah shook her head. "He's not done," she said again.

"Sharlah—"

"You have to stop him. He can't stop himself. Someone else has to stop him." She rubbed her shoulder. "That's how it works. Someone else, you have to stop him, for him."

"The police will find Telly, Sharlah. The police will stop him. This isn't your problem anymore."

But Rainie could already tell the girl didn't believe her.

Chapter 8

CAL NOONAN HAD BEEN A MEMBER of the county's sixty-person volunteer search-and-rescue team, SAR, for a dozen years. Trained in search techniques, land navigation, man tracking, rescue and recovery, and first aid, he was as comfortable in the wilds of his childhood as he was in his family room. Maybe more comfortable. Cal was one of those guys who itched when he spent too much time inside. It had always been that way. His mom had spent most of his youth exclaiming in exasperation, "Cal Noonan, go outside and play before you drive me crazy!" His father had given him his first fishing rod at five, BB gun at six.

It was only in high school that Cal had discovered his love of chemistry, which had led him, much to his parents' surprise, into cooking of sorts. Living in the land of dairy, Cal had become fascinated by the science behind cheese production, yogurt manufacturing, the works. At the ripe old age of forty-seven, he was now the head cheese maker at the factory, overseeing the manufacturing and aging of one of the best high-quality boutique cheeses in the world. It kept him traveling more than he'd like, but pride in the job offered some consolation.

As well as the ability to live in Bakersville, with its rocky beaches, vast green fields, and, of course, towering coastal range. Weekends and holidays still found Cal roaming the woods, fishing the streams, or even strolling on a beach.

And, sometimes, called out as an SAR volunteer.

The sheriff's department was looking for an armed fugitive. What they'd found so far was the suspect's vehicle, abandoned just south of his last known shooting. A suspect on foot meant a good old-fashioned manhunt ranging from the blacktop of the coastal highway to the foothills of the jagged mountains. Some law enforcement officers would be intimidated by such a vast search area. Cal and his team, however, loved this game.

Other SAR members were pulling up as Cal arrived. He nodded in greeting as he moved around his truck. He kept a well-supplied backpack and hiking boots with him at all times. He'd swung by home for his rifle.

The initial call had come thirty minutes ago. Given the sprawling nature of the county-wide organization, it would take an hour to get all SAR members on-site and incident command established. In fast-moving cases, however, the first responders would form an immediate search team and get the party started. As one of their best trackers, Cal expected to be on the trail within the next fifteen minutes. He only required a situational report and a couple of teammates.

He spied the county's mobile command center, a souped-up RV parked across the street from a tired-looking gas/convenience store sporting a great deal of crime scene tape. Shooter's last known destination, most likely. Nodding to himself, Cal headed over to incident command.

Sheriff Atkins stood in the open doorway of the RV, already talking to the assembled volunteers, most of whom were covered in a sheen of sweat.

"Target is a seventeen-year-old male, suspected in four shooting deaths. We believe he's in possession of at least six firearms, including three rifles. Having recently discovered his overheated vehicle abandoned two miles south of here, we also believe he's on foot, which will limit what he can carry with him at one time."

"Cell phone?" a voice asked from the back.

"We recovered the subject's personal cell from the glove compartment of the truck. It's possible, however, that he has a burner phone on him. But nothing we're aware of for immediate tracing."

"Other supplies?" asked Cal's team leader, Jenny Johnson, standing to the right.

"We don't know. Other than the cell phone, the truck's empty, so assuming the kid doesn't want to lug around an arsenal, he could be utilizing some sort of weapons cache. Most recent visual showed the kid wearing a black hoodie and armed with a nine millimeter. Across the street, you'll see his last known location. Given it's a convenience store, it's possible he helped himself to some water, snacks after the shooting. Whatever he took, it's not enough to be readily noticeable, but that doesn't mean he left empty-handed."

The assembled volunteers nodded. First rule in tracking: Think like your target. In conditions as hot as this, hydration would be a major concern. Fugitive would need water, lots and lots of water. As in an entire backpack full of the bottled stuff, or purification tablets in order to make his own on the go.

Next question, from the back: "Outdoor skills?"

"Unknown," the sheriff said.

At the collective groan, she raised a hand.

"Sorry, folks, but the suspect's first victims were his foster parents. Appears he shot them early this morning, then headed out shortly before seven thirty. At this point, the only people he's had contact with, he's shot and killed. Needless to say, this limits our information."

Cal felt himself stand up a little straighter. The call had come in as fugitive tracking of a target considered armed and dangerous. But Cal hadn't realized this armed, this dangerous. He'd hunted a few wanted men in his day, one charged with domestic violence, another B & E, but never a suspected murderer.

"This is what I can tell you," Sheriff Atkins continued now. "The suspect has been in and out of half a dozen foster homes. Rap sheet includes trespassing, criminal mischief, and resisting arrest. At some time this morning, Telly Ray Nash walked into his foster parents' bedroom and shot both dead. From there, it appears he ransacked the gun safe, helping himself to six firearms and an undetermined—but probably considerable—stash of ammo. He then set out north in his foster father's truck, which overheated two miles south of here. From that point, we're assuming he continued on foot, arriving at this convenience store shortly before eight A.M., where he shot and killed both a customer and the cashier.

"And he hasn't been seen since."

The sheriff fell silent, giving them a moment to digest this news.

"Now, if I can bring your attention over here"—Sheriff Atkins gestured to a giant topographical map that had been posted to the side of the mobile command unit—"we have our initial search area. Given it's been three hours since the shooting, we're assuming a perimeter of nine miles, maybe less given the heat."

As Cal knew, first order of business in a search was to establish a perimeter of greatest possible distance traveled. Given that a fugitive moved at an average speed of three miles an hour, the sheriff had accordingly drawn an enormous circle, radiating out nine miles on all sides from the shooter's last known location, the convenience store, which was marked in the center as a giant red X. A three-hour head start had already given the fugitive many more possibilities than Cal would've liked. And given that the perimeter would be expanded by three miles every hour of the search, their target area would only grow larger in the near future. Fortunately, geography was on their side, as the sheriff now explained:

"Looking at our map, you can see that nine miles to the west puts our fugitive smack in the middle of Tillamook Bay. Given that it's beach season and we haven't had a single tourist report a black-clad gunman, it's reasonable to assume our suspect didn't head west.

Likewise, traveling directly north or south puts our gunman along the coastal highway. We've already had half a dozen cruisers patrolling this area since the original call-in, and once again we haven't received a single sighting from any business or residential area. Which, to look at the map, brings us to the east. The foothills of the coastal range." Sheriff Atkins climbed down from the front steps of the command center, crossed to the map, and tapped a huge green swath. "I'm betting our fugitive's gone off the beaten path, hiked up enough to reach the cover of the tree line, where he can run along the foothills in either direction while remaining out of view. Hence, even with every local, county, and state patrol officer on the hunt, we still haven't had any sight of him."

Cal and several members of his team nodded their agreement.

Essentially, command had started out with a sizable search area. With a little help from the coastline, plus some basic logic, the sheriff had already reduced that circle by half. Now the experienced trackers such as Cal would define their target area even further by picking out natural pathways—say, a river that would be logical for the fugitive to follow, or an easy-to-access deer trail through the woods. Starting at ground zero—the convenience store—several search teams would radiate outward in different directions, focusing on locating those natural pathways and seeing who could pick up the trail first.

Which, of course, is when things would grow interesting.

The sheriff wrapped up by promising she had detectives already digging deep in the fugitive's background; the minute they knew anything more, she'd be sure to pass it along. Till then, SWAT would be providing backup for each search team. Dogs were on their way. And yeah, her first priority was that everyone go home safe.

The debriefing broke up. SAR had its own command structure. Cal spotted his team leader. Jenny Johnson was standing at the topographical map, motioning for the rest of them to join her.

One of the biggest misconceptions of tracking: A tracking team itself didn't magically stumble upon the fugitive. Even a tracker as experienced as Cal, working his home turf, could only move at a pace of half a mile an hour.

Given a fugitive's much faster speed of three miles an hour, it would be unlikely for Cal and his team to ever catch up. Instead, a tracking team's goal was to establish the target's directionality. Once they picked up the trail and determined which direction the fugitive was headed, then Cal's team would become a spear, slowly but surely driving the target forward, keeping on his heels, but also, whether the target realized it or not, forcing him to make choices. Pretty soon, leaders such as Jenny Johnson, who'd be following Cal's progress on the topographical map, would get some very strong opinions about where the target would have to head next. At which point, a recovery team would be sent in at a hard hiking pace to intercept.

Having said that, fugitive tracking was still dangerous work. Hounded, panicked targets could decide to double back for an ambush, or, feeling pressured, find high ground and make a last stand. Hence the SWAT team officers who would be assigned to each team, serving as flankers. Cal's job would be to pick up the trail, while the flanking officers worked on getting everyone home safe that night.

Assuming, of course, that the search was over by then. Thirty-six hours of searching wasn't uncommon for an SAR team, and Cal had once headed out for forty-eight consecutive hours. Others would hike in additional water and supplies to the tracking teams as needed. Such was the nature of the hunt.

He felt jazzed. Which might be good. Might be bad. Adrenaline perked a man up, got him moving. Just as long as he remembered that in cases like this, slow and steady won the race.

Jenny started assembling teams. Cal, as a head tracker, was ready to go. He simply needed an assistant tracker—basically a second pair of eyes—then the two flankers from SWAT.

Jenny assigned Norinne Manley as his second. Cal approved. An iron-haired grandmother of four, Nonie could out-hike searchers half her age and spent her free time teaching adult literacy at the local church. To say she was beloved would be an understatement. Certainly Cal was happy to have her on his team.

From SWAT, Jenny rattled off the names Antonio Barrionuevo and Jesse Dodds. Two green-clad men separated from the huddle of law enforcement and made their way to where Cal and Nonie were standing.

Both men were wearing light body armor, which, given the heat, made Cal feel sorry for them. But maybe at the end of the day, they'd be standing over his shot-up body thinking the same. Never knew.

The SWAT officers had .223-caliber rifles on AR-15 frames slung over their shoulders. Based on his own long gun, Cal would guess the rifles were outfitted with EOTech holographic sighting systems. In addition, the officers' vests bristled with supplies—extra magazines, a tactical medical kit, flexicuffs, a baton—while the pockets of their tactical pants were weighed down with protein bars, water tablets, batteries, probably even a knife or two. Cal didn't often get to work with SWAT officers. At this stage, he was mostly interested in their shoes. Nothing hampered a search team's efforts quite like blisters. Annoying in the beginning, agonizing at the end, blisters could grind them all to a halt. But both his flankers appeared to be wearing well-loved boots, one of the most important pieces of equipment, as far as Cal was concerned.

Now Cal delivered his spiel, rapid-fire, ready to go. Fugitive already had a three-hour head start; no reason to give him even more lead time.

Cal hefted up his pack. "Don't leave behind anything you might need, don't bring anything you don't. Pace won't be hard, but once we set out, could be days before we come back."

Nonie, who'd done this kind of thing before, yawned. Antonio and Jesse barely blinked. Tough guys. Fair enough.

"First indication of a hot spot on your foot—speak up! I got moleskin. Better to treat the blister before it ever happens. Because again, once we set out, don't know when we're coming back."

Yep, definitely tough guys.

Cal continued: "I track thirty feet out, looking for signs—which is to say, any disturbance of the natural world. Broken twig, impression in the moss, hell, boot tread in the mud. We had rain two days back, so if we get lucky, conditions in the shade might yield us some imprints. Nonie here will be acting as a second set of eyes, 'cause as the saying goes, two heads are better than one. Lose sign and we backtrack to last known location, work in outward spirals till we pick it up again. There'll be times it'll feel like we're going backward more than forward, but you're gonna have to trust us. And just in case you haven't worked with trackers before—we're not bloodhounds. We don't walk around staring at our feet. Best way to see something is to come at it from a diagonal. So we will be looking out more than down; doesn't mean we're not doing our job."

Antonio and Jesse nodded, still blank faced.

"Look up," Cal advised them now. "There's a lot of hunting in these parts, meaning there's lots of hunting stands. Any of which would make for a pretty good hiding spot at best, or ambush site at worst. If I happen to know of any stands in the area, I'll let you know. But hunters build new ones all the time, and this area isn't exactly on the hiking maps."

Twin nods.

"You hike before?" Cal asked.

"Grew up in Bend," Jesse supplied, which was on the other side of the Cascades and known for its bounty of outdoor adventures.

Cal got the picture. The SWAT officers had been picked with some thought to wildland skills. He grinned at them now.

"Sorry, but you know how command can be."

Which finally earned him two responding grins. They all knew how command could be. And some days it was enough to leave the worker bees shaking their heads.

They finished gearing up, the flankers unslinging their rifles. Then, as a team, they crossed the street.

Cal started by studying the convenience store. Last known location of their target. Ground zero in their search. He stared at it and did what he did best: thought like a fugitive.

Seventeen-year-old kid. Something had triggered him to get out of bed this morning and gun down his foster parents. At which point, he'd gone on the run. Emptied the gun safe, stolen the truck. Headed north.

Why north? First decision worth considering.

Truck had broken down. Overheated in these hotter-than-hell temps. Where were those coastal breezes anyway?

So the kid had headed out on foot. Carrying all six guns? That would certainly be noticeable. So he'd hidden some. Most likely near the truck, where the investigating detectives would find them soon enough. Cal and his team would appreciate that update. As long as you were chasing an armed fugitive, good to know how armed.

Sheriff had mentioned a nine millimeter. And Cal would bet the kid had also kept a rifle. One short-range weapon, one long, a good mix for a suspect hell-bent on destruction.

Which brought him back to directionality. Why had he chosen north? Did he have a destination in mind? Say, the EZ Gas, where he'd killed two more people?

Cal wasn't a criminologist. He didn't fully understand the whys and wherefores of violence. No, his gift was logistics, thinking like a fugitive on the run. And this fugitive, having gunned down two more people . . .

Cal approached the perimeter of the crime scene, the other members of his team hanging back, waiting for his signal. Nonie was doing some looking around on her own, but mostly, having worked with Cal before, she was waiting for him.

Cal stood at the lone entrance/exit of the EZ Gas. Then, putting himself in the mind-set of the shooter, he turned north. He walked around the crime scene tape till on his left the narrow coastal highway shimmered with silver heat, while to his right stood the store's Dumpster, near a hedge of thick, overgrown brush. No identifiable walking path emerged at the end of the property. No sign of recent trespassing or trampling.

And yet, already, he could feel his pulse quicken.

Cal crouched low. He looked for disturbances in the dusty edges of the parking lot. He sought a different vantage point on the overgrown brush. On the other side of the battered Dumpster, he could just make out something. A footprint? A darker patch.

He rounded the Dumpster, and there, just behind it, nearly touching one locked wheel, he was rewarded with his first sign of the day.

He turned to his team, which was trailing fifteen paces back.

"Hey," he called out. "Tell the sheriff: We got vomit."

Chapter 9

Quincy had met the county da, Tim Egan, a number of times. Twice when Quincy and Rainie happened to be consulting on local cases, but more often than not in social situations, a fundraising function here, a cookout at a friend of a friend's there. Quincy would say he knew the DA well enough, while the profiler in him understood you never really knew anyone at all.

Perhaps Egan thought the same of him.

Egan had been the DA for over fifteen years. Meaning he would've been the one who'd made the decision to not prosecute Sharlah's brother for the murder of their parents eight years back.

Currently, Egan was wrapping up a call. He indicated for Quincy to take a seat, something easier said than done given the boxes of manila folders crowding the space. After a moment, Quincy gave up and remained standing. He was grateful enough for the air-conditioned office and bottle of water Egan's secretary had stuck in his hand.

Egan set down the phone, glanced up at Quincy, then seemed to take in his office, the lack of seating, for the first time.

"Sorry." The older man grimaced. "County decided to save some money by downsizing storage. In theory, we're supposed to be going paperless, so we don't need as much space, right? Except last year, county decided to save money by trimming back manpower. Meaning, who do I have left on my staff to magically make all this paper paperless?"

"Sounds like a job for interns," Quincy commented.

"Ah, if only hungry law students believed in such things. This new generation, they've been raised by their parents to assume they'll start at the top. No scut for them. They'll just sit in their parents' basement till the job offer for partner comes in."

Egan belatedly stood, stuck out a hand. Quincy shook it. In public, the county DA was rarely seen without his gray blazer and signature brightly colored silk tie. Today, the jacket was slung over the back of his chair, topped with what appeared to be a stripe of fuchsia silk, leaving the DA in a button-up short-sleeve Brooks Brothers shirt, the top two buttons already undone. He nodded to Quincy's own casual attire.

"Who knew it could be this damn hot," Egan said.

"Egads," Quincy agreed.

Given there was no place for Quincy to sit, the DA abandoned his desk chair and came around to stand beside Quincy. There was a stash of water bottles on top of one of the piles of boxes. The DA helped himself.

"Hear there's been some big events this morning," Egan said. The man wasn't dumb; he and Quincy were hardly the type for social calls.

"Multiple shootings," Quincy stated, avoiding the word *spree*. "Seventeen-year-old suspect shot and killed his foster parents this morning. Then took out two more at a local gas station."

Egan nodded, no doubt already having been notified.

"Sheriff Atkins asked me to assist."

Another nod, another piece of information Egan already knew.

"We have a video of the second shooting. The suspect has been ID'd as Telly Ray Nash. I understand this isn't his first brush with violence. That in fact, he killed his own parents when he was a kid."

Egan's face had gone expressionless. The DA untwisted the top from his bottle of water. Raised it. Took a long sip.

"Telly Ray Nash," Egan repeated. "His parents' deaths."

"Yes."

"There's no file. He was never charged with a crime."

"I understand."

"So you're here . . ." Quincy could hear the wealth of possibilities in that open-ended statement. Most of which weren't pleasant for a man in Egan's position. Quincy was here to second-guess why Egan hadn't prosecuted a kid now suspected of killing four more? Quincy was here to identify all the warning signs Egan had missed? Quincy was here to start the line of questioning that would only be getting more uncomfortable for the DA's office in the days ahead?

Knowing all that, Quincy decided to take pity on the man.

"I believe you know my wife, Rainie, and I are fostering a girl. We've started adoption proceedings and hope to have it finalized in time for Thanksgiving."

Egan nodded, brow furrowed slightly at this change of topic.

"Our soon-to-be-adopted daughter is Sharlah May Nash. Telly's younger sister."

At once, the man straightened. "Oh," Egan said.

"Oh," Quincy agreed.

"So you're here . . ."

"Personally, as well as professionally."

Egan took a swig of water. Finally, he sighed, crossed his arms over his chest. "You know, I didn't feel bad about my decision eight years ago. Some cases you angst over—what's right, what's wrong? Others you suspect right away will come back to bite you in the ass. But Telly Nash, what happened with his parents, his sister . . . By the time the police were done analyzing the scene and the forensic psychologist was done head-shrinking the boy, I didn't have any doubts. Doesn't that just figure? I didn't have any doubts at all."

"Walk me through it," Quincy suggested.

The man did: "Neighbors from the trailer park called it in. Sounds

of a loud argument, followed by screaming. By the time first responders arrived on scene, they found nine-year-old Telly standing in
the middle of the space, covered in gore and holding a bloody baseball bat. Two dead bodies, his little sister—who was what, four,
five?—collapsed in a ball at his feet, crying."

Quincy winced, said nothing.

"Telly wasn't a big kid. Rather scrawny in fact. No history of violence, though the police were familiar with the parents. Calls out
for domestic spats, disturbances of the peace, that sort of thing. Drug
addicts, according to the cops. Child welfare had been contacted
twice. Kids, however, had remained in the home.

"My office was called in. I personally visited the scene, given the
nature of the offense, age of the offender. I remember the boy mostly
stood there, not moving, not speaking. Shock, I suppose. But it was
quite a sight, let me tell you. This thin, blood-covered boy with his
perfectly expressionless face. Made my hair stand up on end.

"Turned out he'd taken a swipe at the sister, as well, broken her
arm. But she still defended him. Claimed her father had stabbed her
mother, then chased both the kids through the house. She'd actually
found the baseball bat, got it to Telly. He took a stand in the family
room. Apparently, once the boy got to swinging, though, he couldn't
stop. Pulverized his father's skull. Then, when little sis stepped forward, nailed her too. She went down and that seemed to snap him
out of things. Or at least end the rampage. He was still pretty shell-
shocked when we got there. Didn't seem to know what he'd just
done."

Egan looked at Quincy.

"I thought he killed both parents," Quincy said. "But you're saying the father killed the mom."

"Which is where the story gets interesting. Because according to
the ME, in addition to a stab wound to the chest, the mom also suffered a single blow to the head. But neither kid would comment on

it. Every time we asked the question, their faces went blank. Closest we got was days later. We confronted Telly once more with evidence from the scene, trying to get him to talk. His single response: 'I must've done it.' Interesting choice of words, though. Not that he did do it. But that he must've done it."

Quincy nodded.

"Would the stab wound have killed her?"

"She was bleeding internally. Anyone's guess if the EMTs would've been able to save her."

"Interesting."

Egan shrugged.

"Do you still have the forensic psychologist's report?" Quincy asked.

"Sure. Somewhere. I can, uh, do some digging around. Off the top of my head, though, there were three main reasons I opted to not press charges. One, parents' known history of addiction and domestic abuse. According to the neighbors and the like, it was only a matter of time before something terrible happened in this house. Two, Telly had several knife wounds, which lent support to his sister's allegations of self-defense. Let alone the mom had also been stabbed before being smacked over the head with a baseball bat, and the blood trail further substantiated the sister's version of events."

"Telly never provided a full statement?" Quincy asked.

"Nope, just his fairly infamous 'I must've done it.' Following protocol, we set him up with an expert, Dr. Bérénice Dudkowiak. The level of violence disturbed me; I definitely wanted a professional's opinion before I decided whether or not to pursue charges. According to Dr. Dudkowiak, once a kid with Telly's kind of history explodes . . ."

"To this day, Telly himself probably doesn't know how many times he struck his father," Quincy filled in.

"She was more interested in what kind of coping skills Telly might have exhibited leading up to the 'tragic incident.' All signs indicated the deaths themselves were impulsive, not planned, and sparked by the father's own drug-fueled rage—"

"Tox screen?"

"Both parents were high as kites," Egan assured him. "Another point in the boy's favor. There was some suspicion the boy suffered from RAD. Reactive . . ."

"Reactive attachment disorder."

"That's it. And of course, Dr. Dudkowiak wanted to check out the possibility of Telly exhibiting signs of the homicidal triad."

"Bed-wetting, arson, cruelty to animals," Quincy provided.

"Exactly. But on that front, the boy was clear. If anything, he showed some signs of nurturing behavior, given his care of his little sister. Dr. Dudkowiak did have concerns about RAD, but given the parents' history of addiction and the children's level of exposure to violence . . ."

"Attachment should be an issue." Quincy knew this well from Sharlah's own file. And, of course, from having spent the past three years with a child who could disappear inside her head for long periods of time, then look at him and Rainie as if they were the crazy ones.

Egan took another swig of water. "Deciding factor for the shrink: Telly's relationship with his sister."

"Really?"

"Really. Based on whatever the boy said, and substantiated by teachers, et cetera, Telly cared for his sister. Was in fact the one raising her. Making her breakfast, doing laundry, getting her to school. He even walked them both to the library after school and read his sister books, apparently, to keep them both out of the house. Also, according to Sharlah, Telly had interceded on her behalf in the past when the father had grown violent, taken the hit himself, that sort of thing."

Quincy nodded. Such a scenario, a young child raising an even younger sibling, was hardly uncommon in households with drug addiction.

"For Dr. Dudkowiak, this proved two things." Egan counted them off on his fingers. "One, the boy had some capacity to bond, as clearly his baby sister mattered to him. Two, Telly had tried. I think that's even the term she used. The fact he'd taken on such adult roles showed he'd made some effort to cope with his parents' issues. In a kid his age, apparently three or four strategies was what you'd expect to see. Telly had used them. Unfortunately, his father had still opted to shoot up, then grab a kitchen knife. At which point Telly abandoned more traditional approaches and went with the baseball bat option instead. Sad, in her opinion, but hardly unexpected."

"What happened to Telly?" Quincy asked.

"I don't know. He would've been in emergency placement the first few days. Then I assume Child Welfare would've found an appropriate foster home for the boy. No living relatives, so family was out of the picture."

"Sharlah was placed without him," Quincy said. "In the file we have, it says she's not to have contact with her brother."

"He did shatter her arm with a baseball bat."

"And yet she defended his actions."

Egan shrugged. He was the county DA, after all, not family services. "One way or another, Telly was out of control that night. Maybe the powers that be thought it would be better to give Sharlah some space. She'd already spent most of her young life with a violent father. Why add to that a violent brother?"

Which, given the events of the morning . . .

Both men fell silent.

"Is Dr. Dudkowiak still practicing?" Quincy asked.

"Has an office in Portland," Egan provided. "My secretary can get you her number. My turn: I just saw the video image from the morning's shooting. The kid, Telly Nash. He's looking right at the camera. No expression, no nothing at all on his face."

Quincy didn't say anything, which seemed to tell the DA enough.

Egan sighed heavily. "This isn't going to end well, is it?"

"Statistically speaking?" Quincy finished his water, set the empty bottle on top of a box. "We'll end up in a shoot-out with a seventeen-year-old suspect. Or he'll kill us first."

Chapter 10

RAINIE WON'T LET LUKA AND ME play outside. "Too hot," she says, which it is, except we both know that's not what she's really worried about. Instead, I take my bowl of yogurt and granola and head down to the basement. If it's hot outside, then she can't argue with the coolness of the basement, can she?

I like this house. I'm lucky to have landed here and I know it. And not just because Rainie and Quincy want to adopt me, or because they have a cool catching-killers business, but because they're successful and have the house to prove it. Don't get me wrong. First foster home was clean and welcoming. I remember number three as also being cutesy in a hand-stitched-quilt, red-cheeked-gnomes-everywhere sort of way.

But Rainie and Quincy's house . . . I like how it sits on top of a hill, with a steep gravel drive that never lets anyone approach without being noticed. I like the mounds of ferns and wildflowers that lead up to the front deck, with its matching Adirondack rockers. When my family worker brought me here the first time, I thought we'd arrived at an L.L.Bean catalog.

The house is big. Not too big, Quincy likes to say. I guess he designed it. But it's plenty big by a foster kid's standards. Open floor plan, exposed beams, massive stone fireplace. Lots of windows and skylights, which during the gray winter months help keep Rainie and me from going insane.

And there are fun little details. A stone-inlaid floor in the foyer. A custom-built staircase with birch-stick banisters. Bringing the out-side in, Quincy explained to me one day. I like the outdoors. One day, I'd like to build a house that brings the outside in. Maybe I can follow in my soon-to-be adoptive parents' footsteps and become an expert in monsters, too.

While I head downstairs, Rainie remains sitting at the kitchen table, tapping on her laptop. She doesn't tell me what she's research-ing and I don't ask. We're that kind of family.

In the basement, Luka opens his mouth wide, like a yawn, except I think he's really trying to pull in as much of the cooler air as possi-ble. The basement has some natural light from windows placed up high on the rear wall. But mostly, the basement is rec space. One corner has exercise equipment, a treadmill and elliptical for the days the two obsessives can't make it out for their morning run. In the middle is a U-shaped soft brown sofa facing an impressive flat-screen TV. Hangout space. As in, I could have friends over, Quincy sug-gested one day, before he knew better.

Even Luka has a space. An oversized kennel, complete with piles of dog beds, a few treasured tennis balls, and of course a massive water bowl. It looks a little dungeony, which led Quincy to make a few ironic observations about profilers and what they had in their basements, before he realized I was listening. As Rainie pointed out to him, "Quincy, you have a kid now. And they're *always* listening."

Luka is supposed to spend downtime in his kennel. At least that was Quincy's plan when he had it installed. But mostly, Luka spends downtime sleeping on my bed or sprawled at Rainie's feet. Quincy will tell you he knows when he's been beat.

Now I set my yogurt on the dark-stained coffee table. Luka won't touch it. He's much too professional for petty theft.

Instead, he's running easy laps around the sofa, getting the lay of the land, reveling in the feel of cooler air. I let him relax. We're be-hind on his exercise routine, let alone training regimen, but I blame it on the outside temps. Who can concentrate in this heat? At least he didn't have to attend swim camp. The moment I got home, I told him how lucky he was, and I could tell from the serious look on his face that he believed me.

I don't turn on any lights in the basement. The bright sun leaking through the top windows is enough. Besides, it feels cooler this way.

With my yogurt in front of me, and Luka running in circles around me, I reach into my back pocket and withdraw the real reason I'm down here. My iPhone. I start my search on Safari. *Shooting, Bakersville, Oregon.* "Breaking News," the first headline informs me. "Two found shot and killed at an EZ Gas. More details to follow."

The stories don't have much information, however, and make me frown. Luka comes to sit beside me. He puts his head on my lap and gazes up at me with his big brown eyes. Luka has expressive eyebrows. He arches one now in question. I pat his head, take a bite of my yogurt.

"Someone must know something," I tell him. "What's the point of an entire Internet filled with news if you can't learn what you need to know?"

Next up, I try searching the web page of the local oxymoron, as Quincy calls it, the *Bakersville Sun.*

Sure enough, there's a photo. Freeze-frame from a security video, I realize, of a teenage boy in a black hoodie pointing a gun. Basic hoodlum material, I would think. Except this hoodlum has Telly's eyes, staring straight at me.

I study it for a long time. Looking for . . . I don't know what. An aha moment? A bolt of recognition? A squeeze in my chest?

I look at the picture and mostly I feel nothing. Nothing at all.

Then, almost on cue, my shoulder starts to burn.

Luka whines softly. I stroke his ears, but mostly to comfort me.

I tear myself away from the photo, move on to the main article. The shooting at the EZ Gas happened shortly before eight A.M. I would've been getting out of bed right about then, dragging my feet, already dreading the day ahead. At eight, I was taking Luka outside, recoiling at the wall of heat, further agitated at having to spend my morning stuck at the Y.

At the bottom of the article came the most interesting information. Suspect identified as Telly Ray Nash, seventeen. Also wanted for questioning in the deaths of Frank and Sandra Duvall. Suspect believed to be armed and dangerous.

I have a response then. I shiver. And whether I mean to or not, I see the knife. I hear my father's voice, crooning from the other side of the couch. And I feel Telly's hands, scooping me up, tossing me through a doorway, out of my father's path.

My hand has curled into a fist on top of Luka's beautiful brown and gold head. He growls, so softly it's more like a rumble in his throat, and I release my fingers, patting him gently once more.

"It's okay," I tell him, but this time, he doesn't believe me.

I don't know what to think. I don't know what to feel. I wasn't lying to Rainie earlier. I don't really remember my brother. Or my parents. I get more like vague snapshots. Yellow Cheerios box. The smell of cigarettes. *Clifford the Big Red Dog*.

My brother taking me to the library, reading me stories while I sucked down apple juice.

My shoulder hurts. I'm sweaty, and not just from the temperature. I don't want to think about him. Or my parents. Yet now I can't help myself, and I'm filled with a mix of sadness and fear and . . . longing.

I miss my brother, my parents. No matter how terrible they were, they were still my family.

Not true, I tell myself. I have Rainie and Quincy now. And neither of them would ever chase me around the house with a bloody knife or smash my arm with a baseball bat.

I have traded up.

But still I'm . . . sad.

I find myself touching the image of Telly's grim face. As if trying to find something that was probably never there.

Back to work. I tap my phone's tiny little touch-screen keyboard. Search: *Frank and Sandra Duvall, Bakersville, Oregon.* Turns out, Sandra has a Facebook page, where she talks about Crock-Pot recipes, shares photos of an older boy wearing OSU orange, and recommends DIY craft projects.

Is she a good foster mom? I wonder. She certainly seems proud of her oldest son. And her husband, Frank? Did they volunteer for Telly? Did they have any idea what they were getting into?

I find one last photo, recently posted. A big guy wearing head-to-toe army camo, a smaller teen similarly clad to his right. I recognize Telly immediately. Both are holding rifles, a dead animal at their feet. "What the boys did today," the post reads. My brother, the hunter.

Once again, I'm confused. Did Telly have fun that day? Quality time bonding with the foster dad? Happy to be outdoors, experiencing the thrill of the hunt? Or was he thinking the whole thing would've been easier if they'd given him a baseball bat?

I don't know I don't know I don't know.

I would like to know how to shoot. I asked Quincy to teach me. He wanted to know why. Self-defense, I explained. You know, just in case.

You have Luka, he told me. *You don't need anything else.*

There are guns in the house, I tried again. *I should at least know basic safety.*

He smiled, and I thought I had him. But he's still never taken me. Later, he says, though I don't know what either of us is waiting for.

Now I study this online image and wonder about my brother. Did he like the Duvalls? Had he been with them a while, thought of them as family? Or had he bounced around the system, an older boy already with a reputation for violence?

He fed me Cheerios, I think.

He broke my arm.

He saved my life.

And he's never spoken to me since. Was that my decision, his decision? I don't remember. I was just a little girl, and that night was so overwhelming. I cried, I screamed, I remember that. Did I yell at him? Call him a monster and tell him I never wanted to see him again?

Or did he blame me? Did he look down at his baby sister, sobbing pathetically at his feet, and think it was all my fault? If I'd been quieter, better, my father never would've snapped, and Telly wouldn't have had to kill our parents.

I'm ashamed now. Or maybe I've been ashamed all along, and this is just the first time I've allowed myself to acknowledge it.

My parents are dead. My older brother killed them.

And I left. Never looked back. Got myself a new family in a better house with a great dog. And forgot all about them.

Final search. I look up the EZ Gas, scene of my brother's last known crime. Then I request directions from my current location to there. Twelve miles to the west, the map tells me. Twenty-five minutes by car, a lot longer on foot.

Close, but not too close.

Which is exactly how we've been living for the past eight years.

I sit back on the sofa, contemplating. I feel like I should do something, but I don't know what.

The past is a luxury foster kids don't have. We're too busy living in the moment. Whatever thoughts I've had about my parents, I don't think them. Whatever emotions I've had about what my brother did, I don't feel them.

Now I wonder if Telly did the same, right up till this morning, when he climbed out of bed, loaded the first gun, and pulled the trigger.

Chapter 11

WHAT DO YOU MEAN you can't find any trace of the missing firearms?"

"Sorry, Sheriff. But we've searched every square inch between Frank Duvall's truck and the EZ Gas. There's no cache of weapons."

Shelly scowled, pushed her wide-brim hat up on her sweaty forehead, and just resisted the urge to scratch her itchy hairline. Or, for that matter, the rope of scar tissue snaking up her neck. Damn heat.

She exhaled, stared at her lead homicide sergeant, exhaled again. "Roy, we need to know everything about this boy. Every pimple, every wart, and sure as hell every single firearm he might be carrying. Those are our people out there."

"I know."

"If the boy is on foot, no way he's walking around with six firearms and dozens of boxes of ammo. It would be too heavy."

"I know."

"Which means either he stashed some of the weapons somewhere or"—she hesitated—"he has an accomplice."

"Or stole another ride."

Shelly sighed heavily. Any of those could be true. Which was why they needed to stop with the theories and start with some answers.

"No calls to the hotline? No hits on the BOLO?" she asked.

"No, ma'am."

"Where is he, Roy? What the hell is this boy doing, and why can't we find one seventeen-year-old kid?"

Roy didn't answer. Shelly gave in, rubbed her neck. She was standing in the mobile command unit, which came with a generator capable of powering the air-conditioning. For now, however, Shelly was more concerned about juice for the array of computers, monitors, and satellite devices. Physical comfort would have to wait.

Shelly was worried. And not just about finding some juvenile delinquent already wanted for shooting four people. She was worried about her search teams. She had three of them, deployed to the woods behind the EZ Gas. Each walking around without any decent intel on the target they were seeking.

"Let's walk through it," Shelly said, reaching in front of Roy to pull up a map of Bakersville on the closest computer.

Roy nodded. He didn't sit. The only chairs available in the narrow space were stick models tucked in at the various workstations. Meaning the sitter was taking up position in front of computers that were throwing off even more heat. Both he and Shelly remained standing as she bent down, zoomed in on the satellite map until they were staring at the immediate area around the Duvalls' home.

"Kid started the day here."

Roy nodded. "TOD on the parents is around six A.M."

"Meaning first thing this morning, Telly Ray Nash shot the Duvalls, stole the weapons. Then loaded up food, water, supplies?"

"Unknown."

Shelly scowled. Roy shrugged. "Kitchen wasn't ransacked, nothing obviously disturbed. Crime scene techs found Frank Duvall's wallet intact on his nightstand; same with Sandra Duvall's purse and jewelry box. There's evidence of dinner last night but no indication anyone ate breakfast this morning. Given there aren't any witnesses to Telly's actions at the Duvalls' house and no supplies left behind in the truck, we don't know what happened between the shooting of the Duvalls at six and Telly walking into the EZ Gas shortly before eight."

Shelly remained disgruntled. But then she frowned. "EZ Gas wasn't ransacked either."

Roy didn't say anything.

"Kind of interesting," she continued. "For a teenager who's running around on a rampage, he's being awfully tidy about it."

Again the silence. Maybe there was nothing to say to that.

Shelly returned to the computer screen. "Telly leaves the Duvalls' and heads . . ."

Based upon the map, there were several roads around the Duvalls' house. Most were dead ends, purely residential roads. Two led back to the main artery, heading into downtown Bakersville, then Highway 101, which ran along the Oregon coast.

"He heads north," Shelly muttered, her gaze following 101 through Bakersville, past the cheese factory, until, eventually, she came to the EZ Gas. "Roughly twenty-minute drive, though he had to walk the last bit, given the truck broke down. Still, that leaves a solid chunk of time unaccounted for. Cell phone?" she asked Roy.

"Family had four phones on a family plan. We recovered the Duvalls' phones from the bedroom and a third in the glove compartment of Telly's truck. Fourth appears to be with the older son, away at college."

"So Telly initially took a phone but left it behind in his father's truck? Why? What self-respecting teenager leaves behind his cell phone?"

"The kind who doesn't want to be tracked. He'd already killed his foster parents. If Telly's watched any cop show on TV, he knows we can use the GPS on his phone to find him."

"Then why take the phone at all?"

Roy shrugged. "Maybe he grabbed it out of habit, then later, while driving around, realized the phone could be used to find him. I don't know. I'm not exactly a teenager."

Shelly considered the matter. "Or he got himself a prepaid phone, another means of communication. Then he didn't need his personal phone anymore." She tapped the map they'd pulled up. "He would've driven right by the Walmart. We should see if he stopped in, made any purchases."

"I'll send an officer. Right now, Dan Mitchell is running down the names and contact info we pulled from Telly's phone. So far, we got his PO, the school office, and his foster parents. But no classmates or obvious friends or associates. Most of the boy's texts seem to be purely logistical stuff, asking his PO what time to meet, telling his parents he's running late for dinner, that kind of thing. Not exactly a kid with a robust social life, at least according to his phone."

"What about Erin Hill, the cashier from the EZ Gas?"

"Not in his contacts. But like I said, not many people are."

"Telly's a loner," Shelly stated. It would fit the model of many mass shooters.

Roy hesitated.

"What?"

"Mitchell did find one thing interesting on Telly's phone. Some photos, taken recently. Not great quality. Looks to him as if the shots were taken from a distance, zoomed in. The images are of a teenage girl. Maybe thirteen." Roy glanced over at Shelly. "Mitchell sent me the copies. I've only met her once, but I think . . . I'm pretty sure the pictures are of Rainie and Quincy's foster daughter, Sharlah."

Shelly paused, straightened. She had to think about this, because already, her gut instinct was this was very, very bad news.

"Sharlah is also Telly's younger sister," Shelly murmured out loud. She'd known something was up the second she'd mentioned Telly Ray Nash's name and watched Quincy's expression freeze. What he'd had to say about their suspect's past, not to mention his own family's connection, had been disquieting. "According to Quincy, Telly Ray Nash killed his parents eight years ago in self-defense— basically saved his and Sharlah's lives. Afterward, the two kids were separated. Sharlah ended up with Quincy and Rainie. Telly found his way to the Duvalls. Quincy swears Sharlah hasn't had any contact with her brother since. Rainie and Quincy haven't ever met Telly, didn't even know he was still living in the area. Which seems to corroborate that Sharlah and her older brother are estranged."

"Gets a little more complicated," Roy said. "Not sure what this means, but the photo stream on the phone had been cleared. As in, the *only* images on Telly's cell phone are the pictures of Sharlah."

Shelly got his point. "That seems rather intentional. When were the photos taken again?"

"Five days ago."

"Browser history? Any sign he was looking up information on Sharlah? Or Quincy or Rainie?"

"Phone's browser had also been cleared."

Shelly stared at her sergeant. She was back to her gut instinct— this was all very bad news. And yet, she still wasn't sure what it meant. "What about the family computer? Anything useful there?"

"The Duvalls had a single desktop, shared by everyone. Initial glance showed the browser history had been recently cleared on it as well. I sent it to state for processing. If something useful was deleted off the family computer, their experts will find it, but it's gonna take some time."

"All right. So Telly grabs his phone when leaving the Duvalls' house. But then he turns around and leaves it behind. Browser cleared, text messages and contact list virtually empty, and the camera containing only images of a sister he supposedly hasn't seen in years." Shelly shook her head. "That sounds less and less like a kid forgetting his phone, and more like a suspect sending a message."

She glanced at the map on the computer screen again. Telly Ray Nash's last known location was more than ten miles west of Quincy's house. If the boy was on foot, there was no need for immediate concern. And yet . . .

"Okay," she said softly, more to herself than Roy. "One last time, what do we know here? Telly Ray Nash shot his parents. Telly Ray Nash raided the gun safe. Then he headed north on Highway One-Oh-One until his truck overheated. At which point, he pulled on a heavy black sweatshirt even though it's already hotter than hell out. He selected a nine millimeter out of a collection of six firearms. And he walked north until he came to the EZ Gas. Where he shot and killed two more people, seemingly at random."

Roy nodded.

"You've searched the area all around the truck," Shelly tried again. "How thoroughly did you inspect the truck itself? Maybe Telly stashed the remaining firearms beneath the seat, or tucked up in the undercarriage?"

"Removed door panels, shredded the upholstery, pried at the undercarriage. Trust me, no guns. Also scoured a one-mile area around the vehicle. Whatever Telly did with Frank Duvall's guns . . . they're not around the truck."

"Which brings us back to our earlier theories. Maybe Telly met up with someone, gave the extra firearms to an accomplice. Even sold them for cash."

"If so, he was smart enough to use a second phone to make the arrangements."

Shelly scowled. "We're missing something. Too many assumptions, not enough facts. Cameras. That's what we need. Traffic cams, video feeds, anything that might help pinpoint Telly's movements between the Duvalls' house and the EZ Gas."

"Not a lot of cameras around this part of the highway," Roy said, but he was already bending over the monitor, studying their options. "Downtown Bakersville, however . . . Here, intersection of Third and Main. Pretty sure there's a traffic cam."

"Next block over." Shelly tapped the screen. "First Union Bank. ATM faces the street. That camera might have caught something."

"All right. I'll get on it."

"Put together a timeline," Shelly said. "Everything Telly Ray Nash did this morning. From what time he got up to what he ate to who he spoke to. Then exactly what happened in the minutes after he shot his parents and before he arrived at the EZ Gas."

Roy nodded.

"After that, full background. Every foster family the kid ever stayed with, every person he ever said hello to, every classmate he bumped shoulders with in the school hall. We need to learn everything there is to know about Telly Ray Nash, and then some."

Roy nodded.

"You said one of the numbers on Telly's phone was his probation officer, Aly Sanchez?"

"Yeah. She's the one who gave us the information on the Duvalls."

"Okay. I'll follow up with her. See if she can shed any light on the kid's state of mind. In particular, does she know if he'd had any contact with his sister or was thinking of contacting his sister, that sort of thing."

"Should we assign an officer to watch Sharlah?"

"Let me talk to Quincy and Rainie first. Good news is, Sharlah has a built-in security team of sorts. And then there's her dog." Shelly shook her head, still trying to make sense of what they knew. "Two shootings. One close to home. One seemingly random. And a cell phone with photos of a younger sister the suspect allegedly hasn't seen in years."

Shelly scrubbed at the roped scar tissue on her neck. "Kid's gonna resurface. Needing supplies, wanting revenge, hell if I know. But one way or another, we're going to see Telly Ray Nash again. Only question is, what'll it cost us?"

Chapter 12

CAL NOONAN HAD FOUND a drainage ditch. Snaking along the road, partially obscured by a thick bramble of blackberry bushes, it was just deep enough to keep a lone occupant mostly hidden from sight. Right now, he and his team were working it northbound, moving from sign to sign—a heel imprint in exposed mud here, a broken spiderweb there, crushed grass everywhere.

Someone had definitely traversed the narrow ditch in the past twenty-four hours. But the question remained: Was it their suspect?

Tracking in the movies generally involved some half-wild, silent loner, gliding effortlessly across a trail invisible to all others and issuing such outlandish statements as "Based on the taste of the wind, the target crossed here, thirteen minutes ago, dressed in flannel and eating a Snickers bar."

Real life, nothing at all like that. Cal had a sign. The sign made him happy. Foot imprints, broken twigs, crushed ferns all told Cal something had definitely passed this way. But that didn't mean his shooting suspect had done it. For all Cal and his team knew, they were currently tracking a thirty-year-old former Vegas dancer who'd walked up the drainage ditch yesterday after visiting the EZ Gas for a pack of gum.

Evidence was what Cal wanted to see now. A shred of black fabric caught in the bramble from a torn black hoodie. A discarded water bottle with a SKU number the detectives could trace back to a batch delivered to the EZ Gas. Hell, brass would be nice. A kid running around with a nine millimeter and a pocket full of ammo, least he could do is drop a slug or two.

Instead, at the beginning of the gully, where it met with the parking lot of the EZ Gas, Cal had found a partial heel print in the softer mud. Size looked about right for a male, but no tread pattern. A casting would be made for future reference. For now, Cal's job remained to identify their target's trail.

He figured he was half right: He had a trail.

Jesse and Antonio moved along slowly behind, a good fifteen feet back, rifles in hand. They didn't like the ditch. By definition, it formed a chute, boxing them in. Strategically speaking, if someone were to appear at the top edge, armed with a rifle . . . It would be like shooting fish in a barrel.

Cal was aware of the danger. Unfortunately for all of them, this was the best lead they had.

Another broken twig, straight ahead. Middle gleamed white, end of the twig still fresh and pliable in Cal's fingers. Recent break, then, the wood not having dried out. Ditch was narrowing now, and slowly but surely growing shallower. Soon they'd be at road level, meaning their target—and they—would have to make choices.

"Cal," Nonie whispered.

He stilled, turning his head to the right, where she was working five feet back. "What is it?"

"Got something, tucked up there in the blackberries."

Cal reversed course, walking back to Nonie's vantage point. No doubt about it, the grandmother had great eyes. Cal had been looking straight ahead when he'd passed through this section. Nonie, however, had had the sense to look up.

But now, following her finger, he could just make out what had caught her attention. At first glance, it appeared to be a darker shadow, maybe even a particularly dense patch of blackberry bush. But it wasn't.

Nonie's hands were smaller than his. He nodded at her to do the honors.

She gloved up first. All SAR team members had training in evidence recovery. Even the most urgent fugitive chase was merely the opening act in a much larger law enforcement drama. Screwing up the evidence risked releasing the suspect they'd spent so much effort hunting down in the first place.

It took her a bit to work it free from the thicket of thorns. Slowly but surely, Nonie eased the wadded-up fabric from its hiding place.

Antonio and Jesse stood closer, rifles still in hand, not watching Nonie but keeping their attention all around.

"Got it," Nonie murmured.

She pulled it down and out. A thick black hoodie. Nonie took an experimental sniff. "Vomit," she reported stoically.

Then, for the first time since starting the hunt, she and Cal broke into smiles.

"We got trail," Cal said.

"We got trail," Nonie repeated.

Cal radioed it in.

Their team leader was happy. Jenny consulted the master map. By her estimate, they had about a hundred more yards of gully, then they'd arrive at an intersection with a dirt road. Road cut east-west, west connecting with the highway, east heading deeper into rural residential. Appeared to be five or six properties from what she could tell. All on large pieces of land.

Cal and Nonie exchanged glances. Not the best news. Out of the gully, they'd be back to hard-packed earth. Tough surface for tracking. Not to mention half a dozen homes tucked away in the deep shadowed woods . . .

Antonio and Jesse, clad in light body armor and covered in sweat, didn't say anything at all.

Cal left the hoodie in plain sight, marked with a bright orange flag to help alert the follow-up officers to its position. A second flag indicated where Nonie had pulled it from the bushes. Crime scene techs would want to retrieve the sweatshirt for analysis, plus work their own magic at the site. For all he knew, they'd clip entire swaths of the blackberry bushes, looking for bloody thorns where the suspect might've scratched himself.

That kind of thing was beyond Cal's pay grade. Command had its job, the detectives and the crime scene geeks had theirs. As for him and his team . . .

They resumed the hunt.

They hiked to the end of the drainage ditch, where it merged with a flat dirt road. Sounds of the highway to the left. Dark green shade to the right.

Cal didn't need the next toe imprint, coming up the side of the shallow ditch, to know which way their fugitive had headed.

Into the cool dark woods, roof of the first home just visible, they went.

Chapter 13

*T*HIS IS A TWENTY-TWO BOLT-ACTION RIFLE. *Training rifle, so you'll notice there's not a big kick. Having said that, a rifle feels fundamentally different from a handgun. Check it out."*

We were out in the woods again. Same clearing. Same setup with the folding table, wood pallet target, litter of spent shells. For today's lesson, however, a long black bag lay in the middle of the table. I could already tell from the bag's sleek shape that it contained a rifle. Now Frank tended to the zipper, and sure enough . . .

The gun was striking. Different from the compact, black-on-black Ruger we'd shot two weeks ago. The rifle reminded me of Western movies, a new sheriff in town. The wooden stock had beautiful golden grain, a diamond pattern etched into the grip.

The barrel was long. Twenty-five inches, Frank told me as he slid the rifle from the bag. As he had with the handgun, he set this out on the table, magazine ejected, bolt removed to reveal the empty chamber.

"I added the scope myself," Frank continued, tossing the carrying bag aside. "Nothing special. Just a basic Bushnell. Will help you get used to looking through the crosshairs. Like the Ruger, this rifle comes with a magazine. This is a five-round magazine. Small, you can see. This button in front, click up and the magazine ejects into your hand. Load the magazine, and simply pop it back into place. It sits in front of the trigger guard, versus being part of the handle, but you won't notice it much. Small little thing, which is why I also pur-

chased a larger plus ten. But that's for later. Right now, you need comfort, not firepower.

"Now, just like the handgun, for safety's sake, you clear the magazine, then check the chamber. In this case, the bolt is all the way out, showing the cleared chamber. The bolt action is what makes this rifle special. No semiauto function to kick in after the first round is fired. No, you're gonna have to feed each bullet from the magazine into the chamber, by racking the bolt after each and every shot. Here, I'll show you."

Frank hefted the rifle effortlessly, feeding the bolt into the top of the barrel, right under the scope. It looked like a tight fit to me, but apparently there was exactly enough room for everything.

Next, he brought out a strange container of bright blue bullets, roughly the size of .22s.

"Load the magazine," he instructed me, nodding his head toward the box.

My hands shook. I tried to keep them close to myself, so Frank wouldn't notice. He seemed to enjoy these sessions. His older son was gone now, off to college. Guess that made me, the troubled foster, the only candidate for father-son bonding. But guns made me nervous. The Ruger, once I'd picked it up, hadn't been so bad. That had been an okay first session.

But this, the rifle. It scared me.

I finally got the blue rounds into the magazine. Awkwardly done. I could feel Frank watching me, noticing. But he didn't say a word.

He took the magazine from me. Popped it into position, in front of the trigger guard. "Bright blue rounds are dummy rounds," he announced now. "No gunpowder. Just to help you get a feel for the weapon."

His eyes looked kind. Maybe. What does kindness look like in a man? Not something I'd had much opportunity to see. I shrugged, shook out my arms beneath my favorite black hoodie, worn with my

*favorite baggy black jeans. Black on black. Johnny Cash, Frank
called me when I dressed like this, but I had no idea who he was
talking about.*

*"Go on," he said now. "Pick it up. Remember what we said about
pretending there's a laser coming out of the end of the barrel. Even if
it's loaded with dummy rounds, don't point the rifle at anything you
wouldn't want to shoot."*

*The rifle was heavy. Awkward. I tried holding the stock against
my right shoulder, right hand around (but not touching) the trigger,
left hand holding up the incredibly long barrel. Immediately, my left
arm started shaking. I didn't see how anyone could hold this for
long, let alone spend a day hunting in the woods.*

*"All right, first things first." Frank moved to stand beside me.
"Move your feet. Sideways stance, left foot forward. There you go.
Now, right arm, bring your elbow out. See how that forms a natural
pocket in the front of your shoulder? Dig in with the stock there.
Yeah, like that. Left arm, bring that elbow down. You want that arm
tight against your side. Better. So, this is a long gun. Almost seven
pounds. A compact seven pounds, say a dumbbell, you could lift no
problem. But by virtue of length, the weight is way out in front of
you. That's what's taxing your arm, making it shake, the effort of
trying to hold up the barrel.*

*"So you need to pull the rifle more into your shoulder. Press it
into the pocket. Notice how that immediately lightens the load on
your left arm."*

*I did what he said, and as he predicted, my left arm stopped shak-
ing.*

*"Good job. Rifle takes a bit to get comfortable with. You're gonna
have to practice more to make it feel like a natural extension of your
body. Now, try putting your right eye to the scope. You can squeeze
your left eye shut if it makes it easier. But find the crosshairs. Place
them on the target and just hold for a bit. Practice breathing in,*

breathing out, with the crosshairs moving the least amount possible. Good job."

He was lying. Being kind again? My crosshairs were all over the place. Left arm back to shaking, each inhale and exhale rocking the system. But he didn't complain. Just nodded beside me as if all was going according to plan.

Last week, Sandra had asked me my favorite meal. I'd told her Kraft macaroni and cheese. No, no, she'd tried to explain. A homemade meal, or maybe something I'd once eaten at a restaurant. I stuck with Kraft. So last night, for dinner, that's what she'd made. Or at least tried to. Instead of buying the cheap blue box with the powdered sauce, she'd purchased the home-style version. Probably as close as she could bring herself to preparing packaged food. Home-style came with a real sauce, though at least it was the same reassuringly nuclear orange color. Frank had eaten his gamely. Sandra had pushed hers around the plate. But I'd eaten all of mine, then asked for seconds, even if it wasn't the right version of mac 'n' cheese. That seemed to please her.

I still hadn't figured Sandra out. She seemed happy when her men were happy. Honestly, it creeped me out.

Time to work the bolt action. I was to take my right hand off the trigger to push up, push forward, pull down with the bolt. It was harder than it looked. First time, I nose-dived the end of the barrel. Guess my fake laser was eating dirt. But with a bit of practice, I got used to the feel of the bolt. The way the "empty" shell spit out the right side, before the fresh bullet was racked into place.

My arms hurt. Especially my left arm. I'd liked the Ruger. The Ruger hadn't been so bad. But this . . .

"How about live ammo?" Frank said now.

"Sure." I gratefully returned the rifle to the table. Hoped he didn't notice me shaking out my left arm, rubbing my right shoulder.

"A twenty-two doesn't have much stopping power. Meaning this

is a good rifle for training, but not much else. Hunting, you're gonna want a three-oh-eight. Self-defense, an AR-fifteen."

I nodded, though I had no idea what he was talking about.

Then, as if he'd read my mind: "Know the difference between a twenty-two and three-oh-eight?" he asked me.

"Bullet size."

"True. Three-oh-eight is larger, makes a bigger hole. But more importantly?"

My foster dad, the science teacher, stared at me.

I shook my head.

"Energy. Three-oh-eight leaves the barrel with way more energy. Say each bullet was a bobsled. Twenty-two is fired by four guys standing in one place, shoving it forward. We watched the Jamaican bobsledding movie the other night. What's the better way of pushing off?"

"Running with the sled to build up speed, then shoving it off."

"Exactly. A three-oh-eight hunting rifle provides a great deal more energy to a larger bullet, resulting in greater efficiency. You'll wound with a rifle like this one." He lifted up the reloaded training rifle. "You'll kill with a three-oh-eight."

And now, armed with live rounds, he moved me into position once more.

I missed the target with the first shot. Snagged a corner with the second.

"Take your time. Focus. Press it back tighter into your shoulder. Breathe in. Breathe out."

Twelve shots later, I hit the target.

"Yeah!" I exhaled before I could stop myself.

Frank clapped me on the shoulder.

"You wanna shoot now?" I asked him, setting the rifle on the table, going about the business of clearing it. I almost felt like a pro.

"Nah, it's getting late. We should get back."

"Come on. Couple of rounds. Your gun, after all."

I was curious. With the handgun, he'd been amazing. And with the rifle?

"All right," he conceded, with a glance at the sky, which was growing darker. "Why don't you set it up for me," he said.

It didn't take him long. Five shots. Five bull's-eyes. And whereas I'd stood ten yards from the target, he'd moved back to thirty. It was impressive enough for me.

"You're really good," I said as we started to pack up.

"Just like it."

"Were you in the military, something like that?"

"Nope."

"Local competitions? Aren't there events for these sorts of things?"

"Just my hobby. Teaching is what I love. This is how I blow off steam. Speaking of which, what do you love, Telly?"

The question caught me off guard. I hadn't seen it coming. I shrugged defensively, working on getting the rifle back into its form-fitting carrying bag. "I dunno."

"In school. Out of school. Everyone loves something."

"I'm okay."

"Not what the principal said when he called about the fight on Friday."

Now my fingers stilled on the bag. I looked away. I should've known. Let's go shooting together. Always a catch.

"He started it," I mumbled.

"Principal thought the same."

I didn't answer.

"But you can't keep making yourself a target. And when you fight back, engage with the enemy, it makes it more likely to happen again."

I didn't say anything.

"You're angry, Telly. I see it in you. I get it. Hell, if I'd been through everything you've been through, I'd be angry too. At my loser parents. Other kids. The system. Even people like Sandra and me. Just passing through, while your entire life, you've had to go at it alone."

He paused. I kept my gaze on the rifle bag.

"Do you have one good memory, Telly? A single good memory of your time with your parents?"

"The library," I heard myself say.

"They took you to the library."

"No. I took myself. My baby sister."

"But your parents read you stories?"

"No."

"Encouraged you to check out books?"

I shook my head, very confused now. He stared back at me.

"So your one good memory of your time with your parents doesn't involve your parents at all?"

I shrugged. "I liked the library. They were good to us at the library."

"All right. Okay. So . . . maybe you'd like to become a librarian?"

Now I did look at him like he was crazy.

But Frank shook his head. "Seriously, Telly, you're a junior in high school. You're barely passing now, and with the fighting in the halls, that prank you pulled in the lunchroom, trashing school lockers . . . Reckoning is coming. You can only be an angry young hoodlum for so long. Next year is your senior year. Then that's it. You're on your own. Who are you gonna be, Telly? And are you ready for it?"

I didn't have an answer for him.

"Your parents are gone. Your sister, too. What happened happened. Hating it, taking everything out on others, out on yourself, it's just a waste of time. Sooner or later, you have to stop being so angry. And sooner or later, you have to stop living backward. That's what this next year is all about. Figuring out who you want to be. Setting yourself up for success. Sandra and me, we're there for you. We get it. So stop thinking you're alone all the time and the world hates you. You have at least two on your side. That's not such a bad thing."

Frank took the rifle bag from me, headed for the truck.

"I can't come out next weekend," he called over his shoulder. "High school science fair. But maybe the weekend after that. I'll bring the rifles again. Good practice for you."

I went to work on the folding table.

He paused, standing next to his truck, eyeing me intently. "You can do this, Telly. Maybe not perfectly. And maybe you gotta make some more mistakes first. But I see something in you. You saved your sister. Now you just gotta figure out how to save yourself. One more year, Telly. Then it's all up to you: What kind of man are you gonna be?"

Chapter 14

SITTING AT THE KITCHEN TABLE, Rainie could hear the sound of Luka's toenails click-clacking on the basement floor as the German shepherd ran around in the cool space. No noise from Sharlah, but that was hardly surprising. The thirteen-year-old preferred silence; anything to keep from calling attention to herself. Sharlah read, listened to music with her earbuds on, played games on her iPad, all very quietly. They spent entire evenings where Rainie, Quincy, and Sharlah all sat in the family room, looking at their individual books/devices, never making a sound.

In the beginning, the quiet had bothered Rainie. Now she chose to view it as comfortable, one more way her and Quincy's soon-to-be adopted daughter was surprisingly much like themselves—most at home in silence.

Rainie got up, paced around the table. She'd just gotten off the phone with Brenda Leavitt, Sharlah's caseworker. It had taken Rainie a bit, but she'd managed to get some information on Sharlah's past. Next, the caseworker was going to look up Telly's previous placements, promising to get back to Rainie shortly.

Rainie was anxious, nerves on edge. On the one hand, she believed what she'd told Sharlah—her daughter didn't need to worry about Telly. That was Rainie and Quincy's job. On the other hand, Rainie's own experience in life was that the worst could happen and often did. Truthfully, the closer they got to adopting Sharlah, to finally making her their own, the worse Rainie's anxiety had become.

Happily-ever-afters, loving families. Those were things that happened to other people, she often thought. For herself, such gifts remained just out of reach.

Which wasn't true, she had to remind herself now. She had Quincy and Sharlah and Luka. She had a great job, a beautiful house, a successful life. She simply had demons as well. To fight every day, to conquer every day. Such was the life of an addict.

Which is why she'd fallen desperately in love the first time she'd met Sharlah. She'd looked into her foster daughter's eyes and she'd known her. Just . . . known her. Sharlah's fears, anxieties, fragile hope, bone-deep strength. Rainie saw all of her daughter. And she loved her, not in spite of her weaknesses, but because of them. Sharlah was a fighter. Just like Rainie and Quincy.

And there was no way in hell Rainie was going to let some estranged, homicidal older brother mess with her family now.

Her phone rang. She glanced down, expecting it to be Brenda Leavitt, calling back. Instead, it was the sheriff, Shelly Atkins.

"We have a development in the case," Shelly said without preamble. Rainie and Quincy had worked with Shelly going back to her first stint as sheriff. None of them were much for small talk.

"We recovered Telly's phone. On it, we found some photos of Sharlah. Dated five days ago."

Rainie stopped pacing. She felt her heart jolt in her chest, her hands fist instinctively. She took a deep breath, forced herself to sit down at the kitchen table.

"Five days ago," she said. She was trying to think; what had they been doing five days ago? Were they home? Out and about? And how had she, a trained member of law enforcement, not noticed some teenage hoodlum snapping photos of her daughter?

"Photos aren't good quality. Taken with the cell phone, probably zoomed in. Dan Mitchell will be e-mailing you copies. He recognized one of the buildings in the background as the library."

That's right, five days ago, Rainie had taken Luka and Sharlah to the Bakersville County Library. Luka was part of the summer reading program—kids reading to canines. The program encouraged children with challenges to read out loud to a dog audience, which was more fun for the kids while also being less stressful.

"Okay," Rainie said.

"You talked to Sharlah about her brother?"

"She's had no contact with him since the night he killed their parents. Furthermore, she doesn't even remember him that well. Sharlah would've been only five when they were separated."

"What about e-mail, texts? Something you couldn't see?"

Rainie smiled. "Sharlah's phone account is attached to mine—I receive copies of all her texts. And we routinely screen her e-mails. Welcome to parenting in the modern age."

"Rainie . . . I don't know what this means, but Telly Ray Nash's phone. He'd cleaned it up—erased the browser history, deleted the photo stream. *Except* for the pictures of Sharlah. It's like he wanted us to see them. He wanted us to know he'd been watching."

Rainie stilled. Her heart was leaping in her chest again. She could feel the spike of adrenaline, the instinctive fight-or-flight reflex. Her anxiety had been right all along—the worst was happening.

Another deep breath. Think like Quincy. At times like this, his relentless logic was as soothing as it could be frustrating.

"Do you have any more information on Telly Ray Nash's whereabouts?" Rainie asked. Her voice sounded reasonably strong. Another steadying breath. Then she got up from the table, made her way down the hall to Quincy's office, which held their gun safe.

"A tracker, Cal Noonan, has picked up the boy's trail heading north from the EZ Gas parking lot. It appears Telly headed into a residential area—few homes, a lot of acreage. They're searching that now."

Rainie nodded, removing the picture of Quincy's oldest daughter from the wall, then holding up her index finger to the exposed biometric reader. The door of the gun safe swung open. Rainie's personal weapon was a Glock 42. The size of the handgun, however, would make it highly noticeable to carry given Rainie's summer wardrobe. Instead, she selected her backup twenty-two. Quincy carried his in an ankle holster. Rainie preferred to tuck hers in the small of her back. More accessible, she thought.

"It's been more than four hours since the gas station shooting," she said now.

"Yes."

"And still no sign of the suspect? No hits on the BOLO or hotline?"

"No."

"In other words, he might still be on foot, wandering this neighborhood. Or he could've stolen another vehicle, hooked up with a friend. He could be anywhere at all."

"Yes." The advantage of one law enforcement officer talking to another. Neither of them had to lie. "I can assign an officer protective detail," the sheriff offered now.

"And reduce the manpower looking for an armed fugitive? No thank you. We're well situated here." And Rainie didn't just mean because she was now carrying a handgun, or that she had a trained police dog at her daughter's side. She meant because Quincy had built this house with just these kinds of situations in mind. The positioning of the windows provided clear lines of sight, while the gravel driveway was its own kind of instant alert system.

Rainie had her fears and demons. Quincy had his.

"I spoke with Sharlah's caseworker," Rainie said now. "Sharlah claims she doesn't remember much about her parents or her older brother. To be honest, we've never asked a lot of questions about Telly or why he's no longer part of Sharlah's life. Given this morning's developments . . ."

Rainie didn't have to be able to see the sheriff to know she was nodding over the phone.

"According to Brenda Leavitt, Sharlah defended Telly's actions that night. Furthermore, the DA, Tim Egan, had a forensic psychologist evaluate both children. Her assessment was that Telly had taken on the caretaking role of his sister. He made her breakfast, got them both off to school, that sort of thing."

"He loved Sharlah?"

"According to the forensic eval, yes. But this is where things get interesting. As the assigned caseworker, Brenda Leavitt conducted her own interview of Sharlah while Sharlah was recuperating in the hospital. Given that Telly had also attacked Sharlah with the baseball bat—in the heat of the moment, the forensic psychologist theorized—Brenda wanted to make sure Sharlah was still comfortable living with her brother. The state rarely breaks up siblings and generally will only do so if the kids are considered better off apart."

"Okay."

"Every time Brenda asked Sharlah about her brother, she became very agitated. 'He hates me,' she'd say again and again. In the end, Brenda had concerns that Sharlah was afraid of Telly. Thought he might hurt her again. Hence the recommendation to place the kids separately."

"So Sharlah was the one to end the relationship, so to speak," Shelly said.

"Yes. Though how much Telly knew about that . . . He was only nine at the time and processing trauma of his own."

"Still. You could argue from Telly's perspective, he killed his own parents to save his sister's life, only to have her say she never wanted to see him again."

"You could say that," Rainie said. "Plus, according to the forensic psychologist's report, after all the time and effort Telly made to take care of and protect Sharlah . . ."

"Her rejection would be that much harder to take. In fact, probably really pissed him off."

"Yes," Rainie said quietly. "Brenda is going to get me a list of all of Telly's previous foster families, but it doesn't sound good. Since losing his own family, he's bounced around all over the place. Antisocial tendencies, oppositional defiant disorder. He's a very troubled teenager."

Shelly sighed heavily. "Is this gonna be one of those cases where all the neighbors appear on the news—'I knew that kid was no good,' et cetera, et cetera?"

"Possibly. Brenda knew the foster family before the Duvalls. The wife struggled with Telly. She thought he was too quiet. He'd do what they told him to do . . . but she never really trusted him. In her own words, she worried he'd kill them in their sleep."

"Great."

"They removed Telly over allegations of theft—some small items around the house went missing. Telly never argued. His probation officer came to get him and he left. I guess to go to the Duvalls'? Months later, however, the family found the missing items. They had four foster kids. Turned out a different one had been taking things, hoarding them, really. They found everything in a box under the boy's bed. They felt bad for blaming Telly but not bad enough to request his return."

"So pissed-off, too-quiet teenager who grew up in a violent household, killed his own parents when he was nine, and was rejected by presumably the only person he ever cared about, his baby sister, then not given a chance by the rest of the world."

"Rampage shooters often have hit lists," Rainie said. "Everyone who's ever wronged them."

"I'm sending over an officer. Seriously."

"And you'll send one to every foster family that ever rejected Telly as well? What about the principal who suspended him or the classmates who teased him? In the people-who've-done-him-wrong department, Telly's list is too long; you'll never have enough officers.

Find him. That's what we need. Pinpoint Telly's location. Make an arrest."

"Got a tracking team on his trail now. Next up, I'm interviewing Aly Sanchez, Telly's PO. Gonna see what she can tell us about Telly's state of mind, plus background on the Duvalls. If Telly's the type to hold a grudge, God only knows what they did to set him off."

"Can Quincy join you for that conversation? I would like to, but I need to stay with Sharlah."

"I never mind a profiler's insight. Especially in a case where it feels we have way more questions than answers."

"Send me the photos."

"On it now."

Rainie walked back into the kitchen. She paused long enough to listen for the sound of Luka's toenails. Then, when she didn't hear it . . .

"Sharlah?" she called out sharply.

"Yeah?" Her daughter appeared, coming around from the kitchen counter, holding a glass of lemonade. Luka was at her side.

And once more, Rainie willed her heartbeat to steady, unclenched her hand on the phone.

"Sharlah," she said. "We need to talk."

Chapter 15

QUINCY WAS ON EDGE. And what Rainie was telling him on the other end of the phone didn't help.

"Telly has pictures of Sharlah on his cell phone?"

"Half a dozen shots, taken in the past five days. Quincy, most are of Sharlah and Luka walking to the library. But the last photo. It's our front porch. He's been to our home."

"I think you and Sharlah need to go on a trip. Drive to Seattle. Canada. Somewhere."

"I understand. I'm talking to Sharlah now. She still swears she hasn't had any contact with her brother. And never noticed anyone taking her picture. Why leave us those photos, Quincy? Why clear his cell phone of everything but that? Shelly thinks it's a message—or maybe a warning. But why?"

Quincy wasn't sure what to say. "He's angry? Sharlah rejected him once. Now he wants her to know he can find her anytime he likes."

"Then why not find her? Why not drive here after killing the Duvalls and be done with it? Why head north and kill two strangers instead? If the photos are a warning . . ."

"I don't know," Quincy said at last.

"Everything I'm hearing about Telly—he's textbook. Quiet, troubled, loner. Grew up in a bad household. Was driven to kill his own parents at nine. Has been lost ever since. It's everything you'd expect in a spree shooter. Yet somehow, I feel we don't know him at all."

"Because you know Sharlah. You love her. And loving her, you can't imagine her brother would be someone that bad."

"Maybe. He took care of her. Her first thought when she thinks of her brother is Cheerios. He fed her breakfast, Quincy. Surely that kind of connection . . . it has to mean something."

"He was bonded with his sister," Quincy supplied. "Which in theory is a good thing. A child who can bond once can bond again." Hence their getting Sharlah a dog. "When that bond was severed, however . . . It's a very real possibility he feels betrayed by his sister. He has a kernel of rage, which he's been nursing for years. And now that he's exploded . . ."

"All bets are off," Rainie said quietly.

"You and Sharlah should go on a trip."

"I know. Let me get some things together. And you? You'll join Shelly to talk to Telly's PO?"

"I'm headed to the mobile command center now."

"We need to understand him, Quincy. And not just because Telly's a threat, but because he is Sharlah's brother. She's going to need answers. I mean, first her father tries to kill the whole family and now her brother's a mass murderer. It's going to make her wonder about her own future. How could it not?"

"I know. We're going to figure this out, Rainie. We're going to catch this suspect, just like we've always done. Sharlah will be safe, life will return to normal."

"And you, are you doing okay?"

The question was spoken softly, by his wife and partner who knew him well. And understood he'd already lost one daughter to a killer.

"I would like you and Sharlah to go on a trip," he said again.

And because Rainie knew him, truly knew him, she said, "Sharlah is not Mandy. You're right. We are going to find Telly, and Sharlah will be safe again. We'll do this, Quincy. We will."

_____

HE DROVE UP TO MOBILE COMMAND.

Telly's PO, Aly Sanchez, was already there, squeezed in beside Sheriff Atkins in the narrow space.

At first glance, it would've been easy to confuse Aly with one of her charges. Petite. Long dark hair. A face that looked closer to fourteen than forty. Currently, she sat cross-legged on a chair in a position Quincy wouldn't have thought possible. Dressed in shorts and a loose-fitting flowered peasant top, she took in his conservative navy blue shirt and tan slacks with a smile.

"You must be the profiler."

"Guilty as charged." He crowded forward long enough to shake Sanchez's hand, then drifted back closer to the door. The space was small enough that where you stood wouldn't affect whether you were heard.

"As I was just saying to the sheriff, I've known Telly for the past year. He was first assigned to me at sixteen. Kid has an explosive temper—someone said or did something wrong, and Telly ended up trashing a school locker. That got him a charge of disorderly conduct. He was also expelled for five days, except being Telly, he showed up two days later in defiance of the principal's order. Another showdown in the halls, then the principal called the police to forcefully remove Telly from the property. Let's just say Telly didn't exit gracefully, earning him a charge for resisting arrest, as well as a file in my office. And around and around we've been going ever since."

"Drugs, alcohol?" Shelly asked now.

"As part of his probation, Telly is subject to random drug tests. I've administered four in the past year. To date, he's passed them all."

"Do you believe those results?" Quincy asked, because experienced addicts knew many ways of defeating such tests.

"Actually, I do. Not that I'm saying Telly's a saint. But of all his problems, I don't think drugs are one of them. In fact, I get the impression, based on his experience with his parents, that Telly is quite antidrug."

"Different," Quincy observed, as children of addicts were much more likely to become addicts themselves.

"Oh, Telly is different. One of my still-waters-run-deep charges. Do I like him? Yeah, I do. Would I have ever guessed I'd be questioned for his involvement in a mass shooting? No. Then again, still waters do run deep. And I've only been meeting with Telly off and on for less than a year. There's more about him I don't know than I do. Plus his temper . . . Telly's too quiet. Meaning once he gets triggered . . ."

"All bets are off," Shelly filled in.

"He didn't remember what he did to the school lockers," Sanchez provided. "He watched the hall cam video as surprised as anyone, though the blood dripping from his fists was probably a hint."

Sanchez leaned forward. "Part of probation is to work on coping strategies. I'm not just monitoring Telly due to prior bad deeds, I'm trying to work with him to develop new approaches to avoid such acts in the future. In his case, Telly has several key challenges. First, he can't sleep. Trauma, overexposure to violence, anxiety, take your pick. So he rarely sleeps for more than an hour or two at night, which, as you can imagine, makes school, focus, that much more challenging."

Living with two insomniacs himself, Quincy could imagine it.

"Sandra Duvall had been doing some research on the subject," Sanchez continued. "Sleeping pills had an adverse effect on Telly. But last time we met, she'd started him on melatonin, a natural supplement, to see if that would make a difference."

"Did it?" Shelly asked.

"I don't know. That was four weeks ago."

"Other challenges?" Quincy asked.

"Telly had a hard time avoiding trouble. Push him, he pushes back. And given his history and what a lot of kids think they know about him . . . Transitioning between classes, another student might say something in the halls, maybe bump against Telly's shoulder, and next thing you know, rumble in the jungle time. In May, I suggested Telly wear earbuds between classes, focus on his music and keeping himself to himself. That seemed to help. Of course, by then, Telly was already failing his junior year, meaning he's spent the past two months in summer school. For Telly, school equals stress."

"Priming the pump," Quincy murmured.

"Exactly."

"Did he like his foster parents?" Shelly asked.

Sanchez shrugged. "He seemed to tolerate them, which for Telly is probably close enough. For the record, I recommended the Duvalls for him, contacted Telly's caseworker myself. In the foster system, everyone has their niche, from the families that are in it for the twenty bucks a day; to people who take in short-term placements, wanting to feel they're providing a safe haven before a kid journeys on to his or her forever home; to the foster-to-adopt families who are looking to offer permanency. Frank and Sandra Duvall were the tail end of the spectrum. They wanted an older kid and were looking to focus on mentoring. For example, a teenager like Telly is too old to be thinking family anymore. On the other hand, he needs support. He's one year from aging out of the system and being on his own. How does he find lodging? A first job? Open a checking account, pay his bills? I work with my charges on some of these issues as well. But it's the next steps in life that often trip kids up. Turning eighteen is challenging for anyone. If you're a foster, it's particularly rough."

"We saw some pictures on Sandra Duvall's Facebook page," Shelly said. "Appeared Frank was taking Telly shooting. Were you aware?"

"Frank talked to me before he took Telly for his first lesson. Frank believed shooting could help teach Telly how to focus. Hitting a target requires discipline and concentration. And, if the kid is any good, it can improve confidence as well, another one of Telly's challenges. At least that was the spiel Frank gave me."

"Did Telly talk about it?" Quincy asked.

"No. Never."

"Was he a good shot?" Shelly pressed.

"I have no idea."

"And Sandra?" Quincy asked. "What did Telly think of his foster mom?"

"He complimented her cooking once."

"Did he talk about his past? About what happened with his parents?"

"No."

"Did you bring it up?"

"Yes and no. We danced around the topic. Technically speaking, no charges were filed, meaning there's no official paperwork attached to Telly's name regarding his parents' deaths. Having said that, I talked to a couple of the officers involved, wanting to learn for myself what had happened. And of course there's the rumor mill. Kids at the high school even made up a jingle: *Telly Nash, armed with a bat, slugged his mother out of the park, then whacked his father till all went dark.* . . . Like I said, earbuds for navigating the school halls were a good thing for Telly."

"But he wouldn't talk about it?" Quincy asked.

"No. And when I tried to press . . . His face would just go blank. I'm not sure I can do the look justice. Just, lights on, nobody home."

Quincy leaned forward. "And his sister? Did he ever mention Sharlah?"

For the first time, Sanchez hesitated. "Telly, no. But Frank Duvall. Five months ago? March sometime. He called me. He wanted to know if I had any information on Sharlah."

"Did you?"

"No. I'm a probation officer, not a family counselor."

Quincy peered at her intently. "Why did he ask that question? What did Frank want to know?"

"Frank had it in his head that Telly couldn't let go of what happened with his birth family. Killing your own parents, even if your father is allegedly chasing you around with a knife, is heavy stuff. Add to that breaking his sister's arm as part of Telly's rampage . . . Frank thought if Telly could see, or at least know, his sister was okay, that might help him move on. Make some kind of peace with what happened. Which Frank felt had to happen if Telly was ever truly going to move forward."

"I want to see the photos," Quincy said. His gaze went to Shelly, his words a statement, not a request.

The sheriff sighed, moving over to one of the laptops to work the keyboard. "They're still processing the phone, but Deputy Mitchell copied the images for me. There's half a dozen of them, taken five days ago to judge by the dates on the files."

True to Rainie's description, the first five photos were taken in front of the county library. Sharlah appeared to be walking across the parking lot, Luka at her side, Rainie trailing behind. Sanchez peered over his shoulder, looking at the photos for herself.

"Telly spend much time at the library?" Quincy asked.

"I don't know that I've ever asked him that question. But he's a reader. Generally has some dog-eared paperback in his backpack. Tom Clancy. Brad Taylor. Military thrillers."

Could it be that simple? Five days ago, Telly had spotted his long-lost sister at the local library. And then . . .

Based on how happy she looked with her dog, decided to shoot up the entire town, starting with his own foster parents? Quincy shook his head. He didn't like this. There were pieces they were not seeing. Still too much about Telly, the shootings, that they didn't know.

The final photo filled the screen. Except this wasn't Sharlah standing outside the library anymore. This was Sharlah sitting on a front porch in one of two matching Adirondack rocking chairs. Her front porch.

Quincy's house.

"When was this taken?" he asked sharply.

Shelly's voice was steady. "Same afternoon."

"He followed Rainie and Sharlah home from the library."

"That's my guess."

"Why?" He whirled on Sanchez now, who'd had the good sense to retreat to her chair. "Why these photos? Why this sudden interest in his younger sister, who, according to you, he'd never even mentioned before?"

"I don't know."

"Did Frank Duvall look up my daughter? Did he pursue the matter?"

"I'm sorry. I don't know. You'll have to ask Frank—"

The probation officer's voice broke off. Because they couldn't ask Frank. Telly had already shot and killed him first thing this morning.

"Telly Ray Nash is an angry kid," Shelly stated, standing between the two of them, trying to get the conversation back on track.

Sanchez pulled her gaze from Quincy, returned her attention to the sheriff instead. "You want me to put Telly in a box: Good or bad. Black or white."

"He killed four people this morning. That makes him bad enough in my book."

"I get that, Sheriff. And given that I personally knew Frank and Sandra, that I recommended they take this boy . . ." Sanchez's voice trembled, and for the first time Quincy heard the emotions she'd obviously been working hard to keep at bay.

"I can't box up Telly for you," the PO continued after a moment. "Yes, he's impulsive and explosive and troubled and pissed off. He's also a seventeen-year-old boy trying to come to terms with a violent childhood while simultaneously being told he only has a handful of months to figure out the rest of his life. Would I want to be walking in his shoes? Not at all.

"Telly trying is not a bad kid. The Telly who took his melatonin and used his earbuds between classes, that Telly was hoping to figure things out. He worked with me. Maybe even listened to Frank. Having said that . . ." Sanchez's voice trailed off. She took another steadying breath. "Telly's stressed. His past, his future, his present time at summer school. Take your pick. Telly is a teenager under a tremendous amount of pressure, and historically speaking, Telly under pressure . . ."

"Explodes," Quincy provided.

"Yeah. And then he becomes the kind of person capable of most anything."

"Including taking a baseball bat to his baby sister?"

"Exactly."

Sanchez fell silent. Quincy wasn't sure he had much more to say himself. He went back to staring at the picture of his daughter, shot on their own front porch, with none of them the wiser.

How had the boy gotten that close? And why now? What the hell did Telly want from his sister?

The radio clipped to Shelly's uniform crackled suddenly to life. The call came in that much louder, given the tight stillness of incident command.

"Shots fired, shots fired! Team Alpha to base. Requesting immediate backup. Repeat, shots fired!"

Chapter 16

CAL NOONAN LIKED TREES. He admired their towering beauty, appreciated their deep shade, and on a day like this one, respected them as strategic cover. When tracking an armed fugitive, it never hurt to have as many trees as possible between you and him.

Which made their approach to the first house that much more nerve-wracking. The house was a small white bungalow, set way back on a dirt drive. The yard had been cleared decades if not generations ago, leaving a vast expanse of real estate between Cal's tracking team and the front door. The house wasn't even what interested Cal the most. He'd found a shoe impression leaving the road and heading toward the left side of the property, where Cal could just make out a ramshackle shed. The kind of building where the homeowner might have a rusted-out truck, an old tractor, or, around these parts, a four-wheeler.

If Cal were a seventeen-year-old on the run, he'd want a four-wheeler.

Antonio took up the lead position. Cal behind him, then Nonie, with Jesse bringing up the rear. They walked upright, keeping themselves tucked as close to the shade of the side bramble as possible. Slow and steady approach. Rifles in hand. Eyes on anything that moved.

Except for Cal, who was looking around Antonio for any fresh disturbances in the ground ahead.

Meaning he never saw the first shot coming. One second, he was studying a particularly compressed patch of grass, the next . . .

Rifle crack. Loud and clear.

Antonio swore. Cal and Nonie dropped where they stood. Then Jesse was belly-crawling past both of them, rifle forward, saying, "Are you hurt, are you hurt? What did you see?"

Antonio was already on the radio calling for backup.

Cal promised himself if he ever got out of this, he was sticking to making cheese for the rest of his life.

Second crack. From the direction of the house, Cal determined this time. Then, just as the third shot exploded the bushes above his head, he saw the glint of a rifle, positioned in an upstairs window.

"This is the police. Cease fire!" Antonio boomed from a low crouch, while signaling Jesse with a series of hand gestures. The second SWAT team member nodded, then rolled three times quick, taking up position behind a rhododendron.

"This is private property!" an older, raspy voice called out. "You leave my house alone. Nothing to see. Nothing to steal. Now off with you."

"Sir! This is the police. We are in pursuit of an armed fugitive. Lay down your rifle. Cease fire!"

"Only way you're getting my gun is to pry it out of my cold, dead hands!" the homeowner yelled back.

Cal lowered his head. He was going to die because of an old man's paranoia. Wouldn't that just figure.

"Sir," Cal called out, making his own attempt. Antonio cast him a grim look. "We are in pursuit of a seventeen-year-old male. He shot and killed a store clerk and a customer at the EZ Gas about a mile back. You might have seen it on the news."

"Someone shot up the EZ Gas?"

"Yes, sir. My job is to track that someone. We have reason to believe he passed through your property."

"You mean that kid who was in my shed? Don't worry, I shot at him, too. Hoodlum. Thinking he can just take whatever he wants."

"Is the kid still in the shed? This is important. The boy is heavily armed and considered dangerous."

"Nah. Couple of shots from my rifle and he took off through the side shrubs. Probably breaking into my neighbor's house now, not that she has anything good."

"Sir, I'm going to stand up. Please don't shoot me. In my real life, I'm the head cheese maker at the factory, so you know, if you ever want to eat cheese again . . ." Very carefully, Cal got one leg beneath him, then the other. He stood, Antonio aiming his rifle at the second-story window as if to cover him.

Cal held up both hands. "We need to find this shooter, sir. Before he hurts anyone else. You said he was at your shed."

"Yeah. Till I targeted his backside with a little lead."

"Did you hit him?"

"Nah. Aimed way over his head. Just like I did with you." The man's voice was calming down. Less confrontational. More conversational.

"We need to search your shed. Check for evidence. Pick up the kid's trail. It's important."

"Who'd he shoot at the EZ Gas?"

"Um, female cashier. Local girl—"

"Erin? He killed Erin? I'll be . . . Son of a bitch, shoulda shot him when I had the chance. All right. I'm coming on down. I'll meet you at the shed."

The rifle withdrew from the window. Crouched in front of Cal, Antonio shook his head, rising much more slowly to his feet. "Some people. Some days . . ."

"Yeah," Cal agreed. "And this day's just beginning."

Cal and Nonie approached the shed first, Antonio and Jesse taking up position between the trackers and the front door of the trigger-happy homeowner. They held their rifles loosely before them, still at the ready, but making some show of faith.

Cal identified two more foot depressions in softer areas of the yard, then they were at the shed.

About the size of a single-car garage, the shed was a dusty, broken-down affair. The side door yawned open enough to reveal the black, grimy interior. Both side windows were missing panes of glass. The hot August sun beat through, showing whorls of dust where the space had been recently disturbed.

A creak from the house behind him. Cal turned to see an older gentleman, jeans, plain white T-shirt, red suspenders, come huffing down the front stairs. At least the homeowner had left behind his weapon.

"Jack," the man declared, crossing to their little group. "Jack George. This here's my property. That's my shed. Now, what do you need to see to find the little bastard?"

At Cal's request, Mr. George allowed them to open the front bay, allowing in more light. Now Cal could see even more disturbances in the dust. Fresh marks on a wide worktable where their suspect had felt his way along, maybe looking for equipment that might be useful, or even another weapon.

The shed held an assortment of lawn tools and power tools, plus a riding lawn mower, relatively new and smelling of fresh-cut grass. The real item of interest was in the back: a four-wheeler, covered in another layer of cobwebs, both tires flat.

"I purchased it for the grandkids," Mr. George provided. "Thought they'd like zipping around the property. But they haven't been around in a bit. The thing needs some air in the tires clearly, probably fresh fuel mix, but it'll run. If I hadn't seen that hoodlum skulking around outside, he would've stolen it, no doubt."

Cal nodded. He could make out a clear outline of footprints next to the four-wheeler, where their target had stood, considering his options. Given that the recreational vehicle was parked in the shadows at the rear of the shed, out of sight of the windows, Cal already doubted Mr. George's assessment of things.

Their suspect had made it into the shed. Most likely, the flat tires and pitted gas tank had convinced the teenager to give up on the four-wheeler. At which point, according to the footprints on the dusty floor, he'd left the shed via the side door. Where Mr. George had finally spotted the intruder and opened fire—catching the boy exiting the building, not entering it.

Now, once shots had been fired . . .

Cal left the shed, resumed studying the grass. The suspect appeared to have spun around the back of the shed. Deeper prints, farther apart, indicating the target was running, no doubt with his head ducked low, trying to avoid gunfire.

On the other side of the shed, he discovered two fainter impressions side by side. The target pausing, catching his breath, and then determining his best route of escape.

Sure enough, straight across from the back of the shed was a thick hedge, with a narrow break where one of the bushes had died and never been replaced. Not the easiest squeeze for Cal or his SWAT team commandos, but for a wiry seventeen-year-old boy . . .

Cal approached closer, inspecting the break in the shrubs. He identified several broken twigs, green wood still showing, and recently shed leaves. He indicated for his team to fall back for a moment, while he returned his attention to Mr. George.

"Your neighbor on the other side, she like rifles as much as you do?"

"Aurora? Nah. I don't think she's even home. One of her kids showed up the other day, packed her off to Portland for a visit. She doesn't have AC in her house, and Aurora's not one for the heat."

"So her home could very well be empty?"

"Yes, sir."

Cal looked at Antonio.

"What time did you see the suspect?" Antonio asked Mr. George.

"Let's see. Was watching the morning news. So a good five, six hours ago?"

Cal nodded. Given the EZ Gas shooting happened at eight A.M. and it was now nearly two, they already knew Telly Ray Nash had a good head start. But to judge by the trail, he was also having to make decisions as he went. Such as turning right toward the residential area, then creeping up on the first house and inspecting his options in the shed before having to flee the premises.

Telly was moving faster than they were, but he also had to pause to consider. And the empty house next door would pose another tempting target. Maybe even a place to hole up and rest . . .

"With any luck," Cal informed Antonio, "the kid made some attempt to break in next door. Looking for water, food, other supplies. Might be our first chance to catch up with him."

Antonio turned to Mr. George. "Sir, is it possible to see your neighbor's house from your upstairs windows?"

"Now, see here, what are you implying—"

"Recon, sir. I'd like to be able to check your neighbor's house for any sign of activity before we go strolling up to the front door."

"Oh. Well. Yes. From the bathroom window, now that you mention it . . ."

Antonio followed Mr. George back to his house. Cal resumed studying the break in the shrubs. They wouldn't pass through it. That would disturb evidence. Instead, they'd go all the way around, pick up the trail from the other side. Now he and Nonie inserted more orange flags for the crime scene techs following up behind them.

Ten minutes later, Antonio reemerged from the house. "No sign of movement. I radioed in our position. The chopper's on its way; it'll conduct an aerial sweep of the neighborhood."

"Good. We're making some progress."

They fell back in line, exiting Mr. George's property, heading back to the shaded dirt road, looping around the hedge.

The neighbor Aurora's house appeared to be a cute cape, set a distance back. Cal took the first step.

A fresh crack of gunfire.

Not from Mr. George's house to their left. Not from the cute cape to their right.

But from behind them. Across the street.

Cal was still pivoting, still realizing the magnitude of his mistake, just how badly he'd been outplayed.

Then Antonio was down in a spray of red. Nonie screamed.

While the distant rifle cracked again and again and again.

Chapter 17

RAINIE AND QUINCY ARE TALKING in the kitchen. Their voices are low; they don't want me to hear. This is not a discussion "suitable for children." And yet, it's all about me.

Quincy arrived home fifteen minutes ago. There was a look on his face. . . . I can't explain it. I want to both run away and rush over and hug him. So me being me, I held perfectly still. While Rainie came to stand beside me, her eyes locked on his face.

"Sharlah," she said quietly. "Please go to your room."

I went. Without saying a single word. Which is not at all like me.

Now my legs are jiggly. I can't sit down. I can't stay still. But I'm doing my best, lying on my stomach, my ear pressed against the slit under my door. They may be talking about things that aren't suitable for me, things that are even terrifying for me, which is all the more reason I have to hear.

"Two down," Quincy is saying now. "One of the flankers was hit in his shoulder. The second tracker, Norinne Manley, was shot in the arm. Both are being medevaced to Portland, the SWAT officer in critical condition."

"You're sure it's Telly Nash?"

"Of course it was him! They'd traced Telly to some remote house where he'd broken into a shed. That homeowner, however, spotted him and fired off a couple of no-trespassing shots. The kid escaped around the back of the shed and appeared to have approached a neighbor's house. Except . . . he didn't. Or did and had already moved on. The tracker, Cal Noonan, is still trying to sort it out. But somehow, Telly ended up behind them. And while they were approaching the neighbor's house, he opened fire from across the street. Now two out of four members of a tracking team are down."

A pause. I hear the muffled sound of movement. Maybe Rainie crossing to Quincy, placing a soothing hand on his shoulder, as I've seen her do many times before.

"Do they know where he went?" she asks, voice quiet.

"Out the rear of the property, where we're told there's a maze of trails. He stole the neighbor's four-wheeler, giving him speed and flexibility. Shelly has a low-flying chopper scanning the area, though how heat-seeking imagery can pinpoint anything in these temps is beyond me."

Sighing. Frustrated. Heavy. Deep. From Quincy, I figure, all fired up, except, of course, he prides himself on never being overly emotional. Maybe my brother has that effect on people. Personally, I'm fighting a nearly uncontrollable urge to rub the scar on my shoulder.

"What do you think he wants?" Rainie continues.

"I have no idea."

"If he's a spree killer," she says, her voice calmer than his, "then his rage is its own endgame. He will destroy, till he self-destructs."

No answer. Because Quincy isn't one to talk? Or because Quincy, the profiler, already knows the answer to these questions, and it's too terrible to say?

"We know spree killers are all about feeling misunderstood and wronged by the world," Quincy states. "Which fits with how Telly has been described."

Is that who my brother has become? Is that how he truly feels?

I see Cheerios again. A cheerful yellow box in the middle of a dingy table. And I'm sad in ways I can't explain. For the boy who brought me those Cheerios. Or, maybe, for the way that made me feel. Like I would at least have him, forever and ever.

Except it hadn't exactly turned out that way, had it?

"According to Telly's PO," Quincy is saying, "Telly can be a good kid when he makes the effort. But under stress, he's also prone to impulsive acts of violence. Taking a baseball bat to his entire family. Destroying school lockers with his bare hands. Under pressure, Telly explodes. And afterward, he often doesn't even remember what he's done."

"So what is his trigger now?"

"From the sound of it, time. He's a year away from graduation with no idea what to do with himself. As well as aging out of foster care without a plan. By all accounts, his foster parents, Frank and Sandra Duvall, were good people. They asked for a teenager explicitly because they were looking for a mentorship role. Now, that all sounds very good, but change, even positive change, can be stressful. It could be that Frank and Sandra's tough-love style was too much for Telly. They pushed too hard, leading to his explosion."

"I don't buy it. All the things you're talking about—the stress of being seventeen, the pressures of adolescence—that's all slow burn. With spree killers, there's always an inciting event. Meaning, if Telly's now on this rampage, what triggered it?"

Quiet now as both consider the possibilities. Quincy furrows his brow when thinking. I can picture him doing that, and it sends another pang to my chest.

My foster dad is stressed. That's part of his job, I guess. But he's also fearful. I can hear it. He's worried. And that's because of me.

Everything about this particular case is more difficult because of me.

"At this time, I know of only one new element in Telly's life," Quincy murmurs finally. "Which is Sharlah. According to the probation officer, Frank Duvall believed Telly needed closure from what happened eight years ago. Meaning Frank himself was pushing for a meeting between Telly and Sharlah. I don't know what happened with that, as certainly no one contacted us—"

"They would have to go through the caseworker, Brenda Leavitt," Rainie murmured. "I spoke to her earlier. She never mentioned any outreach from Telly or the Duvalls."

"So maybe Frank never went through official channels. But clearly he was talking about the idea, putting Sharlah back on Telly's radar screen. Then, five days ago . . . Telly sought out his sister? Randomly spotted her as you guys crossed the library parking lot? I don't know. But he took those pictures on his cell phone. Then he waited and followed Sharlah home."

Silence, neither one of them speaking.

Rainie had told me about the photos earlier. I still feel shocked and faintly violated. The least my brother could have done was walk up to me outside the library and say hey. And yet, at the same time, if I'd been the one who spotted him, would I have that kind of courage? I doubt it. I might snap a photo, though. Which I guess means, all these years later, my older brother and I remain kindred spirits.

Except, of course, I haven't spent my day gunning down innocent people.

"Sharlah? The new variable is Sharlah?" Rainie's voice is clearly distressed.

"She is *a* new variable in Telly's life. But is she *the* thing? We don't know yet, Rainie. There's still too much about this kid we don't know."

"He can't have her. I don't care how many guns he has, how many four-wheelers he steals. She's ours, Quincy. Homicidal maniac or not, Telly's not getting her back."

Given the tone of her voice, I believe her.

"Obviously," Quincy says, seconding that. "I'm back to what I said earlier—you and Sharlah should take a trip. Drive up to Seattle.

Or, better yet, fly out to Atlanta and pay Kimberly a visit. I don't care. But given Telly's interest, I don't want Sharlah anywhere in his vicinity. The boy has now shot six people and killed four. No way he's taking Sharlah down with him."

Rainie doesn't hesitate: "I started looking into options. There's a red-eye flight to Atlanta, eleven P.M. Until then?"

"One of us is with her at all times," Quincy says.

Armed is what he means. I've already observed the bulge in the small of Rainie's back. From the twenty-two she has tucked beneath the cover of her light hoodie.

They will keep me under armed guard, then get me out of town.

So my big bad evil older brother won't get to me.

My shoulder aches. This time, I roll onto my back and give in to the urge to rub it. I wish I could understand all the emotions spinning through my head. Gratitude for Rainie and Quincy, who certainly seem to be in this for the long haul. And yet fear, too. Because getting me away isn't the same as keeping Telly from coming here and looking for me. And a spree killer like him, who shoots innocent cashiers and doubles back to attack the tracking team, he's not going to show up unarmed and open to conversation. If the whole point of these killers is that they're pissed off at the world, news of my absence is hardly gonna calm Telly down.

So maybe he doesn't get a chance to shoot me.

Doesn't mean he still can't hurt me.

Cheerios boxes. *Clifford the Big Red Dog. Go to sleep, Sharlah, I'll take care of everything . . .*

The exact same boy, staring at me with his red-flushed face and bulging eyes as he raises the bat up, up, up . . .

Telly, no!

The last words I ever spoke to my brother.

Telly, no.

At least, I think that's what I said.

Then, no more time for thinking: A fresh sound reaches me. Footsteps coming down the hall. I bolt off the floor and do my best to prepare for what must happen next.

LUKA IS SPRAWLED ON MY BED. When Rainie enters my room, he raises his dark head and yawns. I do, too, from my position sitting beside him, scratching his back. Rainie isn't fooled by either of us.

She moves into the room, pulling out my desk chair, taking a seat. She sits stiff-backed on account of the twenty-two. She follows my gaze, smiles faintly.

"So," she says. "Did you hear half of the conversation or all of it?"

"Most of it," I allow.

"Are you okay, Sharlah?" she asks me softly.

In response, I shrug. I don't know what I am.

"You don't need to be afraid. You know that Quincy and I are trained members of law enforcement. We're not going to let anything happen to our daughter."

"Why are you adopting me?" The question is out before I can stop it. I'm not sure which of us it surprises more. I've never asked this question. Not even the afternoon they sat me down and told me they wanted to be my forever family. *What do you think?* they asked. *Sure,* I said. Because *sure* is as close as I could come to describing all the mixed-up emotion inside of me. Because *sure* is safer than a lot of other words, and a girl like me, I can't help but play it safe. Hence all the new friends I've never made. And my new parents who've never heard me say that I love them.

Cheerios boxes, I think again, and now my eyes are stinging except I don't know why.

I'm on the verge of losing something. I can't see it. I can only feel it. And I know the pain of that loss is going to be deep and lasting. It will *hurt.*

"We love you, Sharlah," Rainie is saying now. She gets up from the chair, moves to the bed beside me. Quincy has appeared in the open doorway. He hesitates and I know it's his own emotions that hold him back. The words he feels the most are the words he has the hardest time saying. He and I share that, just like Rainie and I share sleepless nights and the same taste in superhero movies.

Rainie, Quincy, Luka, and me. We are family.

I turn slightly, rest my head against Rainie's shoulder. This is me hugging, I think, and I know from Rainie's stillness that she gets that.

"I'm sorry," I hear myself say.

"You have nothing to apologize for." Quincy from the doorway, his voice thick. "Telly's actions are his own."

"He's my brother."

"Do you miss him?" Rainie's voice, soft against the top of my head.

"I barely remember him."

"If there's any way to help him," Quincy says, "you know I'll do it."

"He's killed people. A lot of people."

"Not all killers are evil, Sharlah," Rainie counters, her voice ruffling the top of my hair. "Some are sick. Telly may not even know what he's doing. He might be in an altered state, not himself, so to speak."

Like the night he killed my parents? Injured me? That's the unspoken question. And how many episodes of being "not yourself" do you get before people figure out this is who you really are?

I should sit up, ask Rainie about this impromptu trip to Atlanta, what kinds of things I should pack. But I don't. I stay exactly where I am, my head against Rainie's shoulder. And I feel the comfortable bulk of Luka, now pressed against my hip, the steady weight of Quincy's stare.

Family.

Something that can be found. Something that can be made. The caseworker has preached it to me for years. But I've never really believed. Even when Rainie and Quincy first sat me down, I remained skeptical. Maybe, I thought, once we were all standing in front of the judge in November, and the papers were officially signed, I'd feel something move inside me. An understanding. Acceptance.

But I get it now. Family. My family. People who want me, even with my knobby knees and flyaway hair. People who accept me, even when I can't raise my hand in class or talk in front of strangers or do the things I know I'm supposed to do. People who love me, enough to actively plot to keep me safe, because I am theirs and they're not letting me go without a fight.

Family. My family.

I sit up. I wipe my eyes because somehow, there is moisture all over my cheeks.

"I'll go with Rainie," I say softly.

"Give me an hour," she says. "I'll talk to Kimberly, work out the details."

She looks over my head at Quincy, and I feel the pull between them. The years together that allow them to communicate everything they need to say without speaking a single word.

"Pack a little bit of everything," Rainie tells me.

Then she's up and standing. She hugs me. For a change, I hug her back. I close my eyes and wonder if I ever hugged my real mom like this.

For a second, I catch a whiff of memory. Cigarette smoke. Overpowering perfume.

I can see myself with my mom, my arms wrapped around her knees. I loved her, I think. At least, I wanted to. Right before my father stabbed her with the knife. And then . . . madness ensued.

I feel a weight inside me. Sadness, guilt, shame. All these years later, one night, one memory, one set of actions neither Telly nor I can ever escape.

My brother hates me. I remember saying it to the family case-worker standing next to my hospital bed. *My brother hates me,* I whispered, and though I can't talk about it with Rainie and Quincy, though I've never talked to *anyone* about it, I do know why. Is that what this is all about? Eight years later, my brother has decided I should pay?

Rainie follows Quincy out the door. I remain on my bed with Luka, who's already studying me, his dark eyes filled with concern.

"I love you," I tell him, because with Luka, the words have always come easier.

He rests his head on my lap. I stroke his ears.

Water, I think. We're going to need lots and lots of water. As well as dog food and a flashlight and emergency supplies.

Rainie and Quincy have their plan.

Now I have my own.

Chapter 18

SHELLY AND HER HOMICIDE SERGEANT Roy Peterson met up with Cal Noonan outside the house Telly Ray Nash had used for his latest shooting. Cal had disappeared for a good hour after the medevac chopper had left with his team members.

"Be back," he'd said, and Shelly had never doubted for a moment that Noonan had something specific he wanted to check out. He'd had that kind of look on his face: grim, determined.

Now he walked them through his findings.

"The neighbor, Jack George, called it correctly: After checking out George's property, Nash headed next door, where he found the owner's hidden key and made himself at home. Apparently the owner, Aurora, is away visiting her family. She left a fully stocked fridge, however, which Nash raided. Kitchen table is covered with a half-liter of soda, leftover lasagna, and melted ice cream. Means our suspect has refueled and rehydrated—though soda wasn't his best choice. In these conditions, he'll need water again soon enough."

"Theft?" Shelly asked.

"Other than the kitchen, I can't tell anything else in the house was disturbed. While we were told Aurora is out of town, Nash had no way of knowing that, so he probably kept himself on task. He grabbed some food, eating straight out of the containers, then was on his way again. It cost him some time, though—reconning the house to determine it was empty, finding the key, et cetera, et cetera.

After eating, Nash exited Aurora's house and headed across the street, no doubt attracted by the outbuilding, similar to George's.

"Now, this is where things get interesting. The shed contains a four-wheeler, which we know Nash ended up stealing and using for his getaway. But he didn't steal it straightaway. Instead, he reconned this house, too. Determined it was also empty. Then he broke in through an open window.

"The boy's already eaten. He's burned through some time. You'd think he'd want to be on his way. But no, for a seventeen-year-old supposedly acting on rage and impulse, this kid's a thinker. House A provided sustenance. House B gave him supplies. This home belongs to a couple—"

"Joanne and Gabe Nelson," Roy supplied. "Both at work today."

"It appears Nash helped himself to some of Gabe's clothing. Changed out his shirt, grabbed a baseball cap—there's a box of hats pulled out of the closet, and a sweat-stained T-shirt left wadded on the floor. I also found open tins of black and brown shoe polish next to the bathroom sink. So either Gabe Nelson is in the habit of polishing his dress shoes in the bathroom, or, my personal guess, Nash painted his face. Either camouflage one-oh-one for the woods, or even random 'dirt' smears to make him less recognizable should he return to civilization."

Shelly regarded the tracker and her sergeant. She didn't like what she was hearing. "Meaning the boy is returning to town?"

"Meaning the boy's a planner. I'm not the expert here, but when was the last time one of these spree shooters took time out to resupply and strategize? Aren't these shootings supposed to be one long temper tantrum? 'Cause Nash is clearly up to something more, and he's taking the steps to get it right."

Shelly definitely didn't like the sound of that.

"After eating and camouflaging, hell, maybe even catching a si-esta given the amount of time that passed, Nash finally made his way to the Nelsons' outbuilding. There, he found the four-wheeler. Unfortunately, he also became aware of our approach. The boy could've taken the ATV and fled. Instead, he reentered the house, took up a perch in a second-story window, and opened fire."

Cal thinned his lips, stared at the ground hard. "You know what happened after that."

Shelly nodded. They all knew what happened after that. She turned to Roy. "You said we had a witness? A neighbor who saw Telly crossing his yard?"

"Jack George. Also took some potshots at the search team. But now that he's up to speed on what Telly did, Mr. George says he's willing to help."

"All right, let's talk to him."

She and Roy crossed the street. Cal fell in step behind them. Shelly didn't wave the tracker off. Interviewing a witness wasn't usually SAR's domain, but she figured with everything that had happened, Cal now had a personal stake in the investigation. She didn't blame him for wanting to know everything he could about their suspect.

The neighbor, Jack George, was standing outside, watching the show, as police combed the woods for signs of Telly Ray Nash's activities. If Shelly had had support from other departments before, every investigator in the state was flooding her county now, given the shooting of a fellow officer and SAR volunteer. She definitely needed the manpower. On the other hand, the logistics of overseeing so many people, not to mention multiple crime scenes and multiple victims in such a short period of time, were rapidly approaching overwhelming. She was having to remind herself to breathe deeply and step methodically. This could all be done and would be done. She swore it.

George hooked his fingers through his red suspenders at their approach. He was an older gentleman, late sixties, early seventies would be her guess. But there was an alertness to his features Shelly appreciated in a witness. She got straight down to business.

She produced the image of Telly Ray Nash shooting out the EZ Gas security camera. "Jack George, Sheriff Shelly Atkins. Thank you for your cooperation. I understand you had a trespasser earlier this morning. Is this the boy?"

George eyed the photo. "Yes, ma'am."

"What time again?"

"I'd say around eight thirty, nine A.M."

"Was he alone?"

"Yes, ma'am."

"How would you describe him?"

"Well, I mean, he looked just like he does in that photo. Except he wasn't wearing a black sweatshirt. He had on a short-sleeved shirt. I didn't see the front. Maybe it was navy blue in color? But he was wearing a backpack. That's mostly what I saw."

"How big a pack?" Shelly asked.

George motioned with his head toward Cal. "Roughly the size of that guy's pack."

"Day pack," Cal supplied for Shelly and Roy. "Would hold basic supplies and handguns. It's not long enough for a rifle, though."

Shelly returned her attention to the neighbor. "You happen to notice any firearms on the trespasser? Maybe he was carrying a rifle?"

"I didn't see anything. But like I said, I mostly saw him from the back. If I'd known he was carrying a rifle, I might've thought twice about shooting at him." The man paused. "Or taken better aim."

Shelly truly wished he had. "You ever see him before around these parts?"

"Sure, at the EZ Gas. Is Erin really dead?"

"I'm sorry, but yes. She and another customer were shot, we believe by this suspect, early this morning. Now, you're saying you've seen Telly Ray Nash at the EZ Gas?"

"Yes, ma'am. This time of year, with all the tourists, it's too much work to drive into town. So mostly I head to the EZ Gas for my morning paper, milk, and bread, that sort of thing. I saw Erin just this morning." The elderly man's lips trembled. "I teased her about being too pretty to be holed up in such a dingy place. Told her she should run away with me instead. She laughed. She was that kind of girl. Nice to an old man. Is that what this is about? This kid, he like a jilted boyfriend or something?"

"We don't know. How often did you see him at the EZ Gas?"

"Once or twice before."

"Was he talking to Erin?"

"No, last time was in the afternoon. She wasn't working."

"And when was this?"

"I'm not sure." George scratched his thinning gray hair. "Maybe two weeks ago?"

"Was he alone?" Roy spoke up.

"Nah, he had a friend with him. Another young man. Maybe early twenties. They walked in together. They were looking at sodas when I left."

"Can you describe the other man?" Shelly asked, as this was the first time they'd heard of Telly's having an associate.

"Um. White. Short dark hair. I don't know. Just a kid. Dressed in T-shirt, shorts, hiking boots. I remember thinking his feet must be hot in boots like that. Maybe he had brown eyes? I didn't really pay much attention."

"Did they talk to each other?" Cal spoke up. "Maybe one of them called the other by name?"

"Uh . . ." George appeared to be thinking hard. "I can't recall. I'm sorry. I just needed some milk. That's all."

Roy was jotting down notes.

Jack George turned his attention to Cal. "Your friends, are they gonna be all right?"

"Two were hit, one's in critical condition," Cal said shortly.

"I'm sorry. I know I took my own shots at you earlier, but I swear

I was aiming over your head. You have my deepest apologies. If I had known . . . I'm sorry, sir. I really truly am."

"It's okay," Cal said. The tracker was staring at the ground. He was still upset. Shelly didn't blame him. It had been that kind of day. But she appreciated his renewed effort. She could tell he was one of those guys for whom setbacks only made him work harder. For all of his "thinking" this afternoon, Telly Ray Nash had made a major mistake when he'd opened fire on a search team. No way any police officer in the state was going to let this go. Let alone a tracker like Cal, who was now doubly determined to get the job done.

She handed over her card to Jack George.

"You see or think of anything more, please give us a call. And should Telly Ray Nash return, please contact us immediately. I understand you have some skills with your own rifle," she said, thinking it was best to acknowledge it, "but as you can tell, this fugitive is armed and dangerous. We want him. Let us do the hard part."

"Yes, ma'am," George said. He took her card, then shook her hand. His grip was firm. Again, no doddering old man here. She felt good having him on their side.

Roy took down the man's contact information. Then they left his property, walking once more across the street to the Nelsons' house, now cordoned off with crime scene tape.

"We need the name of the second male," she muttered to no one in particular. "Whoever was with Telly in the EZ Gas."

"A BOLO on a white male with dark hair, dark eyes would generate too many hits," Roy said. "We could go back to the EZ Gas. See if there's a security recording from two weeks back."

"Assign an officer. Maybe Deputy Mitchell. He get any leads from Walmart?"

"He interviewed the morning cashiers," Roy reported. "None of them remembered anyone matching Telly's description in the store this morning. And between seven and eight A.M., store traffic was pretty slow. They felt confident one of them would know if he'd been there."

"And the cameras from downtown? Any luck retracing Telly's route first thing this morning?"

"A downtown ATM camera caught a photo of the Duvalls' truck passing by around seven thirty. Image isn't good enough to see the driver's face or if there's a passenger, but there appears to be something in the back of the truck. Maybe a black duffel bag."

"The firearms?" Cal asked. He was still standing beside them. The tracker didn't seem to know what to do with himself. With Telly now traveling on a four-wheeler, Cal's job was essentially done. And yet clearly the tracker didn't consider it finished.

"Could be," Roy said now. "We still haven't found any trace of the firearms, and if Telly is wearing only a day pack—"

"No way he has three long guns on him," Cal finished for him. He looked at Shelly. "Maybe he has himself a hidey-hole. Given the kid's actions, nothing about these shootings is as random as it first appears, especially if Jack George is correct and Telly has been at the EZ Gas before. Maybe his foster parents, the convenience store, these were all predetermined targets. In fact, the only thing unplanned about the day was his vehicle breaking down. That threw him for a loop, forced Nash to improvise. Now that he has a mode of transportation again, the four-wheeler, he's back on track."

Shelly nodded. "Could be. So what's his plan? Who's Telly's friend from the EZ Gas and what's Telly really up to?"

"Something involving his sister?" Roy guessed. "The photos we found on his phone have got to mean something."

"Rainie and Quincy insist Sharlah's had no contact with her brother and never even knew the photos were taken. So if she's part of his to-do list, it's coming from him, not her."

"If I could suggest?" Cal said hesitantly.

"Sure." Shelly spread her hands expansively. "Be my guest."

"I'm no detective. But my job, it's to think like a target, right? Normally, I do that by looking at signs, thinking of the logistics of life on the run, navigating a trail. In this case, however, maybe if I could visit the house, check out the boy's room? I'm a good observer. I might see something, pick up on something. I don't know." The tracker sighed, shook his head. "I don't mean to overstep; I know you guys are working hard. But that was my team. What happened . . . I can't exactly go home, wait for the phone to ring. So if I could be of use, any use, I'd greatly appreciate it."

Shelly studied the man. For an SAR volunteer to return to a suspect's house was unusual. And yet, Cal was right. He was observant. And she did understand where he was coming from.

"We haven't developed a full victim profile," she said to Roy. "Nor have we had the time to thoroughly search Telly's room. With all these shootings, he's kept us in reactive mode. What Cal suggests, stepping back, trying to climb into the boy's head . . ."

"I like it," Roy assured her.

"And now that we know our loner has been spotted with at least one associate, we have something more specific to look for," Shelly continued, thinking out loud. She turned to Cal. "Okay. I'm in. I'll take you there. I wouldn't mind a second look myself."

"In the meantime?" Roy asked her.

"Update the BOLO with the four-wheeler information. See if we can get Mr. Nelson to identify which shirt, which hat of his might be missing. Then we'll let the search choppers work their magic. Sooner or later, the aerial sweeps, ground patrol, a random civilian, someone's going to see something. No one can hide forever. Not even Telly Ray Nash."

Chapter 19

*T*HE TRICK TO COOKING ANY MEAT *is to sear it on the outside, locking in the juices, then bake it in the oven. For really cheap cuts, you can marinate the meat overnight in salad dressing to help tenderize it, or, of course, beat it with a rolling pin. For baking, three fifty is always a good temperature. You can't mess up at three fifty."*

Sandra moved to the kitchen sink. I obediently followed her. Frank was away this weekend. Some kind of school commitment. He wasn't the kind of husband who explained his actions and Sandra wasn't the kind of wife who questioned him. He'd announced this morning he'd be gone till Sunday night, so Sandra had decided we should spend the day on cooking lessons. More life skills I would need for the future ahead.

I hardly spent any time with my foster mom. I still wasn't sure what to make of her. She moved around the kitchen briskly enough. But she wouldn't look me in the eye. Now, as she approached the wrapped chicken sitting next to the kitchen sink, I could see her hands were shaking.

She was nervous. Did I make her nervous? Was she thinking she was all alone with a kid who'd killed his own parents?

She was small. I'd never really noticed that before. But she was barely over five foot two. I practically towered over her. And my own hands, compared to hers, were massive. The kind of hands that could wield a baseball bat.

Sandra picked up a butcher knife.

"*Couple of things you need to know about chicken,*" she said, still not looking at me. "*It's cheaper to buy a whole roaster. Messier, as you have to deal with the innards. But cost matters. Frank and I lived on discounted chicken and nearly expired chuck roast for our entire first year of marriage. And rice, of course. I'll show you how to make a side dish, rice and beans. It's cheap, easy, and you can eat it as an entire meal in a pinch.*"

I didn't say anything. I watched as she took the knife, used it to tear into the chicken's plastic shrink-wrap. Her hands were still shaking.

"*You have to be careful when handling raw chicken. It can contain harmful bacteria, so you definitely want to cook it through. But also, you should never place raw chicken in your kitchen sink. Instead, put the chicken in a colander, place the colander in the sink, and then rinse. Afterward, you can wash the colander with bleach to sanitize it. Otherwise, you risk contaminating your sink; then, if you, say, set fruit in the same sink, now you have salmonella on your fruit.*

"*Also, never use a wooden cutting board with chicken. You want plastic, which you can bleach afterward. Or sanitize in the dishwasher, assuming you have a dishwasher. But you know, twenty-five years of marriage later, I don't even have one of those.*"

She smiled, apologetically, self-consciously. I couldn't tell. But her nervousness was now making me nervous. I didn't know what to do with my hands, where to look. I didn't want to be in the kitchen anymore. Sandra was too small, too delicate. I wished I was out in the woods with Frank, shooting guns.

He'd taken me twice more. I was starting to like the rifle. It felt more and more natural in my hands.

"*You should do this part,*" Sandra said. She pointed the knife at me. I stared.

"*What?*"

"Prepare the chicken. You need to reach into the center cavity. All the innards are in a bag. Pull it right out. Then chicken goes into the colander, colander goes in the sink. Rinse, pat dry with a paper towel."

She was still pointing the knife at me. Did she know she was doing it? I often wondered about her and Frank. Sandra seemed quiet compared to him. Submissive. Frank had ideas. Frank knew what we should have for dinner, what we should do for the weekend. Sandra seemed to go along for the ride. Cook her husband's favorite meal, gaze proudly at the shooting target while Frank repeated the story of our day for the hundredth time.

I wondered if Sandra had even wanted a foster son. Maybe that was another one of Frank's big ideas. And Sandra was once more along for the ride, sharing her home with a troubled seventeen-year-old boy known for his explosive temper.

Maybe she was right to be nervous. Considering all these months later I still didn't know her at all, maybe I had a right to be nervous, too.

"Frank says you like libraries."

I stared at her. The knife trembling in her hand. "What?"

"He said you have an interest in libraries. Maybe you'd like to be a librarian?"

"I don't know about that," I said. I finally reached forward, took the knife. She flinched as my fingers touched hers, then recovered quickly.

"I like libraries," she said, moving to the side.

I approached the chicken. Eyed the small, hollow cavity. With my left hand, I tentatively reached in. The inside felt slimy. I knew I was making a face. I couldn't help it. Sure enough, my fingers connected with a wrapped package. I pulled it out, holding it uncertainly.

"Ugh."

Sandra smiled again. Genuinely this time. She had a nice smile; it brightened her face.

"You can use that to make chicken stock, if you'd like."

I gave her a look.

"Maybe another time," she agreed. She held open the lid on the kitchen trash. I dropped the chicken guts, innards, whatever, inside.

"Does your son like college?"

"Henry? He loves OSU. He's studying computer engineering. They have an excellent program."

When she spoke of her son, Sandra's face brightened even more. Mostly, my foster mom was a plain woman, not the kind you'd notice. But happy, talking about her son . . . I could see what Frank must've noticed all those years ago.

"He's a good student," I said, a statement, not a question.

"Definitely. Gets that from his father. Lord knows his classes are above my head. Okay, before we sear the chicken, we—you—are going to rub it down with spices. You can buy different mixes from the grocery store. Frank's favorite is a cayenne maple, so that's what I use."

She held up the plastic bottle of chicken rub. I took the hint, washed my hands in the sink. She shook out the spice mix on the chicken. Making another face, I started the rubbing process. I didn't like the feel of raw chicken, the goose-pimply skin, the spots here and there of fresh blood.

I didn't do well with dead things. Unless, I guess, I was out of my mind with rage. Maybe I was secretly the Incredible Hulk. All mild-mannered until something set me off, and then . . .

I remembered my baby sister's scream.

I would always remember Sharlah's scream.

"Um, the chicken is done now," Sandra said.

I looked down. I'd been rubbing the chicken so hard, some of the skin had torn off.

"Now, the searing part," Sandra said. "I prefer a cast-iron fryer. Maybe we can find you one at a garage sale. You need an old one,

with years, if not decades, of seasoning. Never wash a cast-iron fryer. Letting it absorb the oils is the whole point. Instead, when you're done cooking, you can remove any leftovers with a plastic scraper, then wipe it down with a damp towel.

"Oh, and you want the frying pan to already be hot. That's the trick for searing. Add two tablespoons of olive oil, then turn the burner to medium high. You can test the temperature by flicking the pan with a few beads of water. If the drops sizzle, then you're ready."

"Why are you doing this?"

Sandra paused, wet hand suspended over the frying pan. Water dripped down. It sizzled. "Doing what?"

"This. Teaching me to cook. Giving me a home. Any of this. You already have a perfect son sent off to college. So what? You're now taking in the world's rejects?"

Sandra didn't say anything right away. She picked up the spice-rubbed chicken from the plastic cutting board, placed it in the frying pan, which immediately snapped and popped.

"I always sear it breast-side down," she murmured. "Same with baking. Allows the juices to flow into the breast meat, keeping it moist. Then for the last half, you flip it to finish browning the top. Here, you flip it."

She moved aside, handing me a pair of metal tongs. In the frying pan, the chicken was hissing away. Hot oil spit onto my hand. I didn't flinch.

I felt flat, detached. I'd asked the question, and in her nonanswer, I'd found exactly what I'd expected. Sandra didn't want me. She was doing this to please Frank. I might as well have been one of his favorite meals, offered up for approval.

"I know what it's like to be alone," she said abruptly.

I turned the chicken, glanced at her out of the corner of my eye.

"My father . . . He was not a nice person. And I don't mean in a 'my father didn't love me' sort of way. I mean professionally. He worked for bad people, doing bad things. He liked it. So much, he rose up through the ranks. Bought a bigger house, fancier cars. Which in turn meant he needed to do worse and worse things to keep the money coming. A man like that, steeped in violence . . . He didn't exactly come home and turn it off. I might understand better than you think about what you went through when you were a child, Telly. We might even be more alike than you realize."

I didn't say anything. She was right; I hadn't thought a woman like her would understand anything about my life. I guess we were both in for surprises today.

"When I was sixteen," she said now, "I left home. I thought any place had to be better than where I was at." Sandra looked at me. "I wasn't entirely right, but I wasn't entirely wrong either. For a bit . . . my life drifted. If there was a poor decision, I made it. If there was a bad situation, I found it. But then, I met Frank. He . . . he loved me. He accepted me. Even the select stories I told of my father—not a lot, mind you, but some details—he accepted those, too. For the first time, I saw myself through the eyes of a good man. And I found hope."

The chicken was starting to blacken. I was no expert, but I took that as a hint to turn off the burner. Sandra moved toward the roasting pan, placed it on the counter next to the stove. I set the chicken inside, breast-side down as instructed.

Oven was already heated up. She opened the door. I stuck the pan in.

"My father is a bad person," she said flatly. "I don't talk to him. Since the day I left home, I severed all ties and never looked back."

"He let you go?" I asked, because it seemed to me a guy that evil might not accept his own daughter's just walking away.

"Let's just say I took steps to give him some incentive on that subject."

"Okay," I said at last, as she clearly wasn't going to elaborate.

"My point is," she said after another moment, "he's the exception, not the rule. You can do bad things and still be a good person." Sandra wiped her hands on a kitchen towel, handed it to me.

"I killed my parents. I trashed school property. I have a criminal record. I think that's more bad things than good-person material."

"But you're not happy about it. You feel remorse. You are trying harder."

I didn't know what to say. I did feel bad. I was trying to do some of the things my probation officer recommended. I just . . . I still got into fights. I still lost my temper.

"If there's good inside me," I said finally, "why does it feel like the bad is always winning?"

"Maybe you just need someone to take a chance on you."

"You and Frank will save me?"

Sandra's brown eyes were serious. "We don't mind helping, but you have to save yourself. That's how real life works, Telly."

"Are you gonna kick me out?" I had to ask the question; it had been preying on me for months. "I'll turn eighteen and that's it? No more lessons? Just . . . shove out the baby bird, hope he can fly?"

"Are you scared?"

"No!"

"It's okay. The future can be scary. Alone is scary."

"I don't mind being alone. Alone is good. Alone is safe. For everyone."

"Frank found your sister."

"What?"

"He looked her up, located her foster parents. You're not alone, Telly. You have family. Me, Frank, and your sister."

"Does she know? Did he talk to Sharlah about me?" My voice was harsh. I didn't mean it, but I did. Sandra took a small step back.

"He wouldn't do that," she said softly. "The first contact, that's up to you."

"I don't have a future."

"Sure you do. Everyone—"

"I don't! Likes libraries. What the hell is that anyway? Some kind of bad dating line? I'm failing high school, meaning I'm never getting into any college. No engineering degree for me. No anything. I'm going to turn eighteen and just . . . join loserville. Maybe I can be a drunk like my mom, or a junkie like my dad."

"You don't do drugs, Telly. We've read your file. You don't touch the stuff, probably because of what you saw with your parents."

"You don't know anything about me."

"I know enough."

"No you—"

She left. Whirled around on one foot, stomped out of the kitchen. I stared after her, fists still clenched at my sides, feeling even more confused. And angry. So, so angry. At . . . everyone, everything.

Because I had failed and messed up and all these years later I still heard my baby sister's scream and no matter what Frank and Sandra said, I didn't know where to go from here. I couldn't see this future everyone else was so sure of. I just saw the past. Opening up cans of cold Chef Boyardee for dinner. Praying my mom wouldn't be too messed up or my dad too violent. Hoping Sharlah, at least, would be okay.

Until the night I hurt her myself.

Some things, there aren't enough Cheerios in the world to make right again. Just ask Bruce Banner.

Sandra was back. Holding a baseball bat.

My eyes widened. She thrust it into my hands.

"Here you go. You're a bad person? That's what you think? Then have at it. Look me in the eye and take a big swing. Frank's not here. He can't protect me. Just you and me. Do it."

"What?"

"I have some jewelry. Not much. My wedding band, of course, a *necklace from Frank celebrating our tenth anniversary. Oh, and there's some cash in the freezer. Look for the tinfoil packet beneath the frozen peas. After beating me to death, you can help yourself to my jewelry, the cash, and the guns, of course. There's good money in guns. Has Frank told you the combination to the gun safe yet? Because I will."*

She rattled off numbers. I remained holding the baseball bat, staring at her.

"All right. What are you waiting for? Time to get busy."

I didn't move.

"Are you not angry enough yet? Is that it? You have to be furious? Because I can help you get mad. You have plenty to be angry about. A father who didn't love you. A mother who didn't protect you. Having to be the man of the house when you were what, five years old? Having to get your own self up every morning, dressed and fed. Then there's your sister. She must've pissed you off, too. All that crying, screaming, wailing. Didn't she know you were doing the best you could? Didn't she realize she already had it twenty times better than you? After all, no one ever took care of you. Walked you to the library, fed you breakfast, washed your favorite clothes."

"I loved her."

"She was a whiny kid. Totally oblivious to how hard you were working, how bad things really were. That burden was on you. Five, six, seven years old and already totally alone in the world."

"She smiled at me. Even when she was a baby. She'd look at me and smile."

"You were alone! Responsible for everything. And scared. All the time. What would your father do next? How much would it hurt?"

I couldn't speak, couldn't say a word.

"The world is not your friend. It's given you nothing, taken everything. Even your sister. After everything you did for her, where is she now?"

"*I broke her arm.*"

"*You saved her life! And she didn't even visit you in the hospital. Not a single phone call, thank-you, 'Hey, big brother, how are you doing?' What kind of sister treats her brother that way? She's your only family left, and this is what you get.*"

My hands trembled on the bat. Suddenly, I was angry. Furious. Because I did miss my little sister. I had done my best. And then . . . it was as if I'd never existed at all. She left, just like that. All these years later, not so much as a backward glance.

I had loved her.

It still hadn't been enough.

"*Do it,*" *Sandra whispered. Her eyes were bright, nearly feverish. I barely recognized her now.* "*I'm your sister. I'm your mother. I'm every person who ever let you down. Now lift that bat, and get it over with!*"

But I didn't. I couldn't. I simply stood there. Staring at my foster mom. Taking it.

A minute passed. Another.

The kitchen was so quiet. Scary quiet.

Then . . .

Sandra smiled. Her shoulders came down and, very gently, she reached out and took the bat from my shaking hands.

"*I knew you wouldn't do it,*" *she said softly.* "*I know bad, and you're not a bad person, Telly. I know, even if you don't, that you would never hurt Frank and me. I just hope you realize that for yourself. Before time runs out for us all.*"

Chapter 20

I CAN'T THINK. Can't wait. Just move.

Quincy and Rainie are back in intense conversation, this time in his office. I can hear their voices, pitched low, as they peer at something on his computer.

"Just gonna take Luka out to pee," I call over my shoulder. "I know, I know, don't leave the front yard."

And I don't. I let Luka do his business while I walk through the side door to the garage, find my bike, and roll it out. I park it out of sight. Whole thing takes less than two minutes.

I walk with Luka back to the house, trying to ignore the fact that my heart is thundering in my chest and my T-shirt is glued to my body and I feel both too hot and too cold. As if I'm going to vomit, or maybe just burst out of my own skin.

I can't encounter Rainie and Quincy when I return to the house. They'll take one look at me and know.

I pause on the front porch. Then I throw my arms around my dog. I hold him as tightly as I've ever held anything. I don't cry, because my throat is too thick and there are some emotions . . . Crying would be too simple and not tell Luka near enough about how I really feel.

Then I steady myself.

I'm a pro, I remind myself. I've lost enough, left enough. If any kid can do this, it's me.

I stand, peer all around. I try to feel eyes on me, some sense of my brother. If this were the movies, I could use the force or something like that. But I don't feel anything. The air is simply too hot, too still. Luka won't even look at the woods.

I take that as a hint and lead my dog back into the blessed coolness of the house.

IN THE KITCHEN, I pour myself a glass of lemonade, making plenty of noise. Nothing to worry about here. I know Quincy and Rainie well enough by now. They can be buried in a book, lost in thought in front of the TV, enraptured in each other's eyes, and if I so much as contemplate evil, they both know it.

Profilers. No wonder the state sent me here.

So no bad thoughts. Instead, fresh water for Luka. Giant bowl. With ice cubes. His favorite.

Hydration is very important in these temperatures. I down my lemonade, stuffing my pockets with some energy bars here, almonds there. Thankfully, no one is that hungry in this kind of heat, because there's only so much I can carry. I drink a full glass of water after the lemonade, feeling overfull and sloshy from so much liquid, but I know I'll be grateful later. Then I find an apple for me, a chew bone for Luka, and head for my bedroom.

Just a girl grabbing snacks for her and her dog.

Rainie and Quincy are still at the computer. For a second, walking past, I think I see a photo of a man in camo, on the ground, blood staining his uniform. Then Rainie shifts slightly, blocking the monitor from view.

"If you don't talk louder," I call out over my shoulder, "how am I supposed to eavesdrop from my bedroom?"

They don't reply, but I can practically feel the twin eye rolls behind me.

In my room, I plug my iPod into my speaker system, randomly

select a playlist, then crank the volume. I've been known to disappear into my room, especially when there's something I don't want to talk about. They'll let me be for a bit, given they have their own "adult only" matters to consider. Crime scenes. Travel plans.

But Rainie will knock on the door sooner versus later. She doesn't like it when I shut myself up for too long. Plus there's the matter of our evening flight, Project Keep the Foster Daughter Safe.

I can't wait. I can't think. I gotta move.

Snacks in the backpack. I have two leftover water bottles in my swim bag. Not nearly enough, given the triple digits, but probably as much as I can carry. I crawl beneath my desk. In an envelope taped to the underside of the pencil drawer, I have my own stash of hidden money. Because foster kids do things like that. Hoard. Secret away. We can't help ourselves. Which makes me wonder what kind of things my brother might have stockpiled, leading up to the days before he did what he did.

He took my picture.

He spotted me. Followed me.

Never said a word.

Just waited five days, then exploded his rage upon the world.

Do I even know this boy? Eight years later, did he look at me and see boxes of cereal and trips to the library? Or did he just remember that last night? Our father chasing us around and around, face red, eyes bulging, bloody knife dripping.

Me, handing Telly the baseball bat.

Both of us staring at our mother, as she moaned from the floor, regaining consciousness.

And I dare myself, for just one moment, to consider the thought that scares me the most: that this is all my fault.

That if my brother is a monster, then I'm the one who set him down that path.

Money. Two hundred and forty-two dollars. I split it into piles.

Some in the backpack. Some in my shorts' pockets. Some in my left sock. You never know.

Then, as simple as that, it's time. Ready as I'm ever going to be for the stupidest plan in the history of mankind.

Luka is watching me. Has always been watching me. My dog.

He will come with me because there's no way I can leave him without him raising the alarm. Which makes him the bravest, bestest, most loyal dog in the entire world. And me . . .

My throat is too thick again. I don't hug him. I can't. I'll break down. I love him. I love him more than I've ever loved anything, anyone. But right now, my entire family is at risk.

Logic says it's better to reduce that number. And if Luka and I get away, then at least Rainie and Quincy are no longer targets. Field is down to two.

Luka and I will find Telly. I don't know why I think this is so important, but I do. Telly's not just my big brother, who once saved my life, who once shattered my arm—he's the one who's been looking for me.

And while I understand why my profiling parents want to get me out of town, the truth is, that doesn't work for me. Because, then what? Telly is finally gunned down and I'm allowed to come home? After how many people are dead? After how many unanswered questions pile up in my head? I can't do it.

I need to see him.

I need to just know. Did my brother become my father? Will it be my turn next?

One last family reunion.

I'm going to lose something. I don't know what yet. I just know it's gonna hurt.

MY BEDROOM WINDOW faces the front of the property. Thanks to Quincy's security concerns, there isn't a single ornamental bush along the front of our house. They're not just pretty plants, you know, but also potential sources of cover for an evil-minded intruder. So our perimeter landscaping consists of low piles of ferns and wildflowers. At night, the alarm system activates for any raised window or opened door. Not to mention the motion-sensitive floodlights that blaze on, capturing any kidnappers attempting to break in, or perhaps a stupid teenage girl attempting to sneak out.

But at three P.M. on a hot August afternoon, the floodlights hardly matter as I gently raise my window sash.

"*Rustig,*" I command Luka, Dutch for *quiet.*

He's already on alert, ears forward, tail straight back. Retired police dog, back on the job.

I have to move my bedside lamp to make room for us to crawl out the window. This is the tricky part, and I can feel myself shaking again, my face literally dripping with sweat. At any moment, Rainie and Quincy could wrap up their conversation. Or decide they have questions for me regarding our travel destination. Or have had enough of that "infernal racket" I call music (Quincy's words, not mine).

I'll never get away with this. They'll catch me half out the window. Or climbing on my bike. Or even fifteen minutes after that, because how can a thirteen-year-old girl and her dog really get away from two trained members of law enforcement?

This is stupid. I am stupid.

Lamp is on the floor. I reach for Luka first, giving him a boost. His claws scrabble for purchase on the bedside table. No way we aren't leaving tons of evidence behind, not that it matters. Luka jumps through the window on his own.

I drop the backpack next, crushing a fern. Yep, plenty of signs of our escape. Then it's my turn to climb through. I'm not graceful like Luka. I'm just me. All pointy elbows and knobby knees, and my eyes are watering so hard I can't even see.

Then I'm down. From this side, I can't reach the lamp to replace it on the bedside table. Does it matter? Will Quincy and Rainie really need more than two seconds to realize what their impulsive daughter has done?

Quincy will thin his lips. Rainie . . .

I can't think about her reaction at all.

Just move.

Backpack on. Jogging lightly, Luka tight at my heels.

Then I'm at the side of the garage, mounting my bike. The woods behind the house are filled with well-traveled deer paths. Luka and I follow them all the time. Even with me on my bike, Luka never has a problem keeping up.

Now I head left, a straight line away from the house, as heading down the gravel drive will be too exposed. Instead, we'll cut through the woods, coming out a little farther down. Left at the road, coasting down to the main street, and then . . .

Open road, woods, it won't matter. The moment they discover I'm gone, Rainie and Quincy will start the hunt. After that, it's only a matter of time before they find me.

I have an hour at best. Thirty minutes at worst.

To pursue a homicidal brother I barely remember.

"*Rennen*," I tell Luka.

We do.

WHEN WE BREAK FREE OF THE WOODS, I turn left onto the small side road and coast downhill. According to my parents, Telly was last seen fifteen miles to the north. By now, given that he stole a four-wheeler, I'd guess he's anywhere but there.

Which leaves me with what?

I could look up his foster parents' house, but he killed those people, meaning he's hardly going to return. What about our parents' home? I have no idea where we lived. I was just a little kid. I kind of recall the interior—how the kitchen, my bedroom looked. But an actual address? Beats me. Plus, why would Telly head there? Not like our parents are around anymore, because, oh yes, he killed them, too.

What am I doing?

I wasn't lying to Rainie. I haven't had any contact with my brother. I don't know his phone number, no 1-800-Big-Brother to magically reach out and say, hey, we need to talk. Plus, I already turned off my cell—otherwise that's the first thing my parents will use to track me.

I try to take a deep breath, pedaling smooth and easy so Luka can keep up, and think like my profiling parents for a moment. I don't have much time. But when they're working cases, it's always the same. Have to move fast. Have to find the fugitive. They talk about this stuff enough over dinner. So what would they do first?

Visit known addresses. Quincy and Rainie would start by looking at known locations for the fugitive. Except I've already reviewed that list, and it doesn't help me.

Next: identify friends and family. Good question. I don't know any of Telly's friends, and except for me, he's murdered most of his family.

I arrive at the T intersection where the side street intersects the larger road heading toward town. Luka pauses beside me, tongue lolling. I take a moment to look him over. So far, my dog appears happy with this unexpected exercise session. Soon, I will have to take a break, give us both water, but for now . . .

In the absence of a master plan, we turn toward town. Just a girl and her dog, biking through the miserable August heat.

I try to recall details from my childhood, something that might help me find my brother. In my mind, it was always just Telly and me. Telly who fed me breakfast and got me dressed and walked me to the bus stop for school. And took me to the library afterward.

I held his hand. I remember that. My hand firmly in my big brother's grip.

And for a moment, I falter, my ten-speed bobbling uncertainly.

Why didn't I ever call or see him afterward? Because he hurt me? Smashed my arm? I was scared. I screamed. I cried. And afterward?

The family services lady was in my hospital room. I was very upset. *Telly hates me,* I told her. I know at the time, the pain fresh in my shoulder, that's how it felt.

And . . .

And.

That's the kicker, of course. The thing we've never talked about.

My brother probably does hate me. And I wouldn't blame him one bit. Which is why, when I arrived at that first foster family and Telly wasn't there . . .

I accepted it as my punishment. My brother had cut ties with me. It never occurred to me that he might view it the other way around, that I had rejected him.

My eyes are watering. Even with my face covered in sweat, I recognize the salt of tears.

I thin my lips, keep pedaling.

Workplace. Fugitives sometimes return to their employers, often to steal resources they know are there. But if Telly has a job, nobody's told me.

Which leaves favorite places. Say a neighborhood bar or local park. Personally, Luka and I have a favorite tree in the woods behind my house. The tree is thick and old, the bark covered with so many kinds of moss it looks like a living rug. Sometimes we sit at the base for hours, just finding new patterns in the moss, while breathing in the moist, loamy air. Afterward, I always feel better.

I know a favorite place for Telly. He always loved libraries. Him and me after school. A female librarian. I remember her faintly. Not even so much the details of her face as the tang of apple juice on my tongue.

The Bakersville library is only five miles from here. It's a reasonable bike ride for Luka and me. It's also where Telly spotted me and took those pictures last week, meaning he's been there before and knows I frequent it, too. Not a bad meeting spot, then, for two long-lost siblings.

Except it's also in the middle of downtown. Traffic lights have cameras, I know this, let alone most of the state's police officers are now on patrol. No way I could make it all the way to the library without being seen, especially with Luka by my side.

How would Telly know to find me there? He has no idea I'm on the run now, too. He's doing his thing, I'm doing my thing, and in an area with this much vast open space . . .

I'm on the move, but I don't have any way of finding my target. Or letting him find me. Meaning I really didn't think or plan ahead.

Mostly I've just gotten Rainie and Quincy very mad at me.

I should go back. Do it now. I could claim I just needed to stretch my legs. The intensity of the situation got to me. Will they believe me? Of course not. But if I return on my own, how can they argue?

Except I can't do it. I should. I'm being stupid and reckless and impulsive. All the bad behaviors I'm supposed to be working on.

But maybe that's the point. I am all those things. And so is Telly. Which is why I have to find him. Because deep down inside, it's not Telly the killer I seek. It's Telly my brother. The only family I have left.

If I could just talk to him . . .

I could change his mind? Get him to repent? Save him?

I really am stupid.

Then it comes to me. When Rainie and Quincy realize I'm gone, they'll issue a BOLO. Maybe even an AMBER Alert, except I'm not sure you can use those for a suspected runaway. But either way, they'll contact official channels even as they start searching for me themselves. After all, the county is now crawling with cops. Might as well take advantage of every available eye.

And Telly? If I were him, on the run, on the hunt, something, I would have a radio. Tuned in to the same frequency as emergency services. Meaning when the BOLO is issued, he'll hear it, too. The report that his sister is officially in the wind.

At which point, I won't have to locate Telly after all.

Assuming I keep out of sight long enough, my brother, the state's most wanted killer, will find me.

Chapter 21

S HE'S GONE." Rainie stood in the doorway, staring at Quincy, who was still hunched over his computer.

"Luka?"

She gave him a look. There was no way Sharlah would go anywhere without her dog and they both knew it. Quincy pushed away from the computer, moving on autopilot, and not just because he was former FBI, but also because this wasn't the first time Sharlah had disappeared on them.

Rainie took the house, Quincy the yard.

They met at opposite sides of her open bedroom window.

"She moved the lamp, opened the window from the inside." Rainie announced.

Quincy nodded; Rainie could tell it was what he'd expected. No way anyone could break into their home and abduct their daughter without Luka's sounding the alarm. Or Sharlah, for that matter, putting up one helluva fight.

That the threat might come from her long-lost brother unsettled her, though. Could it have been Telly, standing right where Quincy was now, tapping lightly on the glass? Luka would have started to growl, but if Sharlah gave the command for quiet, the dog would have listened to her. And followed her through the window, on her brother's heels, if that's what Sharlah chose to do.

Rainie could tell from the look on Quincy's face he worried the same.

"The ferns are trampled," he reported. "Though from how many footprints, I can't tell."

He backed up a step, but the ferns transitioned to the gravel drive, which was even more difficult to read.

"Her backpack's gone," Rainie called, leaving the window to resume examining Sharlah's bedroom.

"The envelope taped beneath the desk drawer?"

She checked. "Cash is missing as well."

Yes, they still searched their daughter's room, invaded her privacy when she wasn't around. In the beginning, it had been unsettling for Rainie—getting a long-awaited foster daughter, then treating her like a criminal. But Sharlah had come to them with that kind of history. And the family counselor had been adamant on the subject. Trust was something Sharlah needed to earn. They would be naïve to approach her any other way.

While it had been a good nine months since they'd caught Sharlah in an outright lie, Rainie knew she was still a child prone to secrets. Frankly, all three of them were like that.

"Other supplies?" Quincy was asking Rainie now.

"Looking. How about her bike?"

Rainie spent five more minutes searching Sharlah's bedroom, then walking through the kitchen. She jogged down the porch steps just as Quincy exited the garage.

"She took her bike," he confirmed.

Rainie added, "And protein bars and snacks from the pantry."

They each took a steadying breath.

"She went after him, didn't she?" Rainie said it first, putting their fear into words.

"If we had a homicidal older sibling on the warpath, it's what we would do."

"How did we end up with an adopted daughter so much like ourselves?"

Quincy gave her a look. "Punishment for something, I'm sure."

Rainie faltered. She wanted to feel strong, in control. And yet nothing had prepared her for the utter powerlessness that came sometimes with being a parent. To love a child so much and yet not be able to protect her from her own mistakes.

"She thinks she's saving us," Rainie murmured. "If her brother comes here . . . she doesn't want us to get hurt."

"We'll trace her phone."

"She's not stupid; she'll have it turned off. And the battery removed."

"Also means she can't contact him."

"I don't know that she can. I don't believe she lied to me, Quincy. I don't think Sharlah's spoken to, maybe not even thought of, her brother in years."

"And yet here we are."

"Here we are," Rainie agreed.

"Even if she hasn't been thinking of him," Quincy said after another moment, "clearly he's been thinking of her. Hence the photos. Maybe she doesn't have to find him."

"If he's watching, he'll find her. Quincy, what does he want?"

"I have no idea. It may not matter anymore. The boy is acting out his rage. His relationship with his sister . . . It's just one more failure in his life."

Rainie didn't say anything. She wanted to argue that it was Telly's fault that he'd broken Sharlah's arm that night. Sharlah had been just a little girl. What had Telly expected after that? Greetings with open arms?

Except being a trained member of law enforcement, Rainie also knew her opinion didn't matter. It would all come down to what Telly believed. The man with the gun.

"I'll contact Sheriff Atkins," Rainie said now. "Ask her to issue a BOLO. A thirteen-year-old girl on a bike with her German shepherd? They won't get far."

"Speaking of which, I'll get the car."

RAINIE WANTED TO SPLIT UP to cover more ground; Quincy wouldn't hear of it. To track a child while driving a car, let alone possibly coming upon a spree killer all alone? Basic safety principles still applied. Besides, they knew more than they thought: If Sharlah was looking for Telly, then she'd head toward his last known location, to the north.

Quincy drove. Rainie sat beside him, eyes glued to the window.

"If she rode straight down our driveway, we would've heard her," Rainie said as Quincy headed down the property.

"Probably started out on the trails in the backyard."

"Easier on Luka's feet. Asphalt is going to be hot."

"And she knows we'll come looking, meaning she won't spend too much time on major thoroughfares." Quincy took a left at the end of their driveway, headed down the hill toward town.

"Should we have talked to her more?" Rainie asked now, searching the horizon for their child. "Maybe if we'd involved her more in the case . . ."

"What, shown her crime scene photos?" Quincy retorted dryly. Because that's what they'd been doing. Analyzing photos of the Duvalls' scene, the EZ Gas murders, and the ambush of the tracking team. Looking for comparisons, some kind of hint to pass on to Shelly Atkins to help her anticipate what Telly Ray Nash might do next.

"I know." Rainie sighed heavily. "I know."

They drove in silence, Quincy going slowly enough that two cars came up from behind and crossed the double yellow center line to pass. They both had their cells with them. If Sharlah changed her mind and decided to call, or Sheriff Atkins received any hits from the BOLO . . .

At the bottom of the hill Quincy came to the T intersection. They looked both ways, then again; operating on the principle that Sharlah was headed toward her brother's last known location, they headed north.

"How long ago do you think she left?" Quincy asked Rainie.

"I don't know. Thirty minutes."

She could tell he was doing calculations in his head. "Technically speaking," he reported, "German shepherds can run at speeds over thirty miles an hour—hence their attractiveness to law enforcement. But Sharlah will be going for distance, not to mention having to adjust for the heat. Given that, I'd assume they're moving maybe eight to ten miles an hour? Of course, cutting through the woods has shortened their travel distance. So say she's made it five miles north of the house. Meaning . . ."

Rainie took her eyes off the window long enough to glance over at the odometer. They'd already traveled three miles. She sat up straighter, eyes on the road, on the lookout for any sign of Sharlah, pedaling away, Luka by her side. Except . . .

Nothing.

A field stretched out to their right, ending abruptly at the rise of the mountains, miles away. To their left, Rainie spied a drainage ditch, high grass, and then more farmland, dotted with grazing cows. She identified copses of trees, old barns, plenty of places to stop and hide, she supposed. Assuming Sharlah had already stopped. Assuming Sharlah had wanted to hide.

Quincy kept driving. After another moment, Rainie reached over, took his hand.

But they still didn't find any trace of their daughter.

"WE TRUST IN THE BOLO," Quincy announced an hour later. They had looped through downtown, then headed south, in case their assumption of a northern route had been wrong. They still had nothing to show for their efforts. "She'll need water, shade, rest for Luka. With all the patrol officers out there, someone will see something."

Rainie nodded. She prowled their kitchen restlessly, cracking ice into glasses. Even driving beneath the glare of the relentless sun had worked up a thirst for both of them.

"We're profilers," she said abruptly. "We need to stop chasing, start thinking."

"Okay." Quincy accepted the glass of water, eyeing her as she took a long drink from her own.

"Unfinished business," she said. "That's what this is about. Sharlah and Telly, they have unfinished business."

Quincy nodded. "Once upon a time, Telly took care of his little sister. According to what we've heard, was bonded with her, versus their parents."

"But then that night," Rainie continued, "in a fit of rage, he broke her arm."

"Sharlah went away. He never saw her again."

"I think it's reasonable they both blame themselves," Rainie said. "In fact, I think guilt is what they share."

Quincy looked at her.

"Think of abusive households. What's the common denominator we always see among the kids? They assume whatever happened to them was all their fault. Meaning it's reasonable Sharlah blames herself, while Telly blames himself, for what happened eight years ago. Hence neither one of them talks about it. And both accepted being separated. Maybe they each thought of it as their punishment, the least they deserved."

"But Telly was starting to reconsider his past," Quincy stated. "Urged on by his foster father."

Rainie shrugged. "Maybe he got tired of feeling guilty."

"Or started feeling angrier and angrier on the subject. He'd done the best he could; it wasn't his fault. Either way, he located Sharlah. He took her pictures."

"And instead of getting on a plane with me tonight," Rainie filled in, "Sharlah headed out to meet him. I'm telling you, there's something more to what happened eight years ago. Now it's driving both of them. If we can figure out that, maybe we can finally figure out Telly. And stop his killing streak once and for all."

Quincy nodded. "Okay. The first time around, a forensic psychiatrist, Dr. Bérénice Dudkowiak, interviewed both Sharlah and Telly. She probably knows the most on the subject of their parents' deaths. I have her contact information from Tim Egan's office. She should have received the subpoena by now, if you'd like to follow up with a phone call?"

Rainie nodded. She wasn't fooled. "And you?"

"I'm going to return to the Duvalls' residence. We need to know more about that household. You were right earlier; spree killers always have a trigger. We know the slow-burn stress Telly was under. But what lit the fuse? I have to believe those four walls hold the secret."

"I'll work on the riddle of Telly past," Rainie murmured.

"And I'll tackle the riddle of Telly present."

"And then?"

"One way or another, we'll get Sharlah home safe. I promise you, Rainie. I promise."

Chapter 22

SHELLY DROVE CAL to the Duvalls' house. The tracker didn't say much, just watched the scenery flash by outside the window. She decided she liked him for that alone; small talk had never been her strong suit either.

She pulled into the ranch, surprised to see a silver RAV4 parked in front of the home and a lone figure loitering near the crime scene–taped door. Young. Early twenties. Casually dressed. Worn cargo shorts, a sweat-stained blue T with an open checkered shirt over the top. Dusty hiking boots.

Shelly exited her SUV, hand on her holster. She'd just opened her mouth to demand identification when the man spoke first.

"Are you the sheriff?" he asked. "Because I'd like to speak to the sheriff. I'd like to speak to anyone who can explain to me"—his voice broke—"tell me what happened here."

"Henry Duvall?" Shelly guessed, coming around her door.

He nodded, running a shaky hand through his dark brown hair. "When I got the call, I wasn't sure where else to go. Other than here, you know. Home. I came home. Then I saw the tape." He closed his eyes, as if still in a daze. "I wasn't sure where else to go," he repeated.

Shelly understood. One of her uniforms had been in charge of contacting the Duvalls' son, but with everything that had happened since, Shelly hadn't had a chance to follow up with either her officer or Henry Duvall. Or, for that matter, with the parents of Erin Hill or the other young man gunned down inside of the EZ Gas. For a moment, the sheer number of fatalities hit her, and she felt a faint shudder ripple through her. Four dead, two wounded, and it wasn't even three P.M.

Cal Noonan moved around the SUV, coming to stand beside her. She took that as a hint to straighten her spine, shoulder the load.

"I'm sorry for your loss," Shelly told the young man. She turned slightly to her right. "This here is Cal Noonan. He's one of the best trackers around; he's helping us find the person who shot your parents."

"You mean Telly, right?" Henry walked toward them, already sounding bitter. "My parents' new project. Perfect."

"You know Telly?"

"Not really. Just met him a few times. Christmas vacation. Spring break. That sort of thing. I was already off to school when my parents decided to get into the fostering business."

"Did Telly get along with your parents?"

"Everyone got along with Dad. And Mom, she wouldn't hurt a fly." Henry shook his head, clearly agitated. He resumed pacing the front yard. Standing beside Shelly, Cal crossed his arms, still not saying a word.

"Why'd they become foster parents?" Shelly asked.

Henry shrugged. "Dad always believed he could save the world. As a teacher, he logged all sorts of extra hours mentoring misfit A or troubled kid B. Crazy thing?" Henry looked up. "He was good at it. Kids liked him. Adults liked him. Everyone liked him. My parents are *good* people. Ask anyone you want. This is no case of evil foster parents abusing some lonely teen. My parents *cared*. My parents *tried*. Whatever happened here, it's all about Telly. Not them."

Shelly thought he sounded very passionate on the subject. Almost too passionate. "Did your parents talk about Telly? It's a big job, taking in a foster child."

"My mom had some problems when she was a teenager. She

doesn't talk about it much, but I know she ran away from home. Except she was only sixteen, all on her own. . . . She'd say she didn't know what would've happened to her if she hadn't met my dad.

"Fostering was her idea. Personally, I think she didn't know what to do with herself once I left home. Too much time, too much empty space. I think if she'd had her way, she would've raised a dozen children. But apparently the fertility gods didn't agree, and in the end they were lucky to have me. She called me her miracle boy." A slight hiccup. Henry drew a deep breath, soldiered on.

"So, uh, last time I was home, Mom was working with Telly on home economics, how to manage a checkbook, how to shop for groceries, do laundry. She'd also taught him some cooking—chicken Parm. Hell, I don't even know how to make my mom's chicken Parm."

"Your parents were preparing Telly to live on his own," Shelly stated.

Henry gave her a look. "Well it's not like he was going off to college."

Take that, foster kid, Shelly thought. Henry still won successful son of the year award, whereas Telly . . . Telly had *project* written all over him.

"You said your mom left home at sixteen. What about her family?"

"Never met them," Henry said.

"They're still alive? She was estranged from her parents?"

Henry shrugged, wouldn't meet her eye.

"Your father's family?" she tried.

"His parents passed away when I was a kid. He didn't have any siblings."

"Close friends, associates?"

"Mom? I don't know. She volunteered some. But did she have a best friend, someone like that? I would argue it was my dad. Same for him. Most of the time, at least, all they seemed to need was each other."

Interesting, Shelly thought.

"I understand you're working for a company in Beaverton," Shelly prodded.

"I took a few days off. I've been in Astoria, camping with some buddies. I was hoping to come home at the end of the trip. Surprise my parents."

Henry's face spasmed. The shock wearing off. Grief taking hold.

"Last time you saw your parents in person?" Shelly asked, taking in his dark hair, dark eyes.

"I dunno. A month ago, Fourth of July? Too long, my mother would say, which is why I thought I'd pop in at the end of camping." Henry scrubbed his cheeks.

"Last time you spoke?"

"Couple of weeks ago. Beginning of August."

"Anything special your parents mentioned?"

A brief hesitation. Henry shook his head.

"No issues with Telly?" Shelly pressed.

Again the pause, then the head shake.

Shelly didn't say anything more. Just waited.

"I can't . . . I can't go inside?"

"No, son. We're still processing the house."

"Have you found Telly? Any leads?"

"I'll notify you the minute we know something."

Henry remained standing in the front yard, hands in his pockets, gaze on the taped door.

"You're gonna have questions, right? Things you'll need to know. Ways I can help?" His voice was faintly pleading.

"If you could remain local for a few days at least, that would be of great assistance to us."

"Okay. I'll find a hotel, campground, something. Let me give you my cell." Henry rattled off numbers. Shelly entered them into her department-issued phone, then provided her own contact info.

Henry drew a last shuddering breath. "And my parents' . . . bodies?"

"The ME will need to conduct a full autopsy, given the circumstances. Unfortunately, things are a little bit . . . busy . . . right now."

"The second shooting. I heard about that. Why is he doing this?" A sudden explosion of rage. "I mean, my parents were trying to help him. And he just guns them down? Then goes off and shoots even more people? Who does that? What kind of person—"

Shelly didn't have any answers. Henry Duvall broke off, seeming to realize the futility of his questions.

"My parents were good people," he repeated. "They didn't deserve this."

"I'm sorry for your loss."

"Check the freezer," Henry said as he finally walked by them, heading for his RAV4. "My mom liked to hide cash in ziplock bags. Under the peas, behind the turkey, that sort of thing. Her own version of a rainy-day fund. Telly would've known to look there to steal the money."

"How much money?"

"Couple hundred I'd guess. And the gun safe, of course. My dad had six firearms: three pistols, three rifles. They should be in the safe in the basement. Unless . . ." Henry suddenly seemed to get it. What had happened to those guns. Which weapon Telly had most likely used to murder Henry's parents.

"I'll be in touch when we have word," Shelly said softly.

Henry didn't say anything more. He climbed into his vehicle, hands shaking visibly on the wheel. The surviving member of the Duvall family drove away.

Shelly and Cal remained standing in the yard, watching him go.

"Dark hair, dark eyes," she murmured to no one in particular.

"Hiking boots," Cal seconded, picking up on Jack George's description of the second male in the EZ Gas.

"And not the most honest answers. Henry Duvall's holding something back."

"Birth son and foster son conspiring to kill the parents?" Cal asked, tone already doubtful.

Shelly frowned, scratched at the scars on her neck. "Not exactly a large inheritance to split," she agreed. "And yet . . ."

More questions than answers. The story of this investigation.

She shook her head once more. Then she led Cal back into the crime scene.

THE HEAT HADN'T DONE WONDERS for the smell. Not to mention the flies had arrived. Where did they even come from? Shelly thought. But given the faintest smell of blood . . . The flies darted through the air in front of them, massing thickly. With the Duvalls' bodies gone and the sheets bagged and tagged, the flies were limited to drying blood pools next to the bed, which clearly weren't big enough to accommodate their demand.

Shelly closed the door to the master bedroom. She felt like she'd spent too much of the day staring at blood. She'd dream about it later tonight, assuming she ever got to bed.

Cal was already in the kitchen. She'd handed him a pair of gloves when they'd first entered the scene. Now he looked over, gloved hand on the open freezer door, and shook his head.

So if there had been any deposits in the rainy-day fund, Telly had helped himself to that cash as well.

She'd stood in this kitchen hours earlier, with Quincy. She stared at it a second time, willing it to tell her more.

The crime scene techs had done a preliminary sweep. She could see black fingerprint powder, some fresh holes in the linoleum where samples had been cut out and taken away. Blood drops maybe. Who knew?

She tried now to see the house through fresh eyes. Not as a sheriff, taking in an unspeakable crime scene. But as a seventeen-year-old boy, in need of a home.

Kitchen was clean. That was the first thing she noticed. Would a teenager care? The modest family room was also neat and tidy. Further evidence that Sandra Duvall took pride in her home. The overstuffed sofa looked comfy, with an afghan arranged carefully on the back.

Was it too neat? The kind of place where a lanky boy would already worry about getting in trouble for setting his bag down here or putting his feet up there? Speaking of which . . .

Shelly cycled back around to the front-door entryway closet. With gloves on, she slid open the door, taking inventory of the coat collection, arranged as his, hers, then, after a small gap, two coats on their own. A rain jacket, plus a worn barn coat. Telly's, she would guess.

Which brought her to the pile of shoes at the bottom of the closet. Mostly sneakers, rubber boots, the kind of footwear designed to slip on so you could exit the house quickly. Again, under Telly's coat, two pairs of tennis shoes, one functional, one high-top, trendy. Maybe as boys went, his good shoes? So what was he wearing now? Hiking boots or some kind of summer sandal, say, Tevas, given the heat? She voted for irresponsible footwear that would slow him down but doubted they'd be that lucky.

She returned to Cal, who was still studying the fridge.

"No backpack," she said, which made sense as the neighbor had reported seeing Telly wearing it.

"Lot of food in the fridge," Cal said. "Good food. Homemade casserole, fresh fruits and vegetables. Certainly better stocked than my fridge."

"A lot of cheese?" she guessed, knowing his full-time job.

"Not even that lucky."

"I have yogurt in my fridge," she offered.

"Living the dream."

Okay, back to feel, Shelly thought. How would it feel to live here? First impression was a worn but well-tended open space. With plenty of personal touches. Photos on the family room mantel from Henry's prom, high school graduation. A pretty flower print, most likely the kind of thing purchased at a garage sale, then hung up because the colors had appealed to Mrs. Duvall, or reminded her of her own garden.

Effort; that's what Shelly saw when she looked around. A family that didn't have tons of resources. No brand-new cars for them or name-brand labels. But still, a charming home. Given some of the other foster situations Telly had encountered—or, for that matter, the threat of a group home hanging over his head—this should've seemed a big step up. His first thought walking through the door should've been that he'd just gotten very, very lucky.

"Computer?" Cal asked from the family room.

"Desktop. Was on that little table in the corner. It's already been sent to the tech geeks for analysis."

"Okay."

"What are you looking for?" Shelly asked, crossing through the kitchen to the family room.

"Telly. I'm looking for Telly. Because so far, all of this . . ." Cal waved his hand around the space. "This is all about the mom. Her house. Her domain. Which I have nothing against. But if you're a teenage boy . . ."

"This isn't his space."

"No. He might sit at the table to eat, hang out on the couch to watch TV. But none of this is him. And a family computer, no way he's putting anything personal on that, not to mention most teens do all their posting using cell phones, not a desktop."

"Telly's cell phone was found inside the abandoned truck—at least the cell listed on the Duvalls' family plan. It's possible he has a burner phone. Teenagers have gotten pretty savvy about using prepaid cells for all the activities they don't want their parents to know about."

Cal looked at her. "Shooters talk, right? I'm no expert, but all these rampages. The killers posted messages online, filled journals with their rage. World failed them. World owes them. So where is that? Where's some sign of the troubled foster kid's . . . troubles?"

Shelly got his point. The more she looked through the house, the more she also saw what Cal, being a male, had picked up immediately. This was a woman's domain. Meaning when Telly needed to get away, escape . . .

"Bedroom," she said.

Quincy had done the honors the first time around, walking the hallway, checking the rooms for bodies. Now Shelly moved through the narrow hall. First bedroom had been the Duvalls', which left two more open doorways.

Next room. Spartan. Dark paneled walls, twin bed, small wooden desk topped with a pile of paperbacks. She noted a charger, as if for an iPod or cell phone, but the device was missing.

"Didn't take his charger," she murmured, though she wasn't sure why it mattered.

"No way to plug and play in the woods." Cal was studying the books, which were about the only personal items in the room. Shelly glanced at the paperbacks. A Lee Child, Brad Taylor, and, of all things, Huck Finn. Maybe a reading assignment for school. Still nothing that ominous.

"Room's been photographed?" Cal asked.

"Yes."

"Searched?"

"Preliminary. We've been a bit . . . busy."

"May I?" He gestured to the space, and she nodded.

She wasn't sure what she thought the tracker would do first. Pull out drawers. Tap the walls. Rip up floorboards. Instead, Cal headed straight to the bed. He lay down on top, tucked his hands behind his head, and stared up at the ceiling.

Imitating a seventeen-year-old boy, lost in his own thoughts. Thinking like his target.

Getting into the spirit of the game, Shelly took a seat at the desk. Not much to look at. Walls were dark, the desk cramped, and she wasn't even that big. But Telly would've sat here, slaving over schoolwork. His files didn't show him to be a star student, but whether that was lack of effort or lack of ability she couldn't say. So far, his crime spree felt plenty smart to her.

She traced her fingers over the wood of the desk. Feeling the impressions and scars of so many written words over so many years, decades, generations. She pulled out the rickety desk drawer. Loose paper, sticky notes, a lot of pens. But no journal jumped out at her.

Maybe he had posted something online. Kids these days seemed to live more on social media than in the real world to someone like her. Computer techs would figure it out sooner or later. Not to mention Shelly's detectives were in the process of subpoenaing records from the Duvalls' cellular phone provider. But thinking once again like Telly . . .

She couldn't picture him online. She didn't know why. She just couldn't. He was tactile, she thought. Telly didn't want to just see the world. He wanted to feel it with his own hands. Hence his choice of reading materials, dog-eared paperbacks versus the e-readers everyone nowadays seemed to favor.

"There's something on the ceiling," Cal said.

Shelly sat up. The tracker had been so quiet, she'd forgotten about him. "What?"

"Don't know. Depending on how the light hits it, I can see a sheen. Looping. In a pattern. Maybe a drawing, doodles of some kind?"

"Hang on." Shelly returned to the desk drawer. The collection of pens. Sure enough. Neon colors. Except they felt unnaturally heavy in her hands, and were round and bulky at the end . . . Heavy from a battery, she determined, which powered a tiny little bulb at the base. Black light. The ink pens all contained a black light on one end.

"Close the drapes," she instructed Cal.

Then she was off the chair, tending to the door, snapping off the light. Cal obeyed without saying a word. Then, when the room was a dull, gray space, light just seeping around the edges of the curtain . . .

Shelly pushed the button on the ink pen. The black light came on, hitting Cal between the eyes. She angled it up to the ceiling and sure enough, writing. Letter by letter. Word by word.

"'Who.'" Cal identified the first word.

"'Am I?'" Shelly managed the second two.

"'Zero.'"

"'Hero.'"

"'Zero or hero,'" they got together.

"'Who am I?'" Shelly repeated. "'Zero or hero.'" Then, beaming the light across the rest of the ceiling and around the wood-paneled walls, they encountered the same words over and over again. A seemingly endless litany: *Who am I who am I who am I who am I?* With an occasional interjection of: *Zero or hero.* But mostly just, *Who am I who am I who am I?*

Telly Ray Nash had been keeping a journal of sorts. All over the confines of his bedroom. A message of doubt and pressure and stress.

Who am I?

Zero or hero.

Shelly really wished the kid had picked a better answer to that.

Chapter 23

Q UINCY HAD SPOTTED SHELLY'S SUV parked outside the Duvalls'
house. He entered the home on his own, discovering Shelly standing in Telly Nash's darkened bedroom and a shadowed form lying
faceup on the kid's bed. He reached instinctively for his ankle holster
just as the pen in Shelly's hand lit up.

And the ceiling.

The walls.

Who am I who am I who am I who am I?

Zero or hero.

Who am I?

The words covered the ceiling, the dark wood-paneled walls.
Large script in places, but also crammed in unbelievably small print
in the corners. Different days, Quincy thought. Different moods. But
the same burning question. Over and over again.

What had the probation officer Aly Sanchez said about her
charge? That Telly was a kid on the edge.

Here, under the illumination of black light, Quincy could practically feel a teenage boy's relentless stress radiating off the walls of
his bedroom.

Who am I, indeed. Zero or hero. For Telly Ray Nash, that had
already proven a tricky proposition.

"Hypergraphia," Quincy said quietly. Shelly whirled sharply,
hand going to her holster. Quincy figured she hadn't heard him come
in. Now she exhaled heavily, lowering the glowing pen while the
second person sat up on the bed.

"I bet if we could find one of Telly's school notebooks, we'd discover every square inch also covered in writings. Maybe even this same phrase. It's a form of OCD. Some people have to wash their hands over and over to ease their anxiety. Telly must write."

"I didn't see any notebooks." The second person rose off the bed, dressed in outdoor gear, long pale hiking pants, green shirt, hiking boots. "Hi, I'm Cal Noonan. One of the trackers. I'm also head cheese maker of the factory, if you like cheese."

The man stuck out his hand. Quincy shook it. "Pierce Quincy. Law enforcement consultant. Shelly brought me in as an expert in deviant minds."

"You a profiler?"

"Guilty as charged." Quincy kept his gaze on Shelly.

She shook her head, knowing his first question without being asked. "BOLO is out, but still no sign of Sharlah." She cleared her throat. "Quincy's foster daughter, Sharlah," she explained to Cal, "is Telly's younger sister."

Cal stood between them, hands on his hips. "And now she's missing? Of her own volition?"

"Most likely."

"To meet her brother, you think?"

"My daughter's thirteen. What I've learned so far is that having a teenager makes it impossible to think."

Cal nodded. "At the moment, my job is to think like a seventeen-year-old boy—Telly Ray Nash. I'll be the first to say, he's getting the better of us."

"Shouldn't you be out in the woods? Or does this mean you think he'll circle back here?"

"Kid's got a four-wheeler. Puts his speed beyond my abilities. Right now, we're waiting for a helicopter sighting, news from the hotline, or lucky break on the patrol front. While we're waiting, I asked Shelly to bring me here. See what I might notice, given my own . . . unique perspective." Cal regarded Quincy seriously. "Boy shot up two members of my search team. Don't think for a moment I'm off this hunt."

"I'm sorry."

"It's been a long day for a lot of people," Cal stated, which said enough.

"So what have you discovered?" Quincy asked. "Other than . . . this?"

"Don't these guys write?" Cal asked. "I don't mean ink doodles all over their walls, but social media posts, private journals, hit lists?"

"In theory, yes. Given what we're seeing here, I would guess journal entries over social media posts."

"No diaries in the room," Shelly reported.

"He took the journals with him?" Cal asked.

Quincy shrugged. "Possible. But . . ."

"But what?" Shelly prodded.

"Most mass shooters, they want their rage to be heard. Hence they make their letters, posts readily accessible. If he really did have a personal diary, he should've left it for others to find. Tucking away such writings would be different, but is it relevant? I'm not sure." He turned to Shelly. "Any luck with the computer?"

"Not that I've heard. But to be honest, the attack on the search team . . . It's frayed us. On the one hand, I got officers pouring in from all over the state to help out. On the other hand . . ."

"Makes it that much tougher to remain focused and on task," Quincy filled in. Shelly nodded and Quincy could tell from the look on her face how much that admission cost her.

"Coming here was smart," he offered up. "When in doubt, re-group. And you're right," he said, including Cal in his pep talk. "No matter what's going on, it all comes down to one thing, one person. Telly Ray Nash. The better we understand him, the better the chance of getting ahead. So what do we know so far?"

"He's a troubled teen," Shelly supplied. "We just met the Duvalls' oldest son, Henry.

"According to him, his parents are great people, fully committed to helping a kid like Telly get his life in order. But that doesn't change the fact that Telly comes from a violent past and is known for an explosive temper when under stress. And according to his bedroom walls, at least, he's under a great deal of stress."

Quincy nodded. "In other words, Telly's birth parents might have deserved what happened to them. But the Duvalls . . ."

"We haven't found anyone with a bad word to say about them," Shelly provided. "Whatever triggered this morning's violence—"

"Probably has more to do with Telly than the Duvalls."

Shelly nodded. "Though just to make things interesting, we have a witness who reported seeing Telly Ray Nash in the EZ Gas two weeks ago, with a young male who matches Henry Duvall's description."

Quincy arched a brow.

"To be fair, the description probably matches a third of the young men out there. But yeah, I think I'll have a detective follow up with Henry's whereabouts two weeks ago."

"Do we know of a reason Henry might want to harm his parents?"

"None at all. Then again, the list of things we don't know right now is definitely longer than the list of things we do. Henry also claims his parents have no close friends or associates. Their love for each other was enough for them."

Quincy didn't respond to the sheriff's dry tone. Frankly, the same could be said of Rainie and him, though such a statement would definitely make Rainie roll her eyes. And yet their social circle remained limited. Most nights, they stayed home with each other, and, of course, Sharlah.

Cal spoke up. "Boy's a thinker. Explosive temper always implies impulsive to me, but I don't know. From what I saw this morning, he's plenty smart. Following the drainage ditch from the EZ Gas was a good move on his part. Then in the third house, taking the time to change his appearance—"

"Excuse me?" Quincy interrupted.

"Kid changed his shirt, grabbed a baseball cap, even smeared some shoe polish on his face. To alter his appearance is my guess. Then, of course, he stole the four-wheeler. If he's doing all of this while in a fit of temper, he's the cleverest hothead I've ever met."

Quincy frowned. He didn't like what he was hearing. He turned to Shelly. "According to Aly Sanchez, Telly's previous episodes of violence were explosive. He snapped, so to speak, and, afterward, didn't even seem to remember what he'd done. But if he's now taking steps to alter his appearance, plus stealing vehicles to help evade law enforcement . . . Mr. Noonan has a point: We're well beyond explosive rage and impulsive acts. Telly knows what he's doing. This isn't some red haze of battle he's going to snap back out of."

Shelly didn't say anything, because what was there to say to that?

Quincy looked around the room again. Following Shelly and the tracker's example, he did his best to put himself in the mind-set of a troubled teenager. One whose early home life had been steeped in violence. But he'd had his sister—even bonded with his sister according to what Rainie had learned. It might sound simple to outsiders, but that kind of early relationship made a big difference. In fact, it should've helped set the stage for Telly to bond again, say, to the Duvalls, who were apparently serious about offering a home.

Instead, he'd killed them, too. Two very different home environments, if reports were to be believed. But both ended with the exact same results.

Quincy didn't like the logical conclusion to that thought. Especially not for Sharlah.

"We need to find him," Quincy murmured, more to himself than to Shelly and Cal. "Telly might've started from a place of impulsive anger—shooting his foster parents due to some perceived threat, then moving on to the EZ Gas out of blind rage. But he's not explosive anymore. Odds are, he now has some kind of plan. And he won't stop until it's done."

"What's his plan?" Shelly asked.

"That's what we need to figure out next."

THEY SPLIT UP. Cal wanted to inspect the garage for signs of missing gear. Given Frank Duvall's reputation as an outdoorsman, he probably had at least a tent, sleeping bag, other basic supplies. The absence of which would mean Telly was better equipped than they'd previously thought.

Shelly moved into the family room to check in with operations.

Which left Quincy alone in Telly's room. He thought of Cal lying on the kid's bed and realized it wasn't a bad approach. Think like your target; that's what Cal had said. Which is exactly what a profiler did.

Quincy didn't take the bed. He sat at the desk instead. For a bit, he picked up the paperbacks, thumbed the worn edges. Military thrillers. Books with clear right and wrong where the good guys always won in the end. Zero or hero. A part of Telly clearly wanted to be the hero. The brother who'd saved his sister. The troubled teen who, according to his PO, was trying to do better. What was it Aly had said? Telly trying was a good kid. Telly trying was his own kind of hero.

So what had pushed him over the edge?

The Duvalls were described as mentoring foster parents. But no doubt that also meant they had rules for Telly to follow, expectations to be met. Had he gotten into another altercation at summer school? Been caught in a lie? Taken up drinking or drugs?

Quincy began to methodically open up drawers. The desk. Bedside table. Old wooden bureau. He and Rainie had had to take a class on kids and drugs as part of their fostering training. They'd laughed—two experts in criminal minds being forced to take a drug abuse awareness class. But in fact, the whole hour had been enlightening. As profilers, they didn't work drug cases. And no, they hadn't thought of hiding rolling papers in the pages of books, or stashing needle tips inside barrels of pens, or tucking baggies of powder behind speaker foam. And teenagers always had electronics in their hands. Making the devices a great way to transport drugs without anyone being the wiser.

If Telly was an addict, however, Quincy couldn't find the signs. And the more he thought about it, the less he liked the idea anyway. According to Aly Sanchez, Telly had seen the toll drugs and alcohol had taken on his parents. Having lived that life once, Telly had more incentive than most to just say no.

There was no way of predicting what might set a shooter off, of course. Telly could've done any number of things that might have earned him punishment. Which in turn had triggered his resentment or rage.

But if the Duvalls were indeed the targets, why had Telly shot them as they slept? In theory, he should have wanted them awake, terrified. Acknowledging their foster son and the command he now held over their lives.

Power. That's what rampage killers really wanted. One moment when they were finally the ones in control.

Vomit. It came to Quincy again, the detail that had niggled at him earlier. The boy had vomited outside the EZ Gas, but not here, in the Duvalls' home. If the boy was squeamish about murder, shouldn't the first round of shootings have bothered him more than the second?

Unless Telly had been in a dissociative state the first time around.

That was possible. Something set him off. Triggered that explosive temper. He acted. Then reacted. Stealing guns, truck, supplies. Probably driven by panic. What have I done? Must get away.

Tearing out of the driveway in his foster father's truck. Driving . . . anywhere. Until the truck overheated and he found himself on foot. And realized for the first time just how much trouble he was in.

Perhaps that was when he transitioned. Killing the Duvalls had been impulsive. But now, standing roadside in the unbearable heat, Telly must've understood the full implications of his actions. No more doubt. In the zero-or-hero debate, Telly had his answer. And having resolved the debate, he was now doing what killers did best.

Quincy lifted the mattress. Searched under the bed. He moved the bureau, the desk, searched for loose floorboards. Nothing, nothing, nothing.

Then, a light rap on the door frame.

Cal Noonan was standing there.

"You'd better see this."

"TENT'S MISSING. Sleeping bag, a larger backpack would be my guess. You can see this corner was where Frank Duvall stored his gear. Now it's at least half-empty."

Quincy stood in the garage with Cal and Shelly. The tracker did the talking. Both Quincy and Shelly nodded.

"I also went to the basement to check out the gun safe. Which got me thinking: Shooters have a lot of gear, too. Table for setup, safety glasses, ear protection, gun-cleaning kits, and, of course, duffel bags for carrying it all to the shooting range. I found a folding table and some protective eye and ear wear. But duffel bag, gun-cleaning kit. I'm not seeing it."

"Telly took a fair amount of supplies," Shelly murmured. She frowned. "None of which we found in or around Frank Duvall's truck."

"Exactly. At this point, we're talking too much gear for him to have stashed it all behind a tree. I'm thinking he must've already delivered it somewhere, before the truck overheated."

"A base of operation," Quincy said.

Cal nodded. "Bad news being he's much better prepared than we thought."

"And the good news?" Shelly asked dryly.

"It's gotta be someplace local, right? And having a camp, the kid won't go as far. He's not just running away. He's got a home base. That can help us."

"We found camera footage of Telly driving through downtown around seven thirty this morning," Shelly said. "There appears to be a large black duffel bag in the back of the truck."

"Puts his base camp somewhere north of town," Cal said. "Next question being, does Telly have a favorite place? Maybe a campsite he's used before? Favorite shooting range?"

"Most of the locals shoot at a clearing in the woods," Shelly supplied. "But it's too exposed for camping."

Quincy spoke up. "Rainie did a quick search on the Duvalls. Sandra posted regularly on Facebook, including photos of Frank and Telly heading out on various outdoor adventures. There might be mention of campsites, fishing holes on the Facebook page. Or enough imagery in the background to identify where they're at."

"Would he go someplace he associates with his foster father?" Shelly asked. "He did just shoot the man."

"He'd go where he feels comfortable," Cal said. Quincy nodded his agreement.

"By now, Telly knows what he's done," Quincy stated. "And in between his bouts of rage and self-loathing, there's also fear. There's no coming back from this. He'll need moments to regroup. He can only do that someplace he feels safe."

He didn't bother to add that if they got really lucky, Telly would use one of those moments to put an end to his fear and loathing once and for all. One pull of the trigger, and Telly Ray Nash would never have to wonder who he was ever again.

Though Sharlah's wondering would be just beginning.

"We should check with people who knew the Duvalls," Quincy recommended. "Better yet, a hunting buddy, fellow gunmen. They should be able to provide a list of Frank's preferred locations."

"His son might know," Shelly said. "Odds are Frank must've taken Telly on some of the same adventures he once shared with Henry. Henry might also know exactly which pieces of camping gear are missing."

Quincy nodded. "Also give you an excuse to question him again, without arousing too much suspicion."

"I like the way you think."

"One more thing," Cal said. He shifted from foot to foot, for the first time appearing uncomfortable. "There's a stack of cardboard boxes on the other side, marked with Telly's name. They seem to be filled with old pots and pans, some household items. Inside, I also found a metal lockbox. Too new to be a resale item. Which made me curious."

Cal held up the box now. Twisted the latch. The lid sprang open, revealing four single items.

Photos, Quincy realized. Similar to ones he'd seen earlier. Sharlah walking with Luka by her side. Sharlah at the front of their house. But a different shirt, he realized now. Different photos, taken on a different day than the ones recovered from Telly's cell phone.

Telly Ray Nash had definitely been stalking his younger sister. Furthermore, these photos had an added element: On every single picture, centered over Sharlah's face, he'd drawn crosshairs.

After photographing his sister, Telly had turned her into a human target.

Chapter 24

LUKA IS SPLASHING AROUND IN THE RIVER, trying to find the stick I just threw to him. I already had my turn in the water. Parked my bike under a tree and waded right in, fully clothed. It's that hot out. The river, in contrast, feels like rushing ice, gurgling over rocks and around fallen tree limbs. It's the best feeling in the entire world.

We haven't made it far. A couple of miles? But the heat . . . Luka started to tire almost immediately and I wasn't that far behind. Then I started to worry about the temperature of the road surface against the pads of Luka's feet. Which meant we needed to get off the road. Except the soft, grassy shoulder made for even tougher going on my bike. My face started dripping sweat. *Dripping.*

Finally, I veered off into the woods. I could hear water and that was enough for me. I got off my bike and walked it into shaded bliss.

Now here we are. All grand plans and minimal execution.

Luka is happy. And I'm . . .

I don't know what I am. Confused. Stupid. Messed up.

Guilty.

Rainie and Quincy are probably out looking for me. Maybe one of them is searching the woods behind the house, the other driving all over town. They'll be worried. Rainie's face will show the strain, though she'll keep moving, gun tucked in the waistband of her capris.

Quincy, his face will appear stern, unforgiving. He'll look angry, because that's his worried face. It took me a good year to figure that out.

What makes you a family?

In the foster system, there's a lot of talk on the subject. Especially from the family counselors. They work with the prospective parents to set expectations (I know because one of my many failings is my tendency to eavesdrop): The child will arrive a total train wreck. While you see yourselves as providing a loving home, remember the child just had to leave another household to come here. It's not unusual for the child to be sad or angry or fearful. But don't panic. You know families aren't built in a day.

Of course, they have similar lines they like to feed us: Don't worry if you don't immediately respond to your new parents. It's not unusual to feel awkward or strained or uncomfortable. You have to take the time to get to know one another. But these people care, that's why they're taking you in. You know families aren't built in a day.

When did Rainie, Quincy, and I become family? I've been thinking about it for a good hour, and I still don't know the answer.

It definitely wasn't love at first sight. Rainie at least tried to smile. Quincy was all stern faced and wearing those clothes, of course. You can identify that man as a former fed a mile away. My first thought was that I'd arrived at boot camp, or maybe one step up from a reform school. At least the house was nice.

Quincy and Rainie started things off by giving me the official tour. Here's the family room, the kitchen, your bedroom. Let's help you unpack. Well, that was quick. Now how about dinner?

Did we talk that first night? I don't remember. I was angry, I think. Or maybe scared, or both. I'd screwed up at the last home. It's what I did. Some crazy, stupid idea would come to me, and even though I knew better, I'd do it. Which made me a problem child. At least I didn't talk much. I actually heard one of the foster units say that. *At least this kid is quiet.*

My guess, Rainie made all the conversation that first night. While

I counted down to when I'd get to escape to my new room and Quincy, no doubt, wondered what he'd gotten himself into.

It definitely wasn't love at first sight.

In the beginning, they tell you to focus on routine. Set up a daily rhythm, stick to it, and things will feel less strained and more natural. Get up, go to school, come home to Rainie sitting at the table, armed with some kind of healthy snack. Rainie would ask me about my day. I would say nothing. She'd ask me about school. I'd still say nothing.

Then she'd take my class binder and read the note from my teacher, summarizing my day and outlining my homework. Because impulsive, irrational children can't be trusted to do their homework on their own.

I wasn't allowed up from the table till my homework was done. Something else to resent. But at least Rainie wasn't a talker. She'd read a book while I plugged away. When I finally finished, she'd proof my work, circle ones I needed to fix, then return to her novel.

Dinner was a very quiet affair. At a certain point, she and Quincy gave up on me, talked among themselves instead. Little things about a case, do you remember when . . .

Which started to catch my attention. Because crimes, criminals, how can you not be fascinated by something like that? Besides, as I explained to them one night, I knew all about psychopaths. Welcome to at least half the kids in my class.

When do you become a family?

Is it a recipe? So many days together, shared dinners, inside jokes? Or is it a moment? The afternoon Quincy brought Luka home and I realized for the first time that Quincy wasn't that stern after all—he was nervous. He'd gotten this dog, just for me, and now he was worried he'd screwed up. I wouldn't like Luka, Luka wouldn't like me.

Except for Luka and me, it was love at first sight. I threw my arms around his furry neck and he licked my face and I loved him.

Loved him more than I'd ever loved anything. And then, looking up at my foster dad, I realized that some of that love now extended to him, for doing this for me.

And to Rainie, who was already laughing and sorting through dog toys, almost as big a kid about it as I was.

Luka made us a family.

Of course, there was that second or third parent-teacher conference, where my teacher was once again explaining everything I did wrong, all my "challenges," and Quincy suddenly announced, "I'm not worried about Sharlah's challenges. Sharlah is a bright, strong, capable girl. Now, you, on the other hand . . ."

Rainie gave him a lecture about that when we got home. Then she gave him a really big hug.

How do you become a family?

The day they announced they were adopting me? I know they wanted more reaction. Maybe I was supposed to cry with relief or throw my arms around them in gratitude. Instead, I just sat there, hands in my lap.

Because I'm not much of a talker, and in that moment, there were too many words to say. And some of those words were about relief and love and joy.

But there was also fear.

Because while I'm still trying to figure out how you become a family, I already know how you lose one. I know exactly what it takes to tear a family apart. Until both your parents are gone. And my brother . . . I don't even know if he's my brother anymore.

The family counselor lady was right: Families aren't built in a day.

But they can be destroyed in an instant.

Luka is back, dripping wet. He drops his stick at my feet, eyeing me expectantly, then giving a vigorous shake. I throw up my hands in protest but still get covered in dog fur and water.

"Really?" I ask him. "Really?"

He gazes at me solemnly. Sticks are serious business in his world. For that matter, so is playing in the river.

I pick up the tree branch but don't throw it immediately. Instead, I study my dog, my best friend in the entire world.

"Luka," I say, my voice as serious as his expression. "I don't know what I'm doing."

Luka doesn't answer; he's always been an excellent listener.

"I mean, Rainie and Quincy are going to be mad. Worse, they're gonna worry. I don't want them to feel bad. But I just . . ."

I just can't sit around waiting to see what will happen first: my brother attacking and hurting my new parents, or my brother attacking and my new parents hurting him.

"Do you know what time it is?" I ask Luka. "I don't even know that much. Not a great plan, if you think about it. But here we are. On the road. Except I don't know where we're going or how we're going to get there."

I could consult my phone. Turn it on long enough to check the time. Maybe even look up our position on Google Maps. Better yet, if I could call up a map of all the ATV trails, then figure out how to access them from my position, maybe I could increase the odds of running into my brother. He's out there somewhere, and certainly sitting around on a random riverbank within miles of my home isn't helping any.

Unless, of course, he's heading toward my house already. In which case, coming from the north he'd have to traverse these woods. Though "these woods" covers a pretty large tract of land. He could be in "these woods" already and unless we actually ran into each other, I'd be none the wiser. Hoping we'll magically collide doesn't seem like much of a plan.

I go back to studying Luka, who's now lying down and chewing on his stick.

"If I turn on my phone," I inform my dog, "they can ping my

GPS. At least that's what they say on the cop shows. 'Ping so-and-so's phone.' I'm not sure exactly how it's done, but on TV, they always end up with the guy in handcuffs." Which leads me to a new thought: "Do you think they'd cuff me? I mean, I am a runaway. Maybe Rainie and Quincy will have me charged. Scare me straight, that sort of thing."

Luka cocks his head at me, resumes chewing.

"But what are my choices?" I ask him. "We sit here all day? Until we run out of food, water? And then what? Crawl home with our tails between our legs?"

Luka's ears prick up at the word *home*. His favorite words he understands in English and Dutch. But I'm already shaking my head. I can't do it. And I don't mean in a that-would-be-awful sort of way. I mean, I *can't* do it. There's this actual physical resistance inside of me. Like a shard of glass I can't take out. This is what gets me in trouble. It's the same rigidity that means I *have* to do something, even after I've been told not to.

I'm not trying to be stubborn or disobedient. I just . . . There are things I have to do. And things I can't do. None of my foster parents ever got this. Sure, they'd read my file. Oppositional defiant disorder, anxiety, blah, blah, blah. But none of them truly got it. How it feels to be me.

Rainie and Quincy did. I could see on their faces, they knew, recognized the symptoms, so to speak, when I got triggered. And they'd back off, give me a chance. Because in these moments, I *can't* change course, meaning something else has to give.

Like now. When I know I should go home. But I can't.

I simply . . . can't.

So here I am, with my dog, on a fool's errand. The only choice being will I turn on my phone, or won't I.

I do it. Don't give myself another chance to think. Just power it on. And if someone somewhere is pinging away, then maybe I won't have to worry about what I can or can't do for very much longer.

I tap Safari, launching the Internet browser before I get distracted by anything else. Say, texts from Rainie or Quincy. Or voice mails begging me to come home.

First up, ATV maps of Bakersville County. I'm in luck; the page loads quickly. The trail network is extensive. On my small phone screen it takes me a bit to figure out where I am on the map in relation to the closest routes.

It turns out, I'm not that far. Maybe half a mile, following the river through the woods. Now, whether my brother will be on this particular trail, given the wide variety to choose from, is another question entirely. But it's a start. Something for Luka and me to do.

I close out of Safari, my hands trembling even though I will them to be steady. Then, of course, I see them: eight new texts. Three new voice mails.

I already know what they will say. No need to check. Just power down the phone, get on with my great escape.

Except that shard of glass inside me now has a new target. The messages from my parents. Things I don't need to check, shouldn't check, and now absolutely, positively have to see. This is the way it works. This is what it means to be me. I sigh heavily, then open the texts. The first few are what I expected. *Sharlah, where are you? Sharlah, please come home so we can talk. Sharlah, we just want to know that you're safe.*

The second-to-last one is from Rainie. Two words that hit me like a blow to the chest: *I understand.*

Nothing more. Nothing less. Pure Rainie.

And for a moment, my eyes flood with tears.

Except there's a final message. One from Quincy. And if I thought Rainie's hurt, this one knocks the wind right out of me.

We found your brother, Quincy's message reads. *Come home, Sharlah. He wants to speak to you.*

Chapter 25

*H*E DIDN'T LIKE ME.

He sat at the table, in the chair next to Frank, trying to look relaxed, loose, college student home on spring break. But his gaze kept drifting to me next to the stove, where I was grating cheese to top the chicken Parm.

Checking out the new kid. The one who'd taken over his house, his parents, while he was off at school.

Henry definitely didn't like me.

I kept my head down. Focused on the block of Parm, cheese grater. Sandra had asked me to help with dinner. Showing off the new kid's tricks? Hell if I knew. I did as I was told, having been through this drill too many times to count. So many foster homes. Foster, birth, adopted siblings. Being hated was a rite of passage. Been there, done that.

In the kitchen, Sandra was all nervous energy. I hadn't seen her like this since maybe my own first day at the house. She had salad going on. Garlic bread. All of her son's favorite foods; that went without saying. And everything had to be perfect. I knew Sandra well enough by now to recognize the pressure she put on herself. Her son was home. With her foster son. First family dinner must be perfect, perfect, perfect.

Since our first cooking lesson, I had given Sandra more respect. So now I worked really hard on grating Parm.

Frank was happy. He sat at the table, a rare beer cracked open in front of him. Henry was going on and on about his classes. All computer-nerd this, engineering-geek that. I definitely didn't understand anything. But Frank, being the science guy, nodded right along. Maybe this is who Henry got it from, because Frank asked questions. Then beamed at the answers, parental pride practically radiating off of him.

I grated a little too hard. Caught my thumb. I moved discreetly to the sink to rinse off the blood before Sandra realized what I'd just added to her Parmesan cheese.

"Telly, what happened to you? Did you cut yourself?" Too late. She was already at my side, grabbing my thumb, inspecting the damage.

"I'm fine."

"Nonsense. Frank, we need a Band-Aid. Go grab a Band-Aid."

Frank obediently pushed back from the table, meandering down the hall. "We have Band-Aids? Where are they? Closet, bathroom?"

"Oh, Frank, how can you not know where the Band-Aids are?"

Sandra headed down the hall after Frank, leaving Henry and me alone in the kitchen. I kept my thumb under the water, gaze forward.

From the table, Henry wasn't feeling so subtle. "Preparing for your future in food service?" he drawled.

I didn't say anything. Why bother? He'd be on his way again. Back to college. And by the time we hit summer, who knew if I'd even still be around? There was only so much cooking and shooting a boy could do, right? Not to mention it was pretty clear by now I'd be spending most of June and July in summer school.

Henry pushed his chair back. Walked around the table toward me.

Standing at the kitchen sink, I felt myself tense. Frank was a big boy and so was his son. Tall, at least. But maybe not as experienced in a fight.

So this is how it would be, then. He'd push till I exploded. Then

Frank and Sandra would return to find their two "boys" brawling in the middle of the kitchen. At which point, of course, they'd rush to their son's side. Henry the golden child.

Good news was, maybe I wouldn't have to worry about summer school after all. I'd already be gone.

I turned off the faucet. Reached for a paper towel to wrap around my shredded thumb. Strained for sounds of Frank's and Sandra's return footsteps down the hall.

"What are you doing here?" Henry stood behind me, his voice low in my ear.

"Cooking dinner."

"Gonna earn their trust? Is that the deal? Be a good little monkey, then rob them blind the minute they're not looking?"

My probation officer, Aly, had been talking to me about techniques for managing my temper. I tried frantically to remember some of them now. Except I didn't have my iPod handy to drown out Henry's taunts with earbuds.

"Come on. Look around. My parents are hardworking, modest folks. Even the computer is five years old and not suitable for anything other than the junkyard. Whatever you're thinking, this is not the house. My parents are not the people."

"Your parents are nice," I heard myself say. A surprise for both of us.

"What?"

"Your parents. They're nice."

Henry stared at me. I found the courage to turn around, stare back.

"I don't have your future. Maybe I don't have any future. But your parents, they're trying to help me figure it out. That's 'suitable' for more than the junkyard."

Henry frowned at me. Still trying to decide if I was for real or not. Maybe I was, too.

Then, *from behind him, a discreet cough.*

We discovered Frank and Sandra back in the kitchen, watching both of us.

"*Well, now that that's out of the way . . . ,*" *Frank said.*

Henry flushed. Sandra giggled nervously, and that seemed to break the ice. Henry and Frank returned to the table. Sandra and I returned to dinner prep.

"*You never could share your toys,*" *Frank told his son.*

Henry didn't argue.

NEXT DAY, *Frank decided the boys should go shooting. We headed to the redneck range, armed with a small arsenal, targets, folding table, and protective eye and ear wear. Upon arrival, I went to work on the folding table. Frank and Henry prepped the guns.*

Henry was talking to his father, voice low, as if he didn't want me to hear.

"*Is Mom's dad still alive?*"

"*Why do you ask?*"

"*Because I am. Yes or no. Do I have a maternal grandfather or not?*"

Frank stilled at the sharp tone. I drifted closer. Sounded to me like Henry was asking for a smackdown. I didn't want to miss it.

"*I believe he's still alive. Your mother hasn't said otherwise.*"

"*But you've never spoken to him.*"

"*You know your mother had her reasons for leaving.*"

"*Which were?*"

"*Her story to tell, Henry. Now, why all these questions?*"

Henry removed the pistol from its case, racked it back to show the empty chamber, then placed it on the table. I made a show of picking up the first target, heading toward the battered wooden pallet to pin it up. Walking away, but not too far away.

I knew Sandra's father was alive. At least I had assumed so. Mean guy. Killed people for money, was my impression. So good at it, he'd risen up the levels, was maybe now the master mobster himself. Was it possible I knew something Henry didn't? Sandra trusted me that much?

"This old guy showed up," Henry said now. "Couple of weeks ago. Was waiting for me after class. Just standing there, staring straight at me. And the crazy thing is that I immediately had a sense of déjà vu. That I'd met him before."

Frank didn't say anything.

"He said he was my grandpa. Said he wanted to get to know me. Invited me to dinner next week."

"What?" Now Frank's voice was sharp. *The wooden pallet was riddled with thumbtacks. I pulled out a blue one, used it to secure the target, not daring to turn around.* "Did you say yes?"

"Maybe. Come on. The old guy . . . He looks so much like Mom. Like . . . part of my family. You think I don't have questions? You think you wouldn't want to know more about your own grand-father?"

"Your mom hears about this, she'll have a fit."

"Well I'm not exactly asking her about it, am I? I came to you for a reason."

"Henry . . . you can't do this. Tell the guy no. What do you hope to get out of this anyway? An extra gift at Christmas? You've made it this long without a grandfather. Don't destroy your mom by starting this relationship now."

"Why would it destroy her? Won't someone please tell me what this guy did?"

"Your mom ran away at sixteen. Left behind everything to live on the street. Doesn't that tell you enough?"

"What if he's changed? He definitely looks older than dirt. Hell, maybe he's dying. Wants one last chance to make amends before he goes."

"He's a lying bastard—"

"So you have met him?"

"Your mother doesn't want him back in her life! That's all I need to know, and all you need to know. You think he isn't aware of that as well? You think there isn't a reason he showed up at your college campus instead of on our front porch? Think about that for a second. If this guy is so anxious to make peace, why isn't he reaching out to your mom?"

"Maybe because she's an even better shot than you are."

This was news to me. Still holding up the target, my back to Frank and Henry, I blinked my eyes.

"Telly," Frank barked.

Belatedly, I stuck a second tack in the bottom of the target, then made a big show of jogging back.

"You heard."

I didn't say anything, because Frank hadn't asked a question. He sighed. Ran a hand through his graying hair. I'd never seen Frank so agitated.

"Of course you heard," he muttered now. "If I was in your place, I'd eavesdrop on everything, too. Henry, describe your grandfather. Everything about him. Go."

Henry opened his mouth, looked like he was about to argue further, then shut it again. "Five foot ten," he said at last. "Steel-gray hair, thin at the top. Mom's eyes." He seemed to relish that phrase. "Moves a bit like her, too. Tan trench coat, brown polyester pants and button-up shirt. Kind of old guy one-oh-one. But you'll know him when you see him. He looks . . ." Henry shrugged. "He looks like an old-guy version of Mom."

"You see this guy," Frank informed me in a clipped voice, "anywhere on our property, you call me. Right away. If he approaches our house, makes any move to speak to Sandra, shoot first, question later. Trust me, a violent death for this guy is hardly gonna raise any suspicions."

"Who is he?" Henry asked again.

I didn't say anything but moved slightly closer to Henry. At this point, I wanted to know, too.

"David," Frank offered up suddenly. "David Michael Martin. You want to know more, try Googling him. But don't be surprised when nothing comes up. Guys like him . . . He's spent his whole life making sure he doesn't exist. Not on paper, and certainly not on the Internet."

"What do you mean he doesn't exist? How can a guy not exist?"

Frank thinned his lips. "He's trouble. That's all you need to know. He's the kind of guy that wherever he goes, death follows."

Henry made a face. "He's an old geezer. I saw him with my own eyes. Whatever he once did . . . He's an old man now, looking to make amends. Shouldn't that count for something?"

"You're a good kid," Frank said abruptly, staring at his son. And he wasn't just throwing out the words. He meant them. "Smart, enrolled in a top computer program. So where was your grandpa fifteen, ten, five years ago? I can give you the answer: He was nowhere. Because at those ages, you weren't as potentially useful to him."

Henry studied his father. "I don't know what you mean."

"Guys like David . . . He doesn't make amends, Henry. He manipulates. Meaning, if he's reaching out, it's because you have something he wants."

"Forgiveness."

"Don't be stupid. He doesn't even know you. What would your forgiveness mean to him? On the other hand, your degree, your smarts, your reputation with computers . . . Now, that's interesting. Next generation of crime is all about the Internet. A kid like you could be very useful to him. The fact that you're family, all the better."

"You think he's recruiting me? For, like, the family business?"

"Why wouldn't he? And I'll tell you now, he'll use all the right terms. Tell you everything you want to hear. You don't live as long as he has without knowing how to be very, very good. But at the end of the day, evil is evil. He damn near destroyed your mom. If you let him in your life, he'll do the same to you. And he won't lose a moment's sleep over it. Once you've lost a daughter, what's a grandson? That's the kind of man he is, Henry. I'm giving it to you straight."

Henry looked at him. "You want me to cancel dinner."

"Your mother has never gone back. For the past thirty years, not so much as a phone call home. She gave up her own mother, Henry. To keep herself safe. And then, after you were born, to keep you safe, too. That should tell you enough right there."

Henry didn't say anything.

"He let her go," I said suddenly. Because this bothered me, had been bothering me.

Both Frank and Henry stared at me.

"You're saying he's some big bad worst of the worst. But his sixteen-year-old daughter walked away and he just let her." I'd tried asking this question of Sandra but hadn't understood her answer. Now I could see from the expression on Frank's face that he understood my point immediately. Henry, however, was still frowning.

"My father," I heard myself say, "if he wanted something and you had it . . . He wouldn't just let go. He wouldn't let you take it."

Henry gave me a look. I could tell it was all he could do to not sneer, offer me a baseball bat.

Frank's gaze, however, was much more assessing. "There are questions," Frank said at last, speaking to me, not Henry, "I don't ask my wife."

I nodded.

"It's not that I don't think I know what those answers are. It's that I understand it's better that she never have to put them into words."

Meaning that Sandra had done something. She hadn't just walked away, as the PG, Henry-approved version of the tale went. She'd done *something*. Perhaps as terrible as beating someone to death *with a baseball bat. And that bought her freedom. Maybe even made her think about taking on a kid like me.*

I felt something then. A rush of emotion. More than gratitude. Maybe love for my new foster mom, or at least the sixteen-year-old girl she'd once been.

"Oh for God's sake," Henry said, "next you're going to tell me Mom's a secret assassin."

Frank held the silence just long enough for Henry's eyes to widen. Then he burst into a smile. "Yeah, your mom. Killing them with kindness."

Henry guffawed. I let them have their fun. But I thought I'd learned something about my foster mom, the secret ace shot, who had more in common with me than her own child. Then I had a second thought, more disquieting than the first. If Sandra had done something once to buy her freedom, what had changed that her father would show up at her son's college now?

But the mood had passed, both Frank and Henry returning their attention to the handguns.

Frank had gotten out the ammo. Now Henry was lining up the first shot with the twenty-two.

Henry was good, almost as good as Frank. Then it was my turn, and though I hated having Henry's eyes upon me, I did okay. I liked the pistol. The rifle still felt awkward. But the Ruger was starting to feel more and more natural in my hand.

Frank ended with a few of his tricks. Then Henry got into the spirit of the game. They shot at shell cases. Turned the paper target sideways. Even took turns seeing who could shoot pinecones off tree branches. Then practiced moving three paces left, drawing, and firing. Three paces right, boom, boom, boom.

They relaxed, and for a moment, I had this surreal feeling. Father-and-son bonding. It did exist. And this is what it looked like.

Then I remembered walking my little sister to the library. Reading her Clifford the Big Red Dog. *Brother-and-sister bonding. It had existed, too. And that's what it had felt like.*

I wondered what Sharlah might be doing right now. Where she lived. Did she like her foster parents? Was she happy?

I closed my eyes, shut it all down. Because it was either that or pass out from the tightness in my chest.

Time to clean up. I put away the guns. Henry folded up the table. Frank packed the truck. No one spoke.

On the way home, Frank broke the silence. He spoke a single sentence:

"Not one word of this to your mother."

Henry and I nodded.

Chapter 26

SHELLY GOT THE LEAD straight from Henry Duvall. She'd wanted to pay the man a visit, quiz him further about his personal timeline and/or family history. But now, given the ticking clock, she settled for a simple phone call. *Did your father have a favorite, semisecret campsite?* Which turned out to be a yes. Right off the same route Telly Ray Nash had driven north toward the EZ Gas.

Next step: recon.

"I don't want any more surprises," Shelly stated. They were back in central command. Herself, Cal, Quincy, the other search team leaders. "When we declared this suspect armed and dangerous, we weren't kidding."

"Choppers," Quincy suggested. "Have one buzz over the target campsite, see if the IR unit picks out any thermal readings. That would tell us if the campsite is already occupied."

Shelly sighed heavily.

Cal did the honors: "Infrared's not working," he supplied, looking at the sheriff. "Or, to be more accurate, generating too many false positives."

"It's very hot out," Shelly said.

Cal translated for the other team members: "One of the drawbacks to IR technology—sun heats up a lot of things: rocks, water in broadleaf trees. Temperatures like this, whole landscape lights up bright red. Kind of like Vegas."

Shelly wasn't feeling so amused. "Maybe."

Cal shrugged. "Agencies like their toys, but end of the day, there will always be work for guys like me."

Shelly couldn't argue with that. In the post-9/11 law enforcement funding world, "toys" such as infrared imaging, choppers, GPS devices, etc., etc., were easy to come by. And yet, here they were, back to the basics.

"I have a canine unit assigned to assist," she said tightly.

Once again, it was Cal who spoke up. "Nothing against Lassie, but have you thought about cameras? Aerial imaging might be out, but ground-level cameras, say trail units, they might be able to help."

Shelly stared at her tracker. Of course. She couldn't believe she hadn't thought of it sooner. Every place had eyes now, even in the wilderness. From state and federal parks installing motion-sensitive cameras to track wildlife, to Shelly and her own detectives installing surveillance devices to catch drug dealers growing marijuana on county land. Yeah, the forest was vast and mysterious and filled with places for a shooting suspect to hide. But it was also dotted with cameras.

"Shit," she muttered. "Where was this idea three hours ago?"

"Situation was different three hours ago. We were talking a suspect on foot, following an unknown path. Now we have a campsite. Known destination, off of known trails. Meaning we can check those trails for cameras."

"I don't know if I like you or hate you," Shelly said tiredly.

Cal smiled. She could tell from his face he understood her frustration, was feeling it himself. They all were.

"I have that effect on people," Cal assured her. "Then I feed them cheese."

Shelly turned her attention to her lead sergeant, Roy Peterson. "Trail cameras," she said. "You find them, we'll start studying the footage."

He nodded.

"Any other bright ideas before we approach the campsite of a mass murderer?" A broader question, which Shelly posed for the entire team.

"Bring surveillance cameras with you," Quincy said. "That way, if Telly's not there, rather than risk keeping a team at the site, you can install equipment to do the monitoring for you."

Shelly nodded. "I like it."

It was also easily accomplished, as motion-activated cameras came with the mobile command center.

"That it?"

A short pause for consideration, then her entire team nodded back.

"All right. Let's get this done."

CAL ASSUMED THE ROLE of lead tracker. Technically speaking, Shelly wasn't in charge of such things; the SAR team had its own leadership and took care of its own. She wasn't surprised, however, to learn that Cal was once again setting out. Given what had happened to his team, he had a personal stake in matters. And despite having already led one effort this morning, he didn't appear any more tired or wrung out than the rest of them.

Quincy agreed to wait at the mobile command unit with her. If Roy could find any relevant trail cameras, Shelly and Quincy would review the footage as fast as humanly possible.

The state's SWAT canine unit arrived. Shelly had met its star, Molly, once before at a demonstration. The stocky black and white mutt looked nothing like any police dog Shelly had ever met. Boxer's awkward body. Pit bull's square head. A blotch of black fur forming a perfect pirate-like patch around her right eye. Combine all that with her panting grin, and "Mollywogs" appeared more like a sidekick in a comedy movie than the state's favorite action hero.

Which, according to her handler, Debra Cameron, made Molly perfect for her job. Rescued from a pair of drug addicts, the young dog had a natural drive to work and an even bigger desire to please. Last year, Deb and Molly had tracked a murder suspect three miles through the streets of Portland, Oregon. The suspect, a strung-out hooker who'd stabbed another working girl, had crisscrossed through various abandoned buildings, even hid for a while in an unlocked car, before finally passing out on the top of the fire escape of a deserted warehouse. Molly had been relentless on the trail. Up, down, all around. The suspect had apparently regained consciousness to discover the dog drooling on top of her. The addict had lunged forward with her bloody knife. And goofy-looking Molly had clamped down hard on the woman's arm.

End of story for the suspected murderer. The beginning of many commendations for Molly and her handler.

Now, as Shelly watched, Deb geared them up. The dog had her own vest. Military issue, it looked to Shelly. Heavy black fabric that fit snugly around the dog's compact frame, leaving only the white legs, tail, and pirate-patched head unprotected. The vest included pockets and straps, maybe for Molly to carry her own gear. For now, however, Deb the handler seemed content to be placing bottles of water, snacks, and a collapsible water bowl in her own pack.

Shelly had seen some search dogs with foot protection as well, but given the conditions—hiking in deep summer woods—Molly's paws remained boot free.

Cal walked on over. He glanced at Molly, who cocked her black and white head to the side and grinned at him.

"Cal Noonan," the tracker said, sticking his hand out.

"Debra Cameron."

"Mmm-hmmm."

The handler smiled, swinging her pack up and on, adjusting the straps. "Don't worry. Molly can keep up."

"What is it?" Cal indicated the dog, who was still panting cheerfully.

"She's most likely some kind of boxer–pit bull mix."

"I've never heard of a boxer who tracked."

"Well, Molly and I have never heard of a cheese maker who tracks, so guess that makes us even."

Cal blinked several times. He turned back to Shelly as if looking for help. She merely smiled. Of course she'd provided his background to the canine unit. Professional courtesy and all.

"Hot," Cal said.

"Yes it is."

"Gonna need a lot of water."

"Understood."

"Our suspect shot two of my team members this morning."

"I'm sorry. How are they doing?"

"One's stable. Other's critical."

"I've been briefed on the situation. I understand surprise is our best option."

"And that beast has a stealth mode?"

"This beast not only has a stealth mode, this beast also has a drool mode. So be careful, or I'll let her at you."

Cal finally cracked a smile. He reached down, scratched behind the dog's ears. Molly leaned into his hand, sighing ecstatically. Cal's smile grew. "Drool mode it is," he murmured. He straightened, did his best to appear more professional. "Ten minutes, then we're outta here."

"Not a problem."

Cal moved off to the side. Shelly watched him check his rifle, then guzzle more water.

Four twenty-five. Thermostat topping a hundred. Around four hours till sunset.

In the law enforcement world, a near-lifetime of possibilities.

Quincy came to stand beside Shelly. "Miss being part of the action?" he asked her.

"Maybe. You?"

"Don't envy them the task ahead." Then, a heartbeat later, just a whisper of a question: "Any word?"

"Sorry. But I'm sure she's all right. Keep your phone on. Sooner versus later, Sharlah will reach out. Especially, you know, since you lied and said we'd found her brother."

"It's only a lie if we haven't located Telly by the time she reappears."

"Parenting has turned you into a Machiavellian master and you know it."

"Sure it was parenting?"

Shelly shook her head. She and Quincy went way back. The profiler was known to do whatever it took to get his man. Or, apparently, draw out his errant daughter.

Roy stuck his head out of the mobile command unit. "Found us a camera. Only one, might not even be the right trail. But still . . ."

Shelly and Quincy took the hint.

Both of them went back to work.

Chapter 27

RAINIE HAD NEVER BEEN GOOD at waiting. As Quincy had requested, she'd called Dr. Bérénice Dudkowiak, the forensic psychiatrist who'd performed the initial assessment of Telly Ray Nash eight years ago, only to learn the doctor was with a patient. Please leave a message.

So she did. Then she paced. Cell phone in hand, rounding the kitchen table, down the hall and back again. Laps around the sofa. Interspersed with long moments when she stood on the front porch, waiting for her daughter to magically return.

Rainie hadn't grown up with the kind of mother who read fairy tales. And Sharlah had come to them too late in life for sharing children's classics. And yet Rainie kept thinking about *The Runaway Bunny,* a story about a little bunny threatening to leave his mother, and his mother promising to find him wherever he went. If he became a fish, then she would be the fisherman. If he became a mountain, then she'd be the climber.

Rainie wanted to be the mother bunny. She wanted to know where Sharlah was right now, simply so she could be that tree, or stone, or flower in a meadow, to be by her daughter's side.

But she wasn't any product of a classic childhood tale. She was an investigator. So, instead, she printed out crime scene photos. Bloody images from the Duvalls' house. Close-up frames from the EZ Gas security footage. Pictures of a search team down in the grass. And alone with her collage of death and destruction, she studied, studied, studied.

This was her job, her legacy. And she'd earned it.

Phone ringing. She was so lost in her thoughts, her eyes zooming in on one image in particular, it felt a million miles away. With effort, she pulled herself back. She straightened, fumbled for her cell, blinking her eyes even as she continued to puzzle over what she was seeing. One thing here was not like the other. But how could that be?

More ringing. She glanced at the phone's screen, then pulled the rest of her thoughts together. Time for focus. The office of Dr. Bérénice Dudkowiak was finally returning her call.

"MY NAME IS RAINIE CONNER. I'm an investigative consultant with the Bakersville County sheriff's department. As you may have heard, there has been a string of shootings this morning."

"Telly Ray Nash," the doctor replied without hesitation. "I saw his face on the news. Meaning, when I received the subpoena a few hours ago, I wasn't surprised." While court-ordered evaluations such as the forensic exam prepared by Dr. Dudkowiak eight years ago didn't fall under the same confidentiality laws as private counseling sessions, they were still subject to restrictions. Hence the county prosecutor, Tim Egan, had volunteered to send over the proper paperwork after speaking with Quincy this morning.

Continuing with the formalities, Rainie stated, "I should tell you that while I'm working in conjunction with the police, I'm also the foster mother to Telly's younger sister, Sharlah. She's been with me and my husband for the past three years. We hope to complete official adoption proceedings in November."

"Congratulations."

"Thank you. We love her very much."

"Which makes you even more concerned about her brother. I'm assuming you've met him."

"Never. When Sharlah was placed with us, we were explicitly told she was not to have contact with Telly. We assumed that was due to his assault eight years ago. She still has the scar on her shoulder."

There was silence on the other end of the line. The doctor thinking.

"To be fair," Rainie continued slowly, "Sharlah has never asked about her brother. Though now, of course, I wonder about that. We have reason to believe Telly is interested in seeing his sister again. In fact, he might be actively looking for her."

"You're scared," Dr. Dudkowiak said softly.

"Terrified."

Another pause. The doctor digesting this latest news.

"I understand you're the one who interviewed both Telly and Sharlah about the events surrounding their parents' deaths," Rainie prodded.

"True. And given the situation, not to mention the subpoena, I'm happy to help. You should understand, however, I only ever spoke to Telly and his sister regarding one situation in one moment in time. Then I never saw either of them again. Given that limited interaction, I'm not sure how much insight I can offer."

"Eight years ago, Telly Ray Nash beat his father to death with a baseball bat, under mitigating circumstances. This morning, he shot both his foster parents to death. Except, based on what we've determined so far, there were no mitigating circumstances. The Duvalls have been described as supportive, mentoring foster parents. And yet . . . Telly murdered them both in their bed. Then it appears he continued on to a local convenience store, where he shot two complete strangers, before opening fire on the fugitive-tracking team pursuing him. Telly Ray Nash is on a spree. Even if you don't have all the answers, we'll settle for any theories, suspicions, niggling doubts. Time matters here."

"You said you believe he's looking for his sister?"

"He had pictures of Sharlah on his cell phone, taken in the past week. My husband just called to inform me they discovered more photos at Telly's house. Taken on a different day, these photos have crosshairs hand-drawn around Sharlah's face."

"But they've never seen each other or spoken in the past few years?"

"To the best of my knowledge, that is correct."

Silence. Then: "That recommendation did not come from my report."

"What do you mean?"

"Separating the children. I'm not sure who made that decision, but I would've advised against it. Eight years ago, Telly Ray Nash was a troubled nine-year-old who didn't have a lot of points in his favor. But he did have his sister. From what I observed, he genuinely loved and cared for her. And she loved him, too. Why the system would sever that relationship, I have no idea. But it probably fractured one of the only true bonds in young Telly's life. After that, he'd have been even more rudderless and angry."

"Telly broke his sister's arm. According to the family counselor, when she interviewed Sharlah in the hospital, Sharlah claimed Telly hated her. The counselor thought Sharlah was afraid her brother might hurt her again, hence the decision to separate."

"Most likely, Sharlah was responding to the trauma of the moment. What matters, however, is the breadth of her and her brother's relationship. Let me ask you a question: How has Telly fared in the eight years since that night? Does he have a history of additional acts of violence?"

"He's been described as having an explosive temper, as well as oppositional defiant disorder. He's currently on probation for an incident at school. Apparently, he trashed some school lockers, then was suspended. However, he returned to school grounds and refused to leave. At which point he was charged with trespassing as well as resisting arrest."

"And his time in the foster care system?" Dr. Dudkowiak continued. "Longest time in any given home?"

"It sounds like he's bounced around. I, um, I know Sharlah did, before she came to us."

"And she's not nearly as angry as her brother."

"She has her own challenges."

"I'm sure she does."

"The Duvalls . . . They've been described as Telly's last chance, but also his best chance. Telly's probation officer recommended them. The husband, Frank, was a high school science teacher, and by all accounts a favorite with students. Their approach was less 'forever family' and more 'the real world is coming, and we're here to help guide you through it.'"

"How was Telly doing with them?"

"Apparently, Mrs. Duvall taught him how to cook. And Mr. Duvall, well, he taught Telly how to shoot."

Very long pause this time.

"All right, I'm going to give you my official Lucy assessment. As in, this is the best opinion you can get for a nickel—or, in this case, with such limited information."

"Okay."

"Eight years ago, Telly already showed signs of RAD. Reactive—"

"I know RAD."

"Growing up with two addicted parents, neither of whom showed much parental instinct—combined with constant exposure to domestic violence—set the stage for a young boy to feel very angry, alone, and, at times, explosive himself."

"I understand."

"The bright note in Telly's world was his sister. According to the children's teachers, Telly and his sister were tight. Telly assumed the role of parent for Sharlah. He took care of her, which didn't have to be the case. If you consider he was four years old when she was born—meaning he'd already suffered four years of abuse and neglect—he could've been angry at his baby sister. Resentful, even abusive."

"Trickle-down theory of pain," Rainie supplied. "The parents abuse the first child, the first child abuses the second. Practices what he's been taught."

"But not Telly."

"Not Telly," Rainie repeated, and found herself already softening toward the four-year-old boy who could've made Sharlah's young life an even bigger hell but had chosen to love her instead.

"It matters," Dr. Dudkowiak said now. "Bonding is a spectrum. From complete inability to bond—the psychopaths of the world who care about no one—to the overly bonded, the Mother Teresas of the world who must save everyone. On that spectrum, Telly would definitely fall closer to the psychopathic end. Except, his relationship with his sister anchored him. And in young kids especially, it only takes one bond. I can't emphasize that enough: one single relationship to make all the difference. By virtue of caring for his baby sister, Telly planted in himself the ability to forge another close relationship later in life."

"Such as with the Duvalls?" Rainie asked. But Quincy himself had already posed this question. If Telly had once loved his sister, had some definition of family, why hadn't it enabled him to feel closer to his supposedly supportive foster parents?

"It's possible. Again, this is the nickel assessment—I've never spoken to the Duvalls, let alone seventeen-year-old Telly. Now, we have to factor in that Telly was separated from his sister while also at an impressionable age, after a particularly traumatic event. I think that would've been incredibly damaging to him. He loved his sister. He killed his own father to protect her. Then the state tore them apart."

Rainie hadn't given it much thought, but now she saw the doctor's point. *Zero or hero*, Telly had written. Proof that eight years later, he was still trying to work it out? What he'd really done that night, trying to save his sister, losing her anyway.

"But he did break her arm," Rainie repeated. "I can see why the state might view that act less than favorably."

"You said Telly is known for his explosive temper?"

"Yes."

"I heard the same thing eight years ago. Which leads me to believe that Telly most likely suffers from intermittent explosive disorder. Do you know what that is, Mrs. Conner?"

"Rainie, please. And beyond guessing it has something to do with someone having a really bad temper, no."

"A child or teenager with IED can't control his own anger," Dr. Dudkowiak said. "Things that you or I might consider small slights or disappointments will instead cause a disproportionate display of rage. At times, the anger, adrenaline, emotional intensity can reach levels where the person suffers short-term memory loss, or a blackout. For example, while Telly admitted that he attacked his father with a baseball bat, the details of the event were difficult for him to recall. He could remember his father stabbing his mother, then going after them. And he remembers Sharlah handing him the baseball bat—"

"Sharlah provided the baseball bat?"

"Telly had had her hide in a bedroom while he tried to lead their father away. Apparently, she reappeared with the bat and tossed it at him. Which he then used on his father. Please understand, Telly didn't just hit his father once. I'm sure you're familiar with the term *overkill*?"

"Yes."

"Telly *beat* his father. Most likely so overwhelmed by adrenaline, fear, and rage he was having an out-of-body experience. At a certain point, Sharlah attempted to intervene. Which was when he turned on her."

"Breaking her arm." Rainie couldn't help herself; she shuddered.

She'd never met nine-year-old Telly. But she could imagine five-year-old Sharlah, having watched her father stab her mother, attack her brother. And then for Telly, her precious older brother, to turn on her . . .

If there were things Sharlah didn't tell them, Rainie understood it now. That her daughter could love them at all, Rainie thought, was a huge act of courage.

"So eight years ago," Dr. Dudkowiak continued now, "I would've said that Telly showed signs of attachment disorder and rage-impulse-control issues, as well as oppositional defiant disorder. But one of the reasons I recommended against pressing charges was because I also saw signs in him of having a protector's personality. His relationship with his sister for one. The way he automatically assumed the mantle of adulthood at the age of four. And that night, he didn't just kill his father out of rage or fear. He killed his father to save his sister. At least according to his account."

"Okay," Rainie said. Except, she wasn't so sure that was okay at all. "But how did we get from protective Telly to the suspected spree shooter we have now?"

"Several possibilities. One, severing Telly's only close relationship—the one he had with his sister—decreased his ability to bond. Two, his journey through the foster care system increased his distrust, lack of empathy, and indifference to violence, until by the time he reached the Duvalls, it didn't matter anymore. Or three, perhaps even more interesting, Telly pulled a fast one eight years ago. He never was bonded to his sister. In fact, he was already a complete psychopath who manipulated the situation to get out of it exactly what he wanted—the death of both his parents."

"He lied about the events that night?"

"He wouldn't have had to lie, just manipulate events. For example, wait till his parents got drunk, then, knowing their triggers, say or do whatever would be necessary to set his father on the warpath.

From there, a violent showdown would be inevitable, providing Telly with the excuse to take care of his abusive father once and for all. I would like to say I would see through such a ruse, but again, I talked to the boy three times over a period of five days. That's it. The forensic evals . . . Experts such as myself are never given as much time and information as we would like. Maybe I should call them Lucy assessments as well."

"So, eight years ago, Telly was either a protective older brother who got a really bad break in life, or was already a budding psychopath?"

"They're not mutually exclusive opinions. Particularly in light of his current actions."

"This intermittent explosive disorder—could it be as simple as something aggravating Telly's temper? He opened fire first, realized what he'd done second?"

"Yes. Though there's no way to determine what will be the triggering event for a mass murderer. We only wish we had that kind of data."

"But he killed the Duvalls in their bed. Shouldn't they have been awake? I don't know. Arguing with him?"

"Not necessarily. They could've laid down some kind of punishment the night before. Telly spent all night churning over the judgment, becoming increasingly frustrated, angry, until first thing in the morning . . ."

"He's driven to act. What about the aftermath?" Rainie asked, because Quincy had given her some questions to run by the professional. "If the first shooting was an act of rage, what about his command and control now? It's been eight hours. He's not only shot more victims, but he's taken very smart steps to avoid the police. If he's in some red haze of battle, shouldn't he be making more mistakes, acting more impulsively?"

"Not necessarily. Someone with intermittent explosive disorder still has intelligence, coping skills, et cetera. The first act might have been the explosive element. But it's entirely realistic for the person to utilize his other skill set in order to avoid capture. The human mind is complex. Telly can be both explosive and cunning. Impulsive and brilliant. One does not negate the other."

Rainie sighed heavily. She understood the doctor's point. Laypeople had a tendency to think of troubled kids as suffering from a single disorder, when more often than not, the diagnosis was all of the above. Hence the difficulty in treatment.

"There was one red flag eight years ago," the doctor said now. "A question which, to the best of my knowledge, has never been answered."

"Which was?"

"The mom. According to the ME, she had been stabbed, as both kids claimed. But she also suffered blunt-force trauma to the head sometime *after* the stabbing. Furthermore, she was still alive at that time, though given the severity of her knife wound, the ME doubted she would've made it."

"Telly struck his dying mom with the bat? When? After he beat his father to death?"

"Sharlah wouldn't answer the question. For the record, neither child was comfortable discussing their mother. The father clearly distressed them. He was all-powerful, frightening. In their minds, most likely evil. But the mom . . . I would say their relationship with her was more complex. As the passive partner in the marriage, maybe she appeared less fearful, more loving. The kids . . . They didn't seem capable of talking about her, and, again, I wasn't given enough time to press the subject. In the end, Telly said he must've struck the blow. Myself, I always wondered . . ."

"Wondered?"

"If that's when Sharlah intervened. Not when he was beating their father to a pulp, but when he struck their mother. Maybe for Sharlah, that was the moment that was too much."

"Telly is in the red haze of battle," Rainie thought out loud. "He hits his father over and over again, then moves on to his mother, except Sharlah gets between him and her after the first blow. At which point, Telly turns on his sister. She screams."

"He snaps out of it. At least according to Telly," Dr. Dudkowiak said. "The minute Sharlah screamed, he realized what he'd done. He put down the bat, then stood there unmoving until the police arrived."

"But you doubt this story?" Rainie asked carefully.

"*Doubt* is a strong word. However . . . Telly's father has the knife. Telly's father is trying to kill them. There are all sorts of reasons for Telly to defend himself with the baseball bat. And once he starts swinging, you can argue that for a kid with his temperament, it's difficult to stop."

"Explosive rage."

"And adrenaline and fear. In a household that volatile, it's all mixed together. Except in this scenario, why turn on the mom? She's on the floor. Unconscious, already dying. What would bring Telly's attention to her? Why stop beating his father and move on to her?"

"I don't know," Rainie agreed. "Maybe she . . . moaned, exhaled."

"Revealed she was still alive?" the doctor suggested.

In that moment, Rainie got where she was going. "The first murder, Telly's father, that would've been explosive. But the second, hitting his mother over the head . . ."

"Calculating. Expedient. Because if their mother lived—their weak, passive, drug-addicted mom . . ."

"They'd never be safe."

"You could say you have a pattern now: the shooting of the foster parents, which could fall under explosive rage, except then there are additional killings that clearly aren't impulsive at all. Maybe this isn't a new pattern. It's simply Telly repeating what he learned eight years ago. Certainly, it would explain why he's looking for his sister."

"How so?" Rainie asked sharply.

"She's the one who stopped him then. Maybe he secretly hopes she can stop him now. Or maybe . . ."

The doctor hesitated.

"What?"

"He wants it to be over. Once and for all. The world has been a cruel, harsh place for Telly Ray Nash and his sister. Now he will end it for both of them."

Chapter 28

THE TRAIL LEADING UP TO Frank Duvall's favorite campsite started at the roadside, cutting through a swath of high grass, then heading steadily deeper into the underbrush, till eventually it shot straight up two and a half miles to a rocky outcropping, which, according to his son Henry, offered one of the best views of the ocean. The trail wasn't on any map. Most likely, it had originally been cut by deer during their own forays up and down the mountain. The forest was filled with such trails. As a kid, Cal had spent countless days exploring new routes in and out of the wilderness. Apparently, so had Frank Duvall.

Given this was a stealth operation, they had parked a single vehicle half a mile back at the turn-in for a bait shop. Second appealing feature of Frank's favorite camping site—it overlooked a popular fishing stream, making dinner easy to catch.

One of the officers had already questioned the bait shop owner about seeing any kid matching Telly's description. According to the owner, no. But Cal had watched the guy's gaze slide away as he answered, then dash nervously to the TV screen.

Cal was no expert, being just a cheese-making tracker and all, but even he thought that was suspicious.

Not that it really mattered. The new search team—Cal, Deb the dog handler, Molly the dog, and fresh SWAT flankers Darren and Mitch—had a plan and they were sticking to it.

At the base of the trailhead, Molly had sat, which apparently meant she had picked up a human scent. Deb had then given the dog the signal to track and Molly had headed straight up the thin, snaking path.

According to Deb, Mollywogs would keep on going, with her curious rolling gait, until the human scent reached some kind of critical mass. At which time, Molly would lie down, alerting them that said human was straight ahead.

Hopefully, Molly would provide that signal before their suspect opened fire.

Cal was nervous. He didn't like it. Wasn't accustomed to feeling this edgy out in the woods, the place he'd always felt most at home. And this deer trail, it was beautiful, everything there was to love about hiking in the Pacific Northwest. Within moments of leaving sun-bleached asphalt, they'd stepped into a shadowed sanctuary, dense with towering fir trees, carpets of thick moss, mounds of lush ferns. It felt cooler in the woods. Smelled better, too—green, which wasn't even a smell but should have been. Because that's how the woods always smelled to Cal: deep green.

Which made him resent the kid even more. For making Cal, in the temple of the great outdoors, still hear the echoing crack of rifle fire, followed by the screams of his fellow teammates.

Cal's hands were shaking. Cal, whose hands never shook.

He spied a mark in the trunk of a tree ahead, motioned for the team to stop. The fir tree neighboring the trail was a relative youngster, tall and thin, having to grow up up up to find sun. Most of its lower branches were gone. Fallen off, maybe removed by other hikers to make the narrow trail more accessible. But none of that accounted for the white gouge near shoulder height.

Cal stuck his finger in the wound, discovering beads of sticky sap—a fir tree's version of first aid. Fresh, no doubt about it.

The team waited, the two replacement SWAT snipers keeping their eyes on the woods, while Deb leaned down and scratched

Molly's ears. The dog had used the break to sit down, legs splayed in front, white throat exposed above her black vest as she arched her thick neck and leaned against her handler, rumbling happily.

"You sure that thing is a dog?" Cal asked, still inspecting the tree.

"Rescued her myself from the heroin den."

"Might explain a few things."

"Like what? That she's a survivor? When I first saw Molly, she was nothing but skin and bones; huge head; emaciated, wiggly body. She reminded me of a pollywog, hence her nickname. She was also pregnant. Turned out she was carrying seven pups, which, given her condition, no one thought would make it. But Molly did it. Gave birth to seven beautiful puppies and tended them every day, no matter her own discomfort. The pups were easily adopted out. But a one-year-old pit bull mix? Molly's road was harder. So I decided to take her in myself. Strictly as a pet. I was already working with my next search dog, a one-year-old Lab.

"I still have him, too. Except now he's the pet, and Molly, who watched all my training sessions, has become the star. Breed is only a starting point when it comes to work dogs. Heart is what really matters, and Mollywogs here, she has the biggest heart I've ever known."

"Bet you she snores," Cal said.

"Like a Mack truck," Deb assured him. "What's with the gouge?"

"See the white wood? Fresh wound. Tree's only begun the healing process. It's the height that has me interested. Can you move forward?"

He didn't want to step in front of them, ruin the incomparable Mollywogs's scent trail. Deb obliged, walking her and Molly farther up the path. Now Cal could stand level with the fir tree, measuring where the mark on the trunk hit halfway between his elbow and shoulder height. It almost looked to him . . .

"Rifle tip," Darren said behind him.

Cal turned to look at the SWAT team officer who'd replaced Antonio. "That's what I was thinking. Kid's hiking up this trail, lugging backpack, bedroll, multiple boxes of ammo. Add to that three rifles." Cal grimaced. "Sure, he could be carrying two strapped to his back. But the third, bet he was cradling that one in his arms, at the ready. Which would place the tip right about . . ." He placed his fingertips in the fresh wood gouge.

None of them spoke for a moment, the two SWAT officers still on watch, scanning the woods.

"Stealth," Deb said at last.

"Yep," Cal agreed. "Simply gotta sneak up on the campsite, seize the guns, grab the mass murderer. Nothing to it."

They resumed their hike.

HALFWAY UP, Cal's radio crackled to life. He motioned to the group to halt, stepping off to the side, where he could answer Sheriff Atkins's summons, volume turned low.

"Progress?" Sheriff Atkins asked.

"The dog, Molly, seems to think she's following a human. Airborne scent particles settle in eight to twelve hours, so according to Deb, that means someone must've passed this way earlier today."

"What do you think?"

"Trail's hard to read. Soft-packed pine needles. Great for hiking but not so good for footprints. Have found a fresh gouge in a tree, some depressions in mossy surfaces, so I suppose I agree with Molly: Sometime earlier today, a human being this way cameth."

"We reviewed camera footage from a nearby trail, as you suggested. The Umatilla doesn't access the campsite but passes just east of it. Unfortunately, the trail camera is set up to capture wildlife, meaning it records everything at ankle height. We've seen the feet of several hiking groups, some twosomes. But no lone hikers."

"Which doesn't mean Telly hasn't returned to the campsite. Just means if he did, he used a different approach."

"True."

"Your camera trail, the Umatilla, on hiking maps?"

"Yes."

"If I was him, I'd avoid it, too. Known trails are busy this time of year. Better to stick to lesser-known byways, such as this deer trail. Sounds like Frank Duvall knew plenty and shared his knowledge with his sons."

The sheriff didn't answer.

"Anything else I should know?" Cal asked.

"According to the son, there are a couple of sites after this one we can check out. They're much farther away, but now that Telly has access to a four-wheeler, they're possible."

"Something's gonna break," Cal said. "In real life the trail does go cold, but sooner or later, we always pick it up again. Remember, the kid's gonna need water. Even if we don't find him at this campsite, we'll find him."

The sheriff didn't say anything. Was she thinking something? Worrying about something?

Cal had never worked with Sheriff Atkins before. He'd heard stories—how she'd single-handedly carried a federal agent out of a burning building. And he'd spotted the shiny scars on her neck that seemed to prove it.

Tough woman, he thought. And interesting.

"Check back in thirty," the sheriff said now.

Cal replied in the affirmative.

Then they were once more headed up the trail.

MOLLYWOGS LAY DOWN.

Just like that. She was walking. Then she wasn't.

It wasn't an exhausted plop, either, which Cal would have fully understood after ninety minutes of hard hiking. This was more like a crouch. Barrel-chested body low but stiff, ears cocked, gaze going directly to the handler. Deb held up a hand, not that it was necessary. The moment the dog had stopped, so had the rest of the team. Up until this point, Cal had viewed their strange-looking canine as little more than a drool machine. But now he saw it. The pit bull side of the dog's mongrel breeding. And the look she had for her handler . . .

Goofy Mollywogs would die for her human. She'd done her first job, tracked the scent to the critical mass looming straight ahead. Now the dog was preparing herself for what would happen next.

Cal unslung his rifle as the two SWAT team officers got busy. Recon. They needed information. Not just that there was a human at the campsite, but how many, how prepared? To get the job done, Darren picked a tree, one of the few broadleafs around with thicker branches. His smaller, younger sidekick, Mitch, got to do the honors, hopping from the ground to a nearby boulder, to the lowest available branch. Mitch didn't say a word as he worked himself higher and higher, seeking the best vantage point. Then, halting at last, he pressed his back against the trunk, peered through his scope, and zeroed in on the camp.

He held up one finger.

One target.

Darren acknowledged, and Mitch settled his rifle into the curve of his shoulder, his vantage point now a sniper's stand.

They had been green-lighted for use of deadly force before they ever set out. Capturing the suspect alive was still preferred. But given their target's history, what he'd done to the last search team . . .

That kind of fugitive, Cal found himself thinking. That kind of day.

And his hands were shaking again. His hands that never shook.

Cheese maker. Tracker. And now this.

Darren gathered Cal and Deb together. A tactical situation was his call, so they listened close as he drew a map in the dirt and illustrated their strategy. With Mitch up in the tree to provide cover fire, they would split up, creep to the top of the trail in sync, then, at his signal, burst upon the camp.

Darren glanced at Molly, then Deb, raising a brow in question. Clearly, he wanted Molly to go first, as a charging police canine made for a very intimidating sight, not to mention a smaller target. If they got really lucky, Molly would take down their shooter before they ever cleared the trees. Or at least distract him long enough for their own ambush.

Deb nodded, her hand resting on top of Molly's square head. A policewoman. A police dog. But even Cal could tell that if things went badly, the loss for the dog and the handler would be well beyond professional.

He kept his own rifle gripped in front of him. He'd asked for this assignment. For his team. For his community. He could do this.

Another flurry of hand signals, more scratches in the dirt, and then that was that. They had a plan. Deb and Molly took the trail. Darren headed left. Cal headed right.

They made their final approach.

CAL PAUSED TWICE TO WIPE THE SWEAT from his brow. The building heat, the growing tension, he wasn't sure which it was. But suddenly, acutely, he was aware of how his favorite hiking shirt was glued to his torso and the rivers of sweat poured from his brow. The woods were no longer a cool, shadowed sanctuary. He didn't even smell the scent of green.

Instead, creeping around boulders, stepping lightly through knee-high ferns, he felt as if the world had gone eerily silent. He smelled earth and rot and decay. The scent of death, which had to be a trick of his imagination.

He'd never shot anyone. He didn't even like to hunt. For Cal, walking through the woods had always been enough.

This, he thought ironically, was what too much volunteering did to a person.

A snap of a tree branch to the far left. Darren. Man better be a good shot, Cal thought bitterly, because he was a piss-poor stealth tracker.

Then, what had to happen next:

A whistle, high overhead. Mitch's signal that their target, alerted by the noise, was on the move.

Followed almost immediately by Darren's own birdcall and then . . .

A deep, rumbling growl as Molly burst up the trail. Barking, barking, barking, former rescue dog, now loyal police canine, charging into the campsite.

Cal didn't let himself think anymore. He picked a break in the bushes and ran toward the madness.

Chapter 29

IT HAPPENED IN A BLUR. Cal didn't see as much as he heard. The sudden snap of breaking twigs and multiple bodies bursting through the underbrush. Barking. Mollywogs, low and fierce. Followed by a man's shriek and Deb's steely command. "Stop. Police."

More barking, more shrieking, then Cal himself was skittering to a halt in the clearing, rifle held before him, blood thundering in his ears. Ambush. Gunshots. Screams of terror. He was braced for it all. Expecting it all. Adrenaline coursing through his veins and something more. Rage. Primitive and raw, because this kid had shot his team. Because Cal had screwed up and walked his team straight into a killer's rifle sights.

Nonie, a grandmother for God's sake, had screamed as she went down. Screamed and screamed. Then Antonio, and all Cal could do was hit the ground and wait for it to end.

He was on the kid before he was fully aware of his own actions. Rifle jammed against the back of a dark-haired skull: "*Drop your weapon drop your weapon drop your weapon!*"

Then it was over. Just like that.

Molly came into focus, standing stiff-legged on the other side of the crouched figure, Deb behind her dog, Darren three feet to Cal's right. None of them were looking at the cowering figure. All of them were staring at him.

Moaning. From the curled-up form on the ground.

"Don't shoot, man. I swear, I swear. Don't shoot."

Cal came back to himself. He realized just how hard he was trembling. Like a man on the edge.

Very slowly, very carefully, he took a step back.

Shock, he thought. Delayed grief and rage over the events of the morning. Maybe even PTSD if one could have it set in within a matter of hours. Why not? He was just a cheese maker and a tracker. And nowhere in all the training did they tell you how to handle becoming the target yourself. Or what it would feel like to watch members of your team drop one by one.

Cheese maker. Fugitive tracker. And now, he thought, also someone else.

Deb took control. Her dog, her catch.

"Hands," she demanded now, in the kind of voice that brooked no argument.

The man was curled up on his knees. A camo-patterned hiking pack obscured most of his back. His arms were wrapped protectively around his head. Probably more in response to Molly's barking charge than any of the humans bursting onto the scene. Now his arms shot straight up.

"Very slowly, rise up from the waist. Stay kneeling! Just straighten up."

Very slowly, the man obeyed. Kid, really. Late teens, dirty-blond hair, sweat-plastered dark green shirt. And definitely not Telly Ray Nash.

Just a terrified hiker, who, by the look and smell of things, had just wet himself.

"Holy shit," the kid whispered now. "Whatever it is . . . I swear, man. I swear."

"Name?" Darren barked.

"Ed. Ed Young."

"What are you doing here, Ed?"

"Hiking, man. I mean, just . . . getting away from the heat.

Thought I might spend a night camping out. Hanging in the river, chilling out."

"By yourself?"

"Um . . . sure." The kid's gaze slid away.

On cue, Molly growled low in her throat.

"Brought my phone," the kid added hastily. "Might've called a few buddies to join later. But uh, no dice, right, 'cause look around. This campsite's always been first come, first served, and someone already beat me to it. That's the breaks, right?"

For the first time, Cal took in the entire clearing. It was a makeshift camp of sorts. The charred remnants of an old fire, still ringed in stones, not far from where their target now knelt. Farther to the left, a platform of old wooden pallets, currently topped with a small pile of gear. The pallets were to keep a camper and his supplies out of the mud in inclement weather, a common enough trick in the Pacific Northwest, where liquid sunshine was the forecast more often than not.

Now Darren motioned with his head for Cal to do the honors. So Cal crossed to the platform, careful to check the ground for any sign of footprints or trace evidence he'd need to mark for later. But the thick carpet of needles held on to its secrets. He'd have to get luckier with the gear.

"Bedroll," he called out as he grew closer, used the tip of his rifle to sort through the pile. "Tent. Backpack."

He knelt down. The tent was still folded up and secured in a green nylon carrying case. He could make out dark lettering at the edge. "F. Duvall," he read off, then glanced up at Darren.

"Frank Duvall. This is his stuff. We found the campsite."

Darren returned his attention to their charge. "Who did you see?" he demanded sharply.

"What? Who? Man, I didn't see anyone. Just got up here myself, saw the stuff, and then, like, the woods exploded. That dog . . ." He looked over at Molly, who was still at attention, and shivered. "Man . . . I'm telling you, whatever it is, I didn't do it."

Which implied even to Cal that the kid had done something.

Darren seemed to agree. He crossed his rifle in front of him, adopting an intimidating stance.

"How old are you, Ed?"

"N-n-nineteen."

"Local? Grow up around here?"

"Yeah."

"Bakersville High School?"

"Yeah."

"Know a fellow student? Telly Ray Nash?"

Frown. "Nah."

"Really? Never heard the name?"

"No. But, I mean, it's a big school."

"Not even this morning? On the news?"

"What happened this morning?" The kid appeared so confused, for once Cal believed him.

"How long you been hiking, Ed?" Darren again.

"Started out first thing. Six A.M., trying to beat the heat, though shit, man, in these conditions, too damn hot even then."

Cal spoke up: "Which trail?"

"The Umatilla. Parked my car couple of miles north of here, hiked in from that direction."

So not the deer trail used by the tracking team, who'd been presumably following Telly Ray Nash.

"You started out at six A.M.," Cal continued, "and you're just now hitting this site? What are you, the world's slowest hiker?"

Kid flushed. "Took my time. Enjoying the great outdoors, you know." The kid went to spread his arms as if to indicate the towering trees and magnificent scenery all around him. Molly growled. Kid jerked his arms straight up again.

From behind Molly, Deb leaned closer, took a few experimental sniffs. "I'd say you've been enjoying more than the great outdoors," she observed wryly.

"Hey, man, I got a prescription," the kid said quickly. Great, Cal thought. They'd set out to catch themselves a homicidal teen and had ended up with a half-baked doper instead.

"You encounter any other hikers today?" Cal asked. "Out on the trails?"

"Well, sure. It's August. Trails are lousy with hikers. Which is why I thought to come here. Off the map, you know. Locals only."

"What about coming across a lone male? About your age."

"Dunno."

"Think harder," Darren said, taking a small but pointed step forward.

"No! Definitely no. Some groups, okay. I saw three or four groups, some younger couple . . . an old guy with a dog. But no loners . . . like me."

"Four-wheeler?" Cal prodded. "See one, hear one in the area?"

Ed regarded them blankly. "No four-wheelers around here. Trails aren't wide enough."

Cal nodded. The Umatilla was marked for hiking only. Traversing it with a four-wheeler would be difficult going and, given the steady flow of day hikers, conspicuous. Meaning Telly would have to ditch the four-wheeler before accessing this camp. Or approach it from a different direction. Being a hoofer himself, Cal wasn't as familiar with the recreational vehicle paths.

Most likely, Telly had accessed this campsite first thing this morning, utilizing the same, lesser-known deer trail they had followed. In which case, he never would've crossed the Umatilla. Once he'd dropped his supplies, Telly would've had to return via the same trail in order to get in his truck. Next stop: the EZ Gas station and a fresh round of carnage.

Which raised the question: If Telly had dumped camping supplies here for future use, had he also stashed the extra firearms?

Cal glanced at Darren, saw the SWAT officer was thinking the same.

Darren whistled once. At which point, Mitch clambered down from his tree perch, and, with Mollywogs keeping an eye on their trembling hiker, they scoured the area in earnest.

A rifle carrying case was hardly a small item. Given Telly had been caught on camera wielding a pistol, then had opened fire on Cal's team with a rifle, that left two handguns and two long guns unaccounted for. For ease of carrying, Cal imagined Telly had packed the firearms into a single duffel bag, then filled the rest of the space with boxes of ammo. A heavy load, especially given the kid had also strapped on a metal-framed hiking pack, a tent, and a sleeping bag.

Upon arrival, Telly had to have been relieved to divest himself of his load. The pack, tent, and sleeping bag had obviously been dropped on the wooden pallet. But a duffel bag? Long gun case, anything?

Darren and Deb took the campsite, while Mitch returned his attention to the trees, in case Telly had thought to stash his weapons up high.

Cal returned to his area of expertise, looking for signs—trampled ferns, broken branches, recent scrapes in the moss-covered tree trunks—anything that might indicate Telly had departed the campsite in search of a more discreet place to hide the firearms. But once again, the dense covering of pine needles made picking up a trail nearly impossible.

They widened their search, working in broader and broader circles. Hot, tedious work.

Which yielded nothing, nothing, nothing.

They returned to the dopehead hiker, emptying out his day pack in case he'd found the guns before they did. Still nothing.

Two rifles. Two handguns. Boxes and boxes of ammo. No way they could've simply vanished into thin air.

And yet.

They'd found Telly Ray Nash's campsite. But still no signs of his arsenal.

ORDERS FROM CENTRAL COMMAND: Return campsite to original conditions, install the surveillance cameras, and retreat. With no reported sightings of Telly or a lone male on a four-wheeler, they had no way of knowing just how close he might be. And Sheriff Atkins was adamant—next time they encountered the armed fugitive, she wanted it to be on their terms, say, when he'd returned to his campsite and, thinking he was finally safe, gone to sleep.

Cal disagreed. Having determined what wasn't present at the suspect's base camp—the guns—he now wanted a chance to discover what was. He gave the sheriff some credit: At least she listened. After a bit of back-and-forth, they settled on a compromise: Deb and her canine would return with the wayward hiker to mobile command, where Sheriff Atkins and her detectives would question Ed in more detail. Mitch would resume his tree perch, where, between the vantage point and his high-powered scope, he would be able to spot an approaching figure way before Telly could spot them. And with Darren also standing guard, Cal would inspect the camp as quickly and thoroughly as possible.

"Then get the hell out," Shelly ordered.

"No problem," Cal agreed. "For the record, however, there's no indication Telly's anywhere in the area. And we need all the information on this kid we can get."

"Snap photos. Document the scene before, during, after. Then put everything back exactly as you found it. We don't want to spook the kid. Ambushing him once he returns is our best chance of ending this."

"Above-average powers of observation, remember? I think I can handle this."

"Really? Then who's that standing right behind you?"

"What?" Cal whirled around, only to discover empty air.

From over the radio: "Gotcha." Then, more soberly, "Fast and efficient. Get in, out, done. I mean it. We've suffered enough damage today."

Deb and Molly set off with half-baked Ed, Molly still in full work mode, dark eyes fixated on her catch. She no longer looked like a panting, grinning sidekick. More like a predator, licking her chops.

With the civilian out of the way, Mitch headed for his tree perch, while Darren took up a crouched position behind a mound of ferns, his attention split between the deer trail they'd used to access the clearing and the direction of the Umatilla trail, which Ed had followed to the camp.

Cal went to work. He started with the gear. Despite his wisecrack to the sheriff, he understood her point: They couldn't afford to spook the kid by revealing they'd discovered his base of operations. And while Cal would have liked to think he could outsmart a teenager, truth was, the kid was clever. All of Telly's steps since the shooting had been surprisingly strategic. So Cal did the sensible thing and snapped a photo of the pile of supplies to serve as a model for reassembly.

He started with the sleeping bag, unrolling it fully, inspecting it inside and out. He followed along the seams, looking for . . . he didn't know what. Anything that might help catch a killer. When the sleeping bag proved to contain nothing but nylon and flannel, he rolled it back up, returned it to its place on the wooden pallet.

Telly's metal-framed hiking pack featured a multitude of pockets, straps, ties. Cal worked his way from the outside in, beginning with a smaller pocket that contained everything needed for hiking 101. Cal recognized the setup of first-aid gear, trail maps, etc. He kept his hiking pack similarly supplied.

Next up, he discovered an inner pouch containing granola bars, two clementines, and a bag of what might've been chocolate-covered almonds but was now a melted mess. Two bottles of water. Not nearly enough for these conditions, which gave Cal some hope. Once Telly consumed these bottles, which would be sooner versus later in these temperatures, he'd be forced to forage for more.

In the pack's main compartment, Cal discovered his first surprise. Books. Telly had set out on a homicidal spree and he'd brought with him . . . books.

Cal reached in, then caught himself and snapped a quick photo of the pile. Would Telly notice if Cal replaced the articles out of order? Better to be safe than sorry.

First item Cal removed was a thin children's book. *Clifford the Big Red Dog*. Apparently, property of the Bakersville County Library. And according to the back page, due back in twelve days. Cal didn't get it. A teenager with a picture book? He photographed the cover, then the library page.

Moving on. A stack of thin, spiral-bound notebooks. Cheap, kind that could be picked up in any office supply store. He counted five of them. He started with the top copy, flipped open to the first page, and was once again caught off guard. No writings, but a photo. A four-by-six close-up of a baby, cocooned in blue, cradled in a woman's arms, only the side of her face visible as she stared down at her newborn. Telly? With his mom. The page didn't offer any captions, just the picture, colors fading with age, taped dead center.

It unsettled Cal to look at such a mundane shot. Cute, innocent baby. Happy, tender mom. And to realize seventeen years later, the baby in this photo would grow into a boy determined to kill them all.

Slowly, Cal flipped his way through, holding up his mobile phone to document each page as the baby became a toddler, then was joined by a second baby in a pink blanket.

Soon, both the little boy and little girl were growing up, with no captions to provide insight into the Kodak moments. And no parents in sight.

"Noonan," Darren growled behind him.

"I know."

Moving faster, he flipped to the final page in the photo album: a lone shot of an older gentleman. Blurred, not the best photo. Maybe the infamous father, or, to judge by the sparse gray, a grandfather. But again, no caption. Just a lone male, who at one time must've meant something to Telly Ray Nash.

Cal set the photo album down, moved quickly to the next notebook in the pile. Any second now Telly could burst into the campsite, guns blazing. Or worse, he could've been hunkered down all along in some hidey-hole they hadn't discovered. And right this minute, he was settling the butt of his rifle into the pocket of his shoulder, deep breath in, deep breath out, as he placed the crosshairs on the back of Cal's head.

Notebooks. Four more to go. He went with the one with the green cover. And finally was rewarded by the content he expected. Text. Every line, margin, top of a page, even the narrow little spaces between the wire binding, was covered with words. Disjointed. Fragments of sentences, repeated thoughts. Probably not written all at the same time either. Some lines held larger, sloppy letters, as if written by a grade schooler. Whereas the heavily inked words crammed into the spiral binding—he couldn't even read most of them. The printing was almost microscopic, very controlled. Older Telly, who'd run out of space at the end so returned to compulsively fill the rest of the page?

He snapped a photo, realizing already there was way too much here for one twitchy tracker to read while waiting for his head to get blown off.

Quicker now, from notebook to notebook to notebook. Scanning, scanning, scanning, while Darren growled at him to hurry up.

Flipping to the final few pages of the last notebook, snap, snap, snap. Intel for the police, fodder for the retired profiler.

Then, because he couldn't help himself, Cal lowered his phone and checked out the page.

He'd expected a litany of rage or petty grievances against the world. Maybe even a list of all the ways Telly had been done wrong. But instead, the final pages of the last notebook mirrored the content from the walls of Telly's bedroom: not a recounting of the day's events or ponderings into the greater universe but, instead, a litany of words:

Zero or hero. Who am I?

Protector. Destroyer. Protector. Destroyer. Protector.

What kind of man, what kind of man, what kind of man?

The writing was heaviest on the final two pages. The letters dark, as if Telly had gone over each word repeatedly, not just inking the page but scoring his anxiety into the paper.

Think, think, think, think, think, think, read the page.

About what? Cal wanted to know.

Then on the very last page. A single word. A single pledge.

Hero.

Cal shook his head.

He replaced all items, restaged the wooden pallets, then set up the motion-sensitive cameras. Work done, he motioned to his flankers, who rematerialized at his side. They headed down the trail.

Best-case scenario: Telly would return to his base camp shortly, triggering the motion-sensitive cameras as he unrolled his gear. He'd close his eyes. SWAT would descend and the community would be able to sleep at night.

Worst-case scenario: Telly would never return to camp. Meaning the mass murderer who labeled himself a hero . . .

Could be absolutely anywhere.

Chapter 30

LUKA IS WHINING LOW in his throat. I don't blame him. I'm tired and confused myself. It feels like we've been wandering in the woods forever. Following the river toward . . . four-wheeler trails, my homicidal brother, nothing at all?

It's late. I know because I keep checking my phone. Quick turns on and off. Checking the time and, of course, messages. But nothing else from Quincy or Rainie. Which proves what I initially suspected: Quincy's text about having my brother in custody was a lie. I figured as much. I mean, they arrest a kid suspected of shooting how many people, and the first thing they do is reach out to his sister for a reunion?

I pay attention at family dinners. I know it's okay to lie to a murder suspect, as well as to your teenage daughter. Whatever preserves the greater good. But the fact that I'm probably right doesn't make me feel any better. Mostly it leaves me sad. And missing Quincy. Because he loves me enough to lie, and I respect that about him.

So Luka and I have been wandering. Along the river so we don't get totally lost. And where there's plenty of water for Luka, who's stuck wearing a fur coat in this heat. From time to time I feed us both snacks. But I'm sparing because not knowing where we are going or how long it might take us, I'm not sure how to ration our supplies.

Luka is accustomed to dinner at five. On the dot. Frankly, at four, four forty-five, he starts hanging around in the kitchen, staring pointedly at his food bowl. Where does he hide his watch? I've never known. But Luka can tell time better than any automated system, and sure enough, about an hour ago, he started getting very agitated with me.

I may not have Luka's sense of time, but my stomach is rumbling. I pause long enough to gift each of us with half a granola bar. Luka eats his in two bites. I, at least, try to savor mine. But it's been a while since lunch. And we're hot, tired, and . . . dispirited.

Looking for a miracle, when I'm not that kind of kid.

Noise. It takes a moment to penetrate. Distant and buzzing, like bees. Except then I register the continuity and how the sound is growing louder. Closer. An engine.

Most likely of a four-wheeler. We've reached the recreational vehicle trails. Just like that, I'm excited, panicked, and terrified all at once. Is that him? My long-lost brother driving closer to us? I've found him.

What do I say? What do I do?

Hey, remember me? Stop, don't shoot?

I pick up my steps. I can't help myself. I'm so agitated and exhausted, I just have to know. Even if it's horrible and I was all wrong and my own brother and last surviving family member shoots me, hey, at least it seems better than being in limbo.

I'm stupid, and rash, and everything Quincy and Rainie have ever accused me of, as I start jogging down the path, Luka at my heels, heading closer to the noise.

I arrive at the path just as the rugged black four-wheeler roars into sight and blows by me. My first impression, not a kid at all. But a big, burly guy, capped with a helmet, tearing up the trails. Then three seconds behind, another vehicle appears from around the bend and whips on by. Good old boys, having a time of it.

Because apparently my brother isn't the only lunatic wandering these woods.

And . . . and I don't know what to do.

I came. I saw. And now I'm utterly, totally done. I want to go home, hang my head in shame, and take my punishment. Rainie, at least, will hug me. I could really use a hug right now.

Growling. So low, it takes a moment to register. Luka has gone stiff-legged by my side. He's peering into a bush, and he's rumbling deep in his chest.

I frown, turn to shush my dog, and in the next moment . . .

I see him.

Holding so still, so motionless, his face painted in streaks of brown and black, he could be the bush around him or the tree right behind him. But he's none of those things. He's my brother.

Standing right there.

GUN. I SEE IT without really seeing it. The next second, I'm on my knees, throwing my arms around Luka's furry neck, as my guard dog starts to bark in earnest. Shush, shush. I need to quiet him, calm him, but my Dutch has deserted me and all I can do is hang on to my dog, block his body with my own as I beg:

"Don't shoot, don't shoot. It's not Luka's fault. I made him come. But he's a good dog. The best dog. Please don't hurt my dog. Please."

"Clifford," my brother says, his voice hoarse, almost rusty sounding.

I nod without understanding it. Then I remember Dutch long enough to give Luka the command to stand down. He does, but I can tell from the stiffness of his body beneath my arms that he doesn't believe me. I keep my head buried in the scruff of his neck. If my brother is about to shoot us both, I don't want to see it. I don't want to know that I led my dog to his death.

Seconds pass. Maybe a full minute. I'm not sure. Eventually, I feel the muscles soften in Luka's shoulders. When I raise my head, I expect my brother to be gone. To have vanished as dramatically as he appeared.

But he's still standing there. Not having moved an inch. With all the fancy streaks and paint on his face, it's hard to make out his features. I see mostly the whites of his eyes. I wonder how he learned to disguise himself this well, become such an outdoorsman. And I realize there is much about this brother I don't know.

"Sharlah," he says.

"Telly," I answer.

Then, for a long time, we say nothing at all.

Luka breaks the silence first. He whines. Licks my face. I realize for the first time I'm crying. It embarrasses me. I pull away from Luka long enough to scrub my cheeks. When I look up again, my brother is still there, the trails, the woods quiet all around us.

"I came looking for you," I say, because someone's gotta do something.

"I heard you got new parents. Cop parents. You should've stayed with them."

"I didn't want you to hurt them. I didn't want them . . ." I make myself look him in the eye. "I didn't want them to have to hurt you."

He doesn't say anything. Just stares at me with his disconcerting face blending into the tree trunk behind him, the rifle loose in his hands. I wonder if this is the same gun he used on his foster parents or those people at the gas station, or the police officers. Guess eight years later, Telly doesn't need a baseball bat anymore.

"Your foster parents," I say at last. "Why?"

He shakes his head, as if trying to deny my words.

"And strangers at the EZ Gas. Telly, what are you doing?"

"You shouldn't be here."

"But I am."

"Go home."

"Or what? You'll shoot me?" I draw myself up tall, proud of how brave I sound, even if I'm quivering on the inside.

My brother looks at me again, and for the first time, I can finally read his expression. Grief. Horror. Sadness. Deep, endless sadness. I can't help myself. I reach out a hand.

That quickly, he fires to life. Rifle, pointed straight at me. Level, steady. Yep, he's come a long way in the past eight years.

Luka starts growling again, and only my fingers, wrapped tight around his collar, keep him in place.

"Damn it, Sharlah—"

"Where's a baseball bat when you need one?"

"Get out. Go home. I mean it! Get the hell away from me!"

"Or what, you'll shoot?"

"You don't understand—"

"Then tell me."

"Get the hell away from me!"

"No!"

"I'll pull the trigger. So help me God, I'll do it."

"Then do it!"

"You stupid— Think of your arm, Sharlah. Want me to break the other one?"

"Mom," I say.

Just like that, he draws up short, rifle bobbing uncertainly. "What?"

"Mom," I repeat.

He doesn't say a word. But then I don't expect him to.

"I remember Mom," I say steadily. "I remember that night. And I know, Telly, I know why you broke my arm."

I don't wait anymore. I let go of my dog. I walk straight forward. Into the bush, into the rifle. I shove the firearm aside. I put my arms around my brother. Then I say what I should've said eight years ago.

I whisper in my brother's ear: "I'm sorry, Telly. It was all my fault. And I'm so sorry."

I wrap my arms around my big brother's skinny waist and hold him as he cries.

TELLY PULLS AWAY. He starts to walk. Without bothering to ask, I scramble after him, Luka close at my heels.

"Where are we going?" I ask.

"Wherever they don't expect me to be."

"That's not much of a plan. Can't walk forever. Especially in this heat. And not to brag or anything, but my new parents, they're pretty good. Quincy even tried to get me to return home by pretending to have found you already. It's only a matter of time."

Telly pauses briefly, shoots me a glance. "They found my camp. Is that what he said?"

"I don't . . . remember."

He nods, resuming his quick pace along the edge of the trail. "Bet they did. After finding Frank's and Sandra's bodies, they'd have to call Henry. He'd notice the missing camping gear. Knowing him, couldn't resist mentioning Frank's favorite campsite." He nods again, more to himself than me. "Good."

"Good?" I ask. "Doesn't that mean the police now have all your camping gear?"

"Can't make an omelet without breaking some eggs," he says. Which makes no sense to me.

"I have an apple left," I offer shyly. He's wearing a navy blue backpack, near the same size as mine. It appears heavy, but whether it's weighed down with food or ammo, I'm too chicken to ask.

Telly shakes his head.

"Water?" he asks instead.

"One bottle." I start slipping off my backpack. He shakes his head again, comes around behind me. I feel the jerk and tug as he works the zipper on my backpack himself, weight shifting and moving as he digs around. After a near eternity he reappears in front of me, plastic water bottle now in hand.

I have a piece of paper in my hand. My cell phone number written on a scrap of notebook. I hand it to him wordlessly. He doesn't say anything, just slides it into his pocket.

Telly glances at Luka. In response, Luka curls up his lip, baring a long, white fang. Far from being fearful, my brother nods in satisfaction. "I heard he's a police dog?"

"Retired. Bum knees."

"Should he be hiking?"

"This kind of walking doesn't bother him. And exercise is good for him. I still have some treats for him, and so far, he's done just fine drinking out of streams. Do you have a plan?" I ask him.

He doesn't answer. Walks faster.

"Gonna do what? Keep roaming the woods, shooting at random strangers? Or are you now only firing at trained members of law enforcement?"

"You can go home anytime you'd like," he informs me.

"But I know where you are."

"Nah. You'd only know where I once was. Like the campsite. Knew the police would find it. Planned on it, actually. Because now they're focusing their efforts up there, while I'm down here." He glances at me. "How well do you know policing?"

"Only a little bit," I hedge. "Just stuff I pick up over dinner."

"I know what I've read in books. Looking for anyone, police start with the known associates. But I don't have any. So maybe they'd talk to my probation officer, Aly. And of course they'd have to talk to Henry. And"—he glances at me—"you."

"But I don't know anything." The "not after eight years" part goes unsaid.

"Exactly," he replies, and keeps on hoofing.

"I didn't know what had happened," I say at last, having to work now to keep up. At seventeen, Telly has grown up up up. Whereas I'm still a mess of arms and legs, he's turned into a real person. Tall, strong, maybe good-looking, but I can't tell with that paint all over his face. I wonder if he looks like our father. Another thing I wouldn't know as I don't really remember our parents. My childhood, my younger years, they're all about Telly. The older brother who took care of me. The older brother I thought would never leave.

"When I got out of the hospital, the lady brought me to the first foster home," I continue now. "I thought you'd be there. I walked right in. So excited to see you. But . . . you weren't."

Telly doesn't say anything.

"They sent you to a different home?" I guess now.

"It doesn't matter. Jesus, Sharlah, that was so long ago . . ."

My eyes are burning again. I will myself not to cry. This is what I wanted. To find my brother, to be with him. To see for myself who he's become. Well, here I am. For once in my life, I've actually succeeded in a plan. I will not cry now.

"I told the police, that doctor lady, you'd protected us. Dad had the knife. He attacked first. The last day I was in the hospital . . . the doctor lady told me you'd be okay. You weren't in any trouble."

Telly stops. The movement so sudden, I bolt by him three steps before I can rein in my own movement.

"Let it go," he says. "I'm not that boy anymore. It doesn't matter."

"Says the teenager with the rifle!"

"This isn't about that!"

"Then what's it about? You killed your foster parents. Good people, Rainie and Quincy said. You shot them in their bed."

"That's what you think?"

"That's what they said—"

"Why are you here?"

"What?" The change in topic confuses me.

"Why are you here? Gonna save me? Like you did *last time*?" The sneer in his voice cuts me to the quick. I start shaking, can't seem to stop myself. "You wanna know what happens to a nine-year-old boy who beats his parents to death, who breaks his little sister's arm? They have homes for everything, these foster care people. Even homes for monsters like me. And that's where I went, and that's where I served my time. Alone. Isolated. Falling asleep every night so I could dream about our dear old dad again. And Mom. Except sometimes, in my dreams, he gets it right. We're the ones who go down, he's the one who wins. Other times it's Mom who grabs the knife, and around and around . . . One thing always stayed the same. You screaming. And that's what I've woken up to every night for years and years. My baby sister screaming as I cracked open her arm with a baseball bat."

He's breathing hard. Me too.

"Go home, Sharlah. Whatever you want . . . It's too late for both of us."

He doesn't sound angry anymore. He sounds defeated. Just like that I'm crying again. "I miss you," I whisper.

"Why? There's no point."

"I didn't know who to call. Who to ask. That first home. It wasn't a good place for me." Nor the second or the third or the fourth, but I having a feeling Telly knows all that. He has his own list.

"You ended up someplace good."

"Too much time had passed. I didn't know how to ask about you anymore."

"You know what, Sharlah? I ended up someplace good, too."

"Where?"

"The Duvalls'."

"But you—"

"You heard right. They're good people. They didn't deserve what happened to them."

"Then why did you—"

"Frank wanted me to find you. He thought if I could see that you were okay, had gotten on with your life, then I could get on with mine."

I don't have any words.

Telly turns, stares at me point-blank. "Are you doing good, Sharlah? Have you gotten on with your life?"

"I guess."

"Do you dream of our parents? Do you wake up screaming at night?"

"No."

"You know, when I first got to the Duvalls', after a bit . . . I had this dream. Fantasy, really. That I'd turn eighteen. Actually get my life together, the way they talked about. And then I'd come for you, Sharlah. Big brother, once more sweeping in to save the day. You'd be in some hellhole home—we both know about those, right?"

I nod.

"But I'd come. Take you away. We'd be a family again. This time, I'd get it right."

I don't say anything.

"But you're okay, aren't you? Good parents, that's what Frank said. Gonna adopt you. Make you real family."

I bow my head, ashamed, though I don't know why.

"That's good, Sharlah. It's great that you're doing great. That you're gonna be okay without me."

"Telly," I try, but I don't really know what to say.

"Go," he tells me now. "Keep your dog close. New parents, too. If you love me at all, find your happily-ever-after. Live it. Then I'll know at least one of us got it right."

He turns, starts walking again, his strides so long, so quick, there's no way I'll ever be able to catch up. His last words float over his shoulder to me.

"Sorry, Sharlah. You got the law enforcement parents. Me . . . I have at least one more person I gotta kill."

I can't keep up. My brother leaves me. Disappears into the woods, a lone figure with a rifle.

I stand there for a long time, Luka at my side, still on guard. My throat is closed up. My chest too tight.

I have this feeling I just can't shake. That this is the last time I'll ever speak to my brother.

That I will never see him again.

My shoulder throbs.

I don't care. I would give up my other shoulder, I would give up anything, I think. . . .

But it doesn't matter. Because he's gone, and I'm still too little to follow.

Minute passes into minute, the woods quiet.

Finally, I reach into my pocket. I get out my cell phone. Power it up. I say what I should've said hours ago.

"Rainie. It's Sharlah. Please . . . I just wanna come home."

Chapter 31

FRANK DECIDED WE SHOULD GO HUNTING.

"It'll be great," he explained to me. "I have this perfect campsite. Found it when I was about your age. But it's not on any maps. Just this little clearing surrounded by nothing but woods. We'll set up a tent. Cook dinner over the campfire. Count the stars in the sky. You'll love it."

I was less convinced. Camping. Sure. Whatever. But hunting implied shooting something. I was still figuring out the rifle. Last thing I wanted in my crosshairs was something people were dependent upon for dinner.

But once Frank had an idea in his head . . .

We were going hunting.

Thursday night we started with the preparations. Turned out, camping overnight involved a lot of gear. Like, half of Frank's garage. My job, Frank explained to me, was to master tent setup before we were in the great outdoors, tired from a day of hiking the woods, maybe soaking wet from the elements—

"The elements?" I asked.

"You know, like rain."

"It's supposed to rain? We're camping in the rain?"

Frank laughed at me. "What? You think Lewis and Clark only went out in good weather?"

"I think if Lewis and Clark had had Google Maps, they never would've gone out at all."

"*You know what the best part of camping is?*"

"*No.*"

"*Some kids think it's the s'mores—*"

"*I'm not six.*"

"*Some guys think it's staying up all night drinking beers around a campfire.*"

"*I'm not some guys.*"

"*It's the silence, Telly. For people like you and me, it's the one place, one time, we can find peace.*"

So tent. Practice setting it up. Practice tearing it down. Whatever. Setup turned out to be pretty simple. Frank liked his toys and the top-of-the-line L.L.Bean dome tent made sense. Thread rods through seams A, B, and C; secure corners; and boom, blue ripstop polyester shelter. Not bad if I did say so myself.

Tent up: check. Next, tent broken back down and rolled into its stuff sack . . . Impossible. Couldn't be done. I tried folding it this way. I tried that way. Damn thing . . .

Frank wouldn't lift a finger to assist. He had out the biggest backpack I'd ever seen. Metal framed. With padded straps around the hips and shoulders, and clips . . . everywhere.

"*You don't carry a pack with your back,*" he explained to me as I finally paused, breathing hard, half the tent jammed into the pack, the other half exploded out like a mushroom. "*That's a good way to wear yourself out, if not cause injury. Instead, you want the weight secured around your hips—carrying it with your pelvis, the way we're naturally designed to operate. So first, you tighten the hip girdle. Then, of course, the straps around your shoulders, keeping the weight close to your body. Final adjustment, the strap across your chest. Trust me, make the effort to adjust the pack right in the beginning, and you'll be able to hike for miles, barely noticing it's there.*"

I eyed the metal-framed monster doubtfully. It already looked to be a good twenty pounds, and that was before adding the frigging tent, sleeping rolls, maps, food, supplies, blah, blah, blah.

"Maybe we should leave the tent behind," I said now. "In fact, maybe you should leave me behind. I like beds. And indoor plumbing, and a roof over my head that doesn't pop open or blow away like an oversized balloon."

"It's gonna be a great weekend," Frank told me. "I just know it."

I set up the tent again. Broke it down again. Over and over. Till it stopped being such a pain in the ass and became almost possible.

Which turned out to be step one of my outdoor training. Here is how you set up a tent. Here is how you load a backpack. Here are the basic supplies for survival—Swiss Army knife, matches, first-aid kit, water-purification tablets. Even a magnet and a string, which could be turned into some kind of mad scientist's compass.

I had to give Frank credit. He really did love his job.

Besides, given how well I was doing at school, living in a tent might have been my future someday soon.

Of course, after mastering the equipment, it was Sandra's turn.

"Just in case," she informed me, "the hunting part doesn't work out."

She gave me a small smile, and I could tell from her expression she understood everything I couldn't say to happy, excited Frank. He could be so childlike in his joy, it seemed cruel to be the one to bring him down.

"You ever go camping with Frank?" I asked now.

We were in the kitchen. First hiking snack: gorp. Or something like that. Sandra had out boxes of cereal, a bag of chocolate chips, and various containers of dried fruit. Basically, I was to mix them all together. So far, this seemed more manageable than the tent.

"Oh yes. When we were first married, we went camping many weekends."

"Let me guess—you can prepare an entire chicken Parm over a campfire?"

She laughed. "Chicken Parm, no. But take a triangle of Pillsbury crescent roll dough, wrap it around a hot dog, then cover it in foil and rotate it on a skewer above the campfire . . ."

"Wow, you really do have a recipe for anything. Henry says you're a great shot, too. Even better than Frank."

Did I sound casual? I was trying to sound casual, but ever since Henry had made that comment, I'd been dying to know more. Sandra, happy homemaker by day, super sniper by night? Or something like that?

Now she merely shrugged, inspected my gallon-size freezer bag of gorp, added in more dried coconut.

"Ever wonder why we never have moles in the yard? Now you know."

"Frank teach you how to shoot?" I asked.

"No." She turned and bustled to the refrigerator, and I understood from her tone that that subject was closed. Of course. Because if Frank hadn't taught her, that left only one other person I could think of: her father. The mysterious criminal mastermind who Sandra said enjoyed being cruel and Frank said I should kill on sight.

I'd been keeping my eye out ever since the conversation with Henry and Frank in the woods. Not because I thought some old geezer dude was magically gonna turn up and cause trouble. But mostly because I desperately wanted to check out the geezer dude for myself.

Sandra's father. Sandra, who wore bright flowered skirts and loved a good Crock-Pot recipe, and yet was also, somehow, the devil's spawn? I'd always assumed I'd cornered the son-of-Satan market. Now I wasn't so sure.

"It's going to be okay," Sandra said abruptly.

I looked up to find her studying me. "What?"

"Everything will work out," she continued. "One day, you will make your own family, and you will be the father you never had. You will give your children the childhood you never experienced. And the *hole, that hollow place inside you, it will go away. You won't need to look backward anymore. You'll have a future."*

"That's what you did."

"Yes."

"And you're happy?" I asked curiously.

"Absolutely."

"But you miss Henry."

"Of course. Someday, I'll miss you, too."

"You'll take in another kid."

"You'll build your own life. It'll be good. I see that in you, Telly. You're stronger than you think, plus you have a big heart. Even when you pretend not to, you do. At least enough to spend a weekend in the pouring rain with my husband."

"That's not caring; that's craziness."

Sandra smiled. Pulled a package of hot dogs out of the fridge. "You're gonna find your happily-ever-after, Telly. I look forward to seeing it with you."

IT RAINED. *From the moment we left after school on Friday, it poured. I got to wear the pack first. Given my strong, young back, Frank said. Which meant the rain pooled on the top of the frame and during unexpected moments, careered down my neck.*

I was wearing one of Frank's old raincoats. Turns out, raincoats have ratings. Whatever mine was, it wasn't enough to stay dry. Within an hour, I started to feel damp. By the time we finished a scenic hike in the woods—"Look at that clearing, look at that stream, look at the moss on those trees!" Seriously, Frank?—I was soaked.

Finally, Frank led me to the infamous campsite. Good news was it had some wooden pallets, apparently brought by Frank years ago, to keep us out of the mud.

"So what you want to do," Frank explained to me, "is set up the

tent on the pallet. Now, as you can imagine, wooden pallets aren't the most comfortable sleeping surface. So you can cover it with a layer of pine needles, ferns for matting, or just keep things simple."

I gave him a look. Kept things simple. And quickly became grateful for the previous night's practice, because there was no way I would've been able to sort out the miles of tent for the first time under such conditions.

I got our shelter up. Which led to the next question. How the hell did you get a campfire going in the pouring rain?

Answer was, you didn't.

Frank had fashioned a small lean-to from downed limbs. Now he had the camp stove going. Just enough heat to cook up four of the hot dogs and not much else.

We sat in the rain, eating barely cooked wieners and passing the bag of gorp back and forth. Frank was grinning. Like, actually happy.

"There aren't any stars," I told him, staring pointedly at the heavy cloud cover.

"Ah, but there is silence. Plenty of silence."

Not much to do, camping in the rain. Needless to say, we retired to the tent early, hanging up our raincoats under the relative cover of some trees, wearing the rest of our clothes for warmth. I'd never been so grateful to crawl into a sleeping bag before. And yeah, our thin sleep rolls didn't provide the best cushion against the hard wooden pallet, but at least I was getting some feeling back in my toes.

We didn't talk. Just as well. I was never the type who knew what to say.

Eventually, Frank must've drifted off, because the tent was filled with the sound of his snores. Deep and rumbly. Like a bear. I was tempted to hit him, jab him with a finger, something. Instead, I just lay there listening. I wondered how many times he'd brought Henry here. I wondered why it bothered me so much.

Then, finally, I drifted off to sleep.

Eventually the snoring stopped. Best I can explain it, that's what woke me up.

The silence.

FRANK WAS GONE. *I didn't need to turn on my little headlamp to see. I could feel his absence in the small space. Maybe he'd gone out to pee.*

Rain had stopped. Took me another moment to realize that. The drip, drip, drip of rain off the door awning had finally relented. Then I realized the dark outside was starting to turn to gray. I glanced at my watch. Six A.M. I'd actually made it through the night. Just like that.

Made some sense. Frank was an early riser. Maybe he'd gone out to fix breakfast. More hot dogs? More gorp?

I got up myself, realizing now I had to pee, not to mention half my body had gone numb from sleeping on a wooden pallet.

I slipped on my still-damp boots, then unzipped the small door, poked my head out into the real world.

The woods were filled with mist. Long gray tendrils wrapping around moss-covered trees, sliding through tall mounds of lush green ferns. Quiet, just like Frank had said. Peaceful. And . . . beautiful.

I'd read a lot of King Arthur in my younger days. Something about the woods looked the way I had pictured Avalon in my mind. Green and gray all at once. Real and ghostly.

And no sign of Frank.

I tended to business first. Then wandered around the small clearing. The camp stove was still cold, so he hadn't started breakfast. No sign of him in the near vicinity. Then I thought to check where we'd hung our coats. Frank's was missing.

Next I checked the rifles, which he'd stashed with us inside the tent—*gotta keep them dry*. Both rifles were present. Frank's twenty-two, however, which he often carried for personal protection, was missing.

I got it then. The real reason we were having a "hunting" weekend. Why Frank would need to get away and take his handgun with him.

I grabbed my wet jacket and hurried down the narrow deer trail that was the direct path in and out of the campsite.

Sliding in places. Stumbling over loose rocks. Once, nearly biting it on a jutting tree root. But moving quickly because . . . just because.

Near the bottom, I slowed. Already, I could hear voices.

I crept the last few feet. Not all the way out of the woods. But keeping under the cover of the bushes, as I did my best to understand what was unfolding twenty feet ahead of me, roadside.

Frank was talking to a man. An older guy, in an old-fashioned tan trench coat, with a fedora on his head. Old geezer dude, no doubt about it. Sandra's father.

They stood in front of a glossy black Cadillac. Geezer dude's car, which he'd driven here, I would guess, as he didn't look to be in any kind of shape to hike to our campsite.

"You need to back off," Frank was saying. "Whatever you want with my family, my family doesn't want you."

"You always speak for your wife?"

"Please. Sandra will never speak to you, and you know it."

"Henry looks to be a good kid."

"Push this, Dave, and I will be the least of your problems. Sandra will come after you herself. You really want that?"

Silence.

"I'm dying, Frank."

"Aren't we all?"

"I got cancer. Bad. It's only a matter of time now."

Frank didn't say anything.

"Death," the guy said at last, "has a way of changing a person. Makes him see things differently."

"Repenting, old man?"

"And if I was?"

Frank shook his head. "Too little, too late."

"At least let me talk to the kid. It's not fair of her to keep my only grandson from me."

"She'll gut you like a fish."

"My daughter—"

"Learned everything she knows from you. Walk away, Dave. Consider the advice as my gift to a dying man. Walk away, or cancer will be the least of your concerns."

"I got money—"

"Don't be stupid."

"I mean I got real money. Legitimate funds. Stay in business long enough, these things happen."

"She doesn't want it."

"I am her father!"

"Which is the only reason she's let you live!" Frank's voice was cold. Colder than I'd ever heard him. I shrunk back, not sure of this hard, angry man.

"I'm dying," the old guy said again.

"Then I hope, for your own sake, you find some peace. But forgiveness from your daughter? That's out of the question. Some sins a man gets to live with. And some sins I guess you get to die with, as well."

The old man didn't say anything. Finally, he expelled a breath, which rattled ominously in his chest. He reached for his waist. I watched Frank move, arm going to the small of his back. Where he had his twenty-two, I realized.

But the old man didn't do anything. Just belted his trench coat tighter.

He stared at Frank with his rheumy eyes.

"My daughter, she's always been stubborn, but she's never been stupid. So you tell her, from me. My dying, it changes things. I'm not the only one who knows where she lives. I'm not the only one who's been keeping tabs."

"You threatening my wife, Dave?"

"My dying changes things," the old man repeated simply. Then he turned and headed back to his car.

Frank didn't leave. He stood there, hand still at the small of his back, as if he was waiting for the other shoe to drop. I found myself holding my own breath as the guy wrestled with the Cadillac's heavy door, took another rattling breath, then worked on climbing inside the vehicle.

Finally, the door shut, the engine fired to life.

Sandra's father drove away.

Frank's hand dropped from his concealed firearm.

"You can come out now," he said, without ever turning around.

Self-consciously, I withdrew from the bushes, finished hoofing it to the road.

"I didn't see anything," I said.

"Exactly."

"Didn't hear nothing, either."

"Smart."

"That really Sandra's father?"

"Yeah."

"And she hates him that much?"

"More."

"Am I still supposed to shoot him on sight?"

"Would save Sandra the hassle."

"Okay," I said.

Frank finally looked at me. "Thank you."

We turned and hiked back up the trail.

"Hey," he said presently. "I brought some face paint. Instead of going hunting, let's spend the day on woodland survival skills, starting, of course, with very important camouflage techniques."

Chapter 32

RAINIE HAD ALWAYS KNOWN parenting would have rough patches. Times when doing the right thing would mean going against her first instincts. When she would be required to be tough rather than loving, the bad guy versus her child's confidante. For example, this minute right now, seeing her daughter for the first time in hours, as the sun started to lower and the woods filled with shadows, and her heart clenched so tight in her chest it was a physical pain.

She wanted to rush out of the vehicle. She wanted to grab Sharlah in a fierce embrace. Then search her daughter, limb by limb, for signs of injury, while reassuring herself over and over that her daughter was safe, the danger had passed, Rainie could breathe again.

Sharlah walked out of the woods, and instead of rushing to her daughter's side, Rainie forced herself to remain inside the car, quiet, calm, and, of course, aware of her surroundings.

Sharlah's brother had to be someplace close. At least until recently. Because she knew her stubborn child. There was no way Sharlah had simply given up on her mission. If Sharlah had called home, it could only mean she'd gotten a chance to finally see Telly. And her older brother had sent her packing.

Her child hurt. Rainie could tell by the slump of her shoulders, the dejected line of her bowed head as Sharlah now crossed a grassy field, working her way toward Rainie's vehicle with Luka by her side. Not the kind of wounds a limb-by-limb inspection would reveal, but still . . .

Rainie climbed out of her SUV, studying the rapidly darkening woods behind her daughter. Telly had a rifle. If he was somewhere in those woods, watching her right now through his scope . . .

The woods were too shadowed to penetrate. She heard distant birds, a light wind rustle the grass, Sharlah's heavy tread. That was it.

Sharlah and Luka approached. Rainie hit the button to raise the rear hatch of her vehicle. Luka didn't need any more invitation. He bounded across the last twenty yards and leapt into Rainie's Lexus. Then, a minute later, Sharlah was there, her face sunburned, her hair sticking out in all kinds of directions, her bare arms and legs covered in scratches.

"I'm sorry," Sharlah said, and she sounded so sad, so disheartened, Rainie felt the hard knot of fear and rage in her chest dissolve just like that.

"He sent you away, didn't he?"

"He told me to live happily ever after, so at least one of us did."

"Oh, honey."

"And then"—Sharlah took a deep breath, looked right at her—"he told me he had one more person to kill."

"Get in the car," Rainie said. "I brought you some food and water. Luka, too."

"We're not going home, are we?"

"No, honey, we're not."

RAINIE DROVE STRAIGHT TO the sheriff's department. Sharlah sat beside her, not saying a word, a peanut butter and jelly sandwich untouched on her lap. Luka, on the other hand, had wolfed down a bowl of kibble. At least one member of the family was happy.

Rainie had spoken to Quincy on and off all afternoon. After the raid on Telly's camp, he and the others had headed to the sheriff's department to analyze their findings. They needed more space for spreading out the tracker's photos of Telly's notebooks, as well as access to a whiteboard for scribbling down questions, random thoughts, fresh leads. Last Rainie had heard, the motion-sensitive cameras remained at Telly's campsite. If they fired to life, SWAT would instantly mobilize. Until then, they were operating more in an investigative mode. Which would make Sharlah's report on her brother all the more interesting, not to mention Rainie's own recent discovery.

"Eat your sandwich," she told Sharlah as they approached the sheriff's office. "You're going to need your strength."

The front of the sheriff's department was still a circus of media vans and blazing lights. Which made Rainie grateful for her clearly civilian vehicle as she turned into the mob. A crush of reporters briefly descended, took in a boring-looking woman and her child, then backed away, in search of bigger prey. Rainie made it to the rear lot, which was quieter, and parked her car.

Sharlah had managed three bites of her sandwich. That was it. At least the bottle of water had been drained.

Rainie looked at her daughter, sighed.

"I love you," Rainie said abruptly.

"You're mad at me. I shouldn't have run away."

"You shouldn't have."

"You're going to ground me." Sharlah's gaze was on her lap.

"There will be consequences. Sharlah . . . Trust is hard. Especially for people like us. You, me, Quincy. We have a tendency to think we know best. And to feel more comfortable going at things alone. But arrogance, comfort, that's not what a family is about. Trusting each other, leaning on each other, that's what we're here for."

"I thought you might hurt him," Sharlah whispered. "Or worse, he might hurt you."

"I know. But that's the trust part. Instead of taking action on your own, you could've come to us. Told us your fears."

"You would've said you could handle him."

"Yes."

Sharlah appeared miserable. "I don't know if that's true," she said, finally looking up. "This new Telly . . . His face, the rifle. I don't know him at all."

"But he didn't hurt you."

"No."

"He still loves you?"

"I don't know."

"Sharlah." Rainie turned in the driver's seat so she was facing her daughter. "Maybe your brother didn't say what you hoped he would say. But did you get the chance to say what you wanted to say?"

"I told him I was sorry."

Rainie waited.

"I shouldn't have let him go, back then. I should've asked for him, demanded to see him, something. He was my brother. I should've fought harder."

"Why didn't you?"

Sharlah shook her head, glanced away.

Rainie remained quiet another heartbeat. Close, she thought. They were so close to the words Sharlah needed to say. What had really happened that night with her parents, eight years ago. What Rainie had started to suspect, after talking to the doctor earlier in the afternoon.

"Trust," Rainie whispered.

But some lessons took more than thirteen years to learn. Her troubled daughter shook her head again. Then Sharlah popped open the car door, and Rainie had no choice but to follow.

LUKA LOVED THE SHERIFF'S DEPARTMENT. He moved in a stiff-legged trot, all keen eyes and pricked-up ears. Retired police officer, returning for duty.

It was too hot to leave the German shepherd in the vehicle, even this time of night. And while Rainie would have liked to think her presence would give her daughter strength for the interview ahead, she already knew Luka made even more of a difference.

They took the stairs to the second floor, Luka leading the way. They discovered Quincy, working with three others in the conference room. The walls were covered in photos. Printouts, Rainie realized. Not the best resolution, but given that the shots appeared to be photos of old pictures and journal entries, they didn't need to be. Clustered in one corner were different images—Telly's campsite, which appeared to be a wooden pallet piled with gear in the middle of a small clearing. Nothing remarkable to her, but then Rainie's idea of a weekend away included room service.

Quincy glanced up as they entered. Luka had already found him, was nuzzling his hand. Quincy patted the dog on the head, while his gaze went briefly to Rainie's, then settled on Sharlah. Rainie could see in his face all the conflicting emotions that had earlier been in hers: relief, mixed with frustration, anger, more frustration, despair.

The joys of parenting. And they'd volunteered for this.

She answered his questioning gaze with a short nod of her own. Her signal that yes, she'd had a discussion with their daughter. Which, for now, would have to suffice, given this was not the time nor the place for Quincy to work out his own differences with Sharlah. Their daughter had returned home safe. For now, that would have to be enough.

Rainie started the ball rolling. "She saw him."

A man got up from the table, slice of pizza in hand. He wore sweat-stained hiking gear and well-used boots. The tracker, she would guess. What had Quincy said was his name? Cal Noonan. Luka trotted over, sniffed the man up and down. Seemed to deem him acceptable. For his part, the man ignored the shepherd, finished his pizza.

"Approximate location?" he asked, selecting a pushpin from the box on the table.

When picking up Sharlah, Rainie had logged the GPS coordinates on her phone. Now she held up her screen for the man to read.

"Rainie Conner," she introduced herself.

"Cal Noonan. Thanks." There was a blown-up map on the wall behind Rainie and Sharlah. Cal used a bright blue tack to mark the coordinates. Then the tracker stood back, frowned.

"That's twelve miles south of the campsite." He stared at Sharlah. "Was he still on the four-wheeler?"

Mutely, the girl shook her head.

"He had it parked somewhere?"

"N-n-no."

"But you're not sure?"

The girl shrugged, clearly uncomfortable with direct attention. "He was walking," she whispered. "Before I saw him. And um . . . afterward."

Rainie studied the floor, the desire to wrap her daughter in a protective embrace nearly overwhelming. But facts remained facts: Sharlah had run off to meet with a suspected mass murderer. And in doing so, she'd sealed her own fate regarding police interrogations, suspicious questions, and the like.

"Is that his camp?" Sharlah surprised Rainie by asking. The girl raised her hand and pointed to an array of photos opposite them.

The tracker nodded. His gaze was not unkind, Rainie thought. Just serious. A man who'd had a long day and seen two of his own shot in the line of duty. She noticed Luka remained at his side. A sign of approval of sorts. While Sheriff Atkins and her lead homicide sergeant, Roy, seemed content to let Cal do the talking. More signs of respect.

"He said you would find it," Sharlah stated now, her voice clearer.

Shelly Atkins studied the girl with fresh interest. She crossed the room, hunkering down next to Sharlah. "Say that again. Telly knew we'd find the campsite?"

"He said Henry wouldn't be able to resist telling you about it." Sharlah took a deep breath, looked the sheriff in the eye. She was trying. Rainie doubted the others in the room got it, except for Quincy of course, but shy, anxious, hate-to-be-in-the-spotlight Sharlah was trying very hard to do right. "Telly said . . . said he wanted you to find it. It would keep you busy. There, you know. You'd be inspecting the camp, while he headed south."

Cal shook his head. "Told you he was smart."

"Why was he headed south?" the sheriff asked, her gaze fixed on Sharlah's.

"I don't know."

"Did he mention a destination?"

"No." Sharlah fidgeted, shifted from side to side. The girl's voice dropped low. "Um . . . he said . . . he said I couldn't go with him. I couldn't follow, 'cause, um . . ." Sharlah's voice became even softer. "He said he had one more person left to kill."

"Who?" Quincy's voice, a whip snap across the room.

Sharlah flinched. She kept her eyes on the sheriff as she answered her father's question.

"I don't know."

"Was he armed when you saw him?" Quincy asked steadily. Not father to daughter, but profiler to witness.

Again, Rainie had to study the floor, force herself not to intervene. She had her approach. Quincy had his.

Luka, on the other hand, returned to his girl, gently nudging Sharlah's hand until it was on top of his head. Sharlah's fingers dug into the dog's fur. It seemed to bring her strength.

"Telly had a rifle," she answered clearly. "And his face." Sharlah lifted the fingers of her free hand, touched her cheeks. "He'd painted it. Streaks. When I first saw him, in front of the tree, I barely knew he was there. He could've been a bush himself. Then he opened his eyes. And that's what you saw: the whites of his eyes . . . glowing." The girl's voice drifted off. Rainie had no doubt what her daughter's nightmares would be in the days, weeks, months ahead.

The tracker spoke up. "Other supplies? Did he have a pack? Food, water?"

"He had a navy blue backpack. Same size as mine. I offered him some, um, food." Sharlah kept her body angled away from Quincy as she said this. "He said he was okay. Took some water though."

"How much?"

"Um . . . one bottle."

"Did you see any other guns?"

"No."

"What about in his pack? Could he have been carrying more rifles?"

"Um . . ." Sharlah crinkled her forehead. "Rifles, no. But the pack was heavy. Like weighed down." She glanced up. "I wondered if he'd filled it with food or ammo."

"What about handguns?" Quincy asked his daughter. "Did you see anything tucked in the waistband of his pants?"

Another head shake.

Sheriff Atkins had straightened. She regarded the adults in the room. "Handguns would fit in his pack. But the two missing long guns . . ."

"Definitely not on him," Cal muttered. "To be honest, doubt he's carrying three smaller firearms either. Would make for a pretty heavy load, and that's not including ammo. As long as he's stashing the rifles, might as well stash one or two of the handguns as well."

"He has another hidey-hole," Shelly said.

"Real camp. Versus"—Cal indicated the photo array—"the fake one he arranged for us to find."

"With a backpack filled with his personal journals and scrapbook," Quincy mused out loud. He had a look on his face Rainie recognized, where the rest of the room was disappearing and only the evidence existed for him. "Why stock a dummy campsite with such personal possessions?" Quincy asked now.

"I have a bigger question." Rainie took a deep breath. It was time. "I spent the afternoon studying the crime scene photos. I don't know what happened at the Duvalls' house this morning or with the tracking team this afternoon. But the shooting at the EZ Gas . . . Telly didn't do it. And I can prove it."

"FORENSIC FRECKLE ANALYSIS," Rainie said. She slipped a folder out of her bag. Now, with everyone staring, including Sharlah, she removed a stack of images from the EZ Gas security camera and started spreading them out on a corner of the conference room table. "Quincy and I once worked a case where a murderer was identified through forensic freckle analysis. Basically, the odds of any other person having the exact same pattern of freckles as the ones seen in the photos the killer had taken of himself with his victims . . . Ever since then, I've had a tendency to look at freckles."

Rainie tapped her photo array. The first photo was of a bare arm, protruding through the EZ Gas door, pointing a gun at the male victim. Next came a similarly awkward view, disembodied forearm now pointed at the cashier. Finally, the main image that had captured their attention first thing this morning: Telly Ray Nash, fully visible, staring straight at the camera, as he pulled the trigger.

"Not great resolution," Rainie said, "given that the security footage records in grainy black-and-white. In each still frame, however, the shooter's wrist and a good portion of his forearm are clearly visible. Look at them. Then you tell me."

Quincy crossed to the photo array first, Sharlah almost immediately behind him. Father-daughter differences already seemed forgotten as they both peered down, studied the images intently.

"In the off-camera shots," Quincy said, "the forearm is thicker. And there's a blemish of some kind, maybe a large mole, two inches above the wrist."

"Telly doesn't have the dark spot," Sharlah said excitedly. "His wrist is clear!"

Now Shelly Atkins and Roy Peterson jostled close. "I don't get it," the sheriff said at last. "Looking at this, Telly shot the security camera—"

"But he didn't shoot the victims?" the tracker finished in confusion, peering over Shelly's shoulder.

Rainie nodded. "When I spoke to the family counselor earlier today, she mentioned an incident at Telly's previous foster home—his placement before the Duvalls. The foster mom accused Telly of stealing. Telly never denied the charges; he simply left. Later, however, the mom learned a different child had been the one taking things."

Shelly stared at her. "You're saying Telly shot up the security camera because he likes taking the blame for things?"

"I think he's *used* to taking the blame for things." Rainie glanced at her daughter. "Which is knowledge that would come in handy if you were a real killer looking for a patsy."

"Someone is setting him up," Quincy filled in. He cocked his head to the side. "You think for the Duvalls' murders as well? A boy with Telly's past . . . He does make for an excellent pawn."

"But why would he take the blame?" Sharlah spoke up, frowning. "Why shoot the camera at the gas station? Why not just ask for help?"

"I have a theory," Rainie said softly. She eyed her daughter again. "Those photos we found of you in the Duvalls' garage. I don't think those were pictures taken by Telly as a threat to you. I think they were taken by someone else and sent to Telly as a warning."

"Telly cooperates," Quincy said.

"Or Sharlah gets hurt." Rainie placed a hand on her daughter's shoulder. "Zero or hero. All these years later, I think Telly is still trying to save you."

Chapter 33

QUINCY FOUND SHARLAH SITTING in the corridor outside the conference room. She had her back against the rough cinder-block wall, one hand on Luka, who was stretched out before her, her backpack at her feet. The dog didn't seem to mind the worn linoleum flooring. Quincy figured he could survive it as well.

He took a seat next to Sharlah. Forearms on his knees. Head against the wall. They stayed like that for quite some time. Man. Daughter. Dog. Years ago, the family counselor had explained to Quincy and Rainie that in no time at all, they would stop thinking of Sharlah as a foster child and simply consider her their own. For Quincy, at least, that process had seemed to happen quickly. Sharlah felt as much his flesh and blood as Kimberly and, to be honest, probably more so than his oldest daughter, Mandy, whom he'd loved dearly but rarely understood at all.

He and Sharlah, on the other hand . . . She was so much like a chip off the old block. Which is why he didn't speak right away. Sharlah preferred silence, and Quincy certainly wasn't one to argue with that. Besides, after the day they'd all had, silence was good.

Luka yawned. Sharlah patted his side.

"Penny for your thoughts," Quincy said at last.

"I want to go home."

"Me too."

She turned to him. "But you won't."

"We still have an active-shooter situation. As long as that's the case . . ."

"Telly's innocent," Sharlah said stubbornly. "You heard Rainie."

"Of the EZ Gas shooting maybe. Yet still, damage has been done. His foster parents, the search team. Maybe soon enough, this mystery person your brother claims he still has to kill."

Sharlah looked down, sighed miserably.

"What do you want, Sharlah?" Quincy asked softly. "If you could rule the world, what would you do?"

"I'd turn back time," she said immediately. "I'd go back to when it was just me and Telly and our parents. Except this time, I'd hide all the alcohol in the house. Round it up, dump it down the sink. Drugs, too. I'd find them. Flush them down the toilet."

"And the knives?"

"I would only allow plastic silverware in the house," she said solemnly.

"The baseball bat?"

"Toothpicks. We'd eat with plastic forks and play little miniature games of baseball using toothpicks and tiny balls of lint."

"You and Telly would grow up with your parents. Do you think they'd love you more?"

"Telly would. He'd take care of me. He always did. Except this time around, I'd take care of him, too. For each other, we'd be enough."

"And your parents?" Quincy asked again.

Sharlah shook her head. "Telly and I, we'd be enough."

"In this scenario," Quincy continued after a minute, "you and I, we'd never meet. No, you, me, Rainie."

"In this scenario, you'd get another kid. One who doesn't run away. Who listens to you. Who even has a gift for, say, um, policing things. I know. Deductive reasoning, like Sherlock Holmes. You and Rainie will train her and she'll turn into a supercop and set records for how many serial killers she puts away."

"You think we wouldn't miss you? Feel this empty hole in our lives, where you would've been?"

Sharlah shrugged. "Maybe. But you'll be so busy with your new daughter's award ceremonies, you'll get over it. Besides, you and Rainie, you'll always be okay, with or without someone. Whereas Telly . . ."

"He needs you?"

"He's alone. He's totally alone. And it's my fault." Sharlah turned away, stroked Luka's fur.

"Where is Luka in this new and improved world order? If you stay with your family, if Rainie and I never meet you . . ."

For the first time, Sharlah's expression faltered. Quincy could see tears gathering in her eyes. She loved Luka with a bone-deep purity that made him hopeful someday she could love another human being that much.

"Telly and I will adopt a stray," she whispered. "A cat. Who will sleep with us at night, flexing her razor-sharp claws if anyone bad tries to open the door. Telly will be the only one able to handle the cat. And my father will back off, just because he doesn't want to make the cat mad."

In other words, in the new world order, Sharlah would sacrifice her dog. Give up her precious Luka, so Telly could have a guard cat instead. Meaning Sharlah would still be serving penance. For what? What had she done that was so terrible, that even if she went back in time and that final night with their parents never happened, she still owed her brother everything?

"I know you love your brother," Quincy said.

His daughter shot him a scornful look. From vulnerable child to full-on teenager, just like that. And yet another reminder that his daughter was only growing in one direction—away from him.

"Whatever he's doing now," Quincy continued steadily, "whomever he's become, he's still your brother and, by all accounts, he cares about you very much."

Less scorn. More uncertainty.

"You don't want your brother hurt. That's why if you were in charge of the world, you would go back in time. To save him. But there's more to it than that, isn't there? You don't just want him safe; you want you two to be together again, big brother, little sister."

She didn't say a word.

"That's why you went to him. To help. To be his little sister. And when he sent you away . . . that must've really hurt. I'm sorry, Sharlah. Sorry you had to hurt like that."

She moved. Just slightly. But it was enough. Quincy lifted his arm and she ducked under, tucking against his chest.

No words again. Quincy placed his cheek against the top of her head and did his best to just breathe in this moment. Rare. Fleeting. And doomed to be over soon enough.

"I don't know who he is," Sharlah murmured against his chest. "This new Telly, I don't know him at all."

"He still loves you."

"Because he didn't hurt me?"

"Because in his pack—in with his journals, the scrapbook, his most personal possessions—he had a library copy of *Clifford the Big Red Dog*."

"Our story. The one he read to me."

"Maybe if Telly could be in charge of the world, he would build a time machine, too. And in his new world, you and he would never go home. You'd stay in the library, together forever."

"Reading books," Sharlah whispered. "While eating the librarian's snacks."

"Sounds like a good childhood to me."

Sharlah drew back. Quincy didn't stop her. He let her retreat, gather her thoughts.

"Rainie's going to take me home," Sharlah said. A statement, not a question. "She and Luka will stand guard there, while you stay here, working on finding my brother."

Quincy nodded.

"And if you find him?"

"Sharlah, do you know what a great profiler does?"

She shook her head.

"He takes all the statistics and probabilities that help define crim-inal behavior and still does his best to think outside the box. Hu-mans are complex. At the end of the day, there is no equation yet for predicting the full spectrum of possible human behavior."

"I don't know what that means."

"It means if there's any way to help your brother, I'll find it. We still don't know at this point what all he's done or not done. But if Rainie's correct and he's being set up, I'll do my best to figure it out. I will do my best to bring your brother home safe."

"Thank you."

Quincy hugged his daughter. Not long. Not hard. She had her boundaries, and it was his job to respect them. But then she sur-prised him by hugging back. He took that moment, recognized it for the magic that it was. A gift. One he'd have suffered through dozens of terrible afternoons just to experience again.

"You were wrong about your time machine," he whispered. "If we'd never met you . . . Rainie and I would've felt more than simply a hole in our lives. Becoming foster parents isn't about changing a child's life, Sharlah. It's about you changing ours. Thank you for being part of our family."

"I'm sorry I hurt you," she said.

"I know. And for what might happen next, you have my apolo-gies, too."

QUINCY FOLLOWED SHARLAH AND LUKA back into the conference room. Rainie was standing in front of the far wall, gazing at the pho-tographs Cal Noonan had taken of Telly's scrapbook pages. Sharlah went to join her, immediately riveted by the collage of Telly's baby picture, school photos, and, yes, images of their family.

Quincy hung back, taking in the scene. It occurred to him that Sharlah had probably never viewed these photos and, being so young when she was removed from the home, probably didn't even remember what much of her birth family looked like.

The first photo, posted eye level, featured a gurgling baby boy. Telly Ray Nash, seventeen years ago. Sharlah paused, then reached up and very lightly touched the baby's pudgy cheek. No one stopped her. The visuals were just printouts, nothing fingerprints could damage. Not to mention . . .

The pictures had been just pictures. Images collected at a crime scene. But now, with Sharlah hungrily gazing at these remnants of her childhood, the photos came to life. They became memories of a family, before the worst had torn them apart.

Sharlah moved along the wall, one hand on Luka, as Rainie, becoming aware of their daughter's presence, stood off to the side. Like Quincy, she studied Sharlah as the girl consumed images from the first five years of her life.

Sharlah's mom appeared ordinary enough, Quincy thought. Five-year-old son balanced on her lap as she held a bottle for her infant daughter, strapped in a baby carrier. The woman was smiling faintly in the picture. She had Sharlah's dark hair, hazel eyes. Her face was thin, hair stringy. Upon closer examination, you could see that the woman's flowered top was frayed at the edges, while the baby carrier appeared secondhand. Definitely not a wealthy family, but still . . .

The wall of photos presented a family. Any family. Every family. Posing for the world, while holding their secrets close.

"Are these my parents?" Sharlah asked softly. She'd paused before the one group photo, taken in front of a white building. Mom, dad, seven- or eight-year-old Telly, toddler Sharlah.

"I would assume so," Rainie provided.

Sharlah leaned forward. Not looking at her mom but staring intently at the image of her father.

"Telly looks just like him," Sharlah said quietly.

"Do you remember your father?" Quincy asked.

"Nah. He's all distorted in my mind. Big red face. Bulging eyes. Like, you know, some monster in a movie."

"And your mom?" Rainie spoke up.

"I think she loved us," Sharlah said, and now her voice wasn't so steady. Luka whined, licked her hand. "She just . . . didn't love us enough."

Sharlah reached the final photo.

"That's my grandpa?" The picture showed an old man in a tan trench coat and dark fedora, standing near a gray-painted garage.

"I guess," Rainie said, looking back at Quincy.

Sharlah touched her face, then the old man. She shook her head.

"I don't know. The other photos . . . Even if I didn't remember them, I *remember* them, you know? They're like . . . exactly as I imagined. But this one, the grandpa. I don't get this one." Sharlah frowned. "Wait, if I had a grandpa, how did I end up in the foster care system? Wouldn't he have taken us in?"

Quincy had moved over to where she stood. Now he studied the final image as well. "You don't remember this man?"

"No. But like I said"—Sharlah shrugged—"I don't exactly remember anyone."

"Maybe he died when you were still a baby," Rainie suggested. "Which is why he wasn't available to take you and Telly in. According to the state, you had no surviving relatives."

Quincy was still frowning. Something about this photo . . . "The background," he said abruptly. "The garage behind the man. Does it look familiar to you, Rainie? Because I'd swear I've seen it before . . ."

Quincy's voice drifted off. Then suddenly, he whirled on Shelly, who was still studying the EZ Gas photos. "The color of the siding. This corner of the garage door. This is the *Duvalls' house*. This man is standing in front of Frank and Sandra's garage. I know it."

Sharlah looked up in confusion as Shelly crossed to them quickly, the tracker as well. Shelly and Noonan had been with Quincy at the Duvalls' house just this afternoon. Now they both studied the background of the photo.

"Definitely could be the Duvalls' place," Shelly agreed.

"Not that long ago either," Noonan supplied. "There in the corner. That green is a clump of daylilies, just growing in. I noticed them this afternoon, because I hadn't seen such a dark orange bloom before. But late spring, early summer, the foliage would look something like that."

"Assuming it's this year," Shelly said.

"Telly wasn't living with the Duvalls last summer," Quincy murmured. "Which makes this year a good bet."

"Meaning?" Rainie studied him. She had put one arm around Sharlah, who still appeared bewildered.

"Telly has a scrapbook filled with images from his childhood, except for this final photo," Quincy said. "This picture features an old man in front of his foster family's house. No foster parents present. Just the old man. Meaning the man came to see Telly, has a connection to Telly, not the Duvalls?"

"Long-lost grandparent?" Rainie tried on. "Had lost contact with Telly and Sharlah's parents? Now trying to reconnect?"

Shelly looked at them. "Wouldn't he have to go through the system? Meaning you would've received a call from foster care as well? Especially, you know, as you've started adoption proceedings."

Which the appearance of a long-lost relative would certainly complicate.

"We didn't get any calls," Quincy said.

"Could the guy be a relative of the Duvalls?" Noonan asked.

"Telly didn't even include photos of Frank and Sandra in the album. Why omit his foster parents but include one of their relatives?"

No one had an answer for that.

Quincy exited the group circle, pacing now.

"Notebooks, journals, personal scrapbook," Quincy muttered, making it one length of the conference table. "No logic to bringing such items to a staged camp. Not like you search a hiker's pack and are surprised he *didn't* bring his photo album camping. So why these items? What is Telly trying to tell us?"

"Zero or hero," Rainie murmured.

Quincy glanced at her. "Last page of Telly's notebook, he wrote *hero.*"

"Because he's trying to save me," Sharlah said stubbornly.

"From a frail old man?" Rainie glanced again at the photo, tone clearly dubious.

"Telly's cell phone," Quincy said. "Left behind in Frank's truck, with the photos of Sharlah on it. He meant for those images to spook us. He wanted us watching Sharlah, keeping her close."

"Because he was too busy shooting up my tracking team to do it himself?" Noonan said bitterly.

Quincy couldn't argue with that. "This photo, it's a message, too. We need to identify this old man. And fast."

A knock. The group turned to find one of the county detectives, Rebecca Chasen, standing in the doorway, holding a sheet of paper. "Ah, Roy," the woman said. "Need you for a sec."

The homicide sergeant crossed over. He lowered his head as Detective Chasen murmured something low in his ear.

"You're sure about that?" he asked sharply.

In response, she held up the paperwork.

Roy nodded, then returned his attention to the room, fax in hand.

"ME ran the Duvalls' fingerprints as a matter of protocol. Got a hit: While Frank Duvall really is Frank Duvall, Sandra, on the other hand . . . According to her prints, Telly's foster mom's real name is Irene Gemetti. And she's currently wanted for questioning in a thirty-year-old murder."

Chapter 34

Henry Duvall had taken a room at one of the cheap motels lining the coastal highway. Given it was the height of the tourist season, Shelly was amazed the man had found a room at all. The motel was basically a long white building, set back from the road, each room opening up to the parking lot. A blinking red light advertised: CHEAP & CLEAN. Beneath that, the promise of free Wi-Fi.

Shelly had called ahead, so Henry was waiting for them, backlit by the glow of his room as he stood in the open doorway, watching them pull into the parking lot. He was wearing the same shorts and shirt from before, but his hiking boots were off. Standing in just his socks, he seemed smaller, more vulnerable. The grieving son, she thought, except she was no longer convinced.

Shelly had taken time to don a fresh shirt, which looked exactly like her original brown dress uniform but smelled better. Quincy hadn't even managed that much. He'd scrubbed his face and arms in the department's bathroom. That was it.

The air in the parking lot felt thick and sluggish when they climbed out of Shelly's SUV. A strange combination for a town that had always associated summers with cool coastal breezes. The ocean was supposed to be their salvation, not their punishment.

Shelly could already feel beads of sweat prickling her hairline, gluing her new dress shirt to her torso, as she led Quincy to Henry's room. The man stepped back, wordlessly inviting them in.

The space offered a sagging double bed, beat-up dresser topped with a flat-screen TV, and little else. A wall-mounted air-conditioning unit chugged sluggishly, making an ominous rattling sound. If it had cooled the room at all, the temperature change was purely incidental.

Henry shrugged, as if reading their assessment of his cheap room on their faces. "I would say it's a step up from camping," he said, "but maybe only half a step up. At least camping, my buddies and I had a stream for cooling off."

Shelly wondered where those buddies were now. Surely if you'd just learned your parents were murdered, you'd call in some friends for support? So far, her detectives hadn't found any records indicating Henry had been in town two weeks ago, hanging with his foster brother at the EZ Gas. But the investigation was still early and her officers were overworked. Shelly wasn't willing to make any assumptions when it came to Henry Duvall. The more they learned, the more she was becoming convinced the Duvall family held the key to today's shootings, not Telly Ray Nash.

"Want water?" Henry asked belatedly. "I have water. Some snacks."

"We have some questions regarding your family," Shelly said. She placed her hands on her hips. Her official sheriff's stance, devised to make her appear larger, more intimidating. In contrast, Quincy hung back. Not necessarily the good cop, but the less noticeable one as he discreetly took in the room, made his own observations. Shelly and Quincy had worked this gig a few times before, hence Shelly's decision to bring him along.

Henry nodded. He moved to the bed, the only available sitting option, and perched awkwardly on the edge of the mattress.

"Does the name Irene Gemetti mean anything to you?" Quincy asked now, voice drifting innocuously over Shelly's shoulder.

Henry frowned. He could hear the profiler but not see the man's face. "No. Should it?"

"What about your mother's past? Friends, family members?"

"My mother didn't talk about her past."

"You mean she never mentioned her parents?" Shelly asked. "Or, like, she never told stories from the good old days?"

"I mean all of the above. My mom had a strict policy about not looking back. Every time I asked, I got the same answer: She'd left home at sixteen, gotten in some kind of trouble, then met my father, at which point her real life began. That's all I needed to know. Beginning. Middle. The end."

"You had to be curious." Quincy again, having moved away from Shelly and Henry completely, now checking out the door to the rear bathroom. "What did your father have to say?"

"'Go ask your mom.'"

Shelly's turn, redirecting Henry's attention, keeping it split between her and Quincy: "She never talked about her parents? Not once?"

"Her father wasn't a nice guy. That's all I was ever told. Bad enough, I guess, that even after leaving, she still wanted no part of him. No visits, no cards, no phone calls. Nothing." Henry shrugged. "Of course I wondered. I mean, what is very bad? Or maybe, what's so bad in this day and age of Oprah that you still can't talk about it? But my mom never budged on the subject. At a certain point, I'm only the kid. If she wasn't going to talk about it, that's that."

"Irene Gemetti," Shelly stated.

But Henry shook his head, appearing just as confused as before. "I don't understand."

"You ever Google your mother's name? Look into her past yourself?" Quincy reappeared from the back of the room.

Henry flushed. "Maybe."

Quincy and Shelly waited.

"There's a lot of Sandra Duvalls out there," Henry supplied at last. "Eight or nine. Only record I could find of my mom was her own Facebook page. Let's just say she was bigger on posting Crock-Pot recipes than family secrets."

"But Duvall is her married name," Quincy pointed out.

"Which occurred to me, too. But where to go from there? Not like she was going to tell me that much. And searching for Sandras in Oregon—"

"She wasn't from Bakersville?"

"No. My father brought her here. That much I know. They met in Portland. Had some kind of whirlwind, love-at-first-sight thing. Married, like, in a matter of weeks. Then my father graduated with his teaching degree from PSU and they came here. Bakersville is my father's hometown. He always said there was no place else he'd rather live.

"You know what I realized?" Henry said suddenly. "There aren't any photos of my mom. I mean, like, anywhere. Her Facebook page doesn't have a profile pic. And all the images she posts—they're of me, my dad, or maybe pictures of food or a flower in the garden. But no pictures of her. I even went around the house, looking for a wedding photo, snapshots of her and my father. Nope. I found my senior class photos, a couple of shots of my dad and me from some camping trips. But none of my mom."

"You ask your dad about it?" Shelly asked.

"Sure. He said it was just how things were—the one who's always taking the pictures is the one who's never in them. But zero photos? Seriously?"

Quincy spoke up. "Why were you looking for photos of your mom?"

Henry resumed his study of the carpet. His shoulders were bunched. Shelly could feel the tension radiating from the young man. The weight of untold secrets.

Shelly took a step forward. "Irene Gemetti. You know that name."

"Swear to God. Have no idea—"

"But you know something."

"It doesn't matter! Telly's the one who shot them—"

"Shot who? Your parents? The mom with no photos, no past?" Shelly piled it on. "Who died in your house today, Henry? Have you asked yourself that? Who was Sandra Duvall? And why the hell are you still protecting her secrets?"

"I don't know—"

"Your mother's real name: Irene Gemetti. A woman still wanted for questioning in a thirty-year-old homicide."

"What?" Henry popped up straight. His eyes widened.

If the kid was an actor, Shelly thought, he was the best she'd ever seen.

"My mother's name is Irene? She's wanted for murder? What?" Then in the next heartbeat: "The bad thing she did when she was sixteen. She wasn't kidding. Holy shit. My mother. Holy shit." Henry sat down again, staring blindly at the carpet.

Shelly studied him, trying to figure out how to proceed, when Quincy came up next to her. He grabbed the case file Shelly had tucked beneath her arm. He flipped through it quickly. Until:

"There." He thrust out the photo of the old man standing before the Duvalls' garage. "Who is that man? You know. Now tell me!"

Henry looked up, back to appearing dazed and confused. "It doesn't matter—"

"*Who is this man!*"

"My grandfather!" Henry suddenly rocketed off the bed, face flushed. "My mother's father. Pop Gemetti, I guess. He found me. Showed up one day outside one of my college classes. Said he wanted to get to know me. That he was excited to learn he had a grandson. But he didn't go by Gemetti. He called himself David Michael, David Martin, something like that. And he never mentioned any Irene anything."

"You met with him? You spoke to your mother's father?" Shelly pressed.

"No. I mean, I saw him that once, but then . . . Damn it!" Henry whirled away, walked two steps, hit the bedside table, and stopped. His head came down. He sighed heavily, clearly realizing there was no place to run, no place to hide. The truth was often like that.

"I came home on spring break. Okay?" He turned back around. "I asked my father about the old geezer dude. Didn't approach my mother, because I knew that would end badly. So I asked my dad if my mother's father was still alive, and hey, could I get to know him, because I was pretty sure he wanted to get to know me. You know what my father said? Absolutely, positively not. That if I loved my mother at all, I'd forget my long-lost grandfather had ever appeared. I tried to argue. I mean, whatever had happened between my mom and her dad, that was, like, thirty years ago, right?"

Quincy and Shelly waited.

"And the guy was so . . . *old*. Maybe he wanted to repent, mend fences, that kind of thing. All these years later, what could it hurt?" Henry shook his head. "No dice. According to my father, my grandfather was some kind of notorious criminal. Or spawn of Satan. Hell if I understood it. If I loved my mother at all, I'd forget I'd ever seen the man and, better yet, never ever mention him. End of story."

"But you're not the man's daughter," Shelly stated bluntly. "You're his grandson. Surely you have a right to a relationship of your own."

Henry immediately flushed again. "I thought about that," he muttered. "But then my dad . . . He wanted me to consider why my grandfather was suddenly appearing now. I mean, if he'd found us after all these years and really wanted to make peace, why not contact my mom directly? Instead, he just happened to track down his one relative with a reputation for computer skills. . . ."

"Your father thought your grandfather was recruiting you," Shelly said. "For his criminal enterprise?"

"Crime bosses need IT guys, too. At least that's what my father implied."

"What did you do?" Quincy asked.

"Nothing. I returned to school. Kept an eye out, but he never showed up again. Then, shortly after I started my co-op program for the summer, my dad called me. Said the matter was over. My grandfather had died. Cancer."

"When was this?" Shelly asked.

"Um, a month ago. July?"

"Did you believe him?"

"I tried Googling the name. David Michael. David Martin. David Michael Martin. Let's just say, lots of Davids out there, but none that come up as evil incarnate, recently deceased."

"Another alias," Shelly muttered, jotting down a note.

Quincy had a better question: "How did your father find out about your grandfather's death?"

"I guess my dad ended up having his own little chat with him. Told him to stay away from my mom, our family. That kind of macho stuff."

"At your house?"

"And risk my mom finding out? God no. Dad took Telly hiking. Arranged for a rendezvous with Gramps in the woods."

"With Telly present? Telly has met your grandfather?"

"Met him? Not that I know of. Heard about him? Sure. Telly was there the day I first talked about the old man contacting me at school. When my father said we were never to speak with the guy, he was talking to both Telly and me. There might have also been something like, 'And if you do see a geezer dude hanging around the house, shoot first, question later, and save Mom the hassle.' "

"And Telly agreed to these terms?"

"We both did."

"So who met with your grandfather at your house?"

"He never came to the house."

"Henry, look at the photo. Where is this man standing?" Quincy held up the image from Telly's scrapbook again. He tapped the garage in the background. Shelly watched as slowly but surely, Henry got it.

"That's our garage. He's standing in front of my house. Before he died, my grandfather came to the house. . . . But why? Dad said my mom would kill him on sight."

"Unless he didn't come to see your mom," Shelly said. "First he tried you. Then your dad. And then . . ."

Henry's face went pale. "Son of a bitch. Telly. Even after everything Dad told him, Telly met with my grandfather. Son of a bitch. He sold out my parents!"

"Henry, are you sure your grandfather is dead?" Quincy asked again.

Henry shook his head.

Chapter 35

I DIDN'T SEE ANYONE *when I first walked through the door. Seven* P.M. *Thursday night. I'd had a meeting with Aly, my probation officer. My junior year officially done, summer school about to begin. She said she was pleased with my progress. I'm glad one of us was.*

Aly liked to meet at this downtown diner, famous for its malts. She thought cheeseburgers and fries were the world's most perfect food. In the beginning, I'd figured that was just something she said to get on a kid's good side. Having watched her eat the last couple of times, I took it back. For a little thing, she could really toss it down.

At least our meetings weren't so bad. Tonight, I'd kind of looked forward to it. Aly understood my relationship with school. She didn't expect me to magically turn into a star student. But she wanted me to learn how to survive. More focus, fewer outbursts. And she'd gotten me permission to carry my iPod in summer school, so I could listen to it between classes.

"Music for you is a tool. Use your tools, Telly. That's what they're there for."

So I had eight weeks of summer classes and hallway music to look forward to. Then my senior year. Last year to get my life on track. Last year with the Duvalls.

I wondered if other kids, the kind with real homes, looked forward to graduation. Or if everyone was as terrified as I was.

I didn't understand the noise at first. I dropped my backpack on the floor of the entryway closet. Kicked off my sneakers. Stuck my iPod in my back pocket. Then it finally registered. Sniffles. Sobs.

Someone crying.

I stilled in the entryway, not knowing what to do.

Sandra. Had to be Sandra. Who else would be crying in the house?

I crept forward, peered into the kitchen. Nothing. Then the family room. Nothing.

Finally down the hall toward her bedroom. Door was cracked open, sound definitely louder there.

I knocked lightly, not sure if I should disturb her. "You . . . um, okay?" I asked at last.

Sniffle. Ragged sob.

Slowly, I pushed the door open. Sandra sat on the edge of the bed. She wore the same summer skirt and frilly blouse I'd seen her in this morning. Now, however, she was surrounded by a pile of used tissues, glass of water in her hand.

She looked up when I walked in. Nose red. Eyes puffy. She didn't say anything. Just stared at me as I shifted from foot to foot.

"Frank around?" I asked hopefully.

She shook her head.

I kind of knew that, though I'd wanted a different answer. Frank had been gone a lot lately. Going where, doing what, I didn't know. Sometimes I got the impression Sandra didn't know either. But she didn't press him on the subject, and neither did I.

"It's okay to be sad," she said abruptly.

"Okay."

"People like you and me. We understand. For every gain, there's a loss. Some days, you have to mourn your losses."

It occurred to me for the first time that she was slurring her words. Sandra, whom I'd never seen touch as much as a drop of wine, definitely had something other than water in that glass. Straight vodka? Tequila? Where'd she even gotten it? The Duvalls were pretty careful about alcohol in the house, fostering a troubled teen and all. Every now and then, Frank would bring home a six-pack of beer. But hard alcohol? No way.

I advanced farther in the room, worried now.

"You, uh, want me to call someone?"

"Do you miss them?" Sandra whispered.

"Who?" But then I knew. I knew exactly who she was talking about. I stilled, hands in my pockets. It finally occurred to me what was going on here. Sandra was having herself a pity party. She was missing her family. Just like some days, every day, I missed mine.

She stared at me now, so hard I had to look away.

"Did you have any brothers or sisters?" I asked.

"No. Just me. Only child. Lucky duck."

"I miss my sister," I heard myself say.

"My mother died."

"Today? I'm sorry—"

"Five years ago. Breast cancer. I heard about it later. Never called her, you know. Never looked back. She died, and I never even got to tell her good-bye."

"You loved her."

"I hated her! I hated her for being so weak. For marrying that man. For letting him raise his voice, raise his fist, for letting him do everything he did. I loathed him. But I hated her. Especially toward the end. When I'd turned just as mean as he was, and she didn't do a thing to stop me."

I didn't know what to say anymore. Or maybe I did. "My mom was sad," I murmured. "That's what I remember the most. That when she was sad, she was so sad. But then, when she was happy, she was so happy. When I was little, I used to wish she'd be happier more."

"Your father killed her."

I didn't bother to correct her.

"With a knife. I read your story and I picked you, Telly. From all

the kids, I picked you. Because I know what it sounds like when a knife slides home. I know what blood feels like, dripping down your hands. Frank doesn't. He tries to understand. But he's only gutted animals. And it's not the same, is it, Telly? Is it?"

"I'm sorry your mother's dead," I said.

"I'm sorry your mother is dead, too," she replied solemnly. Then she started crying again and picked up another tissue.

"You should call your sister," she said after a while. "Frank has the number, he got all the information. You could have her over for dinner. I'll make that god-awful boxed mac and cheese."

"Thank you," I said, which wasn't really an answer. Frank had been bugging me about Sharlah, too. Closure, everyone thought I needed closure. I'd shattered my baby sister's arm. So, like, what? Meeting her now, staring at her scar, would magically make me feel better?

"You're not going to call," Sandra said. "You're scared."

"No."

"Yes."

"I'm ashamed," I said bluntly. Because I could talk to this drunk Sandra. And she could talk to me, too.

"I hit my mom," she said.

This was interesting. I moved closer.

"Frank, I let him think I left home because my father abused us. But that's only half the truth—my father was a cold, merciless son of a bitch. But I mostly left home because one day, I shoved my mother down the stairs. And it wasn't even the first time I'd yelled at her or hit her or slapped her. Probably not even the twentieth. See, by the time I was twelve, I'd figured out I could be the object of my father's torture or his partner in crime. So I made my choice. I became his daughter. And he was so fucking proud of me."

I didn't move. I didn't want her to stop talking. Even if I couldn't begin to understand this strange, surreal truth. Happy homemaker Sandra, cook-your-favorite-meal Sandra, a secret abuser.

"My mother didn't cry when she landed. It was the total silence *that scared me. For a minute, I thought she was dead. I found myself looking at my hands. Realizing, for the first time, what I'd done. And knowing that I could do it again and again. Would do it again and again. She'd never stop me.*

"Did she love me that much?" Sandra whispered. "Or did she hate me that much? That's the question I've never been able to answer. Who lets their kid turn into such a monster? My father, at least he was honest in his cruelty. It was my mother I could never understand. Eventually, she got up. She limped to the kitchen. She started dinner, never saying a word. And I realized . . . I realized I couldn't live like that anymore."

"You ran away."

"It was my only option. If my father knew I was leaving, he wouldn't have hit me. He would've killed me for sure."

"Why?"

"Because I belonged to him. Just like my mother. And my father wasn't the type to share his toys."

"But . . . you're crying over them."

She glanced up at me. "Don't you still cry for yours?"

She had me. I took a seat on the floor. She held up her glass, but I shook my head.

"I don't drink much," she said now, tone apologetic. "And I try not to cry too much either. What's done is done. And Frank, he's such a good man. I was so lucky. I am so lucky. I know that."

"But some days . . . ," I said.

"Some days . . . ," she agreed.

"You told me it would get better. When I got a family of my own, I wouldn't miss my parents so much."

"I lied." She took a swig from her glass. "Honestly, do you really want to hear that you will forever have a hole in your heart, feel your parents' loss like a phantom limb? Does that help you? Make you feel any better?"

"No."

"Then forget I said anything. You will live happily ever after. Some girl will sweep you off your feet. Then you'll have two bright shining children and never know struggle and disappointment. Better now?"

"You're disappointed in Henry?"

"God no. But I do sometimes wish he wasn't such an arrogant little shit. Computer genius. Bah."

I really liked drunk Sandra. "Thank you for teaching me how to make chicken Parm."

"Pissed him off, didn't it? Well, he has his father. They like to speak geek. It's only fair I now have a child, too. So there. To you and me, because for all their book smarts, they'll still never know the kinds of things we know."

She lifted her glass again. I had to look away. She'd called me her child. Her and me. I was crying. I knew I was crying. I just couldn't help myself.

"Is your father really evil?" I heard myself ask.

"Yes."

"Because he drank, did drugs?"

"No, honey. Because God made him that way, and he liked it. Your father had an excuse. My father doesn't."

"My father was drunk the night he attacked us," I said. "But it doesn't give him an excuse. To put it in your words, God made him an addict and he liked it. He was happier that way."

"You had to kill him, Telly. Don't feel guilty about it. You were only a little kid. You did what you had to do."

"Maybe I should've run away. Taken my sister with me."

"And maybe I should've killed my father, saved my mother. See, neither of us will ever know."

"You still look up your family. That's how you know your mother died?"

"Yes."

"And your father?"

"You mean the frail old man now stalking my son at college and scurrying around to secret meetings with my husband?"

My eyes widened. "You know about that?"

"Frank likes to think he's protecting me. But I've never needed his protection. At the end of the day, I am still my father's daughter."

"Are you going to see him? Grant . . . forgiveness?"

"If your father was still alive, if he'd only injured you and you had only injured him . . . would you want to see him now? Would you feel better offering forgiveness?"

"I don't know. I don't have that option." Except that wasn't really true. There was Sharlah, always Sharlah. Would she feel better if she had a chance to forgive me? Would I feel better if I had a chance to forgive her, too?

Sandra knew the sound of a knife snick-snickering against human flesh. But I also knew the sound of a baseball bat, crunching bone.

"My father doesn't want forgiveness," Sandra said now. She raised the glass, downed the final gulp. "Even riddled with cancer, he's not that kind of man."

"Then what does he want?"

"In my wildest dreams: He wants me to kill him before the cancer does. At least it would be an interesting proposition."

I didn't have anything to say.

"My father's rich," she said. "Stinking, filthy rich. Offshore-funds, secreted-money kind of rich. Live-in-mansions-all-over-the-world-on-ill-gotten-gains kind of rich. In theory, it could all be mine. Kill the king. Long live the queen, and all that."

She smiled, but it was grim. And in that moment, she wasn't drunk Sandra or foster-mom Sandra. She was a woman I didn't know at all.

"You're going to kill your father?"

"Well, if he uses his nice voice . . ."

"You spoke to him."

"No." Her voice suddenly faltered. "Because that's the kicker. All these years later, I still don't trust myself to be around him. I think mostly, he will make me feel small and weak and helpless again. Would you do me a favor, Telly? Would you kill my father for me? I could get you a baseball bat."

I shook my head. "Sorry, I only kill drunk guys chasing my baby sister with knives."

"It's funny, isn't it? All the ways we grow up, promise ourselves we'll do better. And all the many more ways we never change at all."

"I'm sorry," I said, though I wasn't sure what I was apologizing for. Declining her offer to murder her father, or recognizing the pain he obviously brought her?

"Thank you for being part of my new family, Telly," she said. "Frank and Henry love me. But there are things I can't tell them. Things I think only you can understand. We are kindred spirits of sorts. And for that, I'm sorry for both of us."

She smiled sadly. But I didn't return the look. I didn't mind being her kindred spirit. It felt like an honor to me.

"If worst comes to worst," I heard myself say, "I'll help you."

"He's going to die," she told me, voice firmer. "He's going to die. And then it will all be over and life will return to normal. Unless, of course . . ."

I waited, but she didn't explain any more. Instead, a look of consternation came over her face.

"Telly, I may need you to keep one more secret for me after all."

Chapter 36

LUKA IS EXHAUSTED from the day's adventures. I lead him into the house while Rainie performs a perimeter sweep. Luka slurps down a bowl of water, then collapses on the family room floor, casting a longing glance down the hall toward my bedroom.

I'm too keyed up to sleep. My legs hurt. My chest, my heart. But I can't shut down as easily as my dog. Instead, I roam the kitchen, pouring myself a glass of water, then investigating the refrigerator again and again. I should eat. I should be hungry. But nothing appeals to me.

I keep seeing my brother, disappearing into the woods, rifle held at the ready.

By the time Rainie returns, I'm walking laps around the kitchen table. She doesn't say anything. Just pours herself a glass of water, too. Outside it's still hot and muggy. But inside the air-conditioning has done its job. She shivers slightly from the shock of it and I can see the outline of her handgun tucked into the back of her capris.

"You really think Telly's still a threat to me?"

"I think it never hurts to take precautions."

"If he wanted to kill me, he could've done it when we were alone together this afternoon. No need to wait for this fuss."

She shrugs but doesn't put away her gun. Not Telly, I realize abruptly. At least she can't be that worried about him, given his actions this afternoon. But she is still worried. Because if Telly didn't shoot those people at the EZ Gas, then who did?

"All clear outside?" I ask now, pretending to only half-care.

She nods. "Are you okay?"

"Right as rain," I assure her.

Her expression softens. "He's your brother, Sharlah. It's okay to worry about him."

"I feel like something bad is going to happen," I murmur. "And if I could just think hard enough, be smart enough, I could avoid it. But I've never been that smart. Or that lucky."

Rainie doesn't say anything. She takes a seat at the table. After a moment, I join her.

"Most people go through life knowing there's violence out there but cushioned by a certain distance," she says after a minute. "Bad things happen, but not to them. You don't have that cushion, Sharlah. Your first five years were a constant exercise in fight or flight, and that was before your father went after you and your brother with a knife. Bad things aren't an abstract for you. They're very real events. And having experienced them once, of course you expect the worst to happen again."

"Telly's in trouble."

"Yes."

"The way he carried his rifle, the way he spoke . . . He's gonna do something serious. Or die trying."

"I'm sorry, Sharlah."

I twirl my water glass. "I don't think he killed his foster parents. I mean, we don't have video or anything from that shooting, but if we did, I bet you it'd be the other guy from the EZ Gas, the one with the mole above his wrist. He did all this."

She doesn't say anything.

I find myself continuing: "The way Telly spoke of his fosters. He respected them. He liked them. He wouldn't just turn on them like that."

"We don't always know what makes people kill."

"But you try to, right? That's what profiling is all about. Determining why people kill, and using that knowledge to identify the killer."

Rainie regards me seriously. "Nature versus nurture," she says abruptly. "That's the most fundamental question in personality development. Especially when it comes to criminals. Is someone born evil, or did something happen to make him or her that way?"

"Telly wasn't born bad," I say stubbornly. "He took care of me."

"He was born into a household filled with violence. Surrounded by addiction and instability, raised by a father whose idea of conflict resolution was brutality."

"Maybe our nurture wasn't so great," I concede. "But his nature . . . My brother is good. I know that. Even when I saw him today. There's still some Telly in him. You have to believe me, Rainie. You have to believe."

"I do, honey. There were many things Telly could've done this afternoon, and of all of them, he chose to give you back. I'm grateful to him."

We fall back into silence.

"I wanted to save him," I hear myself whisper after a moment. "That's why I had to leave this afternoon. Why I had to find him. Just once. I wanted to make things right."

"I know."

"How do you sleep at night?"

Rainie smiles faintly. "I don't sleep at night. You know that as well as anyone."

"Your mother?" I ask, because she doesn't talk about her past much. None of us do. "Did she . . . did she hit you?"

Rainie takes a moment. Not avoiding me, but composing her answer. "My mother could be abusive. She was an alcoholic, just like I'm an alcoholic. These things run in families. But I don't think my mother measures up to the mean-drunk standards of, say, your father. On the other hand, she didn't have good taste in men. And some of them . . . I also know what it's like to have to lock your bedroom door at night."

"I'm sorry," I tell her truthfully.

She reaches across the table, takes my hand. "It gets better, Sharlah. I know it doesn't feel that way at the moment, but life gets better."

I want to believe her, but she's right: It doesn't feel that way tonight.

Her cell rings. Rainie releases my hand long enough to fish it out of her pocket. I can tell from her face that it's Quincy. She doesn't leave the room, however, but sits across from me, nodding. Apparently, Quincy has a lot to say.

"Okay," she says finally. Then, "Yes, I can do that. I'll start right away. . . . Be careful. . . . I love you. . . . Bye."

She puts the phone down, takes a sip of her water.

"He gave you an assignment?" I ask.

She nods. "Remember the photo of the old man at the end of Telly's scrapbook? Turns out, that's really Sandra Duvall's estranged father."

"Sandra Duvall or Irene Gemetti?" I ask.

Rainie smiles. "Which is where things get interesting. Not only has Sandra been living under an assumed name, but apparently her father, an infamous criminal, has been as well."

"Is that why they're estranged? She didn't want to go into the family business or something like that?"

"Not sure. What matters is that according to Sandra's son, Henry, her father had recently reappeared in their lives. Claimed to be dying of cancer and wanted to make amends. Except, also according to Henry, Sandra wanted nothing to do with him. So instead, the man approached Henry first, then Frank, then, when none of that worked, apparently your brother, Telly."

I frown. "I don't get it."

"Neither do the police. Hence my assignment. I need to identify

Sandra's father. If we know more about him, we might have a better sense of what was going on in the Duvalls' house leading up to the morning of their murders. Which, in fact, might tell us more about who killed them and why."

"I want to help," I announce.

She gives me a look. But being me, I return it with one of my own. Sensing a show, Luka climbs off the floor, comes padding over for a better view.

"Sandra's real name is Gemetti, right?" I ask now.

She nods.

"So all the police have to do is search Gemetti, or even go through birth certificates to find Irene Gemetti, then look for the father's name."

"Which Roy Peterson has been doing without luck. Which could mean that Irene was born at a small hospital that hasn't scanned its records into databases, or that in fact there's no record of her birth. Computer searches are great, but there's a saying: Garbage in, garbage out. If the Gemettis really are some kind of crime family, they have incentive to operate under the radar, keeping most of their personal information to themselves. Sandra Duvall is a fake name, correct? An alias she devised to separate herself from her past."

"Yes."

"Her father has done the same. Crime bosses—think of them as wolves dressed in sheep's clothing. As a wolf—"

"Gemetti?" I ask.

"Yes. He conducts certain businesses, engages in certain behaviors he'd like to keep separate from himself. But, if he's successful at all, he might also want a sheep's life, roaming openly in the world, enjoying the fruits of his labor."

"A second name."

"In this case, the man introduced himself to Henry as David Michael or David Martin, or maybe even David Michael Martin, something like that."

"Those are all first names."

"Those are all common names," Rainie corrects me.

I get it. "To make it harder to track him. How many Davids must be running around the world, let alone Martins, David Martins. . . ."

"Exactly. He's hiding in plain sight, adopting a moniker so common, no one would notice or be able to narrow it down if they wanted to."

"You can't search for all the Davids and Martins, so you're going after Gemetti instead?"

"Actually, Sergeant Roy Peterson is digging into Gemetti. That's the wolf name, and Roy is the one with access to criminal databases. Which leaves me with the more time-intensive search: trolling Google for one of the most common names on the planet."

I frown, chew my bottom lip. "You must have a plan."

She shrugs. "You're the student who has to do research on the Internet. What would you do?"

"Well . . . you can't just Google David. Or Martin. Or Michael. You'd get way too many hits. So you gotta add search criteria. Something to narrow down the options."

"What would you suggest?"

"What do we know about the guy? Is he from Bakersville, like Sandra?"

"Actually, we're thinking the Portland area. Oregon, to be safest."

"Okay, so we want combinations of Davids, Michaels, and Martins who live in Oregon. That's gonna be a long list."

She nods.

"He's old? Old David Michael Martins who live in Oregon?"

Rainie smiles. "*Old* is too generic a search term. Ideally, we'd like a birth year. That would be very specific. Sadly . . ."

"You don't have a birth year."

"No. We could try a range, but in my experience, that mostly gets ugly, especially when it turns out the year you needed was just outside your range."

I scowl. "How do you and Quincy ever find anyone?"

"Just like this. Talking it out."

We both fall silent for a second. Rainie speaks next: "He's sick. At least that's what he implied to the son. Sick and dying of cancer."

I brighten. "That's something specific."

"Yes and no. Health records are confidential. On the one hand, there are only a couple of top cancer hospitals in the state. Chances are, our David has seen docs at one of them. But we have no access to that information. We need public information."

"Is he rich?" I ask.

"The implication has been that he's good at what he does."

"Rich people don't just get sick," I say. I know this because I watch TV. "Rich people hold galas and fund-raisers and launch Twitter campaigns and all sorts of stuff. They turn being sick into a major media event."

For a second, I think Rainie's going to dismiss me, then suddenly . . . "Galas," she murmurs. "There's one in Portland. Biggest fund-raiser of the year to support the fight against cancer. Includes local celebrities, the überwealthy . . . Follow me."

She lets me inside the office. Something worth noting—that I'm finally being allowed onto hallowed ground—except the excitement in her voice has captured my attention. Rainie heads straight to the computer, opens the search engine, and the next thing I know, the screen is flooded with images.

"The One Night, One Fight cancer gala costs fifty thousand a table, making it one of Portland's highest-profile events. Of course there are photographers everywhere to capture the glamour and post the photos online, encouraging even more donations next year. Now, we might not know the real name of Sandra's father, but we do know what he looks like. Meaning all we have to do is keep our eyes open and start hunting. What do you think for timeline? We don't know exactly when David got sick, but given how frail he looks in the photo, probably at least a couple of years ago. So we'll start five years back, work ahead from there, and hope we get lucky."

I nod. Rainie enters the search terms and the entire monitor fills with a glittery whirlwind of sequined dresses, bubbly champagne, and dancing lights. One Night, One Fight from five years ago. I feel light-headed just looking at all the images, and we have pages, years to go.

"Picture the old man from the photo in your mind," Rainie advises. "Focus on something tangible—the bridge of his nose, the distance between his eyes. That's who we're looking for. Don't get distracted by all the rest."

We work slowly. There's no choice. I find the moment I rush, the images blur and I don't see faces at all, but start noting that dress or those earrings. Rainie's right, it's easy to get distracted.

After making it through all the images from five years past, Rainie has to load the picture of Sandra's father on her cell phone, so we can refresh our mental image. She blows it up until all we can see is the old man's face. At this magnitude, it's fuzzy, distorted, but Rainie shows me the tricks. On a piece of paper we sketch out the line of his jaw, the shape of his nose, his eyes, and his lips. Not a face, but a template of a face.

"This is who we're looking for," she reminds me. "Don't worry about hair, clothing, jewelry, background. These are our identifying elements."

One Night, One Fight four years ago. She loads the images. We resume our hunt.

I had no idea so many people liked to wear sequins. Even sequined bow ties.

Three years back.

Rainie brings us both eye drops. The images have run together. I hate formal wear and puffy hair and blue eye shadow. I'm also slightly hungry from all the images of food, yet nauseated from the giant blurs of color. I can stop, Rainie tells me, get some rest. But I can tell she's going to keep going, so I'm determined to make it, too. It's like Where's Waldo, and we have yet to spot our target. You can't go to bed without having won the game.

One Night, One Fight two years ago. Rainie loads. We both lean forward, stare at the monitor, start scrolling slowly down the page.

I see him. Not directly. He's standing off to the side. Wearing a black tux just like the other guys. But his hand holding the champagne glass. It grabs my attention. A patch of old in the middle of bright party lights. The photo reveals just his profile, but I study his nose, the way Rainie showed me, and I know it's him immediately.

"There! Look there! That's him!"

Rainie follows my finger as I poke the image on the screen. "Could be," she agrees. She double-clicks on the photo, blows it up larger.

The old man is part of a group, all huddled together. He stands with a trimmer, serious-looking guy, then a younger man with a pretty girl on his arm. They're all together, I think. The way they lean so close, they're not getting to know one another. They know each other already. His family?

But Rainie isn't looking at the old man anymore. Her gaze has gone to the younger one. She frowns. Blinks her eyes. Frowns again.

"I swear I recognize that face."

"What is his name, what is his name?" I'm dying to know.

She reads the caption: "David Michael Martin."

Definitely a great name for hiding in plain sight.

"President of GMB Enterprises," she continues, then . . .

She stops, turns away from the computer, stares at me.

"Sharlah, I do know that young man. We started the day looking at his photo. This kid . . ." She scans the caption, but the names of the other group members aren't given. "This kid is the male victim at the EZ Gas this morning."

I understand what she's saying. "His murder wasn't random."

"No. Someone must've been sent there to kill him. First Sandra Duvall, David Michael Martin's long-lost daughter," Rainie murmurs. "Then this man, David Michael Martin's . . . associate? This isn't a spree killing."

Rainie is already picking up her phone, dialing Quincy.

"Then what is it?" I ask her.

"I don't know. Something bigger, something more targeted." She looks at me, phone to her ear, and I already know what she's thinking: the pictures of me, scope lines drawn around my face.

And I get it then. I really am my foster mother's daughter. Because Rainie is already thinking, how can she keep me safe?

Just like I'm already thinking, Oh, Telly, how do I get you out of this?

But neither of us has the answer.

Chapter 37

WHEN QUINCY AND SHELLY RETURNED from talking to Henry, it was well after midnight. They discovered the tracker, still in the conference room, pushing markers into the blown-up map. Noonan glanced up as they walked in, then returned his attention to his job.

Quincy helped himself to some coffee, then poured a fresh cup of tea for Shelly.

Shelly grunted her thanks, left the conference room to check in with Roy. Quincy crossed to the tracker. Best Quincy could tell, the map of Telly Ray Nash's trail was now covered in a fresh sprinkling of purple pushpins.

"Do I want to know?" Quincy asked.

"Tagging all reported sightings of persons matching Nash's description."

Quincy realized Noonan was holding printouts from what must have been the recently set-up hotline.

"How'd the conversation go with the son?" Noonan asked. "He in cahoots, or our real target?"

"If he is, he's the best liar I've ever met, and I've met some good ones."

"So he's in the clear? Has nothing to do with what happened with his parents?"

Quincy frowned, twisted his coffee cup. "Not sure I'm ready to go that far yet. There's certainly more to the Duvall family than meets the eye. But Henry seems genuinely in the dark when it comes to his mother's real name and family history. He identified our old man from Telly's scrapbook as his long-lost grandfather. Apparently, the man appeared out of the blue several months back looking to establish a relationship with his grandson, maybe the rest of the family. According to Henry, his father forbade it. Sandra Duvall/Irene Gemetti's father was some kind of criminal mastermind. Not to be trusted, even on his self-proclaimed deathbed."

"Nice. Grandfather really dead?"

"Hoping Roy or Rainie has that answer. Name would be nice as well." Quincy nodded with his head toward the wall map. "Any activity on the cameras you left at Nash's camp?"

"Nope."

"But the hotline sightings?" Quincy gestured to the sheaf of papers in Noonan's hand.

"Looking for a grouping," the tracker reported. "Enough sightings in one place to warrant further investigation. Or better yet, a series of groupings that might provide directionality—tell us where Nash is headed next. Maybe even help us identify his next target."

Quincy nodded; it was a solid line of inquiry. Now he eyed the considerable number of purple pushpins spraying across the map, arched a brow.

"Lot of sightings," he said.

"Yep."

"I'm not seeing any groupings."

"Nope."

"I'm not seeing any directionality."

"Exactly."

Noonan picked up the next purple tack, returning to the call logs. Quincy went in search of Shelly and Roy.

———

WHILE QUINCY AND SHELLY HAD BEEN OUT, Sergeant Peterson had dug up the information on the thirty-year-old murder investigation involving Irene Gemetti, aka Sandra Duvall. Roy handed over the sparse file; Quincy gave it a glance.

All pretty cursory. Irene Gemetti was wanted for questioning in the stabbing death of Victor Chernkov, who by all accounts had been a low-level pimp, working the Pearl District in downtown Portland. These days, the Pearl District was known for its multimillion-dollar lofts and trendy delis. Thirty years ago, not so much.

The case file consisted of the ME's report on Chernkov's remains and a single witness statement from another prostitute who claimed to have seen Irene in the area right before the discovery of Chernkov's body. That was it. Irene Gemetti had never been located, and without further information, the case had grown cold. Quincy wasn't surprised. For a lot of detectives, a dead pimp barely counted as a crime. The investigators had moved on; apparently so had Irene Gemetti.

Quincy set down the file, looked at Roy, who was staring blearily at his computer screen.

"Sixteen-year-old Irene ran away from home," Quincy murmured. "She fell in with the wrong crowd. Ended up in a violent situation. Had to run again."

"Straight into the arms of Frank Duvall?" Shelly asked from the doorway.

Quincy turned. "His son said he liked projects."

Shelly took a sip of her tea.

"So instead of turning herself in to the police," Shelly said now, "Sandra turned to Frank Duvall. Convinced him to marry her and take her away to our quaint town of Bakersville. Where she what? Magically transformed herself into the perfect wife and mother next door? No more life on the street? No more acknowledgment of evil Daddy?"

"Beats going to jail for murder," Roy commented.

"What if you Google Irene Gemetti's name?" Quincy asked.

"Nothing," Roy said.

"What about the pimp, Victor?" Shelly tried.

"Same deal. Too old. Or not nearly interesting enough for the Internet to care."

"And the name Gemetti?"

"Too many hits. I need more information to narrow things down. Turns out *estranged grandpa* isn't as good a search term as you might think."

Quincy nodded, unsurprised. The Internet could be a treasure trove of information, if only there weren't so much of it. "Henry Duvall swears he doesn't know anything about his mother's past or his criminally minded grandfather. And yet, in the past year, there were only two major changes in the Duvall household: taking in Telly Ray Nash as a foster son, and the reappearance of Sandra's father after thirty years. Question is, which one of these things led to the shooting death of the Duvalls? In the beginning, we were assuming it was Telly. And now?"

Roy and Shelly nodded. It did feel more and more like Sandra Duvall's family history held the answer.

"Maybe Rainie will have better luck," Quincy said.

Almost on cue, Quincy's phone rang. He downed another bitter gulp of black coffee and hit talk.

Rainie did have information. She and Sharlah were already on their way over.

THEY MET IN THE CONFERENCE ROOM. The official investigative team, Quincy thought. Two profilers, one sheriff, a homicide sergeant, a volunteer tracker, and a thirteen-year-old girl. Definitely the most interesting team Quincy had ever seen assembled.

He eyed Sharlah with concern. His daughter was up well past her bedtime, not to mention the trauma of her day. But Sharlah, much like Rainie, looked far from tired. Both of them, in fact, appeared incredibly jazzed. Quincy felt a rush of pride. For his daughter, for his wife. For this family he was so lucky to call his own.

Rainie plopped down a pile of printouts. More photos, Quincy realized. Obviously from her computer. She started passing them around.

"Meet David Michael Martin," she said. "Former CEO of GMB Enterprises. Died five weeks ago of cancer."

Quincy took in the printed photo before him. The frail old man at the obviously posh gala did appear to be the same person from Telly's scrapbook. His eyes homed in on the younger man standing with the same group.

Already, Rainie was nodding.

"Furthermore, meet the male victim from the EZ Gas shooting: Richie Perth. He didn't have any ID on him at the scene, but once I learned of his connection to David Michael Martin, I called the ME and asked him to run fingerprint analysis." Rainie glanced at Shelly. "Hope you don't mind."

"Not at all."

"Turns out, Richie is also an employee of GMB Enterprises. Their charter fishing division."

"The truck outside of the EZ Gas," Shelly stated. "It was registered to a company out of Nehalem."

"Exactly." Rainie nodded. "All right, GMB Enterprises was first established forty years ago. Small-time import-export business, specializing in olive oil and vinegar."

Already a few brows were raised around the table.

"Since then, GMB has grown into a hundred-million-dollar company, operating in a little bit of this and a little bit of that. Import-export, shipping, charter fishing companies—you name it, GMB does it. At least on paper."

Sharlah spoke up. "GMB is a shell company!" she exclaimed, clearly having been educated by Rainie.

"And a very successful one at that. Now, David Michael Martin, otherwise known as Sandra's father, has been listed as CEO for the entire forty years. Upon his death, however, leadership was passed to the company's CFO, Douglas Perth. Who is also Richie's father."

Noonan held up a hand. "Hang on. I get shell company. This GMB, it's Sandra's father's cover, right? According to what we've heard, this David Michael Martin was basically a criminal. Like a godfather, right?"

Rainie nodded.

"But bad money can become good," Quincy said, "if you run it through a legitimate business enterprise, hence the creation of GMB. It's Martin's legal front, covering for his illegal activities."

Rainie nodded again.

"But Martin dies," Noonan said. He tapped the photo they'd all been given. "Of cancer. And just like when any business leader dies, the company's gotta get a new leader."

"Douglas Perth," Rainie supplied, "who, being the former CFO, would know all the ins and outs of the business, including its legal and illegal operations. As CFO, it would be his job specifically to spin all the illegitimate gains into legitimate profits."

"Okay. But his son . . . Richie . . . He's one of our victims?" Noonan asked. "Because that's where I'm getting lost. If Douglas Perth is the winner from this Martin guy's death, then how did Douglas's son end up being one of the losers?"

"That's what we're here to find out," Rainie assured him. "What we do know is that these shootings aren't random. Sandra Duvall and Richie Perth have a connection: GMB Enterprises. Once run by Sandra's father, and now run by Richie's father."

The table fell silent. Even Quincy had to think his way through this one. "Is there any evidence," Quincy asked at last, "that Sandra was on GMB's payroll, had any current ties to the company?"

"No."

"Even under the name Irene Gemetti?"

"I couldn't find any record of Irene Gemetti having a bank account, meaning I can't find any traces of her receiving payments. If we assume GMB is nothing but a front, however, there's an entirely different business operation running behind the scenes that we have no way of seeing. So I can't be positive. But from the up-front side of things, Sandra and/or Irene wasn't receiving any monies."

Roy spoke up. "I've examined Sandra Duvall's financials. There's no record of her receiving unaccounted-for payments, not monthly nor lump sum. And I also couldn't find any activity for an Irene Gemetti."

"So once upon a time," Quincy said slowly, "Irene was connected to GMB Enterprises through her father, David Michael Martin. At sixteen, however, she ran away, then ended up creating a whole new life, new identity, with Frank Duvall. The lack of financial activity would indicate she truly did cut her ties with her former life and her father. Henry was right about that."

"Until her father found her again," Shelly said. "First approaching Henry, away at college. Then meeting with Frank, then, presumably, Telly."

"Did Henry say why his grandfather reappeared?" Rainie asked.

"Deathbed repentance," Quincy said. "But maybe also to recruit Henry into the family business."

Rainie's eyes widened. "Did he say yes?"

"According to him, no. But do I one hundred percent believe him?" Quincy glanced at Shelly.

The sheriff shrugged. "If Henry really was recruited into the family business, all the more reason to lie to us."

The table fell silent again, everyone thinking.

"To make things more interesting," Rainie said at last, "Richie Perth does have a rap sheet. Assault, trespassing, more assault. His father might be the financial genius behind GMB's criminal enterprises, but Richie comes across more as good old-fashioned muscle."

"I think he killed Telly's fosters," Sharlah said.

All eyes turned to Quincy's daughter. Sharlah wavered but didn't back down. "Telly didn't shoot them. He talked about them to me. They were good to him. He wouldn't have killed them. No way."

Quincy felt for his daughter. For the courage it was taking his socially anxious teen to meet the onslaught of adult stares. For the loyalty she obviously felt for her brother. They had her too involved in this case, he recognized. And yet, it was his and Rainie's nature to work without limits. Hence the fact that his older daughter, Kimberly, was also now an FBI agent.

"Richie is a thug, right?" Sharlah was speaking again, looking at Rainie. "That's what *muscle* means, right? His father is good with numbers, but Richie likes to hurt people. You know, assault."

Rainie nodded.

"So he killed Sandra and Frank," Sharlah concluded. "Because that's what thugs do. They kill people."

"But why?" Rainie pressed gently. "Just because Richie has a history of violence doesn't mean he shot and killed two people."

"His father told him to," Sharlah said.

Quincy and the others blinked.

"I mean, that's how this would work, right?" Sharlah continued. "You said Richie's father is now in charge of the company. So if Richie did something, it's because his father said so."

"Then who killed Richie?" Noonan asked, looking confused.

"Somebody else," Sharlah said promptly. "Not Telly, 'cause we've seen the video and it's a different arm. But maybe Telly saw who did it. He was at the EZ Gas, right? He saw who killed Richie and that's why he had to run away. Because otherwise, that person will kill him."

Quincy blinked again. His daughter's theory was getting crazier and crazier. And yet, there was an outline of a crime he could almost see . . .

"How did Sandra get away?" he asked.

His fellows at the table stopped staring at Sharlah, turned their attention to Quincy instead.

"We're saying Sandra left home at sixteen," he continued thoughtfully. "Ran away from a father who even thirty years ago was clearly building a successful criminal enterprise. What successful criminal lets his sixteen-year-old daughter go? Wouldn't that have made him appear weak? Even made her a liability to him and his organization?"

Sitting across from him, Rainie got it first. "A crime boss would never tolerate that level of disrespect. He would've gone after her."

"But he didn't. Irene got away, admittedly had a rough start, then met Frank Duvall and successfully rebuilt her life. New name, new image, everything. You couldn't find a single tie between her and her father's business."

Rainie shook her head.

Quincy leaned forward, rested his hands on the table. He eyed his daughter, then his wife. "What if David Michael Martin couldn't go after his daughter? What if Irene, who we already suspect was capable of murder, also understood her father's true nature as well? So she took out insurance. I don't know. Stole something, hid something incriminating. As long as he left her alone, she'd leave that alone. But come after her . . ."

"She'd pull the trigger," Rainie filled in.

"Sounds like a chip off the old block," Shelly drawled. "But what does that have to do with what's going on now?"

Quincy sat back. "We keep going over the new variables in Sandra and Frank Duvall's life. Fostering Telly. The reappearance of her father. But there's a third variable. Her father's death, five weeks ago. Which led to Douglas Perth taking over GMB Enterprises and his son, Richie, appearing in Bakersville. What if Irene and her father did have some kind of stalemate, which lasted thirty years? He lived his life, she lived hers. Then he died, and now . . . that balance is gone. Whatever Irene—Sandra—has, did, Douglas Perth wants it. Hence he sent his son to get it."

Quincy glanced at Roy. "Do we have ballistics back yet from the Duvalls?"

The sergeant shook his head. "But I could ask the ME to test Richie Perth's hands for GSR. That would certainly be a hint."

"*GSR* stands for 'gunshot residue,'" Quincy supplied for his daughter. "If Richie's hands test positive for GSR, that means he shot a gun shortly before dying. Which would lend credence to your theory: Richie Perth killed Frank and Sandra Duvall."

Sharlah nodded. Quincy could already tell from the look on his daughter's face that she was certain she was right.

"Still doesn't explain who shot Richie, though," Shelly said. "Hell, how many people with guns do I have running around my county anyway? And why didn't Telly come forward, instead of ending up at the EZ Gas, shooting out a video camera?"

"I'm going with my original theory," Rainie stated firmly. "Whatever's happening, Telly's been set up to be the patsy. He has to take the blame in order to keep his sister safe, so he can't come forward directly. Instead, he's been leaving us a trail of bread crumbs. The photos of his sister on his phone, so we'll keep Sharlah close. Then the picture of Sandra's father at his fake camp. He wants us to figure out what's going on. He wants us to stop it."

"By shooting my search team?" Noonan all but growled.

No one had an answer for that. Sharlah dropped her gaze to the table, sufficiently cowed.

Once again the room fell silent, everyone thinking.

"All right," Shelly said briskly. "We have four victims. Sounds like Frank Duvall and Erin Hill were collateral damage. Real targets were Sandra Duvall, then Richie Perth. Both had ties to GMB Enterprises, which had a major shake-up five weeks ago, with the passing of David Michael Martin. Now we got a new leader, this Douglas Perth, and a lot of carnage going on. If we agree with Telly Ray Nash that our goal is to stop this, then how?"

"I got a theory," Noonan said.

They all turned to stare at him.

"Not about the crime," he added hastily. "I don't know sh—beans about crime. But I've been working the map. According to the best data we have—including Sharlah's contact with her brother—Telly is headed south. All the rest, including the fake camp, has been for show."

Quincy studied the tracker. "How close is Telly's last known location to the Duvalls' house?"

"Couple of miles."

Quincy nodded. "Dark now," he observed. "Quiet. Media's camped out here. Law enforcement is holed up for the night. Meaning, if Sandra had some kind of insurance policy on her father's criminal enterprise and no one has found it yet—"

"You think Telly is heading back to his parents' house?" Shelly asked Quincy and Noonan.

"If that's really what this is all about, then yes," Quincy supplied. "Sandra took something thirty years ago. Douglas Perth wants it. But . . . so does someone else. A rival maybe? Inside the corporation, outside the corporation? Who knows. But Richie must've gone to the Duvalls' home for a reason. And then someone shot him for that same reason."

"But since Richie was at the home first, wouldn't he already have the information? And then the second shooter would have taken it from him?" Shelly asked.

"I don't think he got anything," Quincy said. "Based on the position of the bodies, he shot Frank immediately to eliminate a perceived threat. Sandra he might've left alive long enough to answer questions. But she was still killed in the bedroom, shot in the back, just as she was getting out of bed. No way she went out, retrieved her thirty-year-old secret, handed it over, then walked backward toward her side of the bed. I think the shooter's mistake was killing Frank Duvall. After that, I can't see a woman like Sandra giving up anything. Especially a woman as savvy as she was—she would've known talk or no talk, she was going to end up dead. Why give her killer the satisfaction?"

"Her father's daughter," Shelly said.

Quincy glanced at Sharlah. "It's been known to happen."

Shelly pursed her lips. Quincy could tell the sheriff was considering. Some cases started with evidence that led to theories. Then there were cases like this one. Where they sat around developing nearly outlandish theories, which they hoped would lead them to some evidence. In Quincy's experience, whatever worked.

Shelly must've thought the same. "What the hell, let's go on a goose chase. Not like we got any better ideas. Roy, contact the ME. Ask him to examine Richie Perth's hands for GSR, then run a full background. Also, see if you can't get Douglas Perth in here for questioning. See what the father has to say for his son. As for the rest of us . . ."

Shelly's gaze fell on Noonan. "How do fugitive trackers do when it comes to searching for secret information? Under the cover of night, with the threat of possible imminent death, of course?"

"We'll find out," Cal said.

Quincy stood. Kiss to Rainie, hug for Sharlah. Then he, Cal, and Shelly were back on the road, headed once more for the Duvalls' house.

Quincy wondered if Telly Ray Nash had truly returned to his foster parents' home. And what it was about to cost them to find out.

Chapter 38

SHELLY HAD A HINKY FEELING. Like an itch between her shoulder blades she just couldn't scratch. Taking the back roads to the Duvalls' residence, she found herself driving more slowly than strictly necessary, watching every bend in the road quiver on the edge of her headlights. No streetlights out in the country. Not to mention most folks weren't the type to leave porch lamps burning all night. Which left them with miles of darkness, the towering shapes of bordering fir trees mere black etches against a navy blue night. Plenty of places for a shooter to hide on a night like this. Especially one with a high-powered rifle and hunting skills.

Just because Telly Ray Nash hadn't shot the two people at the EZ Gas didn't mean he wasn't a killer. It just meant there was more than one threat running around in Shelly's county.

Shelly parked several houses back from the Duvalls', pulling off the road, behind a wild hedge of blackberries. She didn't feel like advertising their mission. Not given all the unknowns involved.

From the back, she withdrew her department-issued rifle, plus ammo. Quincy took it without hesitation. As his shirt advertised, he was a firearms instructor, whereas Cal's skills were better suited for searching than, say, guarding.

"I don't have night-vision goggles," Quincy informed them, jamming home the first clip; he slipped two more into his pockets. "So if either of you plan on running toward me, I'd identify yourself first."

"Position?" Shelly asked him.

"No higher ground. Given that, I'll go with the classic patrol model. Circle the house at random intervals. Hope you find what you're looking for before anyone appears out of the gloom."

"Fair enough."

Cal spoke up. "What are we looking for?"

Shelly frowned. She'd been considering this for a bit. "Something feminine," she said at last, which earned her two blank stares. "Think about it. Judging by Sandra Duvall's Facebook page, she prided herself on being a wife and mother. Which means the home is her domain. If she was looking to keep something safe, she'd keep it close. Not in the garage—that belongs to her husband. And not on the computer—that's her son's toy."

"Not to mention," Quincy inserted dryly, "that thirty years ago computers were large, awkward machines. Her father probably didn't even have one in the house—it would've been at his office. So if sixteen-year-old Sandra was looking to run and needed to grab something quickly, she'd have had limited options. Maybe she found a printout of her father's illegal business accounts in his home office. Or, say, an incriminating photo from his bookshelf, or a trophy he saved from one of his crimes."

"Killers really do that kind of thing?" Cal asked.

"Killers really do that kind of thing," Quincy answered. "And in the case of organized crime, keeping such a memento in plain sight can also serve as a reminder to your underlings of just what you're capable of—never a bad management strategy."

"Do you cook?" Shelly asked Cal.

"Other than cheese?"

"That's what I thought. Okay. You take the bedroom; I'm going to start in the kitchen. You like to think like the target, so good luck. As for me, I'm going to think like a cook. Given all the recipes Sandra posted online, food is what she loved. Meaning, if she wanted to keep something close, kitchen is the best bet."

"Weird," Cal said.

"I know. Which is exactly why no one else has found it yet."

Quincy disappeared first, jogging down the road, rifle in hand, till he was lost from sight. They gave him five minutes, then Shelly received two clicks on her radio, the signal for all clear. She and Cal made their advance, Shelly still trying to shake her nerves.

She was a woman who'd once raced into a burning building. No reason for a dark, humid night to put a quiver into her hands. Even if just hours earlier she'd listened to sudden gunfire, the screams of experienced officers caught unaware.

She noticed Cal wasn't exactly breathing calmly beside her.

"It's okay," she found herself telling him. "We get in. We find our evidence. We get out. And we end this thing."

"I'm not nervous," he said curtly. "I'm angry."

"Because of your team?"

"Nah. Because I'm terrified. Frankly, that pisses me off."

"Agreed," Shelly said, and they approached the house.

No sign of Quincy. Proof he was good at his job, she supposed. Crime scene tape was still intact on the door, another good sign. She'd resealed it after her and Cal's earlier visit. Now she slipped out her knife, cut the fresh tape, cracked open the door.

The smell had definitely not abated. She and Cal both took a moment. A last gulp of fresh air before heading inside.

Shelly went first. Cal followed. Closed the door behind them. Then they were both swallowed into the hot, rancid gloom.

THEY USED FLASHLIGHTS, beams held low, out of sight of the windows. Again, stealth mission. If there really were evil henchmen running around—and God only knew at this point—no reason to give them a heads-up.

Cal turned left for the bedrooms. Shelly didn't envy his task. She went for the kitchen.

It would be helpful to know what they were looking for. Picture it in her head, then look for it in the space. She liked Quincy's idea of a memento. Say, the slug from the first guy David Michael Martin had ever killed. That would be an easy thing for a sixteen-year-old girl to snatch from her father's study. Better yet, keep hidden during the months she lived on the streets.

That was the piece of the puzzle that bothered Shelly. Sandra hadn't just run away at sixteen; she'd ended up homeless, forced into prostitution if the dead pimp was any hint. So what could a teenager steal from her own father that she could hang on to while living hand-to-mouth?

Shelly started with the spice jars. Sandra had racks of them hanging above the stove. Very quaint and country looking. Now Shelly took them out and, beneath the beam of the flashlight, shook each one experimentally. She started with the more exotic spices. Anise. She didn't even know what you cooked with anise, making it a good secret receptacle in her mind. But no such luck.

After the spices, she crossed to the freezer. According to Henry, his mother liked to stash cash in the ice box, a common enough trick. So common, Shelly doubted Sandra would've used the same spot for her most secret possession. But it also felt stupid not to look.

Freezer was clear.

Pantry.

Pots and pans. Crock-Pots, drawers of cooking utensils filled with items Shelly didn't even realize were cooking utensils. And then . . .

A bookshelf of cookbooks. Dog-eared, food splattered. From the thin, yellow-edged *Favorite Crock-Pot Recipes* to the classic *Joy of Cooking* to a three-ring binder filled with recipes Sandra had personally clipped and saved from magazines. The collection was clearly well loved and well used. Personal.

This was it. Shelly knew it, without a moment's doubt. These cookbooks were to Sandra what Telly's journals were to him. Her joy and her salvation, but also the source of her resolve. Every meal she cooked, every moment she created for her family, she reinforced the image of Sandra Duvall. The woman she wanted to be. Not her father's daughter after all.

Shelly took them all down. An impressive stack. Then she worked from the top, moving quickly now, aware of the passing time as she flipped each page, faster and faster. Searching for inserted pages, maybe even cut and pasted over a recipe, into a recipe. Say, a list of ingredients for chocolate mousse that suddenly included names of business associates. Or a description of searing chicken that was interspersed with bank accounts, wire routing instructions, something.

Book after book after book.

Nothing, nothing, nothing.

Cal came in, mouth open, breathing ragged. He took a look at what she was doing, then, without a word, crossed to the refrigerator, opened the freezer, and stuck his head in. Trying to clear his head, she thought. Or numb his sense of smell after an hour in a slaughterhouse.

She didn't need to ask if he'd found anything; he would have told her immediately. Just like he didn't need to ask her as she flipped her way through the last book.

"Has to be here," she muttered, closing up the Crock-Pot recipes, staring at the now-completed pile. "This is Sandra Duvall," she stated.

Cal didn't say anything. Kept his head in the freezer.

"These are her books of worship. Frank would never bother them. Nor Henry, or her father, or a hit man."

"I like cookbooks," Cal muttered from the freezer. "There are some really good ones monks wrote on cheese making. Couple good pioneer ones, too."

Shelly stared at the pile. Glanced around the kitchen. She was right. She knew she was right. So what was she missing?

Her gaze went to the empty bookshelf. A perfect shell.

335 BEHIND YOU   335

Of course, because even if someone did think to toss Sandra's cookbooks, who would think to search the space . . .

She stuck her hand in, patting the bottom, the sides, the top, and then . . .

A crack. Sharp, nerve rattling. Followed immediately by another.

"Down, down, down!" Cal yelled.

As more gunshots lit up the night, the kitchen window exploded.

"Quincy!" she cried into her radio, dropping to the floor, yanking out her sidearm.

But there was no answer.

Chapter 39

FIRST THING QUINCY DID on perimeter patrol was identify and search all sources of possible cover. The Duvalls had an expansive lot, well over an acre would be his guess; not a big surprise in this area. Clear-cut, rolling lawn would've been nice. But no, they'd let most of the property naturalize. Clumps of trees here. Wild bushes there. Not to mention the stand of fir trees next to the garage, or the overgrown row of rhododendrons obscuring most of the left front. All perfect hiding spots for an intruder, just biding his time before cracking off a shot.

He walked with the butt of the rifle pressed against his shoulder, end pointed down.

In conditions such as these, Quincy's best tool was his own ears. Adjusting to the rhythms of the night, the hoot of the owl, the buzz of crickets. Noises that soothed when all was well, then fell sharply silent at the slightest disturbance.

He was breathing too hard. If the thermostat had dipped at all, it was only to the nineties. Meaning his shirt was glued to his torso, beads of sweat were running down his cheeks, and every inhalation of the thick, muggy air required effort.

It'd been a long time since his active-duty days, but he remembered his training. Measured breaths. Slow inhalation through the nose. Slow exhalation through the mouth. It enabled the breather to bring more oxygen into the lungs, steadying the heart rate, loosening limbs. His job was to be prepared but not tense. Tensions cramped muscles and burned unnecessary energy, until when the moment finally arrived, the guard was too wrung out to respond.

Breathe in. Breathe out. Sweep the trees. Back of the house. Under the rear deck. Listen to the crickets. Walk up the bedroom side of the house, noting the flickers of light through the windows—Cal's search—then around to the front of the house, sweep the rhododendrons. Repeat. Except maybe in reverse order. Or walk up and down the same side of the house, then the other, then the other.

Changing out patterns, avoiding routine. If someone was watching, Quincy wanted them to at least have to work for it, so he kept his movements irregular and his body in a low crouch.

He'd just paused once more by the corner of the garage. The same spot where Sandra's father's photo had been taken, what, weeks, months ago? A question occurred to him: If the man had been standing right here, in front of the garage, who'd taken the photo? Clearly it couldn't have been taken from the house. It would have been from somewhere in the fenced-in yard. Say, where another clump of rhodies overgrew the corner of the split rails?

He'd just taken the first step forward, when *crack*.

He dropped.

No thought. Just instinct. He was exposed, in the middle of the driveway, yards from the nearest cover. So he dropped, face-planted into the asphalt as a second shot cracked out and the bullet pinged off the ground next to his ear.

He needed cover. Now. He needed an angle of sight to return fire. Now. He needed to get home to his wife and child. Now.

Belly crawl. Rifle held in front, worming his way around the warm asphalt to the line of fir trees bordering the garage. There was a reason the army loved to make recruits spend so much time wriggling around on their stomachs. It did come in handy.

Three more shots. *Crack, crack, crack.* He flinched. Ducked his head, even as it occurred to him these shots were different. From in front of him, not behind. Cross fire? Two shooters pinning him down?

A fresh crack, the sound of a window shattering. He could hear Shelly calling his name. But he couldn't answer. Inching forward, all his weight pressing against his chest, his arms, he could barely draw a breath.

Then he was there. Edge of the asphalt, into the mulch. He rolled. Four quick turns and he was behind the first tree, breathing hard and wishing the trees were younger, bushier, rather than tall, leggy towers, devoid of lower limbs.

He finally got his hand on his radio. "Two shooters," he reported breathlessly. "Do not leave the house. I repeat, do not leave the premises. You will be caught in the cross fire. Call for backup. We need SWAT."

"Roger that." Then Shelly was gone from his radio, but instead he could hear the lower murmur of her voice through the shattered window, fifty feet away.

He was bleeding, he realized. Blood rolling down his cheek. A wet spot somewhere on his left shoulder. A burning sensation from his right forearm. Genuine hit? Damage from ricochet? He couldn't tell, and now wasn't the time for inventory.

First shots had come from somewhere near the end of the driveway. He was sure of it. Someone approaching the property, making out Quincy, and then opening fire. A suspicious neighbor, thinking they'd spotted an intruder? He didn't think so. A neighbor would at least call out first, give some kind of warning.

That still didn't explain the second shooter, coming from the area of the garage. Up in one of these trees? But again, they were skinny and lacked lower branches. A bitch to climb. So some other high vantage point, then.

His gaze went to the roof. There, next to the chimney. A shadow where a shadow shouldn't have been.

Quincy cursed under his breath. Of all the stupid mistakes. He'd never looked up, never thought about the damn roof. And now here he was, his whole team pinned down and he himself bleeding like a sieve. Idiot, he thought. Though again, now was not the time for listing mistakes.

Slowly, he raised his own rifle, adjusting it against his left shoulder. He grimaced slightly, but whatever the damage was there, the wound felt more superficial than deep. Or maybe that was shock and adrenaline doing the talking. Bringing up the scope, he zeroed in on the shape. Definitely a man. Definitely a rifle. But the majority of his form was blocked by the chimney. Smart shooter. He'd chosen his position with care.

Just then, six rapid cracks of gunfire. Not from the roof, but from behind Quincy. Each shot burying itself into the front of the house, the kitchen area, where he'd last heard Shelly's voice.

Quincy whirled around, tried to identify this threat, while behind him the figure on the roof returned fire. *Snap, snap, snap.*

A ping. Metal. Blacked-out truck, Quincy realized. Parked just across the street and barely visible. But the roof shooter's third shot found home, shattering glass. The next instant, the truck's engine roared to life, and the vehicle careered away.

One shooter down, one to go.

But when Quincy turned back around, the roof was empty.

HE KEPT TO THE TREE LINE, following it all the way to the rear of the house. Then, there he was. Even half-expecting him, Quincy found himself tightening his grip on his rifle, breath hitching in his throat.

The boy stood ten feet back, rifle loose in arms, face obscured in the dark. Sharlah had been right. The boy had painted himself up so that now only the whites of his eyes showed against the night. It made for an eerie sight. As if the boy were less than human.

"Telly Ray Nash," Quincy said evenly.

"You're not supposed to be here," the boy said. He didn't sound angry as much as firm. "You need to be home keeping my sister safe."

"Safe from whom?"

"You're the expert, you figure it out. I got bigger priorities, like keeping myself alive."

"You left us that picture of Sandra's father. You wanted us to learn about him."

"Did it help?" the boy asked. He sounded genuinely curious.

"His name is David Michael Martin. He ran a criminal organization. Or at least he did until he died. But you know that, don't you, Telly? You're the one who met him here."

Slowly, the boy shook his head. He was still scanning the area around them, on alert. "She met him. She said she wouldn't. She said she had nothing she needed to say to him. But I knew . . . Family is family. Even if you hate them, it's hard to let go."

"Sandra invited her father over."

"I overheard them talking, then snuck out the front to take that picture, just in case."

"What did he want?"

"I'm not sure. He kept telling her he was dying. She told him to go ahead and do it then. He didn't need her permission.

"But he wasn't trying to ask her forgiveness. Sounded to me . . . He was trying to warn her. When he died, he wouldn't be able to protect her anymore. Except, I didn't know what that meant."

"What happened?" Quincy asked.

Telly shrugged. "Old man died. Just like he promised. Sandra got the note. Crumpled it up, threw it away. That was that."

"Except it wasn't over. Her father was telling her the truth."

Telly looked around again, searching the woods. "I got pictures. I found them. In my backpack. Pictures of Sharlah. Except someone had drawn a target around her head."

"What did you do?"

"Nothing. I wasn't sure what they meant, who they'd even come from. I was still trying to figure it all out and then . . . I came home one afternoon and there was a baseball bat in the middle of my bed. Brand-new. Tags still on. With a note. 'Instructions will follow.'"

"They wanted you to kill your parents, or they would kill Sharlah?"

"I guess. But why, how? I didn't understand." Telly's voice broke. "I didn't know what to do."

"Did you take the bat to Frank or Sandra?"

The kid shook his head. "I checked on Sharlah instead. I already had some information, so one day, I waited at the library and there she was. . . . She looked happy. Really happy. She had that dog, the German shepherd. And I read about you two—you and your wife. Former law enforcement. I figured whoever left the notes, they had to be bluffing. Because no way you two would let something happen to Sharlah."

Quincy waited.

"I put it all away," Telly whispered. "The notes, the bat. I tucked them in the garage. . . . Pretended it never happened, and then . . ."

"This morning . . . ," Quincy prodded, though he thought he already knew the rest. He wanted to hear it from Telly. And keep the boy talking. SWAT should have been on its way. Given Quincy's current condition, blood on his cheeks, more blooming across his shirt, he certainly wasn't in the best shape for apprehending an armed suspect.

"I came home from my morning run and I found them. In their bedroom. Both shot, just like that. Frank . . . He never even got up. Never had a chance. Frank, who could fix anything, and man, if you could see him with a gun. And then Sandra . . . Henry told me she was an even better shot than Frank, but guess I'll never know, 'cause she didn't make it out of the bedroom either. They were gunned down. Just like that. Neither of them stood a chance."

"You grabbed the guns and the truck and fled."

"There was another note. On my bed again. It said, 'You did this.' With it was a burner phone. I got the message just fine. My foster parents were dead and I was to take the blame. All over again."

"Or else?"

"There was another picture of Sharlah. Except this one was taken at her house. On her front porch. I didn't know what to think anymore. I didn't know what to believe."

"You ran."

"I grabbed some stuff. Best I could. The journals, the photos. Figured as long as everyone was going to start looking for me, I'd give you the right things to find. But then after I set up the camp, the burner phone I'd found on the bed rang. Some guy. Said he had another job for me. It was time to meet.

"So I drove to the EZ Gas, except the truck overheated. Had to walk the last quarter mile."

"You'd been there before," Quincy said. "With Henry."

The boy shook his head, but he looked away as he said this, no longer making eye contact. "I got there just in time to hear the shots," Telly said. "I ran. I had a gun of my own now. I swear I tried. But they were already dead. Instead, some old guy was lounging outside, still holding the pistol—"

"Who?"

"I don't know. Never seen him before." But the kid's gaze slid away again.

"He pointed it straight at me," Telly continued now. "He said, 'Remember, you did this.' Then he slapped the pistol in my hand and walked away."

"He gave you the firearm used to murder both victims at the EZ Gas."

"There was blood on it," Telly whispered. "From the girl, I think. Blowback? Isn't that what you guys call it? Blood on the gun, and then me. I tried to wipe my hand clean. But I couldn't. I couldn't. . . ."

The vomit, Quincy guessed. Telly had been in fight-or-flight mode at his home. But then, at the EZ Gas, staring at the blood on his own hands, the horror of the situation finally sinking in, the boy had thrown up. Though what he'd done with the incriminating pistol was a better question.

"I don't have it," Telly said now, as if reading Quincy's mind. "The nine mil, I ditched it first chance I got. I watch enough cop shows. I know he gave it to me to frame me for both murders. I'm not a total idiot."

"We need a description of that man. We need you to come in and work with us—"

Telly was already shaking his head. "Can't do it. You don't get it yet. Why'd I walk into that store? Why'd I shoot out the security camera?"

Quincy frowned. "So we'd see you—"

"Yeah. 'Cause I *did this*. Don't you get it yet? As long as I'm the one police are looking for, I'm upholding my end of the deal and my baby sister is safe."

"Telly, you're not just being tracked by every law enforcement officer in the state. There's tons of yahoos and local boys also running around with rifles at this point. Any of them find you first . . ."

"She's the only family I have left."

"Is that why you shot the search team?"

"I had to! I had to get away, keep them looking. I tried . . . I tried to just wing them, you know, aim for the shoulders. Are they okay? Are they going to make it?"

"One is still in critical condition."

The boy sagged. For the first time, Quincy could see the weight of stress and fear bowing his shoulders. The boy was trying to hold it together, but that didn't mean he was winning.

"You know what the funny part is?" he whispered. "I'm not even that good a shot. Especially with a rifle. Frank just started teaching me this past year. With a pistol, I'm pretty good, standing five yards from a target. The rifle, though, I've never really gotten comfortable with it. See how many shots it took me tonight just to hit a parked truck? But here I am, the most feared gunman in the state.

"I had to do it," he said again, voice stronger now. "I had to fire at those officers to keep them away. These people, they want something. Otherwise, why shoot Sandra and Frank? Why shoot the man at the EZ Gas? They're after something. If I can find it first, maybe I can negotiate. Keep both me and Sharlah safe. It's the only hope I have left."

"Come with me. We'll keep you safe. You have my word."

The boy looked up. Smiled, a flash of white in the night. "After I just saved your sorry ass?"

"Telly—"

"You can't help me. But that's okay, you know. All I need from you is to protect my sister." He hefted up his rifle. "If I can't find what has these people so hot and bothered, they'll go after her. I know they will. Lives mean nothing to them. They just want what they want, and we're all disposable in the end."

Engines roaring. Quincy heard them in the distance. SWAT closing in.

He wanted to say something. Tell the boy it would be all right. Tell him he could trust Quincy, that together they'd figure this whole thing out.

But even if Quincy didn't know Telly, he did know Sharlah. And she would never believe such a line either.

So instead, he said, "I'll take care of your sister. But make sure you take care of yourself. Because she needs you. You are her family, and she needs to see you again."

"I loved Frank and Sandra," the boy said abruptly. "I never told them that. Never knew how. But tell my sister, I found myself a real family. And it was . . . awesome. What we'd both deserved. Sharlah will understand. She'll be happy for me."

Roaring engines, much closer now.

Telly smiled one last time. Sad, Quincy thought. Forlorn. The boy turned, took a half step away.

"Stop," Quincy tried, wiping a fresh rivulet of blood from his eyes.

"Or what? You'll shoot?"

They both knew the answer to that.

The boy walked into the gloom.

Swaying on his feet, Quincy had no choice but to let him go.

Chapter 40

RAINIE AND I ARE SITTING at the conference room table when Quincy and the team finally return. It's way late. One in the morning? I should definitely be in bed. But Rainie hasn't said anything and neither do I. We're holding vigil. I imagine much like other parents and children who've sent their loved ones off to war.

Luka is asleep under the table. The only one of us able to relax, yet still keeping close. When the sound of approaching footsteps hits the hall, his head pops up immediately, one ear pivoting. Police dog, ready for action.

Then Quincy appears and, for a moment, none of us can speak. All I see is blood. His face. His shirt, his arm. My father.

And for the first time, I get it. What's really going on. What my brother might cost me.

"Are you—" Rainie starts, already on her feet.

As I hear myself say, "Did he do that? Did Telly hurt you?"

"I'm okay," Quincy says quickly. "Just banged up. Ricochet." He looks at me. "From another shooter, Sharlah. Not your brother. In fact, he may have just saved my life."

"And Telly?" Rainie asks.

"He bolted right before SWAT arrived," Quincy explains. "Given my, um . . . injuries, I was in no condition to stop him."

I can't get up. I can't move my legs, I can't feel my own body. Rainie is the one who crosses to Quincy. Regardless of blood and sweat, she throws her arms around him. Luka is already there, sniffing hard, whining low in his throat. Quincy winces but returns Rainie's embrace.

He looks at me over her shoulder and I like to think he understands why I can't move, all the things that once again I don't know how to say.

These are my parents, I think. This is my family.

I get up. I cross to Quincy, to Rainie, to my dog. I throw my arms around all of them, best that I can.

I still don't say anything.

I don't have to.

Because Rainie and Quincy have always understood.

Quincy leaves to clean up. Sheriff Atkins is off talking to her sergeant. The tracker guy has joined us in the conference room. He is guzzling water, not really making eye contact. His hands are trembling hard. Whatever happened at the Duvalls' house has shaken him up, but he's doing his best to not show it. I feel bad for him. Luka goes to him, presses against his leg. After a moment, the tracker reaches down, scratches Luka's ears. I am proud of my dog. He's more of a people person than I am.

Sheriff Atkins barely looks up as she walks into the room. She is carrying a sheaf of papers, skimming rapidly through them. Sergeant Roy and my father file in next. Quincy has exchanged his bloody shirt for a spare deputy's top. The sight of him in a brown uniform makes both Rainie and me smile. We quickly look down.

Shelly pauses long enough to wave hi. Quincy kisses Rainie on the cheek, pats Luka on the head, and, of course, gives my shoulder a gentle squeeze.

"Holding up?" he asks me softly.

"Did you really see my brother?"

"Yes."

"Did you shoot at him?"

"Actually, he shot at the person shooting at me. I have to say, I appreciated his intervention."

"I knew it," I say fiercely. "He is good. I told you he's good. He's my Telly. I knew it, I knew it, I knew it."

Quincy squeezes my shoulder again. "Pace yourself, Sharlah. It's going to be a long night, and there's still plenty of discoveries to go."

"All right," Shelly starts off briskly. "As we suspected, when Irene/Sandra ran away from her father and his criminal enterprise at the age of sixteen, she took an insurance policy with her. Before we were so rudely interrupted, I found a series of numbers taped to the bottom of the shelf where she kept her cookbooks. I plugged the numbers into the financial services database, and, believe it or not, I got a hit. Remember the Panama Papers, which revealed a bunch of hidden bank accounts owned by everyone from wealthy businessmen to high-ranking politicians? Well, you can add Sandra's father, David Martin, to the list. Apparently, those numbers match his own offshore stash. I'll work with Homeland to get more information, but the bits and pieces I got from the public doc indicate the account has been dormant for years. No additions or withdrawals. Which maybe goes to show the stalemate Irene had with her father. As long as he left her alone, she left the money alone."

"So how much money are we talking about?" Quincy asks.

"At the beginning of this year, twenty million dollars."

The room falls silent. I blink several times myself. Twenty million dollars. That's . . . a lot of money. More than I could ever imagine. Real money. Serious money.

The tracker speaks up first. "Wait a minute. Her father is dead, right? So as his daughter, doesn't Sandra Duvall get the money anyway? I mean, why keep the account secret anymore?"

"If Sandra came forward as David's daughter and sole surviving heir," Shelly says, "then yes, she'd get the money. But that would mean admitting she's Irene Gemetti and then facing the murder charge from thirty years ago. So reclaiming her identity isn't as easy as it sounds."

"Twenty million dollars would pay for a hell of a defense lawyer," Cal mutters. "I mean, if she wanted the money, seems like some crime committed when she was a minor, maybe even in self-defense against a known pimp, could be taken care of easily enough."

"I don't think she wanted the money," Quincy says quietly. "If she did, she would've raided the account already. But she didn't. Sandra made a choice to leave behind Irene Gemetti. I don't think her father's death changed that for her."

"Meaning there's twenty million dollars sitting in a bank account, just waiting to be claimed." Shelly shakes her head. "Plenty of reasons worth killing for."

"Who would even know of such a thing?" Rainie asks.

"Given the publication of the papers, anyone who takes the time to sort through one helluva long exposé," Shelly supplies briskly. "I'll be the first to say, however, not the easiest reading. So chances are, someone close to David Michael Martin. Which brings us back to"—she waves a new piece of paper in the air—"Douglas Perth, the new CEO of GMB Enterprises. As one of Martin's long-term associates and head of the financial end of the company, seems logical he'd know about both the account and also the reason Martin had for leaving it alone. He'd also be the first to realize the implications of Martin's death—that the account was now available for the taking."

"I don't understand," I hear myself blurt out before I can stop myself. A lot of adult eyes, now staring at me. "If this Douglas guy knows about the account, why doesn't he just take the money? Why involve Sandra at all?"

"Maybe because he can't." Rainie glances at Quincy. "Knowing about the account is only half the battle, right? You'd still need some kind of authority to access the funds. Sandra could do it—if she came forward as Martin's lone surviving relative and automatic heir. But a business partner . . . Douglas Perth might know about the money, but that doesn't mean he could do anything about it."

"PIN code," Cal mutters. He's pushed back from the table, already up again, roaming the room. Maybe trackers don't do well in such enclosed spaces. Now noticing we're all watching him: "Most bank accounts have them, right? I want to withdraw money from savings, I punch in my PIN code. Overseas bank can't be that different."

"No," Quincy says slowly. "Offshore accounts aren't that different." He tilts his head to the side, displaying his thinking face. "Maybe that's what Sandra had that Douglas Perth truly needed—basically the key to unlocking twenty million dollars."

Rainie continues for him: "So, Douglas sent his son, Richie, to hunt down Sandra Duvall and get the PIN code, password, whatever."

"Roy's been trying to reach Douglas Perth for the past hour, ostensibly to notify the man of his son's death, but Mr. Perth isn't answering any of his numbers. Which makes me wonder, of course, if Douglas Perth isn't the other gunman running around my county."

"He's the one with the mole on his wrist?" I ask, frowning. "From the EZ Gas security tape?"

But Rainie is already shaking her head. "Why would Douglas Perth kill his own son? Especially if Richie was running around on his orders?"

"Valid point," Shelly concedes. "For the record"—she looks at Quincy—"ME confirmed that Richie Perth had traces of GSR on his hands. Meaning he probably is the one who shot Sandra and Frank Duvall. Question is, what happened after that?"

"Telly told me he found his foster parents already dead when he returned to the house yesterday morning," Quincy supplies for the group. "There was a note on his bed telling him that he did this. There was also a burner phone. Someone had been sending Telly pictures of you, Sharlah, threatening your life. 'Further instructions to follow.' He hadn't figured out what to do when he found Frank and Sandra dead."

I nod, though this doesn't clear my confusion. I stroke Luka's fur, trying to find comfort, but there's none.

Quincy continues: "I'm fairly confident Richie killed the Duvalls.

We'd need a gun for a ballistics match to be sure, but I think Rainie has it right: Doug Perth knows about this twenty-million-dollar account. He lacked, however, means of accessing it. So he assigned his son to get the information. Richie enters the home first thing yesterday morning. Shoots Frank Duvall immediately, which explains why the man never even sits up in bed. That alone sends a certain message to Sandra: Start talking or you're next."

"So she talked," Shelly murmurs. "Gave up the password. At which point, he shot her as she tried to flee from the bed."

"I don't think so," Quincy said. "I think Sandra might've proved stubborn on that subject. Hence people are still running around town, shooting at the Duvalls' house. Someone certainly didn't want us there. Maybe the same someone who turned around and killed Richie, and is now hunting for the password on his own. He wouldn't want the police searching the Duvalls' residence. We might find the banking information first."

"But why Telly?" I interrupt. I can't help myself. "Why blame him for all this?"

Quincy's tone is gentle: "Because they can't afford to have the police digging into Sandra's past. They don't want any questions about her connection to the recently deceased David Michael Martin or his business practices. And Telly, given his history, presents the perfect patsy. They make him take the blame for the murders—"

"But he didn't do anything!"

"Except he still wants to protect you. He loves you, honey. You were right about that. Your big brother still wants to keep you safe."

I can't take it. I look down, stare hard at the top of Luka's dark head, blinking my eyes rapidly. Rainie, who is sitting closer, puts her arm around me. I want to move away, be stronger, tougher, but I don't. Mostly, I think of my brother, who's still doing his best to protect me. His little sister, who hadn't even bothered to talk to him in years.

I'm not sad; I'm ashamed.

"This is the part I can't quite get," Quincy is saying now. "According to Telly, after finding the Duvalls and the note, he loaded up the camping supplies, took the truck, et cetera. He knew he was in trouble. To keep Sharlah safe, he had to look like a killer fleeing from his crimes. So as long as law enforcement was looking for him, he wanted to give us plenty to find, including the photo of Martin taken at the Duvalls' house."

"He met with Sandra's father?" Rainie asks, her arm still around me.

"No. According to Telly, Sandra did. Maybe at the end, she decided to make amends. Telly wasn't sure. But after Telly fled from the Duvalls', he received a call on the burner phone, with instructions to meet at the EZ Gas. There, he was met by someone who handed him a nine millimeter. 'You did this,' the man said, which was the same phrase used at the Duvall crime scene, then the man left.

"When Telly went inside, he found Richie dead, as well as the cashier. Not knowing what else to do, he walked into the line of sight of the security camera and shot it, maintaining his ruse as the guilty party. He had to, in order to keep Sharlah safe."

Rainie pulls away, her brow furrowed. "So David's right-hand man sends his son, Richie, to get Sandra's banking password. Richie kills Sandra and Frank. And then someone else kills Richie?"

"Yes," Quincy says.

"I don't like this story," I say quietly.

"Hell, I don't completely understand this story," Shelly says. She's rubbing the back of her neck. "Sounds to me like there's someone else in play. Maybe a rival to Doug Perth?"

"A logical assumption," Quincy says.

"So this mystery man takes out the competition. Then once again utilizes Telly as the patsy. Meaning he must know that much about Richie's plan," Shelly states.

"Meaning we're not talking outside competition, but an in-house rival. Someone with knowledge of the original plan," Quincy says. "In an organization such as GMB Enterprises, that kind of competition can't be too surprising."

"But he still doesn't have the password," Rainie says. "So he returned to the Duvalls' house tonight. Found you guys there and opened fire."

"For twenty million dollars, why not?" Quincy shrugs. Then self-consciously touches the gouge on his temple.

I close my eyes. My head hurts. I want to go home and sleep . . . forever. Except, I know when I wake up, nothing will be better. In fact, if we can't figure out some way to help Telly, to identify this mystery rival, things might be much, much worse.

"Telly described the shooter from the EZ Gas as being an old man," Quincy says now. "But he looked away as he said this. He also claimed he'd never been to the EZ Gas before. But again, I got the feeling he was lying."

"Covering for someone?" Shelly asks. "You mean Henry Duvall? But why?"

Quincy looks at Shelly. "Henry admitted his grandfather approached him first. We only have his word that he never followed up with meeting the man. What if he did? And his grandfather told him about the twenty million dollars?"

"You think Henry killed his own parents?" Rainie asks.

"No, I think Richie killed the Duvalls. Which gives Henry double the motive to go after Richie—first for revenge for killing his parents, second to grab the twenty million for himself. Henry also has incentive to set up Telly: Clearly there's no love lost between those two. As long as Henry's world is going to hell, why not make his foster brother pay as well? I think he'd find a certain justice in that."

"But why wouldn't Telly admit that much?" Shelly asks. "Given the mutual love affair, doesn't Telly have just as much incentive to turn over Henry to us?"

"Not if he plans to go after Henry himself."

"One more person left to kill," I say abruptly.

Quincy looks at me. Nods slowly.

"Exactly."

Then the adults are once more up and exiting the room.

Chapter 41

*S*ANDRA AND I DIDN'T SPEAK *of that night. We fell back to routine. Summer school for me, household projects for her, some science camp duty for Frank at the local Y. Three people sharing a house, each waiting for the other to make the next move.*

I started going for a run early in the mornings. Trying to burn off "extra energy," as Aly would say, so I could focus better in class. I didn't know if I really had more tolerance for school, but the running felt good. One of the only times my head cleared and the pressure would lift from my chest. No more wondering what would happen to me in one more year. No more echoes of my sister screaming. When I ran, it became just my arms pumping and my heart pounding. I would focus on my own ragged breath and for a quarter mile, half a mile, four miles, I almost felt free.

I returned early that Wednesday, having made record time. The house was empty. Frank already off to camp, Sandra most likely at the grocery store—she liked to go first thing. I walked into the bathroom, already shedding stinky clothes. Quick shower, then time to head to school. I was in my bedroom, pulling on my T-shirt, when I heard the garage door open. Sandra returning from the store, I thought.

Shorts, socks, lace-up tennis shoes. I opened my door, and I . . .

I heard them.

Sandra, talking in a low voice to someone with an even raspier reply. I knew immediately she was meeting with her father.

He sounded terrible. Even weaker, threadier, than the day he'd met Frank. If I hadn't believed he was dying then, I definitely believed it now.

I crept down the hall, the old man's voice too hoarse to carry. I crouched down low at the very end, where I could just see them. Sandra's father, still wearing his tan trench coat even though it was warm out, collapsed in an easy chair. Sandra standing across from him, her arms wrapped tight around her waist. I couldn't see her face but could tell from her body language she was tense.

"Coupla . . . things . . . ," the man was wheezing. "Not much time . . . You . . . oughta know." He started coughing then. Wet, phlegmy. Sounded to me like a guy drowning in his own lungs.

Sandra didn't move. Offer him water, anything. She just stood there, waiting.

"Doug . . . Remember Doug? Smart man. Doug . . . He'll . . . run business."

Sandra didn't say anything.

"Could arrange . . . make you an officer . . . Put you on the board."

"No."

"Real business . . . Irene—"

"Don't call me that."

"Real company. These days."

She stared at him in cold silence.

"You are . . . my family. . . ."

She remained silent.

"Man . . . wants to honor . . . his family."

Still nothing.

"Your son." The old man switched gears. "Bright boy." Cough, cough, cough. "Going someplace . . . in life. Offered him a job."

"Leave him alone."

"Not really . . . your choice." The old man smiled. It was a hideous sight. His wide, gaping mouth, skeletal cheeks. He looked like

an animated corpse, grinning wildly. I dropped my gaze to the carpet.

"Leave him alone!" Sandra ordered again.

"Whattaya gonna do . . . kill me?"

Sandra stiffened. From where I stood, I could see her trembling with rage. "What do you want?" she asked coldly. "Just tell me, and let's get on with it."

"Your mom," he said, and for the first time, I saw Sandra flinch. "Buried her . . . No one at the funeral . . . Not even her own daughter . . . pay her respects."

"What about Mom?"

"Gonna be buried next . . . to her. That way, if you want to see her . . . gotta see me, too. That's the deal. Visit us both. Honor your parents."

"You always were a manipulative bastard."

The old man laughed. Or tried to anyway. It ended in another wet, ragged cough. When he finally fell silent, so did the whole room.

"Don't hate you . . . ," the man said at last. He sounded . . . reflective.

Sandra didn't answer.

"Admire you . . . even. Heard . . . you killed a man. Your first." He nodded slowly. "My daughter. Raised you right."

With her back to me, Sandra shivered. I couldn't decide if that was because she agreed with his words or was horrified by them.

"Your mom . . . too soft. Too sick for another baby. I wanted a boy. Had to settle for you. But you! Got me. Got me good. Boy would've betrayed me to my face. Knocked me off. Taken over. You . . ." The old man nodded at something only he understood. "Played the long game . . . better than anyone . . . I ever met."

Sandra didn't speak. She seemed to know what the man was going to say next.

"All games end." He looked up at his daughter. Stared at her with

his rheumy eyes. "When I die . . . Others know, Sandra. Doug knows. That account, our little secret . . . got published. Not our secret anymore. Not our little game anymore. Take the money. Just do it. Empty it all out. Don't care. Can't hurt me anymore. But do it. Before real people suffer."

"I'm already hurt."

"Doug'll want the money. Part of the business . . . in his eyes."

"He can have it."

"Don't be stupid!" For the first time the man snarled, reared up. "Didn't raise you to be stupid."

"No! You raised me to be violent, greedy, and mean. Well, too bad. I don't care about your damn money. I don't even remember the stupid pass code anymore. You want Doug to have it, then transfer it all over to him. I'm not stopping you."

"Your boy—"

"Leave Henry alone!"

"Because all children . . . follow their parents' wishes?"

"Time for you to leave." Sandra started to turn.

"Wait! Irene—"

"Don't call me that!"

"I'm trying to do right. Can't an old man . . . repent?"

But Sandra remained with her back to him. Minute dragged into minute. The old man issued another long, ominous sigh. Then . . .

He rose shakily, leaning heavily on his cane. Sandra made no move to assist. Belatedly, I realized they'd be headed through the kitchen, toward the front door.

I backtracked to my bedroom, then, thinking quickly, grabbed my cell phone, shimmied open my window, and climbed out. I ran straight ahead, figuring I could reach the cover of the rhododendrons before Sandra's father completed his painful trek.

I was just rounding the corner, bringing up my phone so I could snap some pics, when I ran smack-dab into Frank's crouched form, also taking cover in the rhodies, phone camera held before him.

"*Shhh*," he said immediately as I dropped to the ground beside him.

The front door was just opening. We didn't talk anymore. Just started snapping photos. I had a branch blocking the view on the front porch. I scooted around Frank, caught up with the old guy as he made his way gingerly down the front steps, came to a halt in front of the garage. Snap, snap, snap.

No driver. This surprised me. In the movies, the big crime bosses always have drivers, bodyguards, minions. But Sandra's father painfully folded himself into his black Cadillac on his own. Then he sat there for several long moments, no doubt gathering his breath.

A man drowning in his own fluids. You could hear it when he talked. He hadn't lied before. Anyone who sounded like that wasn't long for this world.

Sandra remained on the front porch. Just standing. Till at last her father started up his car, put it in reverse, drifted down the driveway.

At the last moment, I thought I saw her raise her hand. I thought, zooming in through the lens of my phone, I might have seen some lines of moisture on her cheek.

A daughter, saying good-bye for the last time.

Then she turned, walked into the house, closed the door.

Frank and I sat together in the dirt.

After a moment, I couldn't help myself. "Did you hear?"

"Enough."

"So what's all this money he's talking about?"

"Doesn't matter, Telly."

"He said something about Henry—"

"Don't worry about it. Henry's a smart boy. He knows who his real family is."

"Old man really is dying?"

"Yep."

"And she really doesn't care?"

"Nope. Old man always did underestimate his own daughter. She *saw this day coming even if he didn't. As for the money and every-thing else . . ." Frank turned to me, finally smiled. "Sandra's already taken steps. Joke's on him. Even dying. Joke's on him."*

I WAITED TILL THE POLICE LEFT, then doubled back to Frank and Sandra's house, resuming my perch on the roof. I didn't have any-place else to go. Couldn't make it far anyway, with only my legs for transportation and having already logged God knows how many miles. Besides, I doubted the night was over yet.

Sure enough, maybe an hour later. Twin headlight beams turning down the road, pulling over three houses back. Driver killed the lights. I waited, on my stomach near the chimney, finger on the trigger.

Figure appeared at the end of the driveway. Moving stilted. I looked for evidence of a gun but couldn't make out anything in the darkness.

I waited until he was nearly at the front porch.

Then I said a single word: "Henry."

Chapter 42

THREE A.M. ON A HOT SUMMER NIGHT, Henry's strip motel was busier than Shelly would've liked. People hanging out in front of their rooms, sitting on folding chairs and drinking beer, which they discreetly tucked behind them as the sheriff pulled up.

First deputy's car had already arrived on the scene. Shelly had Quincy sitting beside her. Roy followed in his vehicle. Plenty of people to confront a single man. As always, Shelly could feel the adrenaline pumping through her veins.

She also felt a corresponding sense of calm. She was the sheriff. This was her town, these were her people. Nothing here she couldn't handle.

She parked outside the manager's office. No flashing lights or sirens. It had already been a long day. Shelly wanted to keep this latest development as smooth and controlled as possible. Not to mention that regardless of their suspicions, Henry Duvall had also had a long, emotional day. In Shelly's experience, tired, stressed people could become very unpredictable very fast.

Assuming Henry was armed—which they certainly thought he was—it was even more imperative to keep things quiet and quick. Knock on the door. Cuff him before he had a chance to blink. Cart him off for further questioning while Roy and Quincy searched the man's room.

Shelly picked up her hat, jammed it down on her head. Final piece of the uniform in place.

Shelly and Quincy got out of the car.

Shelly entered the manager's office first. Her deputy was already there, asking all the right questions. No, the night manager hadn't seen Henry leave his room. And according to the vehicle log, his silver RAV4 was still parked outside. Perfect.

Shelly returned outside, motioned to Quincy and Roy.

"Henry should be in his room. We don't want to make this any messier than necessary. Quincy and I will do the honors. Knock on the door, say we have information regarding his parents. He's already answered questions once today, so hopefully our return won't arouse his suspicions. Once the door is open, I'll take him into custody.

"You"—she directed her gaze at Quincy—"keep your eyes open for a handgun. We don't need any more drama today."

Roy took up a cover position on the other side of the parking lot, tucking behind a vehicle where he'd have a line of sight on the open door but Henry wouldn't be able to see him. Meanwhile, the deputy approached the closest group of loitering guests and quietly urged them to return to their rooms. They picked up their beers without argument.

Then, just like that, it was showtime. Again, that curious combination of surging adrenaline and steady calm.

Quincy nodded once. They made their approach.

Room was dark. Given the time of night, not a surprise. If their assumptions were correct, and Henry had started his day discovering his parents' bodies before wreaking vengeance of his own, no doubt the man needed some beauty sleep.

Shelly stood front and center. A woman with nothing to fear. Quincy stood slightly to the side, having to watch his angle so he didn't block Roy's line of sight.

She rapped the door hard. "Henry Duvall," she called out loudly. "Sheriff Atkins. Sorry to disturb you, but we have news about your parents. Thought you'd want to hear."

Nothing.

She knocked again. Authoritatively, she liked to think.

Nothing.

She glanced at Quincy, who was frowning. Slowly, he moved to peer through the window. Curtains were half-drawn. He worked his way to the exposed slit in the middle, then shook his head.

"Too dark," he mouthed.

Shelly's turn to purse her lips.

"Henry Duvall," she called out again. "This is Sheriff Atkins. Open up. We need to talk. This is urgent."

Then, when seconds passed into minutes, "Get me the key," she murmured to Quincy, who motioned to the waiting deputy.

He jogged over shortly, manager's master key in hand.

"Henry," she tried one last time. "This is Sheriff Atkins. I'm coming in, okay? Just need to talk. It's about your parents."

She slid the key into the lock, feeling Quincy tense slightly beside her. But his breathing remained slow and even. She concentrated on that as she twisted the key, felt the lock give. Moving to the side now, so the door would offer her at least some kind of cover, she slowly eased it open.

"Henry," she called out again, voice softer now, eyes already sweeping the room.

She knew, though, before ever snapping on the light, that the room was empty. It had that kind of feel. Which didn't make a whole lot of sense, given the man's vehicle was still in the parking lot and his pack next to the bed.

"Shelly," Quincy said softly.

Then she spotted it, subtle at first, mixed in with the mottled pattern of the comforter. Bloodstains. Even if they were hard to see, one step closer brought her the smell.

"Telly got here first," she murmured.

"Then where's the body?" Quincy asked.

They searched the whole room but still didn't find an answer.

Chapter 43

THE MINUTE I SAID HENRY'S NAME, his head whipped up, his face briefly illuminated by the moonlight. Dressed in shorts and a dark-stained shirt, he looked nearly as exhausted as I felt. He was also shifted awkwardly to one side, his right hand pressed against his left ribs.

"Telly. You stupid son of a bitch." Henry never did like me. Now I continued to search him for signs of a weapon. Both hands, however, appeared clear. So why had he come back to the house? I wondered. Unless, of course . . .

"I didn't kill them," I said.

"Like hell—"

"I didn't kill them!"

I screamed the words. At least, I tried to. I think what might've come out was more choked with tears. Frank and Sandra. Sandra and Frank. My first and only real parental units. It would've worked. I know it would've worked. Except now . . .

Henry was still standing there, growling at me.

I did us both a favor. I rose to full height. Gave him a clear target, in case he had a handgun tucked unseen in the small of his back. Why not? And I said: "I know your mother's secret. I was there when she met with your grandfather. I know what's going on here."

He didn't answer, nor did he reach behind himself. If anything, he pressed his right hand tighter against his side, swaying slightly on his feet.

"Did you join them?" I pressed. "Are you part of this other *family* now?"

"I would never—"

"*You betrayed her!* Your grandfather told her. I was right there in the house when he tried to warn her. What did you do, Henry? *What the fuck did you do?*"

"I don't know what you're talking about! I never met with the old man. You did. You did this . . . all of this!" Henry's turn to scream at me, but I wasn't buying it.

"You wanted the money for yourself!"

"What money? What the hell, Telly? Do you have what he wants? Do you understand what's going on here? My mom . . . I don't understand. My mom—" Henry's voice broke off. He dropped his head, sagging hard against the side of the porch.

He sounded angry but also genuinely confused. A flicker of movement, out of the corner of my eye . . .

And then I got it. For the first time. Henry was not alone. There at the end of the drive stood a second figure. From this distance, I had a momentary impression of a heavyset fellow in night-vision goggles. Just as he raised his rifle.

Once last glimpse of Henry, clutching his side.

Where he'd been wounded, I realized. Shot by the same man, most likely the guy from the EZ Gas, who'd handed me the bloody handgun and set all of this in motion. He was supposed to be my target, if only I could find him. Except now . . .

I stood on the roof, totally exposed. The hunter becoming the hunted.

As the man looked straight at me and pulled the trigger.

He didn't miss.

Chapter 44

B Y THREE A.M., Rainie could tell Sharlah was dragging. The girl put up a good fight, sitting at the conference room table, spinning a bottle of water in front of her. Luka was already crashed at her feet, the big dog stretching in his sleep, as if reveling in his slumber.

The third time Rainie caught Sharlah nodding off, she made her decision.

"Come on," she said, rising to standing. "Shelly has an over-stuffed recliner in her office for a reason."

"I'm okay," Sharlah mumbled.

"You're asleep sitting up. If your head hangs any lower, you're going to give yourself a concussion. Besides, it's okay to sleep on the job. Look at him." Rainie gestured to the tracker, who was sacked out in the corner of the conference room, hat covering his face, head on his pack.

"Quincy—" Sharlah mumbled.

"Will be back at any time. Then it's all official questioning and piles of paperwork. Nothing for you to do anyway. Might as well get some sleep. You can be the lucid member of the family in the morning, because God knows Quincy and I won't be."

"Telly—"

"What will happen will happen," Rainie prodded gently. "There is nothing you can do for him tonight."

She could tell Sharlah was less than convinced. But Rainie made one last motion with her hand, and Sharlah reluctantly climbed to her feet. Luka came awake instantly, already falling in step beside her as Sharlah picked up her backpack and followed Rainie to the sheriff's office.

As head muckety-muck, Shelly Atkins got the proverbial corner office. Not huge, but it did offer windows overlooking the back and side parking lots. Better yet, it featured an old, battered gray recliner. Straight out of the nineties, with one corner chewed off and mauve pin-striping, it promised the best hope for snagging a few hours' sleep.

Sharlah didn't even bother to recline. She curled up in the thread-bare seat and was asleep with her head on the arm in seconds. Luka collapsed in front of the chair. Single sigh, and he was also out like a light.

Rainie paused. She stroked her daughter's rumpled hair. Marveled at the peacefulness of Sharlah's features at a time like this.

There was so much they still needed to say to each other. Present issues to resolve. Past issues to unravel.

But she loved this girl, loved her in a way she'd heard about but, even when they'd agreed to foster a child, hadn't been sure she'd really feel. Sharlah had come to them all rough edges and awkward silences and stubborn defiance. Intent on doing everything she could to put them off.

Instead, Rainie looked at her and saw herself thirty years ago. Was that love or was that ego? She didn't know. But the more Sharlah attempted to push them away, the more determined Rainie became to keep her close.

She saw the child beneath. She knew that girl. She'd been her once herself.

Someday, as she and Quincy often discussed, Sharlah would be a remarkable young woman. Assuming they all survived that long.

Now Rainie tucked a strand of brown hair behind her daughter's ear. She kissed two fingers, brought them to Sharlah's cheek. She wished her daughter sweet dreams, even though for both of them, that was easier said than done.

Then she returned to the conference room, having more work to do and wanting to let her daughter sleep undisturbed. She started once again with the crime scene photos. The Duvall residence, the EZ Gas station. What did they definitely know, and what had they missed?

Phone rang. Once. Hers? Someone else's? She must've dozed off. Groggily she made her way down the hall to check on her daughter.

But Sharlah, Luka, the backpack . . .

Sheriff Atkins's office was empty.

Sharlah was gone.

Chapter 45

WHEN MY PHONE FIRST RINGS, I'm disoriented. Gotta wake up, late for school. I fumble with my backpack, encountering Luka's head before I finally grab the strap, pull the pack up onto the chair with me.

More chiming. The generic tone, not one of the personal songs I've selected for Rainie or Quincy. This is all the warning I have before I finally get my phone out, tap answer, and hear a strange man's voice say, "If you want to see your brother alive again, you will bring me what he put in your backpack. Now."

I freeze. I can't breathe. I can't talk. I sit, soundless, motionless, in the dark. In front of me, Luka issues a low growl.

"Bring the dog and I will shoot it," the man says.

"Who are you?" I ask. I can't help myself. Stupid question. He'll never answer it, but I can't get my brain to function. My brother's life has been threatened, and I've gone stupid.

The man laughs. "Now," he repeats.

"Wait!" I gotta say something, do something. Think like a profiler. What would Quincy or Rainie do? "How do I . . . Proof of life! Proof that you have Telly. That he's alive. I need that."

Muffled sound. Maybe the phone being passed on the man's end. Then a voice I do recognize: "Don't do it," Telly says. His voice sounds strained. Stressed, I wonder, or hurt?

"Give it back," the man orders harshly in the background. "*Now!*"

"Remember Mom," Telly whispers. Then he's gone, and I'm left with a man I already don't like.

"Henry Duvall?" I try now, finally starting to think. Though I pictured Henry as a young guy, and the voice sounds more like an old man to me.

"Is that who the police are looking for?" Short laugh. "Glad to see all my hard work wasn't in vain. Nah. Henry's a little busy right now. Bleeding to death. But not before he led me back to his parents' house, straight into the arms of your brother. 'Fraid I got the drop on him, too. Youngsters these days. Spend all their time shooting up the bad guys on video games. Then hesitate when it matters in real life. Come on, now. According to your brother, you have what I want, and you're gonna hand it over before more people get hurt."

"I can't drive," I say, because honestly, that's all I can think of right now. Not will I meet this person, nor will I hand over Telly's secret, but *how* can I do such a thing.

"Brother says you know the library."

"Yeah."

"Not that far a walk from the sheriff's department. Be there in twenty."

"But—"

"Be there in twenty."

Then the phone blinks off. Call ended. I'm back to being alone in the dark.

"Luka," I whisper.

He whines, licks my face.

"Luka," I say again. Then I throw my arms around his neck and hold him close, because I'm going to need his strength and training for what will happen next.

TELLY TAMPERED WITH MY BACKPACK in the woods. He didn't just get out a bottle of water, he added to the contents. I knew it at the time, felt the shift in weight. And he knew that I knew. But I didn't ask any questions, because I didn't want to know what I didn't want to know. Then later, with Rainie keeping me so close, there simply wasn't the time to inspect my pack and confront the obvious.

Now I unzip the main compartment. I eye the heavy metal object I've been expecting to see. A handgun. The handgun, I suppose, used to kill those people at the EZ Gas. Then hidden in my pack by my brother, who couldn't afford to be found with it on his person.

And now the caller wants it back again?

I don't understand. Who is this guy anyway, especially if he *isn't* Henry Duvall? And why does he want his gun again?

I reach in with a pencil. I hook it through the trigger guard, like I've seen them do in cop shows, and, very gingerly, I pull the weapon out. I eye the open door, willing Rainie not to appear as I inspect my find. It is what I expected, and yet . . .

Why would some guy be holding my brother hostage for this? A handgun is not a key to twenty million dollars.

Then, all of a sudden, I get it. My own foolishness. Telly needed to part with the gun, sure, but he also used it as a red herring, its obvious weight disguising what he really needed to hide. What, most likely, he expected me to find, maybe even turn over to my law enforcement parents, except I was too busy being hurt by my brother's rejection to inspect what he left behind in my pack.

Now I peer back inside the main compartment. Beneath the half-empty bottle of water and granola wrappers, I see what I was meant to see hours ago. Small, innocuous, and, yeah, most likely the key to tens of millions of dollars.

It takes me another five minutes. Creeping around the sheriff's office, firing up Shelly's computer, belatedly doing my homework. But while I might be slow, I'm not a total idiot.

I can read a computer screen. And I understand now the full danger my brother is in.

The mystery caller is smart: The library is a good meeting place.

Only a six-block walk. Deserted this time of night. The parking lot surrounded by enough bushes and trees to cover up a secret meeting.

I guess that's good. Disturbances would be bad. Maybe goad the man into shooting Telly and/or me? Or maybe he will kill us anyway. I don't know the man's true identity, let alone what he's capable of.

I'm going to go. Does that make me stupid?

Or are the events to come simply . . . inevitable?

My father's beet-red face, bulging eyes, as he chased Telly and me with the bloody knife. Eight years apart, and now, here we are again. Another madman. Another night of do-or-die.

Remember Mom, Telly said.

I do.

I pull Luka close. I whisper in his ear, fiddle with his collar.

Then I slip the awful handgun in the back waistband of my shorts, sling my backpack over my shoulders, and tiptoe down the rear stairwell.

Luka has his instructions, I have mine. Library, here I come.

I START TO FEEL ANTSY within a block of the target. The Bakersville County Library is a two-story building with a yawning foyer and some clock tower thingy. The tower looks really cool, but it strikes me now as the perfect place to stand with a high-powered rifle. Maybe the caller is already watching me through the scope. What is to stop him from simply pulling the trigger, then grabbing my backpack?

I don't know. I'm nervous and scared and . . . exposed. I miss Luka, always trotting by my side. But I'm also grateful he's not here with me, because if the guy really is watching me from the clock tower . . .

I couldn't bear for Luka to get hurt.

Besides, he can't be here for this moment. Eight years ago, Telly and I didn't have a pet.

I slow as I arrive at the street corner across from the library parking lot. Strain my ears for the sound of something, anything.

The streets are empty. Up ahead, a traffic light goes from red to green without any audience. Bakersville is hardly a busy place during the day, let alone this time of night.

Crossing the street, I have a small moment of inspiration. I unsling my pack, then turn it so it hangs from my shoulders in front of me. Now my torso has a makeshift shield. Shoot the pack, risk damaging Telly's secret.

I would like to feel brilliant, but mostly I'm forcing some guy I've never met into taking a head shot. I'm pretty sure Quincy and Rainie would have a better master plan than that, but at the moment this is the best I can do.

Parking lot. I slow, approach the turn-in. There are lampposts in the lot. At least, that's my memory. But either he's done something to tamper with the bulbs or the lights automatically turn off, because currently the expanse is completely dark. I search the space, my eyes already adjusted to the lack of light, but I can't make out anything.

Once again, my gaze goes up. Studying the roof, the clock tower.

Remember Mom, Telly said.

I do, I do, I do.

And I wish I had one moment in time to go back, hug Rainie, and tell her I'm sorry.

Ahead it is.

I walk through the trees now, easing in and out of the border plantings. I'm here, I've done as instructed. Next step is his problem, but I don't want to be any bigger of a target than I already am.

Then, just as I'm getting close to the front doors of the library:

"Stop."

The man's voice is behind me. I turn, making out the shape of a truck in the rear corner of the parking lot. Maybe a man is standing beside it. Hard to tell from this distance.

"Set down the pack," he says.

I don't move.

"Set it down and get out of here, or I'll shoot you and your brother both."

I still don't move. He definitely sounds like an old guy, but who?

"Did you hear me—"

"I want to see him. I'm not doing anything till I see him."

Silence. My turn to wonder if he heard me. My back is very sweaty now. And my shoulders twitchy.

"Listen, girl—"

"There's a rain gutter here. Probably dumps into the ocean. I don't know, but this close to the coast, wouldn't you think?" I hold up a small metal object. I don't know if he can see it in the dark, but I don't care. "Show me my brother, or down the drain it goes."

"You little shit—"

"Show me my brother."

Sigh. I recognize the tone. Another adult clearly not happy with me. If I weren't so terrified, I would feel proud of myself.

The sound of a vehicle door creaking open. Then:

"Sharlah."

Telly. His voice sounds awful. He's hurt, I think. The man hurt my brother.

"Are you okay?" I ask softly.

"Good enough," he says, but I already don't believe him.

"Henry?" I ask, still trying to understand.

"Come toward me," the man orders now, interrupting.

"No."

"Then I shoot—"

"And down the drain it goes!" My turn to interrupt, equally hostile. "Shoot my brother, shoot me, step left, step right, down the drain it goes. The key to twenty million dollars, right? That's what this is all about. Twenty million dollars. It is a lot of money," I assure him. "Would be a shame to lose it now."

The man doesn't speak. He doesn't have to. I can feel his rage and frustration from here. Welcome to oppositional defiant disorder, I want to tell him. If this is how you feel now, imagine my poor parents, who have to deal with it every day.

"You don't know—"

"It's a thumb drive," I interrupt. "I know thumb drives. And how to stick them in computers and how to read them. She moved the money, didn't she? Sandra Duvall took the twenty million dollars out of her father's account and used it to start a foundation. The Isabelle R. Gemetti Foundation. Is that her mother? She's going to use the money to help other women like her mom? Because that would be ironic, right? I know irony, too. Just like I know rain gutters."

A hoarse rattling sound. I think it is coming from Telly. He's laughing. Is he proud of me? I hope he's proud of me, because I'm still not sure exactly what to do next.

"Where is Henry?" I ask. "What happened to him?"

"House," Telly rasps. "Duvalls' . . . He's shot."

"Shut up," the man says. "That is my money. I don't care what it's called or what fund it sits in. It's mine and I'm taking it back."

"Send my brother over."

"No."

"I'm not leaving the rain gutter. You want your thumb drive, come and get it."

The man doesn't move. Can't decide. Thinking it through?

I'm glad the parking lot is dark and empty. My hand is shaking uncontrollably now. I'm not sure what to do next. The rain gutter is my only leverage. I leave it, I'm dead, so I'm not leaving it. But still, he comes to me, and then what?

Telly crawls away while the man's back is turned, man gets the thumb drive, then shoots me, then tracks down Telly and shoots him?

Telly won't leave me. We are in this together, just like eight years ago.

Remember Mom, he said.

My back, soaked through. My shoulders twitchy.

The man approaches. Hard, steady footsteps. Emerging from the shadows. Closer, closer, till I can see the rifle held in his hands. While it's too dark to see, I'm already willing to bet there's a mole above his pale wrist.

"You're the shooter from the EZ Gas," I blurt out. I still don't recognize the man. He's definitely old. Potbellied, some kind of suspenders holding up sagging jeans. Even from this distance, however, I can feel the intensity of his gaze. A former associate of Sandra Duvall's father, I would guess. The kind of guy who was bad enough in his day and, based on the current levels of carnage, clearly remembers how to pull a trigger just fine.

"Your father is the FBI profiler," the man rasps. He's fifteen feet away now, advancing steadily. My arm drops to my side. I don't want him to see what I'm holding. Not yet. "Police know about the money, then."

"You killed Richie Perth," I say, doing my best to sound certain. "After he shot the Duvalls. You wanted to keep the money for yourself."

"Police have been busy."

"But then when you went to access the account, the money wasn't there. Because Sandra had moved it. But she didn't tell Richie that, did she? She held out."

"Richie was always a bit stupid," the man says. "Kind of idiot that shoots first and questions later. Me, I know better." He levels the rifle at my chest.

"Who are you?" I ask, genuinely curious. I mean, if this guy is going to kill me . . .

"Jack George. Met the search team earlier today. Might say I knew Dave from the good old days. We rose up through the ranks together. Before retiring, I was his first lieutenant."

"Gangsters are allowed to retire?"

"Trusted fellows, sure. David got a bead on Sandra's new life years ago. Right around when I retired. Asked me to settle here, keep one eye on his daughter, the other on the Nehalem operations. Bakersville's a nice enough place. Not to mention a guy my age doesn't like to be too bored."

I don't know what to say to that.

"Then Dave was diagnosed with cancer," Jack George continues now. "Decided he wanted to make amends. Sandra, as she liked to call herself, never relented though. She might've thought of herself as better than her father, but if you ask me, the whole problem was they were too much alike. Hardheaded, and just plain hard, both of them."

"You knew about the money? The stalemate she had with her father?"

"Like I said, Dave and I went way back. You're stalling," he says.

Of course I am. Jack George draws to a halt ten feet away. From this distance he can see I'm definitely standing on a rain gutter, and I have something clenched in my fist. He scowls, for the first time appearing uncertain.

Behind him, I can watch as my brother slowly starts limping forward. He's moving awkwardly; it appears his hands are tied behind his back. Meaning he's both wounded and restricted. In other words, I'm on my own. In a stare-down with a man with a rifle.

"Doug Perth called me with the plan," Jack George continues now. He's studying me intently, looking for a sign of weakness. "He wanted me to help out Richie in return for a cut of the money. After all these years, however, why settle for a cut? Not like my retirement years have been that golden. Richie called me after he shot Sandra. Whined she'd tricked him. Pretended to give up the information, so he shot her. Of course, then he looked up the account and realized it'd been emptied. I knew Sandra, though. She was always plenty smart. If the money was gone, she'd done something with it. Just a matter of finding the trail. So I eliminated my rival—"

"You shot Richie and the cashier."

"And went to work on your brother. I already knew of Richie's push to have Telly take the blame in order to save your life. Richie had sent him some threatening photos of you, left a baseball bat on the kid's bed. Not a bad idea. In fact, why mess with success? I met with Telly at the EZ Gas and delivered the new and improved terms. He could now take credit for Richie's death as well, in order to protect his little sister. Better yet, he could locate the missing money to save his own life. Turns out, though, Telly might have learned a trick or two from Sandra. He tried to play a game of his own, leaving hints for the police, stashing the thumb drive with the new account information in your pack, a girl who basically lives in police custody.

"Family is powerful, though, don't you think? Oh, the things we'll do for family."

The old man smiles at me. Then he levels the rifle at my chest. This close, no way he'll miss.

"Your brother didn't want to give up your name or your phone number. But a guy like me, I spent years being paid to be very persuasive. 'Sides, once I realized Henry didn't have the account info and Telly didn't have the account info, only one other person Telly would trust with such a secret. Which brings me to you, and our little rendezvous. Time's up, girl. Give me what I want, and maybe you'll get to see your family again."

Jack George stares at me across the short space. I take a deep breath. This is it. Moment of truth. Because I already don't believe anything the retired gangster is saying. Second I hand over what he wants, both Telly and I are dead. Which is what I suspected from the very start.

"I got bad news," I whisper.

"No, you don't."

I bring up my left hand as I reach behind me with my right.

"I don't have the thumb drive." I show what I'm really holding in my hand, metal fingernail clippers I keep stashed in my backpack.

Remember Mom.

"What?"

"I gave the thumb drive to my dog. He's a really good dog. Smart, too. He's delivering the evidence to the sheriff, even as we speak. No money for you."

"You stupid little—"

A muted roar from behind him. Telly finally close enough to make his move, just as I figured he'd try to do. No baseball bat for my brother this time. Instead, he's staggering toward the man, arms tied behind his back, head lowered to make himself a human battering ram.

I don't think. I don't hesitate.

Remember Mom.

I whip out the gun from the small of my back. The other item Telly stashed in my pack.

I don't know how to shoot. I have no idea what I'm doing.

But then I didn't know eight years ago, when I took the bat from my dazed brother's hand and stood over my mother's waking form.

The woman who loved us. The woman who laughed and sang and danced us around the kitchen. The woman who never protected us, not even when my father was beating Telly so badly, my older brother begged for his life.

If she still lived . . .

Raising the bat then.

Aiming the gun now.

Telly's stubborn roar.

The man's echoing cry of rage.

A single shot ringing out into the night.

Jack George goes down.

As Luka charges into the parking lot, Quincy, Rainie, and the others on his heels. Quincy is holding his twenty-two. His winning shot, because my handgun did nothing but issue an empty click. Which just goes to show how little I know about firearms; Telly removed all the bullets and I was none the wiser.

I don't care. I don't care about anything but Telly.

I run to him now, as he staggers, drops to one knee.

My brother. My proud, strong, means-everything-in-the-world-to-me big brother.

I throw my arms around him just as he pitches forward.

We both go down, down, down.

Telly doesn't get up again.

Epilogue

I HAD A FAMILY ONCE.

Sandra and Frank, they tried to do right by me. But Sandra had her own ghosts, hunting her down. She told me about them, after her father's visit. Her last night at her childhood home. How she made her great escape, taking with her information on her father's hidden bank account.

For thirty years, that knowledge served as her insurance policy. He didn't want anyone to know about the money, so if she kept his secret, he'd keep hers.

A year ago, however, the offshore account became public knowledge, with the publication of some foreign law firm's business papers. Suddenly, her father was ratted out even to his own lieutenants. A couple of them, including Douglas Perth, knew what Sandra had done all those years ago, stealing the account information.

Sandra's father tried to warn her that when he died, she'd lose what protection his presence still offered her. Sandra didn't believe him, though. She had her own idea. The day of his death, she transferred the hidden funds out of his account and set up a foundation in her mother's memory to help support battered women's shelters across the country. She liked the irony of it. Twenty million dollars of ill-gotten gains finally being put to good use.

What she didn't plan on was her father's business associates' determination to get their hands on the money for themselves. Quincy explained it to me later. How Martin's successor, Doug Perth, sent his own son to track down Sandra and gain access to the funds.

How Richie Perth killed Frank and Sandra in their own bed, then framed me, the troubled foster son, for his crime.

What Richie didn't know was that Jack George, Martin's former lieutenant, had plans of his own.

I'd never even met the old man before. Didn't know who he was when he summoned me to the EZ Gas, handed me Richie's murder weapon, and informed me I would once again be the fall guy. Or my sister would pay the price.

What could I do about it? I shot out the security camera, took the blame to keep Sharlah safe. Then I tried to find Jack for myself, knowing only that he'd headed north on foot. When I walked into the neighborhood and some crazy guy took potshots at me while screaming at me to get out of his yard, I didn't realize how close I was. I really did think he was some lawn lunatic. I fled, hid out across the street. Where the tracking team eventually found me, and I was forced to take actions I will regret for the rest of my life.

I didn't lie to Quincy—I really wasn't that great a shot with a rifle. I did my best to aim away from center mass, maybe scare the team away. I hit two instead. Both lived, but I got more screams to keep me awake at night. Not to mention a longer criminal history. But we'll get to that in a sec.

Jack must've figured he was good to go at that point. Police are chasing me. Giving him plenty of time to complete Richie's failed mission—find the twenty mil.

So he returned to Frank and Sandra's house that night. Except the police were already there. He tried to scare them off with rifle fire, only to end up with me shooting back. After that, he went with plan B: track down Henry, who must surely have known his mother's secrets.

Except Henry had been away from home for a long time. Sandra hadn't had a chance to tell him anything yet. Henry got shot in the side as encouragement to talk. Realizing the next bullet might be in a knee, he bluffed the best he could. Sure, twenty mil, he knew everything . . . Just let him return to the house.

Where Henry found me. And Jack gave me a matching wound in the left shoulder. Then I did my own kind of bluffing. A Hail Mary pass, really.

In the woods that afternoon, not knowing what else to do with the handgun the old man had given me, I'd stuck it in Sharlah's backpack. I'd removed the bullets, plus the firing pin. Didn't want the gun to be a threat to her. But I also used its weight to cover for my bigger secret, stashing Sandra's thumb drive with the new account information. I figured eventually Sharlah would find the drive, share it with the police. Maybe if they had the old account information, realized what Sandra had done thirty years ago, that in turn would lead them to Jack George and what was going on now. Though of course, I didn't want them to find George too quickly. By hiding the thumb drive versus handing it over, I gave myself time to find him first. I'd meant what I'd said to Sharlah that afternoon. After what he did to my family . . .

I really did have one more person left to kill.

Did Sandra know someone would come for her all these years later? Did she expect that it couldn't really be that easy? That nothing in life came for free, or, maybe simply, the more you run, the more the past has a way of catching up?

Sandra had used the home computer to handle setting up the foundation, then transferring the money. Then she'd copied all the info onto a thumb drive before erasing it from the computer's hard drive—she didn't want Henry seeing anything before she had a chance to talk to him herself. Or so she said. Personally, I think she was simply so accustomed to keeping secrets, she couldn't approach the money any other way.

After discovering her and Frank's bodies first thing in the morning, I'd hunted down the thumb drive, stashed in the binding of one of her cookbooks. I didn't know what I'd do with it. But if Sandra had a habit of keeping secrets, then I had a habit of keeping her secrets safe.

Later, encountering Sharlah in the woods, I realized this was my best moment to hand off the information. If the gun and the photo didn't lead Sharlah's parents in the right direction, the thumb drive should.

Later, lying wounded on the ground in front of my parents' house, with Jack standing over me, ready to finish the job, I realized I had only one hope left: reach out to the sister I'd been trying so hard to protect. Hope her parents really did live up to their reputation, do some protecting of their own.

I didn't realize Sharlah would honestly come on her own. Or that she'd bring the toothless gun.

When I told her to remember Mom, what I meant was for her to let me take the blame.

But Sharlah had her own memories. More than I realized. She was the one who delivered the deathblow that night. Before I took the bat from her and, in my grief and rage, turned on the sister I swear I loved as much as our mother.

Except our mother . . .

I don't know. There are some relationships, some kinds of love, I still can't explain.

I wouldn't have hurt our mom that night. I would've called an ambulance. I would've saved her. And as Sharlah and I have discussed since, our mother would've hooked up with the next pill-popping asshole, and we probably would've ended up right back where we started.

But she was our mom. And as I told Sandra, I still remember those moments when she was happy.

I miss that mom. I mourn her every day.

And my baby sister?

She saved me. Again. She had her own family, and she used them well. Deploying her beast of a dog with the thumb drive and a note to her mother, telling Rainie Conner exactly where Sharlah was going and the help she needed next.

Family is about trust, Sharlah told me.

So her cavalry came. Rainie and Quincy and the sheriff herself to the rescue.

Family helps family, Sharlah told me.

Which is why she walked to an empty library in the middle of the night and why she stood up to a madman, just for me.

Sharlah, Rainie, and Quincy all visited me in the hospital. Quincy even contacted my probation officer, Aly, who, by virtue of being my already assigned caseworker, was the one who held my legal future in her hands.

I didn't shoot Frank and Sandra. I didn't kill anyone in the EZ Gas. But I did fire on a tracking team, wounding a SWAT officer and a volunteer searcher, even if I didn't mean to. Charges included attempted murder, first-degree assault, and reckless conduct involving firearms. All felonies. In adult court, I could have been looking at up to fifteen years.

As a seventeen-year-old juvenile, however, I could have stayed in the juvie system, served out my time in lockup, followed by years of probation, community service, and mandatory counseling.

Interestingly enough, it was Henry who spoke up on my behalf. Wrote a letter to Aly herself, talking about how much his parents believed in me. Frank and Sandra wanted to help me get my life on track. To have it thrown away instead, because I got caught up in drama from Sandra's past . . .

Henry healed first, then spent some time hanging out in my hospital room. I told him what I knew about his mother, what she'd done as a girl. These days, Henry has his hands full, the sole heir to and executive director of a twenty-million-dollar foundation.

He offered me a job, but his heart wasn't really in it, and we both knew it. We were trying, more for Sandra's sake, but other than his parents, we didn't exactly have much in common. We're not family. Just two people who happened to love Frank and Sandra Duvall.

Their funerals. You should've seen the number of people who came out. Frank's students alone . . .

He would've been proud. So proud.

Aly invited me to live with her for a bit. She got me my juvie trial, scheduled in a couple of months. Quincy helped. Wrote up how I saved his life. Then in the zero-or-hero debate, a judge will get to make the final ruling. For now, I'm going to counseling, doing my work, as Aly puts it. 'Cause life is choices and consequences and I gotta get better at my choices, so I can earn myself some better consequences.

I want to go to culinary school. I wanna bring Sandra's chicken Parm to the world, 'cause when I'm in the kitchen, I can feel her beside me, and that feels good.

I want to give a hand up to other struggling kids. If I was my own chef, I could offer jobs as busboys, dishwashers. I could teach, because when I reach out, I feel Frank beside me, and that feels good.

I want to get to know my sister again. Spend more time with her and her family. Because when she smiles at me, I don't remember that night anymore. I remember Cheerios and *Clifford the Big Red Dog*. I feel proud and strong, like a big brother should, and that feels good.

I want to do better.

I want to be better.

I had a family once.

Now, with a little bit of work and effort, one day . . .

I'm gonna have a family . . .

Again.

Acknowledgments

The genesis for *Right Behind You* started close to home. First and foremost, I must thank my readers for suggesting it was time for another Quincy and Rainie book. As a novelist who's somehow managed to write several series—the FBI Profiler thrillers (aka the Quincy and Rainie books), the Detective D. D. Warren novels, and the Tessa Leoni books—I decided to conduct a Facebook poll in the spring of 2015 to see who should star in my 2017 novel. I'll be the first to say, I thought it would be a toss-up between D. D. Warren and Tessa Leoni. But no, the hands-down winner: Quincy and Rainie. Which led to spending my fall rereading my own novels, as it had been so long since I'd written about the FBI profilers, I had plenty of catching up to do!

Once I knew I was writing a profiling book, I needed a crime. Hardest thing about being a suspense novelist—coming up with something I haven't already written about. In this case, I decided to research spree killers, a new type of killer for me, but certainly one that's topical. As fate would have it, I sat down on my sofa, picked up my husband's copy of *SWAT* magazine, and discovered an article on fugitive tracking, written by Pat Patton. I loved his point that for all the technology now available, there's still no substitute for good, old-fashioned trail work. Being the optimistic type, I fired off an e-mail to Pat, suggesting he spend some of his valuable time educating a bumbling suspense novelist. And he agreed! So my deepest appreciation to Pat Patton, whose insights and expertise taught my fictional tracker, Cal Noonan, everything he needed to know. Any mistakes and/or fictional license are my fault alone.

A spree shooter needs to be armed. All these years and multiple firearms classes later, I'm still not comfortable with guns. On the other hand, my husband and daughter are excellent target shooters. So continuing my quest to write a novel without ever leaving my sofa, I picked their brains for Frank Duvall's gun collection and, of course, shooting lessons. My husband and daughter are very smart and did their best to bring me along. Once again, any mistakes and/or fictional license are my fault alone.

For Sandra Duvall's cooking tips, I owe a big thank-you to my own mother, whose roasted chicken is an exercise in perfection. Oh, and Telly grating his thumb—that would be my daughter again. See what happens when you hang out with a thriller author? Anything, everything, becomes fodder for the next novel.

Next up, developing Telly and Sharlah's troubled past. My deepest appreciation to Dr. Gregg Moffatt and Jackie Sparks, M.S., OTR, ECMHC, for their insights into childhood trauma and proper evaluation of youthful offenders. I also spent a lot of quality time interviewing probation officers and family social workers. The system is not perfect, but as Telly and Sharlah can attest, there are great families out there, and forever homes waiting to be found.

On the subject of family, why not include our canine members? I owe a huge thank-you to New Hampshire state trooper Gregg DeLuca and his gifted Belgian Malinois, Tyson, who provided the background for Luka. I could've listened to stories of DeLuca and Tyson's accomplishments all day long. As Trooper DeLuca put it, Tyson is a once-in-a-lifetime dog. I understood what he meant perfectly.

Which brings us to the incomparable Molly, a shelter dog who found her forever home with Deb Cameron and Dave Klinch. Thanks to their generous donation to the Conway Area Humane Society,

Molly received her star-making turn as a tracking dog extraordinaire, with her dog handler, Deb, of course. Molly, aka Mollywogs, is one of the sweetest, bravest, goofiest dogs I've ever met. In real life, Molly might be more likely to snore loudly than take down an armed fugitive, but she is still a hero. Discovered abandoned, emaciated, and a day away from delivering puppies, Molly was taken in by a dog rescue group in Tennessee. Despite her own poor health, Molly gave birth to seven fat, healthy puppies and nursed them proudly. Upon arrival in New Hampshire, the pit bull mix's sweet disposition made her an instant favorite at the shelter. In the end, shelter manager Deb couldn't part with her, and Molly became a beloved member of her family. For more information, you can check out Molly's Facebook page, www.facebook.com/mollywogwalks/photos. I think you will agree she is one very photogenic dog!

David Michael Martin also won naming rights in this book thanks to a donation to the shelter. As a man with three names, he thought he'd make an excellent serial killer. I have to agree. His original donation, however, was in memory of his beloved grandmother Norinne Manley, aka Nonie. Nonie was also the mother of Carol Manley, whom readers might recognize as a detective in *Find Her*. To summarize, David's fictional family now includes a criminal mastermind, a Boston detective, and a fugitive tracker. I might have to write their family reunion next. Thank you again, Dave, for your generosity to the Conway Area Humane Society, and I hope you enjoy!

Once again, I invited my readers to get in on the murderous fun. Erin Hill won the annual Kill a Friend, Maim a Buddy Sweepstakes on LisaGardner.com, nominating herself as the lucky stiff. Isabelle Gerard won the international edition, Kill a Friend, Maim a Mate, selecting Bérénice Dudkowiak for a role as a forensic psychologist. Never fear, the contest is already back up and running for 2018. Best wishes for your own shot at literary immortality!

TURN THE PAGE FOR AN EXCERPT

The home of a family of five is now a crime scene: four of them savagely murdered, one—a sixteen-year-old girl—missing. Was she lucky to have escaped? Or is her absence evidence of something sinister? Detective D. D. Warren is on the case— but so is survivor-turned-avenger Flora Dane. Seeking different types of justice, they must make sense of the clues left behind by a young woman who, whether as victim or suspect, is silently pleading, *Look for me*.

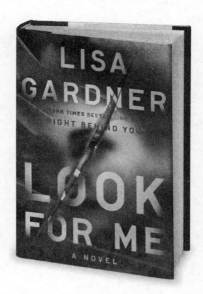

"Lisa Gardner is the master of the psychological thriller."
—Associated Press

 Penguin Random House

Prologue

A YEAR LATER, *what Sarah remembered most was waking up to the sound of giggling.*

"Shhh. Not so loud! My roommates hate it when I bring boys home. Killjoys need their beauty sleep."

"So, no making noises? Like this?" A wolf howl from outside Sarah's bedroom door.

Fresh giggling. Then loud thumps as someone, probably Heidi, ran into the coffee table, the couch, the standing lamp.

"Oh well," Heidi announced. "Quiet was never gonna happen. I'm a screamer and proud of it."

A man's voice: "Knew I picked the right girl at the bar. I like screamers. Always have."

More giggling, more thumps.

Sarah groaned, rolled facedown on her tiny mattress, and pulled her pillow over her head. On the opposite side of the wall, no doubt Christy and Kelly were doing the same. Heidi Raepuro had been a last-minute addition to their apartment. A friend of a friend of a friend, qualified mostly by the fact Heidi was willing to pay extra for her own bedroom, and Sarah, Christy, and Kelly, who'd known one another since freshman year, had really wanted the three-bedroom unit. Walking distance to Boston College, bay windows, hardwood floors, crown molding. When Sarah had first walked into the space, she'd felt like a grown-up. No more minifridge, no more standing-room-only dorm room. No more bare mattress shared with two younger siblings in an overcrowded slumlord's paradise.

The long nights studying when the rest of her friends had been out partying or repeating their parents' drug-fueled mistakes had finally paid off.

Which was the other reason she'd fallen in love with the brightly lit apartment. Because after spending her entire childhood sharing, sharing, sharing, this place offered her the greatest luxury imaginable: her own room. Granted, it was barely the size of a twin mattress, more a closet than a bedroom, most likely converted by an enterprising landlord looking to charge a three-bedroom price for what was originally a two-bedroom unit, but Sarah didn't care. Tiny fit her budget. And with Christy and Kelly able to split the largest room, and silly, vapid Heidi cashing out the other main sleeping space, everyone was happy. Especially Sarah, ensconced in her minuscule slice of paradise.

Except for nights like tonight.

More crashing—then moaning. Good God, didn't Heidi ever get enough?

A curious scrape.

"Hey now." Heidi's voice, hiccupping slightly as she panted from exertion.

Sarah rolled her eyes, pulled the pillow tighter around her ears.

"Wait . . . I don't want . . . No!"

Sarah sat up just as Heidi screamed. Loud, piercing, and . . .

Do screams have a taste? Fire? Ash? Red-hot cinnamon candies, which as a little girl Sarah liked to let melt on the tip of her tongue?

Or is it more that screams have a color? Green and gold giggles, purple and blue cackles, or this? Molten white. Melt-your-eyeballs, singe-the-hair-on-your-arms, bright, bright, white? A color too brilliant for nature, searing straight to the core.

That's what Heidi screamed. Molten white.

It pierced the thin walls, threatened to blow out the windows. It jolted Sarah, sitting bolt upright.

And completely, totally, unable to move.

THIS WAS THE PART *she still didn't remember well. Not even a year later. The police asked her about the details, of course. Detectives, a forensic nurse, later more investigators, crime scene specialists.*

All she could tell them was that the night started with green and gold giggles and ended with molten-white screams. Heidi's the whitest and brightest but also blessedly short.

Christy and Kelly. Two girls in one room. Best friends, members of the lacrosse team. Forewarned, forearmed, they fought. They hurled trophies. Was the sound of crashing metal a taste or a color? No, just a crash. Followed by screams, all kinds of colors and flavors. Fear, rage, anguish. Determination as one nailed him with a lacrosse stick. Horror as he came back with his blade.

He got Kelly right in the gut (Sarah read the report later), but Kelly got him by the ankles. She rolled herself into him, around him, a human armadillo. And he slashed and he slashed, glancing blows off her ribs, which allowed Christy time to grab the comforter from the lower bunk bed and to throw it at him, tangle up his arms.

"Sarah!" they were screaming. "Help, Sarah! Nine-one-one, nine-one-one!"

Sarah called. Another one of those things she didn't remember, but later she listened to it at her own request. A recording of her voice, trembling, barely a whisper, as she reached the dispatch center: "Help us, please help us, he's killing them. He's going to kill us all."

She left her room. It had to be done. In her tiny room, she'd be trapped, the proverbial fish in a barrel. She had to get out to open ground.

To protect herself?

To save her roommates?

She didn't know. A question to ask herself during all the sleepless nights to come.

She left her room.

She went toward her roommates' bedroom. She saw an open hand through the doorway, Kelly's splayed fingers, and without thinking Sarah grabbed it. Was she going to pull her roommate to safety? Man up and carry each and every one of them out to the hall? No time to think. Just do. So she grabbed Kelly's hand and pulled hard.

And found herself holding an arm. Just . . . an arm.

Because, apparently, when a girl armadilloed herself around a madman's ankles, sooner or later he got tired of slashing his victim and simply dismantled her instead.

Screams ahead of her, Christy, still fighting. Followed by a plea behind her.

"Sarah . . ."

She didn't know which way to turn. These sounds, these sights, this night, it didn't register for her. Couldn't.

Slowly she twisted toward the voice behind her, holding Kelly's warm, wet arm tight against her chest. She found herself face-to-face with Heidi. The girl had crawled from her bedroom. The skin of her naked shoulders appeared silver in the glow of lights through the windows. Unmarred, untouched. But the blonde was hunched forward awkwardly, cradling her stomach, and already Sarah could pick up the whiff of perforated bowels.

More screaming from the bedroom. Not molten white. Lava red. Pure rage from a star athlete refusing to be cut down in the prime of her life.

And Sarah knew then what she had to do. She turned away from beautiful, stupid, gutted Heidi. She tightened her grip on poor Kelly's arm, and she joined the fray.

Christy, backed into a corner against the bunk bed, armed with her lacrosse stick. Madman, freed from the comforter, dancing around the body splayed at his feet, enjoying himself, taking his time.

"*Excuse me,*" *Sarah said.*

He darted toward Christy. She swung her stick down. Last minute, he twirled left, jabbed the blade into the soft spot beneath her ribs. A wet, squishing sound, followed by Christy's hollow grunt. She jerked the stick back, tapped him on the side of his head. Not hard, but he retreated.

No screaming now. Just the sound of exertion. Everyone breathing hard.

"*Excuse me,*" *Sarah said again.*

For the first time, the blade man stilled. He turned slightly, a frown on his blood-flecked face. Sarah stared at him. She felt as if she needed to see him. Needed to register him. Or none of this could be real. Especially not this moment, when she held out her hands and offered her friend's severed arm to the man who'd murdered her.

Dark hair. High cheekbones. Sculpted face. Exactly the kind of guy Heidi would bring home from a bar. Exactly the kind of guy who would forever be out of Sarah's league.

"*You forgot this,*" *she said, still holding out the arm.*

("*What?*" *the first officer had interrupted.* "*You said what?*"

"*I had to.*" *Sarah tried explaining to the woman.*

Except maybe there was no explaining such a thing. She'd just known she had to do something. Stop him. Interrupt. Make all those red and white screams go away. So she'd walked into the room, and she'd offered up the only thing she had: Kelly's bloody arm.)

He came for her then. Turned fully, blade dripping at his side, lips peeled back from his teeth.

She watched him advance. She didn't move. She didn't scream. She felt like a little girl, standing in the kitchen as her father picked up the boiling teakettle. "What the fuck, you stupid-ass woman? When I ask you for my money, you give me my money! I'm the one in charge here. Now do as I say, or I'll throw this whole damn pot into your bitch-ugly face. Then we'll see who's willing to take care of you after that!"

Don't look away, don't make a sound. This is what she'd learned from her mother over the years. If they're going to hurt you, make them do it while staring you in the eye.

The madman halted directly in front of her, blade at his side. She could smell the blood on his cheeks, the whiskey on his breath.

He said to her: "Scream."

As slowly, so slowly, he lifted the knife. Up, up, up.

Behind him, Christy fumbled with her lacrosse stick. Tried to move. Tried to take advantage. But the stick fell from her trembling fingers. It clattered as she slid down the wall, sank to the floor. A sigh in the distance: no more rage from the star athlete, just acceptance. So this is what it felt like to die.

"Scream," he whispered again.

Sarah stared at him, and in his gaze, she knew exactly what he was going to do. He was not her loser father. Not subject to a quick temper or drunken rages. No, the hunting knife in his hand, the blood on his face. He liked it. Felt no shame, no remorse. Heidi's screams, Christy's fight, her own silent stand—this was the most fun he'd had in years.

"Though I walk through the valley of the shadow of death," she heard herself whisper, "I will fear no evil."

Then she closed her eyes and clutched this last piece of Kelly close, as with a laugh, a chortle of glee, he slashed the knife straight down toward her chest.

An explosion. Two, three, four, five. More pain, her shoulder, her chest, her throat. He'd stabbed her, she thought, as she collapsed to the ground. No, he'd shot her. But that didn't make sense . . .

A ragged sob behind her, followed by the stench of death growing ever closer. Heidi dragged herself across the hardwood floor.

Holding a small pistol, Sarah noticed now. Heidi had a gun.

"I'm sorry," Heidi whispered. She was crying, tears mixing, smearing with the blood on her cheeks. "Never . . . shoulda . . ."

"Shhh," Sarah said.

Heidi put her head on Sarah's shoulder. Sarah winced; Heidi had shot her while shooting him. But it hardly seemed to matter now. Blood pooling on her throat, blood dripping from her back, so much pain, and yet it seemed far away, abstract.

The madman was still. The molten screams had ended. Now, there was just this. A final moment.

Sarah and Heidi both placed their hands on Kelly's arm.

"I'm sorry," Heidi mumbled again.

As Sarah listened to her last gurgling breath.

"I will fear no evil," she whispered in the ensuing silence. "I will fear no evil, fear no evil, fear no evil."

The police finally burst through the front door. The EMTs rushed to their rescue.

"Jesus Christ," the first cop said, coming to a halt in the middle of the apartment.

"I will fear no evil," Sarah told the woman.

And, once more, offered up Kelly's severed arm.

A YEAR LATER, *what Sarah remembered most was waking up to the sound of giggling.*

DO SCREAMS HAVE A TASTE? *Fire? Ash? Red-hot cinnamon candies, which as a little girl Sarah liked to let melt on the tip of her tongue?*

"EXCUSE ME. YOU FORGOT THIS."

SOUND OF GIGGLING. MOLTEN-WHITE SCREAMS.

I WILL FEAR NO EVIL . . .

ONE YEAR LATER, *one year later, one year later . . .*

A KNOCK AT THE DOOR. Hard. And then again.

Sarah bolted awake in her tiny studio apartment. Drenched in sweat, breath ragged. She lay perfectly still, ears straining. Then it came again. Knocking. Pounding. Someone demanding entrance.

Slowly, she reached for the top drawer of her nightstand. No stashed knife. She couldn't even look at a blade. No gun. She'd tried, but her hands shook too much. So a canister of pepper spray. Meant to chase off bears when hiking in the woods and available at any outdoor gear or camping store. She had the canisters stashed all over her single-room apartment, in every bag she carried.

She drew out the canister, sliding off the mattress as the knocking started again.

She stank. Could smell the reek of her own sweat and terror. Night after night after night.

Screams *did* have a color. It was the only thing she truly understood anymore. Screams had a color, and she was now intimately familiar with all the shades of despair.

"I will fear no evil," Sarah told herself as she put her eye to the peephole and gazed into the dimly lit hall.

A lone woman. Late twenties, early thirties maybe. Dressed casually in jeans and a sweatshirt, she looked like someone Sarah should know. Had maybe met once upon a time. Then again, two A.M. was a strange time for a social call.

"It's okay," the woman spoke up, no doubt sensing Sarah's gaze on her. She held up both hands, as if to prove she was unarmed. "I won't hurt you."

"Who are you?"

"Honestly? You're gonna have to open up to find out. That's part of the deal. I'm here to help you, but you gotta take the first step."

"I will fear no evil," Sarah said, clutching her bear spray tightly.

"That's stupid," said the woman. "World is full of evil. Fear is what keeps us safe."

"Who *are* you?"

"Someone who's not going to stand here forever. Make your choice, Sarah. Hide behind platitudes or make the world a better place."

Sarah hesitated. But then, her fingers landed on the first bolt lock. Then the second. The third. There was something about this woman. Not what she said so much as the way she stood.

Christy, she found herself thinking. The woman stood like Christy had, once upon a time. A challenger, ready to take on the world.

Slowly, very slowly, Sarah eased open the door until she stood face-to-face with her unexpected guest.

"Nice pepper spray," the woman commented. She strode into Sarah's tiny apartment. Rotated a full circle, looking all around. Nodded once to herself, as if all was what she expected.

She turned, faced Sarah directly, and stuck out a hand.

"My name is Flora Dane," she announced. "A year ago, you survived. Now I'm gonna teach you how to live again."

LISA GARDNER

"No one owns this corner of the genre the way Lisa Gardner does."

—#1 *New York Times* bestselling author Lee Child

For a complete list of titles, please visit
prh.com/LisaGardner